TEXAS HUNT

BY
BARB HAN

First Published in Great Britain 2016
By Mills & Boon, an imprint of HarperCollins*Publishers*
1 London Bridge Street, London, SE1 9GF

© 2016 Barb Han

ISBN 978-0-263-91899-1

46-0316

Our policy is to use papers that are natural, renewable and recyclable products and made from wood grown in sustainable forests. The logging and manufacturing processes conform to the legal environmental regulations of the country of origin.

Printed and bound in Spain

Barb Han lives in north Texas with her very own hero-worthy husband, three beautiful children, a spunky golden retriever/standard poodle mix and too many books in her to-read pile. In her downtime, she plays video games and spends much of her time on or around a basketball court. She loves interacting with readers and is grateful for their support. You can reach her at www.barbhan.com.

My deepest thanks go to Allison Lyons for the amazing talent she brings to make each story the absolute best it can be—I am beyond grateful. I'm incredibly blessed to work with Jill Marsal and I'm looking forward to many more years together.

There are three people who cheer me on through late nights and weekends, who are always quick to build me up if my spirits dip, and who inspire me to reach deeper every day so that I can be half the person I see reflected in their eyes. Brandon, Jacob and Tori—my three beautiful gifts!—my world is so much brighter because of you!

And to you, Babe, because the life we've built together is so much better than I ever thought possible—and you are at the center of it all. I love you!

Chapter One

Lisa Moore woke with a start. She tried to push up to a sitting position. Motion made a thousand nails drive through her skin and her head split four ways. Bright fluorescent lights blurred her vision. Her arms gave out and she landed hard on the firm mattress.

"Whoa, slow down there." Before she could shift her position enough to try sitting up again, Ryan Hunt was kneeling at her side. She didn't want to acknowledge just how much his presence calmed her rising pulse.

"What are you doing here?" she asked. Looking around, realizing she was in the hospital, she added, "What am I doing here?"

"I came as soon as I got the call," Ryan said, his low, deep timbre wrapping around her. An emotion flickered behind his eyes that she couldn't immediately pinpoint. At six foot two with the muscled body of an athlete, Ryan could take care of himself and anyone else around. She told herself that was the reason him being there comforted her…but comforted her from what?

Reality dawned on her as a full-body shiver rocked her. She'd been attacked by Beckett Alcorn, son of the most prominent man in town. His father had recently been named a person of interest in the fifteen-year-old kidnapping case that had rocked the small tight-knit community of Mason Ridge, Texas. News broke yesterday that Charles Alcorn had escaped before questioning and a manhunt was under way to find him.

Fear seized her, cramping her stomach. What if Beckett came back? No one would suspect him, the grieving and confused son. Too bad she couldn't tell Ryan what had actually happened, what she really knew. She'd done her part. She hadn't told a soul what Beckett Alcorn had done to her. So why was he trying to deliver on a fifteen-year-old threat now?

"Who else has been here?" She glanced at the door.

"Our friends. Your sister." The questioning look he gave her reminded her that she couldn't afford to give away her true emotions. No one could know about Beckett.

"What really happened to you?" The sight of Ryan—his gray-blue eyes and hawk-like nose set on a face of hard angles softened by rich, thick, curly dark brown hair—settled her fried nerves enough to let her think clearly.

Beckett had misjudged her this time. She'd distracted him long enough to escape. He'd be better prepared next time. Lisa and her family were in grave danger and she needed a plan.

"A guy came out of nowhere and jumped me. I'm guessing they didn't catch him." Playing dumb with Ryan was her only choice. Otherwise, Beckett would hurt her sister or nephew as he'd promised.

"Must not've." Ryan's cell buzzed, his gaze followed hers to the door. "People have been dropping by or calling every half hour to check on you."

"Where's my sister?" Panic beat rapid-fire against her ribs.

"At work. Said she'll stop by when she gets off at three." His dark eyebrow arched.

Lori would be safe as long as she was in a public place. Beckett would strike in the dark when she was alone. Lisa had to make sure that didn't happen. She tried to sit up, but her arms gave and her head pounded.

"Hold on there. Where do you think you're going?" Ryan asked. His suspicion at her reaction evidenced in his tone.

"Nowhere like this." She tried to adjust to a more comfortable position.

"Do you know who did this to you?"

"No. Of course not," she said a little too quickly. It was true that she didn't remember much after escaping. Her mind was as fuzzy as her vision. One thing was crystal clear. Ryan asking questions was a bad idea. She needed to redirect the conversation. "How'd I end up in the hospital?"

"You crawled into the street as Abigail Whitefield drove past on Highway 7. She stopped and called 911 on the spot."

"I'll have to stop by and thank her on my way home," Lisa said, wincing. Speaking shot stabbing pains through her chest.

"The deputy wants a statement. He's been waiting for you to wake up." Ryan's cell phone buzzed. He checked the screen and then responded with a text.

"Everything okay?" she asked.

"It's work. It'll hold," he said without looking at her.

She'd heard that his construction business had been booming. "How long have I been out?"

"Just a day." He chewed on a toothpick.

"What?" She tried to sit up again with similar results, pain forcing her to still.

"Whoa, take it easy there. You shouldn't try to move until the doctor checks you," Ryan said, locating and then pressing the nurse's call button before tossing the toothpick in the trash. There was compassion in his eyes and sympathy in his tone, and for some reason she didn't like either. She didn't want to be the one he pitied. She wanted to be something else to him, something more meaningful than a friend. The thought appeared as out of the blue as a spring thunderstorm in north Texas. Both could be dangerous. They'd known each other since they were kids. Besides, relationships were too risky and Lisa didn't go there with anyone.

But it was Ryan, a little voice inside her head protested—a voice she quickly silenced.

Waking in the hospital was messing with her head. Her nerves were fried and she was reaching for comfort. And those thoughts about Ryan were as productive as harvesting burned corn.

"I just need a minute to clear my head. I'll be okay." The last thing she remembered was seeing Beckett's face as she ripped off his ski mask while he was trying to strangle her. He'd panicked for a split second, which had given her the window of opportunity she needed to push him away, kick him in the groin and run. Lisa was lucky to be alive.

"We'll find the person who did this to you. He won't get away with it. You have my word." Ryan's voice was barely a whisper, but there was no mistaking the underlying threat in his tone. "In the meantime, the doctor or nurse should make sure you're okay."

"So, what's the verdict so far? Have you spoken to anyone?" She scanned her arms for bruising, remembering the viselike grip that had been clamped around them. Black and blue marks were painted up and down both. "I'm guessing I have cracked ribs based on how painful it is to breathe."

"Let me go find that nurse." He made a move to stand, but Lisa grabbed his arm, ignoring the piercing pain.

"Please stay." The words came out more desperate-sounding than she'd planned. "It's just nice to see a friendly face." She added the last part to cover, praying he believed her. In truth, she was scared to be alone in her current condition.

Ryan followed her gaze to the door again.

"I'm not going anywhere." When his gray-blue eyes intensified, they looked like steel.

She didn't want to acknowledge the relief flooding her or how much his presence sent tingles of awareness deep in her stomach. Whatever spark he might've felt had to be long gone by now, replaced with sincere friendship. He showed no signs of experiencing the same electricity humming through her when she touched his arm. Maybe if she'd handled things differently between them years ago...

A young dark-haired nurse wearing glasses and aqua scrubs entered the room, shuffling to Lisa's side.

"I'm Shelly. How are you feeling today?"

"Good, considering I've been dead to the world for the past twenty-four hours."

"You've been drifting in and out. There've been times when you responded to questions. The answers didn't always make sense." Shelly smiled and the look made her plain round face more attractive.

Had Lisa muttered something in her sleep she shouldn't have? Panic rolled through her. If she had, Ryan would be asking very different questions.

Shelly asked a few questions that were easy to answer, ensuring Lisa knew who she was and where she was from.

"Are you sure you don't want something for the pain?" Shelly asked.

"I can manage."

Ryan stood and took a step back to give the nurse room to work.

"How long before I can get out of here?" Lisa checked the door again, half-afraid Beckett would show.

Ryan's eyebrow lifted for the second time.

"The doctor will be in to see you shortly and talk to you about your injuries. Your numbers are strong, but I'm sure the doctor will want to keep you awhile longer for observation. You took a couple of big blows to the head." There was sympathy in her voice, too.

It shouldn't annoy Lisa. Maybe the bumps on her head affected her mood. She should be grateful that everyone seemed genuinely concerned about her.

Except that she knew this was far from over. Beckett must believe she'd told someone or was planning to start talking. With his father in trouble, Beckett might do anything to keep his family's name out of the papers. Either way, she wasn't out of danger.

"I'm sure you'll be up and around soon," Shelly reassured her.

"That's the best news I've heard so far. Think there's

any chance I'll be discharged later today?" Being at home in her own bed sounded amazing about now.

A thought struck her. Beckett knew where she lived. No. She couldn't go there. She'd have to find a safe place to stay until she recovered from her injuries and could do something about Beckett. A flea could take her down in her present condition, and leaving herself vulnerable would be foolish.

"The doctor can explain everything to you when she comes in, but I'd put money on you staying here another night." Shelly had stopped playing around with gadgets and stood sentinel next to the bed. She'd be all of five feet two inches in heels, or in this case thickly padded tennis shoes. "Do you have family in the area other than your husband?"

My husband?

"Why?" Lisa glanced at Ryan, who shot her a look before intently studying his cell phone screen.

"We like to have additional contacts on file in case your husband has to leave," Shelly said casually.

Hold on. Did that mean what Lisa thought? Her dad hadn't been up to see her? She might understand her sister, Lori, being preoccupied with her infant son or work, but wouldn't Dad come by to make sure she was okay? Ryan had said people had been stopping by. She made a mental note to ask him about it as soon as the nurse left the room. "I can give more names. There are others here in town."

"Great. I'll send someone up from Records to take more information."

"Perfect," Lisa said, trying to sound casual.

"The doctor should be in soon." The nurse paused at the door.

"Terrific." Lisa shot a look at Ryan. "I'm sure my husband will bring me up to date in the meantime."

His lips were thin and his arms folded. He fired off a warning look. She understood. He didn't want to be caught in a lie. He must've felt that he had no choice. Ryan was one of the most honest people she knew. He wouldn't take giving false information lightly.

"What else can I get for you while I'm here? Another blanket?" Shelly asked.

"No, thank you. I have everything I need." Lisa glanced from the nurse to Ryan. If he'd been a cartoon character, steam would've been coming out of his ears from embarrassment.

"Press the button if you change your mind," Shelly said before closing the door to give them privacy.

"Was it a big wedding?" Maybe it was the pressure mounting inside her that needed release, but Lisa couldn't stop herself from poking at him.

"Cut it out," Ryan groaned.

Even when they were twelve he didn't like hopping a fence to retrieve a ball in a neighbor's yard without asking first. More than that, he detested outright lying. His older brother hadn't had the same conviction before he'd cleaned up his act. Lisa figured most of the reason Ryan despised untruths had derived from living through the dark periods in Justin's life.

"Sorry. I couldn't resist. I know why you did it and I appreciate you for it. I'm sure they needed consent to treat," she said.

"Yes. You're welcome." The corners of his lips upturned in a not-quite smile. Something else was bothering him. She could tell based on his tight-lipped expression. Whatever it was, he seemed intent on keeping it to himself.

"Has anyone contacted my dad?" she asked.

He shrugged.

"What a minute. How did you even know I was here?"

"Mrs. Whitefield called. She said you asked for me right before you passed out on her. She needed help getting you in the car." He cocked an eyebrow at her. "She said it seemed like there was something you wanted to tell me."

"You could've called my father," Lisa redirected.

"Guess I didn't think of it at the time." Something dark shifted behind his eyes and he looked uncomfortable.

A light tap at the door sounded and then Lori rushed in.

"I came as soon as I heard you were awake. Thank God you're all right." Her hands were tightly clasped and her gaze bounced tentatively from Lisa to Ryan.

"I thought you were at work." Had Ryan really sent a work text earlier or was he covering for connecting with Lori? Why would he do that?

Oh no. Something had to have happened. Lisa's heart raced thinking about her nephew. "Is Grayson okay?"

"Yes. He's fine. Great actually." Lori's face muscles were pulled taut. "It's Dad."

No. No. No. "What happened?"

"He had an accident." Lori shifted her weight to her right foot and bowed her head.

"Where is he?"

"He's gone." Huge tears rolled down her pink cheeks. *Wait. What? No.* This couldn't be happening. She stared at her sister waiting for the punch line. If this was some kind of joke, it was beyond twisted. Tears already streaked her cheeks. Deep down, she knew her sister wouldn't say something like that if it wasn't true.

"What happened?" Lisa forced back the flood of emotions threatening to bust through her iron wall and engulf her.

"He was on the tractor, drinking again," Lori said, raw emotion causing the words to come out strained. "He must've had too much because he flipped it and was pinned. The coroner said he died instantly."

Ryan had moved to her side, his hand was on her shoulder, comforting her. She needed to know the details, to know if Beckett had anything to do with it. Dozens of thoughts crashed down on her at once. She also had to think of an excuse to get her sister and nephew out of town and far away from any threat.

Of course everyone would assume he'd been hitting the bottle again. It wouldn't be the first time he'd relapsed. No one would believe her if she denied it. And yet Lisa knew he'd been clean. There was always a pattern. He was on an upswing. Lisa forced back the flood of tears threatening to overwhelm her. A few streamed down her face anyway.

"Do they know for sure Dad was drinking? Did they perform an autopsy?" she pressed. She'd seen on TV that the coroner could screen for alcohol level.

"Why would they do that? Isn't that for, like, people who are murdered or something?" Lori's voice rose with her panic levels. Her grip on Lisa's hand had tightened to the point of pain.

Lisa gently urged their fingers apart.

"Oh, sorry. This is just happening so fast. First, what

happened to you yesterday morning. Then Daddy later that afternoon." Lori broke down in a sob. "I'm scared, sis. He's gone and I didn't know if you'd—"

"I'm here," Lisa reassured, fighting back her own emotions. She'd always tried to be brave for her little sister. "I'm not going anywhere."

"I know. It's just all…surreal or something. Everyone keeps saying that bad news comes in threes and I keep waiting for the other shoe to drop. It's crazy. I mean, who would want to hurt you? You're like the nicest person. Everyone loves you. You're a kindergarten teacher for heaven's sake. Who would do this to you?"

"Random mugging, remember? I have just as much chance as everyone else. It's like lightning striking," Lisa said even though her heart wasn't in the words. When it came to lying, she fell on the same side of the scale as Ryan. Her father's drinking binges had always been preceded by lies. In bad times, she and her sister would be hauled off to stay with a relative. In the worst cases, they'd end up in the foster care system for a few months until their dad straightened out.

Even though she hated lying, she had no choice. She had to protect what was left of her family. "Where's Grayson?"

"I'm sorry. I didn't want to bring the baby here. I know he's still little, but I thought he might be afraid if he saw you like this," Lori said. The words gushed out. She always spoke too fast when she was a nervous wreck.

"You did the right thing, sis," Lisa said in her most calming voice.

"He's with Dylan and Samantha. Maribel's keeping an eye on him. She calls him her little brother. It's cute." Lori broke into another sob. Dylan and Samantha were longtime friends. Maribel was Dylan's three-year-old daughter. The three of them made a beautiful family. Grayson would be safe in their care. "I know he wasn't always there for us, but he was our dad. And now he's gone."

"I loved him, too." It was surreal to speak about him in the past tense. "It's okay to cry."

"No, it's not. I should be more like you."

"Calloused?" Lisa said quickly before she shattered into a tiny thousand pieces. The only thing worse than holding on to her horrible secret was seeing her baby sister in pain.

"I was going to say brave." Lori leaned into Lisa and sobbed.

With Beckett's father being hunted, this might be the right time to expose the family for the monsters they truly were. And yet she hadn't reported the crime fifteen years ago. Could she come forward now and accuse Beckett? Would anyone believe her?

Maybe Ryan knew about Beckett's family. Hadn't the Alcorns tried to take his father's land? Then again, if she asked him too many questions he might just figure out she was hiding something and force her hand. He was more persistent than a pit bull searching for a bone when it came to finding the truth. She'd also seen how dedicated he'd been to his brother when Justin had been in trouble. Would he do the same for her?

If anyone could understand or help, Ryan could.

He'd been devastated when his own mother walked out on the family. He'd acted tough on the outside, but Lisa saw past the front he'd put up. She'd seen the pain buried deep down because it was just like hers.

Lisa knew pain.

On second thought, exposing Beckett now was a bad idea. First of all, he'd take away everything she loved. Then he'd kill her. Or worse, he wouldn't.

She needed to figure out a way to keep her family safe without alarming them. The Alcorns' number was almost up and she'd be on the front row of the court trial when it happened, cheering when the sentence was delivered.

Until then, she had to figure out a way to keep her family safe.

Every fiber in her being urged her to warn her sister about what might come next, that she and Grayson could be in grave danger. But what if no one believed her?

She lay in a hospital bed with possible head trauma. She had no evidence for an accusation against Beckett. Most people believed him to be a good person and felt sorry for him after news broke about his father.

Lisa had to weigh her options carefully. If she told Lori and Ryan the truth and they questioned her, the risk would only increase. Beckett's attack on her family wouldn't be straightforward, either. He'd watch Lori. Hide. Strike when she least expected it. Considering she had a baby on her hip most of the time, she'd be an easy target.

Doing nothing was a pretty lousy option.

There had to be something she could do to keep her family safe. Lori and Grayson were all Lisa had left and she'd trade her life for either one.

LISA'S EMOTIONAL PAIN hit Ryan far deeper than her physical bruises did. He didn't like those, either, but experience had taught him the stuff on the outside healed. The marks on her heart wouldn't go away in a few weeks. He fisted his hands and then shoved them in his pockets so he wouldn't punch a hole in the wall.

The promise he'd made to Lori to keep quiet about their father had been sitting sourly in his stomach since Lisa's eyes opened. Ryan had wanted to be the one to tell her what had happened, but it wasn't his place. The news about her family needed to come from her sister, not from him. All he could do was be there to help pick up the pieces.

Seeing her lying there, helpless, had stirred more than a primal need to protect a friend.

Instead of acting on it, he'd watched her sleep as he'd held back from stroking her rosy skin as it shone even under the harsh fluorescent light. Her long brunet hair with light streaks that caught the sun seemed brighter.

Listening to the pain in her voice as she spoke to her sister was the second time he'd nearly been done in. He shouldn't allow his past feelings for Lisa to cloud his judgment. Because if they had their way he'd be in that hospital bed with her, holding her until she stopped shaking, comforting her until she felt safe again. It was obvious that the attack had left a serious mark. The way she kept looking at the door as if expecting her assailant to walk through even had Ryan jumpy.

As far as anything else between them went, Lisa was a puzzle in which he'd never quite fit the pieces together. There was no way he could risk his heart twice trying.

Get a hobby, Hunt.

Besides, he had other, more pressing things to focus on, like why she kept checking the door with that frightened look on her face. She had to know a person from a random mugging wouldn't follow her to the hospital. Ryan bet there was more going on than she let on.

"I better go. Grayson needs to nurse soon," Lori said.

"I've been lying here thinking about getting away for a few days. You should, too. Especially now. It's not good for the baby to be around all this and stress can affect your breast milk," Lisa said, looking as though she was grasping at straws. Her sister was almost militant about breast-feeding. Since Grayson's dad wasn't coming back, Ryan figured her sister compensated by throwing all her energy into being Grayson's mother. It was beyond Ryan how a father could walk out on his family. Then again, it didn't seem to have bothered his mother all that much.

Lisa made a good point but when did she have time to think about a getaway option? She'd only woken up a few minutes ago.

"I don't know. I'd rather be here for you. Plus, we need to make arrangements for Dad." Lori's voice hitched on the last couple of words.

"All we need is an internet connection to do that. It'll take a few days to settle everything anyway before the service. I can meet you somewhere. The nurse said I might be out of here later today."

Ryan had no idea why Lisa was skirting the truth, but after all she'd been through he figured he'd toss her a lifeline. "A buddy of mine has a fishing cabin a couple hours from here in Arkansas. It's right on the lake. I'm sure he wouldn't mind if you took it over."

"Are you sure that's such a good idea?" Lori glanced from Ryan to Lisa. "I have Grayson to think about."

"It's nice and big. The place sleeps eight. He bought it so his wife would want to bring the kids," Ryan said.

He intended to have a heart-to-heart with Lisa as soon as her sister left. Then again, her attack was followed by devastating news about her father. Maybe she needed to get her bearings and figured this was the best way. Plus, the Mason Ridge Abductor was still out there and even though Grayson was a baby, not a seven-year-old, which was the usual mode of operation for the kidnapper, she had to be thinking about his safety. With Lori on her own with a baby and Lisa the overprotective older sister, maybe Ryan shouldn't be surprised at how out of sync her reactions seemed to be.

He needed to reassure her that he intended to make certain she was okay.

"It might be nice to take the weekend," Lori said. "There's been so much going on that I don't even want to go to the grocery anymore for fear of running into people. They're well intentioned and all, but my phone's been ringing like crazy. I answered it a few times and it's a game of twenty questions. I can't talk about either one of you without bawling. Plus, work gave me time off to make…arrangements." She wiped away another tear.

"Then it's settled. Ryan will call his friend." Lisa turned her attention toward him. "I'll owe you big-time. You're certain this will be all right?"

"More than sure. He gave me a spare so I could check on the place for him this month while he's out of town for work." Ryan fished in his pocket and then produced a key. "I'll text the address. You should probably take off now. There's a small corner store at the turnoff to get to his place. They're used to weekenders, so they'll have everything you need to get by for a few days with a baby."

"Okay." Lori stopped chewing on her lip and took the offering.

Ryan zipped off a text with the address, waiting for her smartphone to ding.

When it did, she said to Lisa, "Good. Will I see you tonight?"

"I hope so. I'm out of here as soon as I get clearance," Lisa replied.

"Then I'll feed the baby, pack a bag and head out," Lori conceded. The idea seemed to be growing on her when she smiled at her sister.

"Be safe driving. Let me know when you get there, okay?"

They hugged and both had tears in their eyes when Lori left.

"Thank you," Lisa said as Ryan settled into the chair next to her bed.

"You're welcome." Whatever was on her mind, she had no intention to share just yet. He could tell by the set of her jaw and the look in her eye. Lucky for her, he was a patient man. "The deputy should be here shortly to take your statement. You hungry for anything? I could run out and pick up whatever sounds good."

"I doubt I could eat anything," she said. Those bluish-green eyes pushed past his walls—walls he'd worked damn hard to construct.

Lisa was attractive. Only an idiot would argue that point and Ryan didn't put himself in that particular category. He'd be lying if he didn't admit to a certain pull he felt toward her every time she was around.

But that was where it ended. Where it *had* to end.

Sure, a few of his friends had found true partnerships with other people recently. Even though Ryan had been against Brody and Rebecca's relationship early on because of their history, the two were the happiest he'd ever seen them. Dylan and Samantha seemed perfect for each other. Love seemed to suit his friends. Denying the nose on his face wouldn't change anything. Besides, Ryan was truly happy for his best buds.

But only a man with a need for punishment did the same thing over and over again expecting a different result. Lisa had shot him down before when he thought he'd picked up on a mutual attraction. Even though he felt that same sizzle between them now, only a fool would act on it. And not only because she was in a hospital bed, hurt. That just made it inappropriate.

Ryan had other reasons not to get involved with anyone. For one, he didn't need anyone to take care of him. He was perfectly fine living the bachelor's life.

Brody and Dylan might have found their other halves and taken up relationships, and Ryan didn't begrudge them. No two people deserved that kind of bliss more than his friends. He had to admit that they seemed happier than they'd ever been. And that was all pink lemonade and roses *for them*.

Ryan didn't need anyone else to "complete" him. He'd come into the world a whole human being and planned to leave the same way. Living on his own suited him. He liked waking up with the sun and going where he pleased. Was he selfish? Maybe. He was so used to taking care of family members for most of his life that he didn't have much left to give anyone else.

Had his life seemed a little lacking lately? Sure. It would cycle around again.

And if it didn't, he'd get a dog. People were so damn disappointing.

Chapter Two

A hospital was no place to sleep. Even with the lights
turned off Lisa couldn't relax, especially since Ryan had
gone home. To make matters worse, a nurse or technician padded in every hour on the dot to wrap gauges
around her arm or take more blood. After what felt like
the fiftieth time but was more like the fifth, Lisa was
beginning to lose patience.

Lack of sleep and constant ache did nothing to im-
prove her mood. Plus, the news of her father...she
couldn't even go there. Grief would engulf her if she
allowed herself time to think about it. Emotions were a
luxury she couldn't afford. Beckett was still out there.
The rest of her family was in danger. As difficult as it
was, Lisa had to maintain focus.

At least she'd convinced her sister to leave town.
Lori and Grayson were in a swank fishing cabin on a
lake in Arkansas. That was the only bit of good news
in what had been one of the worst days of Lisa's life.

Dad.

Thinking about him, about what had happened
brought a whole new wave of sadness crashing down
around her.

She tried to ease to a sitting position, searching her

memory for any sign he'd been relapsing. Pain pierced her chest, her arms and her back with movement. No use. She'd refused pain medication, needing a clear head. She was still reeling from the news of losing her father while trying to sort out why any of this was happening now. She'd kept Beckett's secret, dammit. Shouldn't that have bought her a pass?

One of the lab techs padded in. *Great.*

Trying to sort out the day's events while Prickzilla jabbed another needle contributed to a dull ache in the spot right between her eyes.

Take a deep breath. Count to ten.

It wasn't a magical cure but she felt better.

"Try to get some sleep," Dracula-in-an-aquamarine-jumpsuit whispered before she closed the door behind her and disappeared.

If only it were that easy.

Lisa tossed and turned for another half hour at least. As frustration got the best of her she resorted to counting sheep.

Still didn't work.

Just like when she was a kid, the darn things shape-shifted into snakes, their slimy bodies slithering after her. The closet had offered a perfect hiding spot when she was six. Another half dozen years later, Beckett Alcorn had been the beast that kept her awake nights. There wasn't a closet big enough now for the monster she faced.

In the category of "not making it better," she was wide-awake at—she checked the clock—three fifteen in the morning. *Great.* Even the chickens were conked out at this hour. Lisa had been drifting in and out, but every time she got close the door would creak open and a nurse or technician would pad inside. It was probably just as well. Anytime Lisa got anywhere near real sleep, she'd jolt awake from one of several nightmares ready to cue at a moment's notice.

In one scenario, hands were closing around her throat. She woke screaming, giving the nurse who was attending to her quite a scare.

In another dream, fists were coming at her from every direction and she felt blood spilling out of her cracked skull with each jab.

After the last round of fifty ways to beat up Lisa, she gave up checking the clock. There was no use realizing just how late it was and how little REM she was getting.

The worst-case nightmare involved being held under water, drowning, only to bob to the surface and find that it was Ryan holding her down. There was no doubt in her mind that he would never try to hurt her in her waking world. Absolutely no way could she even consider him doing her harm on purpose. The dream must represent something she feared. Didn't need a phycology degree to know she'd been afraid of the opposite sex ever since that summer, ever since Beckett.

What did it say about her that even a male friend scared her to death?

She thought about that as she drifted off to her first real sleep.

A hand clamped around Lisa's throat so hard she feared her windpipe would crack. She struggled against the crushing grip. It was like trying to peel off custom-fitted steel.

Her fight, flee or freeze response triggered as she railed against the force pushing her deeper into the mattress. She tried to scream, but no sound came out. In her other dreams she'd always been able to shout.

Coughing, she had the frightening realization that this wasn't a dream.

She was wide-awake.

A soft object, maybe a pillow, was being pressed against her face, suffocating her.

More coughing came as her lungs desperately clawed for air.

Could she somehow signal one of the nurses? Where were they? How had someone walked right past them in the middle of the night and gotten into her room? She felt around for the call button, but came up empty.

Oh. God. No.

Desperate and afraid, she reached for her attacker. Her hand stopped on denim material. Must've been his leg, meaning he was most likely straddled over her. Beckett?

At twelve, Lisa had blamed herself for what he'd done to her. She'd been too embarrassed and too scared to tell anyone. Beckett had threatened to kill everyone she loved if she so much as breathed a word of his actions, and he had the power to follow through with his warning. He'd threatened to do worse to Lisa's little sister. And if Lisa told, he'd said it would be her word against his, and who would believe her, anyway? He'd made a good point. She'd been a shy girl, in and out of the system, who'd mostly kept to herself. Worse yet, she was daughter of Henry Moore, the town's constantly rehabilitating alcoholic.

Lisa wasn't a little girl anymore. No way did he get to destroy her. She followed the inseam straight up to his groin, grabbed and squeezed with every ounce of strength she had.

He muttered a curse as he shifted position long enough for her to take in a swallow of precious oxygen. She clasped harder and he groaned, cursing her.

The weight on top of her lifted for a second as he wriggled his groin out of her grasp. His hold loosened on the pillow pressed against her face so she fought the pain burning through her as she drew her knees to her chest and then thrust them toward his face. They connected with his chin.

His head snapped back.

Lisa screamed for the nurse. She tried to launch another attack, pushing through the agony that came with every movement. Her arms felt like spaghetti and even a boost of adrenaline didn't give her enough strength to keep fighting.

The mattress dipped and then rose as he pushed to his feet.

"I'll be back. You'll regret this, bitch." The voice wasn't Beckett's. It was too dark to get a good look at the details of his face.

A fresh wave of panic seized her as she searched for something, anything on the side table. Her fingers reached the landline phone, so she hurled it toward the stranger's back. "You won't be able to hurt me from jail."

What was taking the nurse so long?

The dark silhouette slipped out of her room and disappeared moments before the door reopened and the night nurse rushed in.

"Someone was here. He's out there. In the hall," Lisa said through coughing fits.

Light filled the room as the concerned nurse's face came into view.

"I was just out there and didn't see anyone. My name's Alicia. I'll be your nurse this evening." She spoke slowly, calmly, as if she were talking to a three-year-old in the heat of a temper tantrum.

"I'm not making this up. I swear." Lisa sat upright, heaving.

The way the nurse stared at Lisa, the questioning look, she knew Alicia was ready to call for a psych consult.

"I promise. A man was just in here. He had a pillow over my face. Can't you see what he did to me?" Her breath came in bursts.

Alicia's forehead crease and raised eyebrow gave away the fact that she was skeptical. With a quick look communicating that Lisa should be grateful Alicia was about to indulge the fantasy, she retreated toward the door. "I'll check again, but I was just out there and I didn't see anyone."

All Lisa could think about based on Alicia's reaction was that she most likely attributed this outburst to a very realistic nightmare or head trauma.

The expression on her face when she returned convinced Lisa of the latter.

"I know how this must seem to you but someone was in here," Lisa said defensively. She glanced around on the floor. "Look. The pillow he used is there."

"It's okay," Alicia soothed. The words came out slowly, again.

Great. The woman thought Lisa was crazy. Lisa wasn't about to let the nurse get away with it.

"Look at me. I must have red marks or bruising. He

shoved that pillow in my face and held me down." She held her hands out to check herself over. A pillow on the floor wasn't exactly a smoking gun. Even Lisa rationalized she could've knocked it off the bed during a nightmare.

The only real evidence was a black-and-blue display up and down both arms.

"You've been through a lot recently. Let's see if we can get you to lie down again," Alicia said as she began her exam, evaluating Lisa's injuries.

She moved to the computer. "We'll send someone down to speak to you."

Either Alicia believed Lisa or the nurse was following hospital protocol. Neither mattered; the only person Lisa wanted to see right now was Ryan. He'd said to call if she needed him, day or night. As much as she didn't want to push the boundaries of their friendship or drive him away she needed to be with someone she trusted.

Would he even pick up at this ridiculous hour?

What choice did she have? Her father was dead. Her sister was more than four hours away, not that calling her in the middle of the night was an appealing thought anyway. Lori would have too many questions and that could be deadly.

Once again, Lisa was frightened into silence. Could she call the sheriff? Tell him everything even after she'd lied to Deputy Adams earlier and said she didn't know her attacker?

The deputy had simply shaken his head while taking down the details for his report, cursing the luck of her family to have both of these things happen within twenty-four hours of each other. He'd warned her to watch out because bad things usually came in threes.

And with her father's alcohol history, maybe the deputy had really wondered why something like this hadn't happened sooner.

Adams had confirmed that her father's death had been considered an accident. No one had argued differently. Her heart knew better.

Lisa knew for certain that her attack yesterday hadn't been random. She'd seen Beckett with her own eyes after ripping off his ski mask. But whoever had slipped into the hospital wasn't him. Maybe her brain was damaged and she'd imagined another person's voice. Who else would do something like this?

Beckett could've hired someone to do his dirty work for him. Attacking her in a hospital setting was high risk. There'd be cameras. Maybe he feared getting caught this time. It might not have been him carrying out the actual crime, but her instincts said he had to be responsible.

What good did it do her to know? If she told anyone he'd be back to kill all the family she had left—her sister and nephew.

Panic gripped her. She couldn't even think about anything happening to them.

They were safe. *For now.*

Lori and her infant son were everything to Lisa. And if she gave up the name of the man who did this to her, both of them would be dead in a heartbeat.

There had to be another way.

Calling Ryan was a risk she had to take. He'd be even more suspicious and he might think she was a little crazy. What was the alternative?

Stay there, unprotected, and she'd be dead by morning.

Try to leave by herself and she wouldn't make it out the door.

As soon as Alicia stepped into the hallway, Lisa grabbed her cell from the side table.

Calling Ryan was the only reasonable option. He'd volunteered his assistance. She'd take him up on his offer.

If he pressed her for more information, she'd have to cut him loose or risk putting him in danger. She hoped it wouldn't come to that.

Chapter Three

The sound of fear in Lisa's voice when she called had shocked Ryan out of a deep sleep.

All she'd said was "I need you."

Those three words had kicked Ryan into action faster than buckshot. Her voice had blasted a different kind of heat through his chest, sent it spiraling through him. He'd dismissed it quickly as an inappropriate reaction and focused on the terror coming through the line. He'd hopped out of bed, ignoring the aftershocks of sexual awareness, thrown on clothes and raced toward the hospital. He'd made the drive in record time, parked and still hadn't come up with a plan to get past security.

Something had happened to Lisa. He intended to find out what was going on. She'd convinced him she'd been too tired to talk earlier that day and he hadn't wanted to put undue pressure on her, given all that she'd been through. This was different. No way could he go back to sleep without answers. And no one could stop him from getting them, not even her.

"Sir, visiting hours are over," the nurse warned as he stalked toward Lisa's wing.

"I received a call from a patient of yours. She's expecting me." Like hell he wasn't going into her room.

"I can't allow it. Hospital policy." The nurse sprang from her seat and moved around the desk too late to block him from entering Lisa's hallway.

"Call your supervisor if you have to, but I'm not leaving until I know my wife is okay." Ryan used the earlier lie he'd given in order for her to receive treatment. He'd had to think quickly then. Surely they wouldn't refuse a husband access to his spouse now. He figured he had at least a few minutes before hospital security could catch up in order to toss him out of the building.

"Sir." Her voice trailed off, which meant she wasn't following him. She'd most likely doubled back so she could call the security desk.

Ryan pushed Lisa's door open and rushed to her side. Desperation was a net, casting a wild animal look over her normally soft, feminine features.

"I don't have long. The nurse will have me evicted in a few minutes. Tell me what happened," he said.

"Someone was here, Ryan." The urgency in her words nearly knocked him back a step.

"Who?"

"I'm not sure." An emotion he couldn't quite put his finger on flickered behind her eyes. It was more than fear.

"Was it the guy who attacked you?"

"Yes. No. I don't know." Her bluish-green eyes were wide and scared.

"I need you to tell me what's really going on." When he sat on the edge of the bed, he realized she was shaking. It took every bit of strength not to pull her into his chest and comfort her.

"I would if I could." She looked away.

What the hell did that mean? He'd been exposed,

firsthand, to people in trouble. Make no mistake about it, Lisa was drowning. He couldn't do anything to help her unless she gave him something to hang on to.

If he'd learned one thing from trying to save his brother, it was that people helped themselves. Sure, sometimes they needed an extra pair of hands. Ryan never hesitated to be there for a relative or friend in need to offer support. But drowning people were notorious for pulling others down with them. Ryan had learned to keep a healthy distance until they took those first few strokes on their own.

"Why can't you?" Seeing her looking so small in that damn oversize gown overrode rational thought. He fisted his hands to keep them at his sides.

Didn't work. He brushed the hair from her face, ignoring the urge building inside him to hold her until she stopped shaking.

"Believe me, Ryan, you're the only one I would tell if I could, but this is…complicated and innocent people will be hurt if I don't play this right." Her words broke at the end and sobs racked her shoulders.

Ryan didn't debate his next action. He just hauled her into his arms, where she buried her face. "I'm here. It's okay."

He half expected her to push him away and tell him she was fine. She didn't. Instead, she pressed deeper against his cotton T-shirt while he whispered reassurances in her ear he couldn't guarantee.

There was no worse feeling than watching someone he cared about in pain and not being able to help.

Against his better judgment, he told Lisa he would do whatever she needed.

She broke away and stared him directly in the eyes.

"If you really want everything to be all right, take me home with you."

Hold on a minute. She couldn't leave the hospital. The determination in her bluish-green eyes said otherwise. Maybe he could talk her off the ledge.

"Is that wise?" He glanced at the bruises on her arms.

"I'd walk out of here on my own if I could," she said, and he had no doubt she meant it.

Could he convince her otherwise?

"The doctor wants to keep an eye on your head injury." Was it safe for her to leave the hospital against medical advice?

"I can't stay here. He'll come back, or send someone. I'm in danger here. You're the only one I trust."

"Did you tell the nurse?"

"Yes, I did. She didn't believe me. She's most likely calling in a psychiatrist. I won't make it that long. He'll slip right back in and…" She bit her bottom lip as if to stop if from forming the next words.

"Tell me exactly what happened." They were running out of time. Security would burst through that door any second now. Ryan believed something had happened and he needed to know more. Whatever it was had scared the bejesus out of her. But how could it be the same guy who'd attacked her earlier? That was supposed to be a random occurrence. Ryan had been sitting in this very room when she'd given the deputy her statement.

"Maybe he works here." Her shoulders sagged and she looked to be in considerable pain every time she moved. "That's impossible, isn't it?"

"Security will be here any second. What if we explain what happened to them? Maybe we can get them involved."

"It's no good. The nurse will tell them not to believe me." She held her arms up as though she wanted him to inspect them. "She thinks I'm crazy and she's sending me for a psych evaluation. End of story. It's the middle of the night and my doctor isn't here, but what would she do, anyway?"

She gestured toward her arms again.

Ryan didn't want to say the bruises could've been from the earlier attack. She needed to hear that someone believed her. Otherwise she'd jump out of her own skin if someone sneezed. "I see what happened and I believe you. I won't let him get to you again. I promise."

He didn't say that might not be an option if he was booted out. He'd figure something out. Lisa had been afraid before, but there was a grasping-at-her-last-straw quality to her voice now that didn't sit well with him.

Touching her was a bad idea because his emotions started taking over his logical thought. Nothing good could come of that.

There was more than her reaction that bugged the hell out of him. The persistence of this guy was unsettling. It took guts to attack at a well-staffed hospital even in the middle of the night. Then again, dress in scrubs or a maintenance uniform and he might blend right in. Ryan needed to get into contact with their friend Dylan, who owned a personal security company. He might have enough contacts to get hold of the footage at the hospital.

The questions of the day were…who was doing this and why was he being so persistent?

Lisa had never been a liar, but one look at her said

she was at the very least holding back something that could get her hurt or killed. Plus, she'd practically forced her sister out of town for a few days. A storm was brewing and Ryan needed to know just how big this squall was going to get.

"Take me out of here. *Please.*" The way Lisa emphasized the last word shredded Ryan's resolve. This was a bad idea. Being there was sketchy enough. Walking her out the front door in her condition was borderline insanity.

Leaving her there, alone, was out of the question.

Voices down the hall neared. Security would walk through the door at any second. Ryan had about two seconds to make a decision. All of his experiences, instincts railed against doing what he was contemplating. He'd be stepping in a boot full of sludge trying to justify this.

Not to mention the fact that his feelings for her clouded his judgment. Logic told him to bolt, to let authorities handle this. And yet she hadn't trusted them enough to tell them everything.

Only a fool or someone in serious trouble would do that.

"What if I stay here with you? I'll stay awake and keep watch." He'd be irresponsible if he didn't put that out there as an option. The fear widening her eyes said she wouldn't take the offer.

"So he can come back and kill us both?" She sank deeper into the bed like a deflated airbag. "I didn't consider this before, but I'm putting you in danger. You can't be here. I didn't think this through all the way. I'm sorry. Forget I ever called you."

Wait a minute.

Was she kicking him out?

"Fine. Where's your stuff? I'll grab a bag." He stood as she stilled, staring blankly at him in disbelief. "We need to get moving. Several people are going to come through that door and none of them are going to be happy to see me in here."

"I can't let you do this. It was a mistake to get you involved." She stared toward the window, blankly.

"You've already told me the risks. Consider me informed. I'm going to take you home with me, but we gotta go now."

The door opened so hard it smacked against the wall.

A guy close to Ryan's height wearing a blue security uniform with a squawking radio filled the frame.

"Sir, I need to ask you to leave," he said. His polite words were delivered with a clipped tone. "You can come back to visit between the hours of eight a.m. and seven p.m."

"My wife is ready to go now," Ryan said, folding his arms across his chest as he assumed a defensive stance. The name on the security officer's badge read Steven. If Steven wanted to go a few rounds, Ryan had every confidence in his own fighting abilities. That said, he preferred to save his energy for more important things. It would be up to the big guy which path they took. "I'm not walking through that door without her, Steven."

"I'M LEAVING." With great effort, Lisa pushed off the bed and stood. Ryan was by her side, urging her to lean on him for support before she lost her balance again. All kinds of heat fizzled through her where they made contact, but she pushed it out of her thoughts.

"You heard her. She's ready to leave."

Steven glanced at Alicia.

"That's not a good idea," Alicia said. "Let's all settle down and think this through."

"You're assuming I haven't already." Lisa winced as she took a step forward. Ryan was there to catch her as her knee gave out, his steadying arm around her the only thing keeping her from falling flat on the floor. "You aren't keeping me safe here."

"I'm afraid I can't allow you to go. Doctor's orders." Alicia's resolve was steady.

Panic overwhelmed Lisa. Ryan couldn't help her and deal with the big security guard at the same time. The air in the room was thinning. Her heart thumped wildly in her chest in part from stress and the very real feeling of contact with Ryan. What was it about him that could calm her and send her body into such a pinball machine of awareness all at the same time?

Trying to take another step toward the door, she faltered.

Ryan hauled her against his chest and made a move to kiss her.

He was giving them a show. She understood that on some level, but his hand guiding her lips toward his sent heat rocketing through her.

Ryan's moment of hesitation—a brief pause to catch and hold her gaze for a split second—sent her heart soaring and caused a hundred somersaults to flip through her stomach.

His lips, tentative, barely touched hers. Her breath caught and she could've sworn she'd heard him groan right before deepening the kiss.

She tilted her head back to give him better access as she parted her lips for him. For one dizzying moment when his tongue slid into her mouth her pain disintegrated and all she could feel was his lips moving against hers and how right it felt to be in Ryan Hunt's arms.

The thought was startling. She didn't belong there.

Breaking away first, she forced her mind to the present because for a moment she got lost—lost in the moment, in the feeling of awareness, in the feeling of life being right for just a second.

Turning toward the folks intent on keeping her in that room, Lisa put one hand on Ryan's shoulder and the other on her hip. No way could they push past Alicia and the big guy. Ryan was not small, nor was he incapable of handling himself. She was the weak link. She was the liability. Anger surged through her for being the one to hold them back. "Do you have a court order keeping me here, Alicia?"

The nurse's lips thinned as she shook her head.

"Then I suggest you step aside." The look of approval on Ryan's face, the way he smiled out of the side of his mouth shouldn't make her this happy. It did. She told herself it was because he was putting himself on the line for her. She owed him this at least.

He squeezed her waist and more of that fiery electricity shot through her, warming her in places she didn't want to think about with him standing this close. Or maybe it was just that she didn't want to go there with other people in the room.

Her thoughts couldn't be more inappropriate under the circumstances. Because that kiss made her wonder if Ryan was feeling more for her than he'd let on.

And what exactly was she supposed to do with that? Her life was a mess and he deserved so much more than she could give him.

In times like these, Lisa had to remind herself to take it one moment at a time.

"Well?" she asked point blank. Her confidence had returned.

"We can't keep you here against your will. However, I would like to ask you to stay, anyway," Alicia said flatly.

They couldn't keep her safe. They didn't believe her. They gave her no other choice.

"I'm fine." She looked up at Ryan. "Let's go. They can throw away the rest of my things for all I care. There's nothing in here that can't be replaced."

He gently leaned her against the bed and she missed his warmth as soon as he took a step away from her.

"Hospital regulation requires her to leave in a wheelchair," the nurse said. "Will you at least sign the paperwork and let me take you out?"

Lisa nodded. "As long as it's quick."

The nurse disappeared, taking the security guard with her.

"My clothes are over there." She motioned toward the tall cabinet next to the wall-mounted TV. "That's all I have with me other than my cell, which is nearly out of battery."

Ryan retrieved her folded-up outfit of shorts and a halter top along with her underclothes.

She hoped he didn't see her cheeks warm with embarrassment at the idea of him handing her underwear to her.

Once they got outside, she'd breathe much lighter. As it was, tension threatened to crack her already bruised and hurting shoulders.

"I can step into the hallway for a minute to give you

privacy while you dress if you'd like." Ryan placed the clothes on the bed next to where she stood.

"Here's the thing. I'm going to need your help." She smiled weakly.

His gray-blue eyes darkened to steel. An almost-pleading look crossed his features for a nanosecond. Then he half smirked. "I guess it would be weird for a husband to leave the room while his wife dressed."

"Hadn't even thought of that. It shouldn't take too long and I probably only need help getting things over my big size eights." Did she just complain about her shoe size? Was she rambling? The thought of Ryan in the room with her while she was completely naked was almost too much.

"I happen to like your feet." He helped her ease onto the bed and then he pulled the blanket over her, covering her midsection. With athletic grace he moved around to the other side of the bed, behind her, and then untied each bow on her hospital-issued gown.

Gently, he rolled the material down her arms. His breath was so close it warmed the sensitive skin along the back of her neck.

The white cloth hit the floor in front of her. She secured her sheet as Ryan moved in front of her. She was so aware of just how naked she was beneath her cover and how thin the material was that kept her cloaked. She white-knuckle gripped the seam with one hand while she reached for her clothes with the other. Thankfully, her ribs weren't broken, just a hairline fracture on one, the doctor had said, but the pain was still excruciating.

Without saying a word, he bent down and then cradled her ankle in his hand. He slipped her black lace panties over one foot, then two and she could've sworn she heard him groan.

Her body went rigid trying to fight the attraction overwhelming her senses.

His hands moved up the sides of her legs, his eyes trailed and when his skin touched hers it blazed a hot trail.

She lifted her bottom long enough for him to slide the panties around her hips. He didn't immediately move. His hands rested on either side of her.

Lisa couldn't remember the last time she felt this intimate with a man. Maybe never.

A few seconds later and with similar ease, Ryan slipped her shorts on.

At least for her bra he stood behind her and she couldn't see his intense expression—intense because they both had to know deep down that anything more than friendship between the two of them would be a bad idea.

After her bra and then halter had been secured, he moved to her side, eyes down. Was he thinking about the kiss they'd shared, too?

He lifted his head and made a move to speak.

The door opened, interrupting the moment. And that was probably for the best. The last thing Lisa needed to hear was just how much he regretted their lips touching. Or worse, an apology.

The nurse pushed a wheelchair in front of her. She helped Lisa into the seat and then handed her a stack of papers on a clipboard. The words *Against Medical Advice* had been scribbled in huge letters across the first page.

Lisa initialed all the places the nurse had highlighted as Ryan positioned himself behind the chair.

When she'd signed for what felt like the hundredth time, he wheeled her out of the room, off the floor and into the night.

The air was still hot. It was the time of year in Texas when she went to bed and it was hot, she woke and it was hot. Midday, the rubber soles on her shoes could practically melt against the sweltering pavement.

"I'm parked in the front row," he said, his voice still husky.

"That was lucky."

"Turns out there aren't that many visitors in the middle of the night," he said, and she could tell he was smiling without looking at him. She could hear it in his voice.

"Thank you for breaking me out. If Nurse Ratchet had her way, I'd be zonked out with an IV drip that would have me slobbering down my chin as she spoon-fed me mashed potatoes."

"Not a problem." He chuckled. "I'm not that big on sleep, anyway."

"Either way, I owe you a big favor for everything you've done today."

"It's nothi—"

"Hold on a second. What the hell's going on?" He abruptly stopped. Based on the shift in tone, this wasn't going to be good news.

"What is it?"

"Someone slashed my tires."

"You haven't been here for long. Whoever did this must be close." Lisa glanced around and gasped. "He must still be here."

"I'll arrange another ride. We need to get you inside." He spun her chair around and wheeled her toward the hospital as she kept watch for any signs of movement in her peripheral.

Ryan parked her near the elevator, away from the automatic sliding glass doors. His cell phone was already at his ear by the time Lisa could see him again.

"Who are you calling this late?" she asked, panic written all over her features.

"Dawson lives close," Ryan said, the line already ringing.

"Please don't say anything," she begged. That damn desperation still in her tone.

Their friend picked up on the third.

"I'm at the hospital with Lisa and we need a ride." He paused, not eager to lie to his friend. "Must've picked up a nail on my way over. Left tire's flat."

Ryan said a few uh-huhs into the phone before he ended the call. "He's on his way."

She couldn't quite feel relief yet; maybe it was hope. Her danger radar was on full alert after everything she'd been through. Every noise made her jumpy.

"Is there any way you'd consider not sharing any of this with Dawson yet?" she pleaded.

"I don't even know what's really going on." Ryan kept his fisted hands at his sides as he kept watch.

A few quiet minutes later, Dawson pulled up in his SUV.

Ryan looked Lisa dead in the eye before he made a move to help her. "I won't force you to say anything in front of Dawson. We're going to my house. And when we get there, you're going to start talking."

Chapter Four

"I'm sorry about your father," Dawson said once they were safely inside the truck. Based on the look in his eyes, she knew he meant it. He had questions. Ditto for Ryan.

"Thank you," she said, unable to suppress a yawn. Exhaustion had worn her body to the bone and for the first time since this ordeal began she felt that it was safe to go to sleep. The burst of adrenaline she'd felt during the struggle in the hospital was long gone.

Dawson seemed content to leave things at that for now. She leaned against Ryan, put her head on his shoulder and closed her eyes. By the time she opened them again, they were parked in front of Ryan's house.

"No need to go out of your way for me. I'll be good on the couch," Lisa said to Ryan as he helped her up the few steps to his house.

He turned and waved at Dawson, who'd been waiting for a signal that it was okay to leave.

Lisa was grateful that Ryan hadn't forced her say anything in front of their friend. More than that, she was thrilled that she'd been able to let down her guard enough to fall sleep.

"Okay." Ryan unlocked the door and led her inside.

It was the first time she'd seen his house, a bungalow on an out-of-the-way street five miles from town. He'd already told her that the place sat on three acres and that he especially liked being on the outskirts of Mason Ridge. He was close enough to get anything he needed and just far enough to feel that he was away from it all when he went home.

He flipped on a light, walked her right past the leather sofa and moved toward the hallway instead.

"Ryan. What are you doing?" She tried to stop, but he nudged her forward.

"Giving you a place to sleep, remember?" He had the upper hand. He knew full well she couldn't walk into the other room without support.

"You said I could sleep on the couch."

"Did I?" His grin shouldn't make her want to laugh. Maybe she just needed to think about something light for a change.

She should throw more of a fit about sleeping on the couch, too, but she didn't have any fight left inside her after all she'd been through. Fatigue weighted her limbs, making it difficult to hold on to Ryan, and the new bruises she'd acquired were already tender.

"Can we close those blinds?" she asked, biting back a yawn as Ryan helped her ease under the covers.

"If that would make you feel better." He paused. "No one can hurt you out here."

He was already moving toward the window.

"I feel rotten for kicking you out of your own room. Are you sure you don't want to put me on the couch? I'd be fine."

"You're in my house. That means we play by my rules. You get the bed." He winked at her, but she could see the storm brewing. "I'll leave the door open in case you need anything. Just give me a shout."

"Where will you be?" She must look pitiful for him to hold off his questions until morning. Maybe she'd figure out what to tell him by then.

"On the couch." He walked toward the hallway. "It's not the first time."

Even so, it didn't feel right.

"No, Ry—"

His hand came up before she could finish her protest. "My rules, remember?"

She was biting back another yawn as she conceded. For tonight, she wouldn't argue. However, she hoped to stay a few days, at least, and she had no plans to force him out of his bed for that long.

"I'll be in the next room," he said, turning off the light. "Unless you need me to stay until you fall asleep."

"I'm good. Thank you, though." Lisa knew that Ryan wanted answers and normally she'd trust him with her life, but more lives than hers were on the line. She had Lori and Grayson to consider. Maybe she could get word to Beckett that she had no plans to reveal his secret. Leave her family alone and she would never bring the truth to light. Would it work?

No. Wasn't that the deal they'd had all these years?

There had to be a reason for the change. A family like his would be savvy. Maybe he figured she would come forward. No way could he allow this accusation to come to light given the depth of trouble his father was already in. The Alcorn name was worth a lot of money. Their reputation was big business. Between that and ruining their family name, their history in the town, maybe Beckett figured he needed to ensure only positive press for him and his father in the coming months. It was the only thing that made any sense.

If a plea wouldn't work, then she'd threaten him if she had to. If he didn't leave her family alone she would go to the law and then to the media and tell them everything.

His voice echoed in the back of her mind. What were the chances the sheriff would believe her? And especially after all these years? Would the media? It wasn't as if she could produce any tangible evidence, not now. She'd believed Beckett's threats as a little girl because she wasn't aware of rape kits and forensics.

A good attorney could turn her testimony upside down. And then she, Lori and Grayson would have to watch their backs for the rest of their lives. Wealthy men had long reach and she doubted she'd be safe no matter how far away she moved, which was precisely why that plan wouldn't work.

Either way, she couldn't see an out. Plus, there was this new guy to worry about. The man who'd attacked her in the hospital was not Beckett.

Trying to think made her brain cramp. Frustration ate at her. Exhaustion threatened to pull her under. She was toast. No way could she think clearly.

For now, Lori and Grayson were safe.

She let that thought carry her into a deep sleep.

LISA WOKE THREE times throughout the night, screaming from nightmares. When she opened her eyes for the fourth time, the sun was bright in the sky. She glanced over and saw Ryan, shirtless, still sleeping in a chair. He'd stayed after the first round, saying he wanted to be close if she needed him.

His presence comforted her.

Her lips tingled with the feel of the kiss they'd shared. She didn't want to be thinking about that first thing when she opened her eyes. And yet there it was all the same.

His chest was a wall of muscle and she had to force her eyes away from his sculpted abs. That body was built from hard work and she admired him for it. There were other marks on his body, too, and she didn't want to think about the scars left behind at his father's hand. She'd witnessed one of the beatings as she was skipping home from school one day. Thinking about it even now caused her heart to squeeze and anger to flair through her.

She didn't ask, didn't know what had triggered Ryan's father that day. Everyone knew how bad the man's temper had been. Ryan was quick to step in to cover for his brother, Justin, and she wondered if Ryan had done it on that day, too.

It had been two weeks until summer break, and the Texas heat had arrived early that year. Lisa couldn't have been more than ten or eleven at the time. She'd stayed after school to finish a science project and passed by Ryan's house on her way home.

His father had him around the side of the house, his hand clamped around Ryan's arm as the man beat his son with a belt, buckle still attached.

There were no screams from her classmate, no begging for mercy, and that was a fact that would haunt her for years.

Ryan's pain was endured in silence, like hers. He never spoke about that or any other beating afterward, either. She could see in his eyes when they'd been exceptionally brutal. His father was always careful to hit Ryan in places where the bruises wouldn't show in plain sight. Every time Ryan had worn long pants in ninety-eight-degree temperatures to school, she'd noticed. Every time he had eased onto a chair, she'd noticed. Every time he'd worn long sleeves in the summer, she'd noticed.

And she'd known why.

Fire burned through her veins, boiling her blood at the memories. Only a coward hurt a child. Ryan's father had been one. And so was Beckett.

"How'd you sleep?" Ryan's voice surprised her.

"Good," she said quickly, trying to slow her racing pulse. She'd slept better than good actually, even with the nightmares. She didn't want to tell him how comfortable she felt in his bed. The sheets were soft against her skin. The mattress was like sleeping on a soft cushion. And his clean, masculine scent was all over the pillow.

The pain was messing with her mind. This bed was no nicer than the one at the hospital, she tried to tell herself.

He stood and fastened his jeans, and she forced her gaze away from the small patch of hair on his chest leading down toward the band of his jeans.

Walking toward her, he yawned and stretched, and she noticed just how powerful his arms were. There was enough muscle there to hold off a bear, let alone a man who liked to hurt women. She told herself that was the only reason she noticed—to see if he could protect her—and not because of the awareness she felt every time he was in the room.

The mattress dipped under his weight as he sat on the edge of the bed.

"Are you hungry?" he asked.

"I think I can eat."

"What sounds good?"

"Don't put yourself out. Anything is fine. A piece of fruit or yogurt would do." She hated feeling so helpless.

"I can make an omelet," he offered.

"No. That's too much work, seriously."

"Would you stop worrying about being a pain already? I don't mind. I can scramble some eggs and heat sausage. But first, how does a cup of coffee sound?"

"Like heaven on earth." She waited for him to leave the room before she tried to sit up. Pain shot through her with every movement. She fought through it. No way was she asking him to help her to the bathroom.

Carefully, she inched her legs toward the side of the bed until her feet hung off.

How long did the nurse say it would take before Lisa felt better?

At this rate, it was going to take a long time to make it to the bathroom let alone go for a run again. She shook it off and forced her legs over the side of the bed.

Pushing up on her arms, she winced. A good look at the bruises there only made things worse. At least she could use her anger to fuel her determination to get up. She focused all her energy on standing.

The first few steps were like walking on stilts for the first time. A few more and she started getting the hang of how to lean in order to reduce the pain that came with movement. By the time she returned to the bed, she was energized. Being able to do something for herself so soon was a huge win.

"Hold on there. Let me help you." Ryan stood in the doorway two-fisting cups of coffee.

"No problem. I got this," she said, in too much pain to outwardly express her excitement.

"I'd ask if you're always this determined, but I already know the answer." His genuine smile was better than any painkiller, and that probably scared her more than anything else.

"I hope it's okay that I opened the toothbrush on the counter. I figure you left it out for me." She eased onto the bed and pulled the covers up.

Ryan returned to his earlier seat near her and handed over a cup of fresh brew.

"Good," he said, and his voice was husky. He cleared his throat and took a sip.

This close, she could see the horrible reminders of his painful childhood up and down his back and her heart nearly exploded.

"How's Justin?" she asked to distract herself.

"Good. He's living in Austin now with a wife and a pair of kids. The oldest is about to start school and Maria isn't thrilled." Ryan perked up.

"It's good that he got out of here," she said. She'd never met Justin's wife. Once he left, he never turned back.

"Too many memories, I think."

"What about you? You ever think about leaving Mason Ridge?" She sipped the coffee, thinking it was about the best thing she'd tasted all year.

He leaned back, positioned his elbow on the bed and said, "All the time."

"Then why do you stay?"

"Not sure. Work's here. Still have a little bit of family in the area, friends."

"You know you can stay in touch via cell phones and social media now. People don't have to live in the same area to keep a friendship going anymore." She wondered if a little piece of him waited for his mother to return. He'd been hurt the most when she left.

"I have a cell phone, which is brand-new, but I use it to as a means to call people so we can meet up somewhere. Call me old-fashioned, but I like to look my friends in the eye when I talk to them, have a beer together and not have to plug in a device or stare at a screen to do it."

"Wow. You really are sounding like a relic now," she teased, enjoying the easy conversation. The heavy discussion would come and she'd have to figure out a way around giving straight answers.

"I'LL LEAVE YOU with that as I make your breakfast, in the kitchen, using old-fashioned machines like a toaster," Ryan said.

She laughed, which shouldn't have put a smile on his face as he left the room. It did. If he had any sense at all, he'd wipe off his silly grin.

Talking to Lisa came easy. It had always been the case with the two of them. He'd misread that to mean something more in the past. Being wiser now, or maybe just older, he realized that their conversation flowed when everything was light, right up until they tried to talk about anything important.

Then there were the nightmares she kept to herself. She woke screaming, traumatized, but refused to talk about them.

He'd also noticed last night that she recoiled when he touched her. If his arm so much as grazed her skin, she involuntarily tensed. What was that about?

There was an electrical current running between them, too. The chemistry that had existed before was as strong as ever, and that just confused the hell out of him.

He might have maturity on his side, but that still didn't explain why he couldn't accurately read her intentions even after all these years. And it wasn't as if that had ever been a problem for him with other women. His relationship was Lisa was the definition of complicated.

Right now there were more pressing questions that needed answers. And he had a feeling he was about to make her uncomfortable.

Right after he fed her.

Ryan brought in a plate of toast and scrambled eggs, which she made short work of.

He'd been reviewing all the possible reasons she'd wound up lying in a hospital bed, none he liked. In fact, most made him downright angry because if this wasn't random, then his mind snapped to the very real possibility that a boyfriend or someone she cared about had done this to her. Fire raged through his veins, burning him from the inside out at the thought. He'd nearly caught on fire last night thinking about how she'd kept watching the door yesterday, afraid. She'd evaded all of his questions even when he'd made sure her back was against the wall. She would rather toss him out than give him the truth. He'd suffered enough at the hands of his father to know when someone was covering for an abuser. Ryan had been that person.

Giving a false report to the law could get her in real trouble. They needed to have a discussion about that.

"So, tell me what's going on with you, Lisa. Are you seeing someone?" She wouldn't come out and tell him she was being abused. He'd need to let her know she could trust him first.

"No." She shook her head for emphasis.

Okay, fine. Looking at her expression, he believed her. Lisa was a bad liar and it was mostly because she had no practice at it. After dealing with his family, Ryan appreciated that about her. But that didn't mean a guy from her past hadn't resurfaced. Maybe even someone who knew her sister. He thought about how protective she'd been over Lori and Grayson.

"Then what?" he asked, not wanting to own up to the relief he felt knowing she didn't have a boyfriend. It shouldn't matter. He had to be hands-off when it came to her.

"I appreciate everything you're doing for me, Ryan, I do." She paused, looking as though she was searching for the right words. "Maybe I should go."

"No, you don't." She was in too deep, and he needed to be delicate with what he needed to ask. "You're staying here. Just give me a reason why you won't tell me what's going on."

"I would if I could. Can we leave it at that?" There was that fear in her eyes again. If he said, "Boo!" she'd bolt. Anger roared through him.

"We can for now." He needed to know what he was up against, but there were other ways to get at the truth without pushing—pushing would only drive her away. Ryan knew that from personal experience, as well. Lisa looked as if she might explode from fear and he didn't want her getting the idea that she had to go home. At least while she was at his place he could keep an eye on things, make sure she was okay. They already had history and he could build on that to get her to trust him. Then, as soon as he found out that bastard's name, Ryan would make sure the guy never touched anyone else ever again.

"Promise me something?" she asked, and he could hear the fear in her voice no matter how much she tried to mask it.

He nodded.

"Don't tell anyone I'm here. Or where Lori and Grayson are staying at least until I get my head around everything that's happened and we make arrangements for my father." A few tears fell, streaking her cheeks.

He thumbed them away, ignoring the impulse to lean forward and kiss her.

"You have my word. I won't tell a soul. But if I'm going to protect you, then I need to know what I'm up against." That seemed to strike a chord.

She pursed her lips and then nodded.

Chapter Five

"The swelling is worse on my cheek, isn't it?" Lisa
asked as she walked into the kitchen, where Ryan was
doing dishes.

"Let me help you." He made a move toward her but
was met with a hand.

"I want to do this on my own. Can't stick around
here forever."

"You just got here last night." Ryan was used to people leaning on him. This was the first time he met a wall
every time he tried to help. Lisa and her sister had been
bounced around when they were kids and he suspected
that was the reason she kept everyone at arm's length.

"It doesn't hurt as much to do this, though." She
stretched her arms out and then lifted her hands above
her head.

The move caused her breasts to press against the
fabric of her shirt. Spending 24/7 together wasn't doing
good things to his hormones. Those feelings from the
past had resurfaced and that was most likely because
he hadn't spent much time around her since then. You'd
think he was still eighteen for how much his body reacted to her. He needed to keep himself in check.

"That's a good thing. Do you want a couple of pain

relievers? I have over-the-counter stuff, but it'll take the edge off." Ryan handed her a fresh cup of coffee. She'd been tight-lipped so far about what was going on. She kept reassuring him that she'd be fine, but those nightmares told a different story.

Ryan had a fleeting thought that her attack could be related to Charles Alcorn slipping out of police custody. His capture brought up the old trauma from their friend and her brother being abducted fifteen years ago.

Would that cause Lisa to wake up in the middle of the night screaming? Ryan's gut instinct said no. Something like that came from deep-seeded fears. He knew all about those.

"No, I'm fine. I need to check in with my sister. Have you seen my cell?"

"Spoke to her this morning. She and Grayson are doing great, enjoying the view of the lake."

"When did you do that?" She moved to the kitchen window, wearing his boxers tied off at the waist and an oversize T-shirt, drinking her coffee.

"Early. Figured she'd be up with Grayson."

"How long has your SUV been here?" The fear was back.

"Since about eight o'clock. I called in a few favors to expedite the process. Having a friend in the private security business helped. Why?"

"No reason." She shrugged off the comment, trying to make it look as if she didn't care.

This might be the opportunity he'd been looking for to get her to open up a little more. He needed to find the right words or he'd scare her into her shell faster than a sea turtle being hunted by a shark.

"What made you become a teacher?" he asked.

"It sounds corny but I like working with kids. Seeing their eyes light up when something clicks is the best feeling," she said, and her mood instantly improved. She settled down at the kitchen table with her coffee.

He'd found a less threatening subject. Good.

"I can see in your eyes that you love your job." He joined her at the table. He wondered how much her own difficult childhood played into her career choice.

"I can't imagine doing anything else," she said, her face glowing.

And that shouldn't make Ryan smile, but it did. He chalked it up to enjoying seeing his friend happy.

"Did you know that my dad never finished high school?" she asked.

"I probably should know that. You know me. I'm not one for gossip." Hadn't he always had his hands full with his own family?

"He didn't. I think it always bothered him, too. He always pushed me and Lori to graduate and go to college." Tears welled in her eyes.

"I'm sure he's proud of you both," Ryan said.

She turned her face toward the window and he could see that she was struggling to control her emotions.

He gave her the space she needed, resisting the urge to move across that table and haul her into his arms.

"You know what keeps me awake at night?" she finally asked, turning to face him. "My sister and Grayson. I worry about her bringing up a child alone."

"Lori isn't alone. She has you." Don't think he didn't notice that she'd just changed the subject before he could dig deeper. Okay, fine. He didn't have it in him to press when she was barely able to tamp down her emotions. But he was determined to make progress with her at some point today. He'd go ask her coworkers if school was in session. Maybe he could dig around a little, anyway. Surely someone knew about her personal life.

"True, but Grayson needs a father and that doesn't look like it's going to happen." She took a sip of coffee. "Jessie cut off all contact with her when he found out she was pregnant."

"Better it happen now than later."

"How do you know it would have happened later? He never gave her a chance." She shot fire at him through her eyes.

He held his hands up in surrender. "That didn't come out right. I'm just saying that it would hurt less now, while Grayson's little, than if he had the chance to get to know his dad before he took off."

She hesitated for a second. "I can see why you'd think that."

"I know what you're thinking and you're exactly right," he conceded. How in hell's name did she flip this into a conversation about his family? "I learned that lesson the hard way."

"I remember when your mom left. It changed you," she said softly. He hadn't expected her to remember, or to hear so much compassion in her voice when she talked about his family.

"A mother choosing to walk out doesn't do good things to a ten-year-old boy."

"No, you're right. That never should have happened." Lisa didn't add the fact that she'd left her sons with a cruel man, and he appreciated her for it. "For what it's worth, I'm sorry."

Those last two words spoken from Lisa did more to ease the ache in his chest than almost two decades of going over and over it in his own mind, reminding himself countless times that it wasn't his fault.

"Have you spoken to her since then?" she asked, studying her coffee mug.

"No. I don't even have a good address on her." This discussion wasn't the one Ryan wanted to have. The only reason he'd keep going is that it just might help bridge the gap between them, help her to trust him to talk about deeper issues.

"It's not hard to find people these days. All you need is a name and you can search the internet," she said.

"Sure. If you want to find them."

"And you don't?" she glanced up from her mug, curious.

"I've already told you. I'm not that good with technology," he countered.

"Oh no, you don't, mister. You're not getting away with it that easily. Nice try, though."

"You got me, then." How did he put this without sounding like an SOB? "She's the one who walked out. Why on earth would I go chasing after someone who could just as easily find me if she wanted to? Just in case you haven't put it together yet, she hasn't even tried."

"How do you know?" Lisa's brow furrowed in the way it did when she studied something intently. She might have been looking at her coffee mug, but she was carefully considering his responses. And from the look of it, she was also holding back her true opinion.

"Why is any of this important to you?" He didn't mean to sound so clipped. Talking about his mother never seemed to get any easier.

She glanced up at him.

"I'm sorry. I shouldn't be so nosy." She ran her finger along the rim of the cup. "I guess I was thinking of all the good times I would've missed with my own father if I hadn't forgiven him for some of the things he did when he was drinking."

"There is one big difference between our parents."

"Which is?"

"Yours cared enough to stick around."

LISA NEEDED TO change the subject. Witnessing the hurt in Ryan's eyes when he spoke about his mother was a shot to the heart and she feared she was only making the situation worse by dredging up the past. Some topics weren't good to revisit.

Ryan did it for her when he stood and took his mug to the sink, mumbling something about making plans for the day.

And it could just be the fact that she was missing her own father that made her want to heal Ryan's relationships. Speaking of her family, she needed to talk to her sister.

"Did you say that you saw my cell?" she asked while he seemed to intently focus on whatever he had going on in the sink.

He stopped what he was doing for a second.

"Is there something going on with my phone?" she asked.

"Are you sure you want it? That thing hasn't stopped vibrating and buzzing."

"What did you do with it?"

"Nothing. Well, I turned it off. You needed to rest and I was afraid it would wake you. I brought it out here and then it kept me up, which is the other reason I slept in that chair last night."

Normally, the thought of her smartphone being stuffed inside a drawer or tucked away on a counter would create a level-five panic. In this case, she was grateful. Everyone would most likely be trying to figure out what was going on with her or sending their condolences. Even though people were well-intentioned and she would get back to them as soon as she could, she wasn't strong enough to face it yet.

"We need to stop by the funeral home later today to make the arrangements," he said.

"Did they call?"

"No. I made contact with them. I knew you and your sister weren't in the right place to be able to handle it yet. I didn't want them leaving messages, so I figured I'd reach out and keep them posted on your progress. They said they'd have someone available early evening today, after closing, so you'd be assured privacy."

Ryan had no idea how comforting those words truly were. "Can we go see Lori and Grayson after?"

"I have a few things to take care of tonight. We can leave for Arkansas first thing in the morning. We'll go at first light."

"Great." She could live with that. Besides, that would give her another night of rest to heal. As it was, she was afraid that she'd scare her nephew. She could hide the bruises with makeup.

Most of the day she spent curled up on the couch watching TV.

Lisa was determined to dress herself. Ryan had washed her clothes and it felt good to have on something clean that fit. The drive to the funeral home went by quickly.

There were only two cars in the parking lot when

they arrived. She noticed a late-model blue sedan parked near the front door. The second, a pickup truck, was positioned around the side of the building. The bed was loaded with mulch and equipment that looked like gardening supplies. The sun was bright. It wouldn't be dark in this part of Texas for three hours and yet the place still had a creepy feel to it.

Maybe it was the knowledge that there was so much death around her that made the hairs on her neck prick. Or the fact that she knew her father lay inside, breathless, gone.

Tears welled, stinging the backs of her eyes.

"Can we stop by my place on the way home?" she asked. "I need to pick up clothes and makeup."

Ryan seemed to pick up on her anxiety because he leaned forward and kissed her on the forehead before helping her out of his SUV. He held out his hand. She took it, the warmth in his touch calming her, and ignored the pain shooting through her chest with every step toward the sales office. This pain was different than what she'd felt for the past few days. She felt that, too. This hurt from the inside out, sucked the air from her lungs in one whoosh and made her want to fold onto her knees and cry without stopping.

The emotions that she couldn't afford to allow herself to feel about her father's death threatened to explode. The inside of her head felt like raging storm clouds gathering, clinging thickly in the air, making it difficult to think.

Her father's body had already been identified. At least she didn't have to do that. Oh, but Lori had and Lisa hated that her baby sister had been the one to do it. Even worse was that Lisa had been in the hospital and Lori had had to deal with it alone. Ever since their mother had died, it had always been the two of them together, supporting each other through their dad's antics. Lisa had stepped up to try and fill their mother's shoes.

The door was locked, so Ryan tapped on the glass.

An older man appeared from down a hallway, waving and smiling. He opened the door and shook each of their hands, beginning with Lisa's.

"Please come inside. I'm pleased to meet both of you. My name is Arthur." His spoke in a soft, even tone. He was a short man in his late fifties. He wore a simple suit with a button-down shirt and no tie.

Inside, the walls were painted taupe, a calming color, and the decor was simple. There was a cherrywood desk with matching bookcase and cabinets. The leather executive chair was tucked into the desk. It was eerily quiet and no one else appeared to be inside the building.

"Thank you for agreeing to meet this late," Lisa said. "I'm Lisa and this is my friend Ryan. I believe you two spoke on the phone."

"It's my pleasure to assist you in putting your loved one to rest." Arthur's hands were clasped, his shoulders slightly rounded.

He isn't at rest, Lisa thought, *he's dead*. Tension tightened the muscles in her shoulders and back. Arthur was being polite, doing his job, so it wasn't him causing her to tense up. Maybe it was the thought that her father didn't have to be…gone.

She took in a deep breath and refocused.

"Please, follow me." Arthur turned and then walked down the hallway, stopping at the second door on the right. There was a Bible verse written on one wall that she remembered from her childhood. On the other was a poster that read Celebrate the Life of Your Loved One. Ask Your Representative for Details.

Two chairs sat opposite the cherrywood desk in Arthur's office. Ryan helped her to the nearest one. He bent down so only she could hear him and said, "You say the word and we're outta here."

She nodded slightly.

He took a seat next to her, and then turned so that he was facing her more than Arthur, bent forward and clasped his hands together. The older man seemed unfazed and she imagined he'd seen stranger things. She glanced backward toward the door, not liking that she didn't have a clear view.

There was a small table between her and Ryan with a few brochures promoting add-on services like all-maple caskets and the use of their on-site chapel for viewing along with a tissue box.

Arthur clasped his hands, mimicking Ryan's gesture, and placed them on top of the solid desk.

"How may I assist you today?" he asked, his voice calm and soothing.

"My father wanted to be cremated." Those six words threatened to unleash a torrent of tears.

Arthur nodded, gave another compassionate look. As genuine as he seemed, he'd probably done this thousands of times over the course of his career. He'd seen an equal number of grieving families bury someone they loved.

Lisa opened her mouth to speak but was silenced by a noise that sounded from behind. Ryan turned at the same time she did, watching the hallway.

"It's probably nothing. Fred, our groundskeeper, is

still here working," Arthur dismissed the interruption, focusing on Lisa again.

"Stay right here." Ryan was already on his feet by the time they heard a second noise.

Lisa didn't want to wait. Besides, the thought of Ryan going out there to investigate alone didn't do good things to her blood pressure. Her father was dead. She'd been in the hospital. Any number of things could happen to Ryan. And the thought of bad news happening in threes was fresh in her mind.

She pushed herself up and followed him. He must not have noticed because he said nothing to stop her. And if he'd known, he would've stopped to help her. He was locked on to something.

Only a few steps behind him, she still didn't get a good look at what had caused the noise. The front door was closing, though.

Someone had been in there.

"Fred?" Ryan called out as he bolted through the front door.

She couldn't get there fast enough to catch him. By the time she made it across the room with Arthur's help, Ryan had returned.

"You expecting anyone else?" Ryan asked the older man.

"No. We get kids running through shouting inappropriate things sometimes for laughs." This was the first time the old man broke form. Disgust was in his eyes.

"Don't they normally say or do anything?" Ryan's gaze moved from Arthur to his SUV. He must be remembering what had just happened to his tires at the hospital.

"Yes. But you never know what's going on in the

mind of a teenager." Arthur shrugged, his compassion-ate demeanor returned.

Ryan turned to Lisa. She tried to command her body to stop trembling.

"You want to do this by phone?" he asked.

She nodded.

"I'm sorry to have wasted your time, Arthur. This isn't a good idea for her right now," Ryan said firmly, leaving no room for doubt that they were about to walk out the door.

"I understand. Call when you're ready to talk." Arthur produced a card from his pocket.

Lisa thanked him and walked to the SUV with Ryan's help.

Once they were inside and he took the driver's seat, she said, "I've had a bad feeling the whole time we've been here."

He turned over the ignition. The engine hummed to life.

"That's because we were being watched."

Chapter Six

"I need to ask this straight out, Lisa. Did an ex-boyfriend do this to you?" Ryan knew he might make her retreat by being straightforward like that, but he needed to know.

"No."

"Are you being honest with me?" Again, he had to ask. It was the only thing that made sense to him, given everything he'd witnessed so far, and especially the way she'd watched the door at the hospital as though she was expecting someone to come in. Expecting wasn't the right word. It was more like fearing.

"I've never lied to you, Ryan." She sounded hurt.

Maybe he should've trusted his initial judgment and left it alone. This was a no-win situation. She wasn't giving him anything else to go on.

"Then tell me what's going on with you. Who hurt you? I know it's not random." He pulled the SUV onto the county road, checking the mirrors in case anyone followed them.

"I'm afraid to tell you. I don't want to make everything worse. I just need a few days to heal and figure this out."

"Figure what out?" he parroted.

"Can't we just leave it at that?"

"No. Not when you could get hurt again. Not when I can't protect you. Not when some unknown threat can pop up at any time."

"It's not a boyfriend, but it is something from my past. I can assure you that I'm the only one he wants," she said quietly.

"Tell me his name." Ryan kept his gaze focused on the road ahead, waiting for her to give him a name.

Neither spoke for the rest of the ride.

As soon as they got to his house, Lisa asked if he minded if she went to bed early.

"Eat first." He grilled a simple meal of beef kabobs with pineapple chunks and slices of green bell peppers for her while she was in the shower.

The plate he'd fixed for her was clear in a few minutes.

"That was delicious," she said with the first half smile since the ordeal at the funeral home. "At least let me help with the dishes."

"No. I got this." He waved her away. No way was he letting her help in her current condition. Besides, he liked cooking for her and taking care of her more than he wanted to admit, even if she was making it difficult by withholding information.

"I kicked you out of your bedroom. I haven't lifted a finger since I got here. The least you can let me do is earn my keep in the kitchen." Her voice rose at the end, angry.

What was that all about? She was injured and he was trying to take care of her.

Lisa started toward the bedroom. He made a move to help her.

"I can do this at least, Ryan," she said.

Ryan bit back a curse as he watched her struggle on her own.

"This is silly. Why won't you let me help you?" he asked, frustrated.

"Ask yourself the same question, Hunt."

If Ryan lived to be two hundred and fifty years old, he'd never understand a woman. All he was doing was trying to help Lisa. She was hurt and he was able. End of story. If she could do more for herself, he'd have no problem letting her pitch in to do the dishes or whatever else the heck she wanted to do around his home. Why had she turned it on him?

There was another thing that had been bugging him. She'd made a big deal about putting him out by taking his bed. He didn't mind. Hell, he'd slept in worse places than his comfortable couch. What was she getting crazy about?

Rather than spin out on questions he couldn't answer, he decided to watch a little TV before turning in.

Ryan must've dozed off because he woke to Lisa screaming. Another nightmare? He pushed off his blanket, did a quick head shake to get rid of the fog and jogged toward his bedroom.

A crashing sound. Ryan broke into a full run.

Ryan smacked at the light switch, missed as he darted to her side. The room was completely black.

Lisa was struggling…and someone was on the bed hovering over her.

Ryan dove at the male figure from behind, knocking him off balance and off Lisa.

Both he and the intruder rolled off the bed. Ryan

fired off a couple of jabs into the guy's ribs, taking a blow to the chin.

Lisa screamed in what sounded like anger and pain rolled into one.

The attacker was smaller in stature than Ryan, but he was quick.

A knee to Ryan's groin had him cursing and fighting off nausea. He had a decent grip on the jerk, and Ryan had no intention of letting go.

"Call 911," he shouted to Lisa.

Another knee to the groin, a little higher this time, and Ryan saw stars. He couldn't get a good look at the attacker in the pitch-black. The blow caused him to lose his grip just enough for the guy to push off and get to his feet.

Ryan rolled onto his shoulder and wrapped his arms around the guy's ankles. He prayed like hell that Lisa was calling the sheriff.

Still on the floor, he couldn't see what she was doing and the guy was kicking and squirming. At this rate, it wouldn't be long before he broke free from Ryan's grip. Unless Ryan made a move. It was risky. Give this guy an inch and he could break free and sprint away.

Damn, Ryan's shotgun was in the second bedroom he used as an office. Lot of good it was doing in there.

All Ryan could see was outlines and dark figures.

An object slammed against the guy's head, knocking him back. The guy tried to rebalance by shifting his feet. Ryan tightened his grip, locking the guy's stance. The attacker fell backward.

"Call 911. Now!" Ryan shouted to Lisa.

He climbed on top of the guy, pressing him into the floor with his weight advantage.

Without warning, the muscles in Ryan's body seized up. What the hell? Every muscle suddenly became rigid and he heard a ringing noise in his ears.

Pain shot through him and he couldn't move. He was paralyzed.

The charge stopped after a few seconds and his muscles relaxed, but it felt as if they were vibrating and he still couldn't coordinate movement.

His attacker wriggled free, elbowing Ryan in the process, catching him in the neck. Ryan still couldn't budge.

The guy took off down the hallway.

There were the sounds of a struggle that lasted only a few seconds. Then a door slammed. A dirt bike engine roared to life.

Ryan still couldn't move, couldn't speak. He could only lie on the floor, frustrated and helpless.

Light filled part of the room. Lisa must've flipped on the hallway light. She was next to him a few seconds later.

"What did he do to you?" Concern laced her raspy tone.

At least another full minute passed before Ryan could respond.

"Taser gun." Those two words took more effort than he imagined. Normal feeling was beginning to return to his extremities. He flexed and released his fingers, wiggled his toes.

Once the recovery process started, it moved quickly. He had full possession of his faculties within minutes.

Ryan pushed himself up to a sitting position. His nightstand had been cleared in the struggle and his alarm clock and lamp tossed onto the floor.

How had the guy gotten past Ryan to get inside in the first place?

His legs were shaky, but he moved to the window in the bedroom, realized it was open and stuck his head outside. He couldn't see anything moving and figured the guy was long gone.

"The deputy should be here any minute," he said to Lisa.

She pursed her lips.

Wait a second. She didn't call?

"We don't need to get them involved, do we?" she asked. The fear had returned.

"As a matter of fact, we do. I still have no idea who we're dealing with and this is the third incident. I don't know what kind of jerk you got yourself involved with, but I'm bringing in the law this time." Ryan didn't wait for her to respond. He located his cell and called dispatch.

He checked the front rooms, locked the door and returned to the bedroom when the house was clear.

She just sat on the floor, facing the wall.

He moved to her side and helped her onto the edge of the bed.

"It's not safe anymore," she said in a monotone, sounding as if she was in a trance.

"Whoever is doing this to you belongs behind bars. We talk to the deputy, bring in the law and they'll lock him up. It's that simple." He stared at her. The hallway light lit up one side of her face. The other was cast in a shadow. "He's bound to have left some evidence behind. They'll figure out who this is."

"You're right," she said.

Finally, he was getting through to her.

"I'll meet you in the living room in a second. I want to get dressed before the deputy gets here," she said.

"Okay." He moved into the kitchen and then brewed a fresh pot of coffee. She was starting to see logic. He was making progress. Now he might actually be able to help Lisa. All he'd done so far was provide a refuge.

But how did anyone know she was staying at his place?

His mind snapped back to the incident at the funeral parlor. Someone had been watching. Waiting to see if she showed so they could follow her and find out where she was staying.

Crazed boyfriends, if that was the story here, were known to go to all kinds of lengths to get revenge on their so-called loved ones. He'd read stories about abused women and the fear stamped on Lisa's face certainly fit the description. Her actions did, too.

The thought of anyone hurting her on purpose boiled his blood. A real man didn't raise a fist to a woman. Give Ryan a few minutes alone in a fair fight with the bastard and see what would happen.

What didn't add up was that Lisa didn't seem like the sort of person who would get mixed up with an abuser. Then again, based on the stories he'd come across, there was no type. Domestic abuse covered every race, religion and income bracket.

He'd nearly finished his cup of coffee by the time the deputy knocked on the door.

The intrusion and the fight must've shaken Lisa up pretty badly, because she hadn't emerged from the bedroom yet. If Ryan was being honest, he'd admit that his adrenaline was still pumping. He wished he'd gotten a good look at the guy. All he could give the deputy was a general description.

Ryan opened the door and invited Deputy Barnes to come inside. Barnes had been in Justin's grade and Ryan hoped the officer wouldn't hold Justin's teenage years against the whole family. Barnes was five foot nine, slim and wiry.

"Lisa Moore is also a witness. She's a friend of mine who's staying with me while she recovers from a hospital stay. I'll let her know you're here." Ryan started toward the hallway. "Coffee's fresh. There's a clean mug on the counter. Help yourself."

"Thank you," Barnes said.

Ryan nodded and then moved down the hallway. He didn't want to surprise Lisa, especially if she was in the bathroom, so he stepped heavily and called out to her.

When she didn't respond, his pulse kicked up a notch. No way the attacker could have returned, Ryan reassured himself.

He knocked on the bedroom door.

Nothing.

She could be in the bathroom, running sink water or flushing the commode. Even so, Ryan didn't have a good feeling about this.

"Lisa." He knocked once more, a little louder this time, before opening the door.

Heat hit him full force as soon as he stepped inside the room. The window had been reopened.

An ominous feeling settled over Ryan. The bathroom door was open and the room was empty.

What had she done?

He raced to the window. The porch light illuminated

a small part of the front yard, and that was about all he could see.

There was no sign of movement or Lisa.

Ryan needed to get out there and find her. He darted into the next room, where Deputy Barnes waited.

"My guest isn't here. She might be in trouble."

"What does that mean exactly?" The deputy, who was standing in the kitchen with a mug of coffee in his fist, blinked at Ryan.

For a split second he feared that the attacker had come back and snatched her from right under his nose. But, no, that couldn't be it. She would've screamed. Or fought. In which case, he would've heard something. It had been quiet. He'd been listening for any signs that she might've fallen. She could be so stubborn and insisted on taking care of herself.

Now he had no idea where she could be.

Chapter Seven

"She's injured and something's happened. Either she got spooked and ran or she's been taken." Ryan was already at the front door by the time he finished his sentence. "I need to search the grounds."

"Hold on a second. Talk to me about what we're dealing with before you trample all over my crime scene." The deputy set the coffee mug down and trailed behind Ryan, who'd stopped.

"I'm sorry. Someone broke in and attacked my guest," he said. "She's already hurt and I'm afraid she's in worse trouble."

"So this is a kidnapping?" The deputy's brow arched.

"I think she could be hiding, afraid the guy will return," Ryan hedged. He wasn't being completely honest. There was a thread of truth in his statement. She couldn't have gotten far, and hopefully she hadn't gone into the woods. That was where the attacker had gone.

"If that were true, wouldn't she come out now that I'm here?" Barnes asked.

"That's why I'm afraid she can't move. If we don't find her soon, it could be life or death."

Barnes nodded.

Within the first five minutes, he and the deputy had

cleared the shed and the yard. The deputy had insisted on going first and Ryan didn't have time to argue.

Being injured, she couldn't be moving fast. He thought for sure they'd find her somewhere on the grounds.

"There's no sign of her," Barnes said after fifteen minutes of searching. The deputy took his notepad from his front pocket and moved closer to the lights on his SUV. "Tell me what happened."

Ryan did.

"Show me where the struggle occurred," Barnes said.

Ryan followed the deputy as he examined the bedroom.

"Looks like the point of entry was the window. The latch is broken." He checked the other window and all the doors anyway, taking pictures as he worked the room. "We might be able to lift a print."

After collecting evidence there, he moved outside and examined the ground beneath the window, flashing a light around the hard dirt.

The deputy's cell phone buzzed. He took the call while Ryan turned toward the shed. He needed to think. Where would Lisa go at this hour?

"Do you have somewhere else to stay tonight?" The deputy stood and pocketed his flashlight when he was finished.

"No, sir. I'd rather stick around and protect my belongings." Ryan had every intention of finding Lisa.

"Let me know if your friend turns up," the deputy said, producing a card from his pocket. "In the meantime, call my cell if you remember anything else."

"Will do," Ryan agreed, anxious to continue his

search. He had every intention of locating her. More scenarios ran through his mind. None of them he liked.

Ryan pulled supplies from his shed to board up the window as he thought about where Lisa might go as the deputy's SUV backed out of the drive.

Thirty minutes later, he'd secured his house and put away extra nails and his hammer.

Walking back toward his small porch, he realized that they'd checked everywhere but his SUV. It was a long shot but one worth investigating.

The doors were locked. Another sign something was off. His personal belongings had always been safe on his land until tonight.

Ryan jogged into the house and retrieved keys from his jeans pocket. He heard the distinct sound of a vehicle door closing. He broke into a run.

Lisa was halfway across the yard when he returned.

"Stop," he shouted.

She froze but didn't turn to face him.

"What in hell's name is going on, Lisa?" Ryan caught up to her, put his hand on her arm to support her and blew out a frustrated breath when she recoiled.

"I'm sorry. I need to go."

"Not so fast. The only place you're going is inside. There's a fresh pot of coffee on and you're going to tell me what has you acting like a scared child." He urged her to turn around and he was surprised she did.

The look on her face, the resignation, should make him feel bad. He didn't want to go down this road with her. The one where he was basically forcing her to talk. But she was in danger and he couldn't put up with this any longer.

"He'll come back." There came the fear in her eyes again.

"Not tonight, he won't. The deputy said he'll be watching just in case. Plus, I have no plans to sleep. I won't be caught off guard again. And we're going to talk about what's scaring the hell out of you."

THERE WAS NO avoiding the discussion that Lisa didn't want to have with Ryan. Her stomach ached, not from physical pain, but the emotional kind. Everything had spiraled out of control faster than she could wrap her mind around it. In trying to keep her sister and nephew safe, she'd inadvertently put Ryan in danger.

Damn. Damn. Damn.

Once inside, Ryan helped her settle on the couch and brought her a cup of coffee. His steel eyes pierced right through her and she knew she could never lie to him. She had to tell him the truth, but she wasn't ready to share everything.

Seeing him retrieve and load his shotgun tied her stomach in knots.

He put two filled coffee mugs down on the coffee table in front of them and then took a seat next to her on the couch. He clasped his hands and rested his elbows on his knees. He was so close his left knee touched her right and she ignored what the contact was doing to her body.

"You already know about what has happened to me, the attack," she said.

He nodded, kept his gaze focused on a patch of hardwood floor to her left.

"This runs so much deeper than that." She took in a

fortifying breath and then released it. "I don't believe my father's death was an accident."

"Murder?" He sounded too stunned to say much else.

"Yes. I know it probably sounds crazy and I haven't given you any reason to believe me so far."

"Has someone been stalking you or your family?" He must've put a few things together, because his head rocked. "They have. That's why you won't talk about it."

"This person has been threatening to hurt my family if I tell anyone."

"And you think they staged your father's death to look like an accident?" he asked.

"That's part of why I was so apprehensive at the funeral home. Is it too late for an autopsy?" She took a sip of coffee, thankful for the burn in her throat.

"It never hurts to ask. I'll call first thing in the morning."

"I want to know what happened, but I'm afraid if I ask too many questions, he'll come after..."

"You?" Ryan paused. "They already have, so that can't be it." He paused again. "It's your sister, isn't it? You're trying to protect her and Grayson."

She nodded.

"No one else in your family is going to be hurt. Your sister and Grayson will be safe in Arkansas. No one knows about the cabin but me," he reassured her.

"What if she decides to come back to town and doesn't tell me?" Lisa asked.

"Lori needs to know the truth. It's the only way to keep her safe. But first, you have to tell me who's after you."

Fear made her freeze. She couldn't form the words. She shook her head instead.

"Lisa, I'm on your side, remember?" he asked with a calmness belied by his features.

She did know that on some level. And on another she knew Ryan wouldn't let up until she told him everything. Plus, he was a good guy. Why was it so hard to tell him?

Maybe it was the fact that she hadn't told anyone about the past…not her sister…not her father…not another soul.

She'd held it all inside for so many years now she'd lost count. Telling Ryan who was after her would force her to tell him why. And her unwillingness to talk about the past had so little to do with Ryan and so much to do with her.

As much as she loved her father, he hadn't exactly been someone she could trust. She'd known at twelve that she couldn't tell him what had happened. And then there was that time in high school when she'd started to talk about it with her friend Angela. Lisa figured she'd explode if someone didn't know what had happened to her.

When Lisa had brought up Beckett's name to test the waters, Angela had spent the next twenty minutes gushing about how wonderful he was. How fantastic his family was to donate so much to the town. Lisa couldn't deny it. Every year, they gave large sums of money to aid disadvantaged kids. Mr. Alcorn always graced the cover of the *Mason Ridge Courier* around the holidays for his generosity. Whether it be feeding the homeless or rounding up toys for kids, Mr. Alcorn could be counted on to give big. All carefully choreographed PR schemes, Lisa figured.

There was also no denying that Beckett was attractive. At least, before she knew what a monster he was on the inside. After that summer night when he'd abused her, she'd never looked at him in the same way again. Him or any of the Alcorns for that matter. She'd thrown out the newspapers featuring one of the family members, refusing to keep them inside the house.

Turning to look at Ryan, she noticed a cut high on his left cheekbone.

"You're hurt," she said.

"I'll live. And you just changed the subject."

"I'm sorry. You deserve to know everything. It's really hard for me to talk about it."

His hand came up to her face and he tilted her chin so she was looking directly at him.

"I'm not going anywhere. There's nothing you can tell me that will make me run away. I have every intention of seeing this, whatever *this* is, through until you're safe again."

Letting Ryan touch her was a bad idea. Her heart already pounded no longer from fear but with awareness. Being this close to him, allowing him to be her comfort, stirred up confusing emotions. And she found that she wanted more from him than loyalty, which made it that much more difficult to say what she needed to.

His expression was unreadable. All she could see in his eyes was determination and anger. His set jaw told her everything she needed to know about where his mind was at the moment.

"Now, we've been friends a long time. You can trust me. So I want you to tell me what's been going on. When did this start? And who has you this scared?" His hand touched hers and she pulled back immediately. She'd seen it plain as the nose on his face. The only thing Ryan felt for her was compassion.

Hope of anything but friendship between them shriveled as she squared her shoulders and took another sip of coffee before trying to figure out where to begin. No brilliant words came to her, so she decided to spit it out.

"Beckett Alcorn has it in for me. Has for quite a while now." There. She'd said it out loud. It was both terrifying and freeing all at once and her heart thundered in her chest.

She waited for Ryan to laugh. He didn't. His gaze intensified. He seemed to take a minute to contemplate this information. After taking a sip of his coffee, he asked, "Why you? Why now? Why your father?"

"All great questions. I'm still trying to figure out answers to those," she said.

"There must be some reason you can think of." His tone had a sharp edge to it.

What was up with that?

She shrugged.

"Have you two dated?" he asked pointedly.

"Me and Beckett?" She had to choke back vomit. The thought repulsed her, especially after what he'd forced on her. Beckett had called what he'd done to her a date. Just thinking about it again made her stomach churn. She set down her cup of coffee. "No."

"I can see that you're terrified of him. Heck, I used to think you were terrified of me with the way you flinch every time I touch you… Hold on…" Ryan stood and then began to pace. It was clear that he'd put two and two together. "That son of a bitch. I'll kill him myself."

He produced a set of keys from his pocket and started toward the door.

"Ryan, no!" Lisa stood, pushing through the pain, and blocked his path.

"Let me through that door, Lisa."

"Hear me out first. Please, listen to reason." She couldn't contain the panic in her voice.

"He hurt you, Lisa. That's all I need to know." Anger pulsed from him as he spoke through gritted teeth.

"Thank you, Ryan. You have no idea how much that means to me." She broke down in tears. Someone actually believed her about Beckett. For so many years she'd been convinced that if she'd told anyone, they'd laugh at her or say she was just trying to get at the Alcorns' money.

"What?" His right eyebrow hiked up.

"For believing me." How long had she feared that no one would? How many times had she wanted to say something to someone but stopped herself? How many times had she been on the edge of sharing but couldn't force herself to say the words?

Tears that had been stuffed deep down far too many years spilled from her eyes, down her cheeks. She couldn't stop them as she released another sob. They were sweet tears of release and her chest felt as if the boulder that had been parked on it was lifting. There was something magical about another person knowing, believing, that made Lisa's heart push out the darkness and begin to fill with light.

"Hold on there. Of course I believe you. We've known each other a long time, right?" He stood in front of her, his arm around her, comforting her.

"I didn't think anyone would." She buried her face in her hands and cried.

"It's okay. We're going to make this right." His hand came up to cradle her neck as he kissed the top of her head.

Her body tensed involuntarily. She had to force it to relax. He whispered other reassurances that her heart needed to hear.

Thankfully, he didn't ask for details and she figured none were needed. Him knowing everything that had happened wouldn't make him hate Beckett any less than he seemed to just knowing that the man had hurt her. There was something so very comforting about that. She would tell Ryan everything in good time. Eventually, he'd want to know and she desperately needed to speak the words out loud.

Sharing as much as she had so far was exhausting emotionally and physically.

"There's more that I need to tell you, Ryan. Let's sit down." She motioned toward the sofa.

He helped her to the couch.

"It's about my father. I know he wasn't drinking."

His gaze intensified.

"There are signs leading up to his binges. First off, he lies about little things. Then he gets irritable in the mornings. It's like there's a battle going on inside him every day. Also, he wouldn't let me see him drunk. Granted, I don't live at home anymore, but I always check on him on my way home. I know the signs."

Ryan seemed to seriously contemplate her words. "Why didn't you tell anyone about this before?"

"I was scared. I still am." And yet this was the most free she'd felt, too. "There's my sister to consider and Grayson. Beckett threatened me all those years ago. Said he'd do worse to my sister if I told anyone about our 'date.'"

Ryan's hands fisted. "You know, there's an easy way for me to fix this."

"Except the person who came to the hospital was not him," she said, needing to push Ryan out of his emotional state and back to a logical one.

"That doesn't mean the guy knew anything. He was probably hired by Beckett."

"That's what I thought, too. But what if he wasn't?"

"Then this would be bigger than Beckett."

"Exactly. So, if I take down Beckett, how do I know that I'm safe? That my sister won't still be a target?"

"First things first. We need to convince her to stick around the fishing cabin for a while longer. You and I need to head up there, too. I have to make sure we're not followed. I'm sure that's what led them here. They had someone watching the funeral home. I should've seen it coming," he said, frustration clipping his words.

"Beckett's a rich guy. He can afford to hire a lot of hands. Even if they put him in jail, what's to say that he won't hire someone to hurt my family from there through a friend or his lawyer? Not to mention the fact that the crime occurred more than fifteen years ago," she said, struggling to breathe while she spoke so freely for the first time. He'd had such a hold on her for so long that she'd barely whispered his name. "Let's sit down."

"Which is a good point. Why would he surface now?" Ryan followed her to the couch.

"My guess is that he's afraid I'll talk while his father is being hunted," she said.

"You think he's closing a loop?"

"If I went to the deputy and gave a statement, I doubt it would matter much. But if I went to the media while all this is going on, it could hurt his father," she said emphatically.

"He's still on the run. Turning himself in would go a long way toward helping him prove that he's innocent. Everything else is just hearsay." He paused. "You make great points, though. There are those in town who would believe that you're kicking Alcorn while he's down."

"Charles Alcorn isn't stupid. He has to be hiding somewhere, right? At least until his lawyer can straighten out this mess he's gotten himself into. Beckett might think they can't afford any bad press right now. That's the only thing that makes sense. He must believe I might come forward," she said.

"Happens all the time when bad news about a person or family surfaces," Ryan agreed.

"I'm guessing he's trying to protect the integrity of his family name and I'm certain they'll fight this charge. His father is probably out there hiding until this PR nightmare can be cleaned up." She couldn't hide her disgust.

"Why attack your father?" Ryan asked, rubbing the stubble on his chin.

"To send a direct message to me. I got away from Beckett when he tried to kill me."

"And he didn't want to get caught with his hand in the cookie jar at the hospital, so he hired someone to do it for him."

"Then it would just be two accidents in one week. Unlucky family," she confirmed. "That's what everyone thinks, anyway."

"We have to go to the sheriff."

"Except that we have no evidence, remember?" She tapped her finger on the table, still shaky from everything that had happened. "It's my word against his and my background isn't exactly solid."

"They have to believe you." Ryan captured her hand in his. "Deputy Barnes is already looking for you. I told him that I'd bring you to the station as soon as I found you."

"I'll call in my report. I can do that, right?" She ignored the shivers running through her fingers and up her arm from contact.

"I believe so," he said, and then glanced down at their fingers as he looped them together. "Is this okay?"

"Yeah, it is." Her fingers tensed, belying her words.

"Being touched bothers you, doesn't it?" he asked.

"I like it when you touch me," she said a little too quickly. "I mean, sure, it still catches me off guard if I'm not expecting it, but I actually do like it."

"Then, can I touch you here?" With his free hand, he pointed to her cheek.

She nodded.

He ran the backs of his fingers down the side of her face so tenderly they were like whispers against her skin.

"Can I move a little closer?" he asked.

She nodded.

He slid toward her until the outside of their thighs touched. Heat burned through her, but she tried to suppress it. He was trying to comfort her without scaring her and she appreciated the gesture. It would do neither of them any good for her to overanalyze the situation, or wish for more than light contact.

And yet her heart did wish for more.

It didn't help when she glanced up at him and saw something besides friendship darkening his eyes.

THE LAST THING Ryan wanted to do was scare Lisa. As he moved closer, he felt an almost overwhelming need to touch her. He shouldn't want to be her comfort. And yet she'd trusted him with a secret that she'd kept inside for more than fifteen years.

So much made sense about her past and present behavior to him now. Scars were still fresh with no way to heal them. He couldn't imagine how she could ever trust a man again. That look he'd seen in her eyes, the one that said she never would, made him realize she needed a friend more than ever now.

Yes, a very big part of him wanted to march out the door and arrive in Beckett's yard, unannounced, and then show him just how it felt to be afraid.

With her settled on his chest, his arm around her, he could feel her trembling. If that didn't make a man want justice, nothing would.

Act on it and Ryan would be the one tossed in jail while Beckett enjoyed his freedom. Lisa's family would be left unprotected. She was too frightened to confide in anyone else and if what she said about her father was true, then the Alcorns were far more dangerous than anyone realized. The town was still reeling from the fact that Charles Alcorn might have been involved in the abductions in the first place.

Ryan had personal reason to dislike the family. It was high time others saw the Alcorns in the same light he did.

What's done in darkness always comes to light.

Those bastards needed to pay.

Lisa tilted her head up and he could see an emotion behind her eyes that he couldn't quite put his finger on.

Ryan kissed her forehead and refocused.

"We'll figure this out. In the meantime, I want you by my side at all times," he said. Without evidence, her case would be a hard sell. Not to mention that he'd hate to open her up for public scrutiny. It didn't matter that she was a kindergarten teacher now. Her painful youth would be dug up, chewed on and spit out. She was strong, but no one deserved to be treated like that.

"I don't want to interfere in your life." She sat up, looking a mixture of exhausted and relieved. "You have a job."

"It's fine. Taking time off when I want is one of the benefits of owning a business."

She'd been there through the weekend, so he'd think that he'd get used to her being around. Yet every time she entered a room his body reacted. Her being at his place was right on too many levels and he told himself that it had been far too long since he'd gone on a real date with a woman who held his interest.

Or maybe it was just companionship he missed. If he was being honest, his house had had an empty quality to it before Lisa showed up. He hadn't paid much attention to it before but he was already dreading the day she would leave.

Being with Lisa 24/7 made Ryan realize how lonely he'd been up until now. When this whole ordeal was behind them, it might be time to swing by the animal shelter and pick up man's best friend, he conceded.

Until then, he needed all his attention on this case. He cursed himself for not realizing sooner the depth of what was going on with Lisa. She'd been scared to death at the hospital. She'd checked the door every few seconds. He'd brought her to his home and she imme-

diately made him promise to lock the doors and close
and lock all the windows.

"Try to get some rest. We'll leave in the morning."

Lisa leaned her head against his shoulder and he
tried not to think about the citrus shampoo that smelled
so good on her. Instead, he focused on the facts so far.
While Lisa was healing the rest of the town was on alert
to locate Charles Alcorn. The man who was wanted for
questioning, believed to be the Mason Ridge Abductor,
had disappeared. But where?

Given Alcorn's considerable resources, he could be
anywhere. Ryan couldn't rule out the fact that Alcorn
might be out of the country by now, too. If Ryan found
Charles, would he be able to find Beckett? The idea was
worth playing around with.

Whoever had broken into Ryan's house was neither
of the two, which meant there was a third party. With
Alcorn money, they could hire someone to do their dirty
work. And it would be safer at this point, since they
couldn't afford to be linked to Lisa.

Knowing this, Ryan figured that his place would be
clean of fingerprints.

Therein lied another problem… Ryan knew the Alcorns on sight. But they could hire anyone to attack
Lisa.

That meant every stranger from now on was a suspect.

Chapter Eight

Lisa's eyes widened as they approached the grand home in Arkansas early the next morning. The fishing cabin looked more like a five-star resort than a family get-away.

Ryan pulled up to the house and parked on the pad.

Lori came running from around the front of the house, Grayson bouncing on her hip.

"This place is amazing," Lori said to Ryan. "Thank you for helping us get away."

"You're welcome. I'm glad you can get some use out of it," he said in his characteristically reserved tone.

Last night, it would've been too easy to get swept away with emotion. Luckily, they'd both had better sense than to act on the chemistry firing between them.

Instead, she'd fallen asleep in his arms.

A visit with her sister and nephew was just what Lisa needed to regain her bearings. So much had gone on in the past few days that she couldn't begin to process it. Then there were all those intense emotions to deal with when it came to Ryan.

Was she falling for him? Even if she was, what on earth would she do with those emotions? She never let anyone past her walls and even though she felt a certain amount of reciprocation from him, there were lines that friends shouldn't cross. She thought about the kiss in the hospital and how much her blood heated when he'd held her in his arms.

Since then, he'd mostly kissed her on the forehead or top of the head, which screamed *big brother* more than anything else. And yet his lips touching anywhere on her sent a fiery reaction coursing through her, electrifying her.

"Are you okay?" Lori's mouth was twisted with concern as she came closer.

"Yes, of course." Lisa reached over and hugged her sister, fighting against the pain that movement still caused. Grayson leaned toward her with his arms extended, but she wasn't strong enough to hold him yet. She kissed his forehead instead.

"I'll run out and pick up lunch. There's a great barbecue place up the road. They cook all the meat outdoors. Give you two a chance to catch up," Ryan said.

Lisa thanked him and followed her sister into the house as he pulled away.

"Mind if we lock the doors?" she asked.

"Since when have you been so paranoid?" Lori asked. "And there's no one around here for miles."

"It's just—"

Lori held up her hand and made a face. "I'm sorry. That was really crappy. Of course you're still on edge."

Grayson threw his hands out toward Lisa, frowning when she didn't take him from her sister. He looked as though he was working up to crying.

"Here, let's sit on the floor," Lisa said, easing down onto the rug in front of the sofa.

The place was as spectacular inside as it was out. A

floor-to-ceiling tumbled stone fireplace was the focal point of the space. The plan was open concept, so she could see clearly into all the main rooms. The decor was rustic chic and the kitchen was fitted with all the modern appliances for a gourmet cook, including a five burner stove.

A gorgeous crystal chandelier hung over the center of the living room, with a metal installation circling it.

"I made pancakes this morning," Lori said proudly. "You?"

"That kitchen inspires me to cook."

"Maybe we should see about installing one in your apartment," Lisa teased.

Lori's smile faded. "How are you *really*?"

Lisa hugged Grayson and handed him one of the big blocks from the basket next to them. He immediately stuffed the corner of the block in his mouth, just as he did everything else. Two of his bottom front teeth had already peeked through and the others were most likely coming soon.

"Better. I guess. I keep thinking about Dad and…"

"I know. I cry myself to sleep every night after putting Grayson down. I can't help it. It's so hard to believe that he's gone." She wiped a loose tear away, then grabbed a tissue off the coffee table. "Did you know that he was drinking again?"

"No." How much should Lisa tell her little sister? *Enough to keep both her and Grayson safe*, a little voice said. "In fact, I don't think he was."

"I'm so glad you said that because I don't, either." Lori blew her nose. "Sorry, I get emotional just thinking about it. I'm trying to be strong for Grayson. I don't want to confuse him. It's just all so sudden."

"You're a great mom, Lori. I hope you know that. If Mom were here, she'd say the same thing."

"Now you're really going to get me all blubbery," Lori said.

"It's true."

"So, what's going on between you and Ryan?" Lori changed the subject.

"That question seems out of the blue."

"Does it?" Lori asked. "I see the way he looks at you. Don't tell me you haven't noticed."

"Yeah, as a friend. That's how he looks at me. I'm pretty sure he thinks I'm a pain in the butt."

"I doubt that," Lori said. "Give him a chance. I can't remember the last person you let take care of you."

"How'd we get on the subject of my personal life?" And when did her little sister get so observant?

"You say that as if you have one." Lori cracked a smile. "Maybe it's this cabin or looking at pictures of this gorgeous family, but I've been thinking. No one should be alone and that's what we are. Neither one of us is in a relationship. When was your last? Mine?"

"I hate to break it to you, but you already have a man in your life." Lisa nodded toward Grayson.

"And I love him with all my heart. Believe me, I wouldn't change a thing about having him."

"I know that."

"Except the part where he grows up without a father. I thought maybe Dad could fill the void, but he's gone now, too." Lori wiped away another tear. Raw emotion bubbled under the surface.

Lisa didn't want her sister to break down in front of the baby. She needed to change the subject, but nothing immediately came to mind. "Dad wasn't perfect but there was a lot of good about him. If he was drinking again, and I don't believe he was, then I missed the signs."

"So did I."

"You knew them?" Maybe Lori was stronger than Lisa had given her credit for.

"It always started with the little lies. I can't stand liars to this day because of it." Lori's chin quivered as she held back emotion.

"I always covered for him so you wouldn't know." Or at least she thought she had. Maybe her baby sister was more perceptive than Lisa realized.

Lori rolled her eyes. "You really think I couldn't see things for myself?"

"I guess not. Why didn't you say anything to me before?"

"You were always working so hard to protect me after Mom died. I didn't want to take that away from you," Lori said.

Wow. Lisa had completely underestimated her sister.

"It would've been nice if you'd spoken up before. You would've saved me a lot of angst at trying to hide things from you, kid," Lisa teased.

"And spoil the fun for me? Are you kidding? Playing dumb had its benefits. I mean, who else got served chocolate ice cream in bed when they were sick? Not one of my friends is who."

Lisa laughed out loud, ignoring how much it hurt.

The back door opened and she let out a scream before she could suppress it.

"Are you okay?" Lori asked, eyeing her sister suspiciously.

"Fine." Lisa tried to slow her racing heart with a few deep breaths.

"No, you're not." She glanced down at Grayson, who'd jumped at the loud shriek and was winding up to cry. She immediately picked him up and patted his back to soothe him. "We're not done discussing this. I need to feed him and then he goes down for his nap."

"I can help," Lisa offered.

Ryan came over and took the baby from Lori's arms. Both women's jaws fell slack at how easily Grayson took to Ryan.

"This is how it's done, ladies," Ryan teased.

"Didn't realize we had an expert in our midst," Lisa shot back. "The least I can do is set out the barbecue. It smells wonderful."

Lori moved to the cabinets and pulled out three plates.

By the time Lisa set the food out on the table, Ryan had Grayson in his high chair and was feeding him mouthfuls of a green puree.

"Since when did you get so great with babies?" Lisa asked as she piled ribs and brisket on Ryan's plate.

"Since Maribel. I figure if Dylan can take care of a three-year-old on his own, the least I can do is pitch in once in a while."

Lisa stared at him.

"Okay, I've watched him feed her a few times. Figured it couldn't be that hard if Dylan can do it by himself," Ryan admitted.

"Well, then I really feel bad, because I'm exhausted," Lori said. "And I never get him to eat peas. What did you do?"

"Mixed them in applesauce." Ryan supplied a wry

grin as he brought another spoonful to the baby's mouth. "I didn't like the smell of them before, either, big guy."

Lori laughed almost as hard as Lisa. Her sister was doing an amazing job with Grayson. And there was something about seeing Ryan with her nephew that made Lisa's heart ache.

Her past experiences with men had taught her that feelings could lead her right down the rabbit hole where everyone deceived her.

Chapter Nine

"The funeral is tonight," Lisa said to Ryan as she walked into the kitchen on the third morning since arriving at the cabin. Not only was he already awake, but he looked as though he'd gone out for a run.

"Are you sure you're up for it?" he asked, holding out a mug of fresh coffee.

"I need to be." She took the offering and thanked him, thinking how easy it would be to get used to this every morning. And then chided herself for having the thought in the first place.

"Just so you know, you don't have to do this," he said, his dark eyes trailing down her face, lingering on her lips.

"I can't say that I especially want to leave this place." She took a sip of coffee. "It's gorgeous here. And with the lake view out the front window…just wow."

She moved to the living room to take full advantage of the view, and to mask the flush heating her cheeks at being near Ryan. She'd thought about the kiss they'd shared too many times since the impulsive moment at the hospital. The worst part was that he'd done a little too good of an acting job. He almost had her believing he felt more than friendship.

She sat on the oversize white sofa and pulled a throw pillow in her lap.

"How are you feeling today?" Ryan sat down next to her.

"Much better." The swelling was starting to go down and her body was far less tender. He'd convinced her to take a couple of over-the-counter pain pills before bed, too.

"You slept the whole night," he added.

"It was amazing." She stretched out her legs in front of her. "No pain when I do this, either."

"You're healing fast."

"Because you've taken such good care of me." A piece of her didn't want to leave this cabin to return to real life ever.

"How long is your summer break?" he asked.

"Teachers go back two weeks before students. It's generally the first week of August. I haven't even looked at a calendar in days. This is not exactly the summer vacation I had planned," she said.

"Can I ask you a question?" Ryan asked.

"Sure."

"Why on earth would you want to become a teacher? I mean, it's one of those noble professions, so don't get me wrong, and I admire teachers for putting up with kids like me—"

"You weren't so bad." She knocked her shoulder into his.

"Then you're looking back with rose-colored glasses on," he shot back.

"We got into our fair share of trouble, but we weren't inherently bad kids."

"That's probably true of the girls in the group. Me,

Brody, Dawson and especially Dylan wouldn't exactly be called angels back then."

"What did you ever do?" she asked.

"Plenty."

"You don't even like to lie. I saw your face in the hospital after fibbing to the nurse. In fact, what did we used to call you back then?"

"No reason to dip that far into the past." He made a move to get up, but she put her hand on his arm.

"Not so fast, mister. You're not getting away that easily. Let me think… Oh, I remember now, reliable Ryan."

"Great. Thanks for that. Bringing up all my painful scars from childhood now. I've gotten into plenty of trouble in the past," he countered.

"Of course you did. You'd never lie about something like that," she retorted, playfully tapping him on the arm.

"And what about you? You were a little holier-than-thou back then if I remember correctly."

"No, I wasn't."

"True story." He put his hand over his heart. "Remember, I can't tell a lie."

"You're making this up."

"Scout's honor." He held two fingers up like rabbit ears.

"You were never a Scout and that's not the hand sign."

"Doesn't matter. I can use the oath, anyway," he said with a grin.

It was good to see Ryan smile. He'd been a serious kid who'd grown to be a serious adult. There hadn't been a lot of laughter in his childhood home. She liked being the one to put a smile on his face.

"Fine. Give me an example, then." She took a sip of coffee and waited for his response.

He seemed to take a minute to think. "Weren't you the one who went around correcting all our grammar in fourth grade?"

"Hello, what do you not understand about me becoming a teacher?" She laughed despite the pain. "I had to try to inspire the next generation of Mason Ridge youth to actually learn something while in school."

"Can't argue your point there." He took a sip of coffee. "We were pretty thickheaded even back then."

"We all had a lot going on." She thought about those beatings he'd endured and she wanted to reach out to him, to somehow make it better. "Do you see your brother's family very often?"

"I get out there as much as I can. He doesn't like to come back to Mason Ridge."

"Is it because of the way your father treated you two?"

"I imagine so. That, and other bad memories about the way he acted. Justin's changed. He's a family man now and I think he wanted to get away somewhere he could wipe the slate clean. Can't say I blame him. Some folks will never forgive him for the past. Small towns have long memories."

"He got into trouble, but he wasn't a criminal, for crying out loud," she said with a little too much emotion. She stopped short of saying that everything he'd done was rebelling against their father, feeling lost and unloved.

Ryan didn't immediately speak. He seemed to be contemplating her response and she was afraid he picked up on her heightened emotion.

"What about you? Why'd you come back to Mason Ridge after college?" he finally asked.

"I don't know." She shrugged. "My sister left for college. Dad was here alone. I was afraid he'd start drinking again. Figured I could teach anywhere and be happy, so I came back to keep an eye on him. He's getting older and I didn't want to get settled somewhere else and be uprooted if his health started failing, which it already had."

"That must've been tough. Did you want to go somewhere else?"

"I didn't want to come back to Mason Ridge," she said without thinking.

"Too many bad memories?" He looked at her curiously, as if he was trying to see something deeper.

"Yes."

"With your father or what we talked about earlier?" Those intelligent, penetrating eyes threatened to see right through her.

And that scared her to death.

"No, nothing like that." She shrugged it off, hugging the pillow tighter to her chest.

"I don't know if I said this before, but I'm sorry about everything that's happened." He nudged her with his shoulder.

Surprisingly, her muscles didn't go rigid this time. There was only a slight hesitation with contact and that was mostly because of the trill of awareness his touch shot through her. Her body warmed and her thighs heated.

"You've done so much for me. I'm not sure how I would've gotten through all this without you." Against her better judgment, she reached over and hugged him.

She must've known that he would come through for her all along and that's why she asked for him when Mrs. Whitefield found her.

Ryan leaned into the hug until his lips were so close to her ear that she could feel his breath on her neck. A thousand tiny volts of electricity coursed through her.

"You would've done the same thing for me if I was in trouble."

"Friends, right? Like you said before, we go back a long way." Lisa reminded herself that this wasn't the time to notice just how much reliable Ryan had filled out since high school.

With one easy movement, he pulled her onto his lap. His muscled arms wrapped around her waist, sending all kinds of sparks through her body. She could feel his thigh muscles through the denim of his jeans against her bare skin.

She repositioned on his lap to face him, stopping when she felt his body go rigid.

"Am I hurting you?" she asked.

"Not exactly but that would be a fun twist," he shot back with a sardonic grin.

"What does that mean?" She scooted her bottom again, worried she'd sat funny on his leg. She was stilled by two powerful hands on either side of her hips.

"You don't want to keep doing that." There was a low, husky quality to his voice.

"Oh." She paused, temporarily robbed of her voice. "And here I was worried you weren't attracted to me all this time."

"That's what you thought?" His face was stamped with shock. "Finding you desirable has never been the problem."

RYAN SHOULDN'T ALLOW himself to get caught up in the moment. But it was Lisa. His better judgment knew not to let this happen but that had gone out the window, taking his self-control along for the ride.

Spending time with her at his friend's cabin made matters worse. He'd figured spending a few days with her would be enough to quash the attraction he felt every time he thought about her or she was in the room.

The plan that had worked with so many women who had come and gone through his life had failed miserably with Lisa. In fact, the only thing he'd succeeded in doing was wanting her even more than before.

All it generally took was a few days of alone time with a woman to see what she was truly about. He'd done well for himself, so some wanted his money. Others wanted his body—them he didn't mind so much. He hadn't met one who had truly stimulated his mind or that he could joke around with so easily. He'd figured the others out in a flash and gotten bored.

Lisa was different. She was intelligent, beautiful and funny. They had history, so he didn't feel the need to put on airs for her. She disarmed him, causing his defenses to drop. Ryan didn't think a woman could get past his carefully constructed walls. But then, no one knew him like Lisa.

Was he falling for her? Again?

Not smart, Hunt.

Or maybe a better question was…had he ever really stopped having feelings for her?

When she looked up at him with those bluish-green eyes, he dipped his head and kissed her.

Her lips parted as she nibbled his bottom lip and he thrust his tongue in her mouth, wanting to taste her sweetness. Heat roared through his veins and need engulfed him like a raging wildfire.

"He turned himself in," Lori said, walking into the kitchen, breaking into the moment and staring down at something in her hand.

"Who?" Lisa scampered off his lap and pushed to her feet, ignoring the pain quick movement had to have caused.

Ryan needed a minute, or both ladies would know the effect Lisa had on him.

"Charles Alcorn." She looked up from her phone and her gaze bounced between Ryan and Lisa. Didn't seem that Lori had seen them kissing, and he sensed Lisa's relief over that fact.

"We were just enjoying the view this morning," Lisa said a little too quickly. Her voice was shaky, too. As far as liars went, she was a bad one. "That's great news."

Ryan cracked a smile. Turned out he wasn't the only honest one in the bunch.

"Yeah, maybe now the town will get some answers and that jerk will finally live out the rest of his life in jail," Lori said.

"He deserves whatever they do to him," Lisa said, her hopeful gaze on Ryan.

"I wouldn't count on it. That family has money and they can afford the best defense attorney in the country. He might just get away with it and he wouldn't turn himself in unless he had a plan. We'll have to keep watch over the next few days on what happens with him." Ryan didn't want to be the one to put a damper on their excitement.

"Well, he shouldn't be above the law." Fire raged across Lisa's face.

"Agreed."

At least he'd gotten her to open up a little bit more about her past. He suspected that he'd only scratched the surface, but she'd trusted him and that went a long way in his book.

They'd made progress, although she still froze up on him in certain situations.

The only reason he'd touched her a few minutes ago was that she'd made contact with him first, and he couldn't stop himself once she gave the green light.

She'd tensed just a bit when he had, so little that he almost hadn't noticed, but his body was in tune with hers. That wasn't something he could shut off, and he didn't want to, but would he ever hold Lisa and feel her trusting surrender?

Chapter Ten

Ryan didn't like the thought of going back to Mason Ridge, where Lisa would be exposed. He understood that she needed to bury her father, to put that piece of her life to rest, but being anywhere near Beckett Alcorn wasn't exactly high on Ryan's list.

He walked outside and called his friend Brody.

"How's Lisa doing?" Brody asked after exchanging greetings.

"It's been a rough couple of days," Ryan said, and then updated Brody on the funeral service.

"You know we'll be there," Brody said solemnly.

"Good. Because we'll need extra security."

"What's that all about?" Brody's serious tone dropped to outright concern.

"It turns out that random mugging wasn't so indiscriminate after all."

"With all the craziness going on, I thought about that. But she seemed so adamant in the hospital," Brody said.

"This is personal between her and Beckett Alcorn."

"Beckett?" Brody repeated, surprise in his voice. "What's up with that?"

"They have a history but she won't tell me exactly what it is. Suffice it to say that she's scared to death of the guy." Ryan didn't think it was his place to go into details.

"Does this have something to do with his father?" Disgust laced Brody's tone.

"No. I don't believe so." It seemed that family liked to prey on people weaker than them. "This is personal and it goes back a long way."

"I can ask Rebecca if she knows anything," Brody offered.

"Good idea. Keep me posted on what you find out." Trusting Brody to keep this quiet was a given. Ryan had always been able to rely on their friendship and maybe that was because both came from families with seriously messed-up mothers. Brody's had ripped off half the town before pulling her disappearing act. Ryan's had left her sons with an abusive father.

"Will do," Brody said.

"We'll talk more when I see you."

"Be safe driving in today," Brody warned. "Any chance you got another vehicle stashed out where you are?"

"As a matter of fact, I do." Ryan didn't think his buddy would mind if he borrowed the Jeep he kept at the fishing cabin. The spare key should be in the junk drawer in the kitchen. "Good idea."

"See you in a few hours."

"Will do." Ryan ended the call and turned toward the lake. The conversation with Brody had Ryan thinking about his own mother, a subject he deemed best left alone.

If Ryan was being honest, he'd admit that he felt no real pain at losing the man he'd grown up with when he buried his father two years ago.

Thinking back now, he'd been sure his mother would show at the funeral. He'd heard the same rumors for years that she'd only gone because of his father's cruelty and hadn't been allowed to take her children with her.

If that had been true, wouldn't she have returned? The old man was gone. He couldn't hurt her anymore. The coast was clear.

If she'd loved Ryan and Justin to begin with, wouldn't she be the first one in town when she'd heard the news?

Her answer had come in the form of complete silence. Distance.

Even then, Justin had tried to justify her actions as being afraid to come back. Ryan knew better. If she'd cared she would have found a way to contact her children or get a message to them that she loved them at some point over the years. Wouldn't she?

How many birthdays had gone by without so much as a phone call or a card? How many nights as a child had Ryan wished on a star that his mother would return? How many times had he denied missing her when Justin brought her up?

Too many.

Lisa opened the back door, breaking into his heavy thoughts.

"Breakfast is ready," she said.

"I'll be right there."

Lori sat next to Grayson, feeding him breakfast, her eyes red-rimmed and swollen. Lisa was busy at the massive island in the kitchen. The scene felt like family and Ryan was shocked it didn't make him want to turn and run right back out the door. It was friendship, he reasoned. "I hope you like biscuits and gravy. Breakfast is one of the few things I know how to cook," Lisa said, holding out a plate. Her smile was weak at best, but at least she was making the effort.

"You didn't have to do all this," he said, surprised at how thinking about his mother still affected him.

"Yes, I did. I can't let you do all the work. Besides, it feels good to be productive, especially today."

"Let me help you put out the food, then," he offered, needing something to take his mind off his heavy thoughts and noticing how difficult it was for Lisa to let anyone do anything for her.

"I already said no." She was being stubborn and he figured half the reason was that she looked as though she'd stayed up half the night crying with her sister. Ryan didn't want to upset her, so he moved to the table and took a seat next to Lori. Between him and their old group of friends, Ryan felt a lot better about their odds of keeping her safe later. He'd live off that win for now.

After breakfast, they piled into the Jeep and made the silent trek back to Mason Ridge.

Everything about Lisa's body language said she was scared as they walked into the funeral home. At least she had Lori and Grayson to keep her busy this time.

Lori unhooked Grayson from his car seat and pulled him into her arms. Lisa stood close by, watching everything around them.

They weren't the first to arrive, just as planned. Dawson and Brody hopped out of Dawson's black SUV. Texas was a conceal-and-carry state, so Ryan knew those two would be ready for any trouble that arrived. His shotgun was stashed under the seat in his SUV.

"Thanks for coming," Ryan said to Brody and Dawson as they walked over. His friends were similar in height and build. Brody still had a tight cut, no doubt left over from his time in the military, blond hair and blue eyes. By contrast, Dawson had pitch-black hair and dark brown eyes. Both carried themselves like warriors.

"Dylan should show up in a few minutes. He wanted us here first. He already checked the place out. Called it recon and I left it at that," Brody said, leaning in for a bear hug.

Dylan was most likely pulling from his own military experience.

Ryan was grateful for his friends' support. This entire summer had been hard on their friendships. First, when Brody's fiancée, Rebecca, was attacked in a grocery store parking lot and it was believed that the Mason Ridge Abductor had returned after fifteen years. That ordeal was followed by Samantha, Dylan's fiancée, being targeted by the same person—and that person turned out to be one of the most powerful men in Mason Ridge, Charles Alcorn. Now Beckett Alcorn was targeting Lisa.

When Ryan really thought about it, everyone had been on edge since the whole ordeal began earlier this summer and all his friendships had been challenged. It had become difficult to know who to trust anymore, save for a few solid friendships.

"I'll go inside with Lisa and Lori," Dawson said. "Why don't you two walk the perimeter until Dylan gets here?"

"Now you're starting to sound like him," Brody said, rolling his eyes in an obvious attempt to lighten the tense mood.

Everyone knew he was only pretending to be disgusted. Of course, they would all do everything it took to keep Lisa and her family safe and Dylan would know how to get that job done.

Lisa gave a tentative look toward Ryan, who nodded it was okay to separate. Her anxiety was written all over the worry lines in her face. Tension practically radiated off her small frame.

As soon as she disappeared inside, Brody turned to Ryan and asked, "How's she really doing?"

"She's strong, as you already know. I think she's holding a lot inside. I know that something's going on in the back of her mind, but she's not sharing."

"Give her time," Brody said as they scanned the area. "Rebecca seems to think that something traumatic happened to her when we were kids."

That was an understatement.

They kept pace with each other, rounding the corner to check out the back of the funeral home.

"Did she say what happened?" Ryan asked.

"She wishes she knew. All she remembers for sure is that Lisa started pulling away from the group weeks before the kidnappings." Brody was referring to when Rebecca and her younger brother were abducted. The event had turned the little town of Mason Ridge upside down.

"Does she remember anything else?" Ryan asked as they walked.

"The rest of her memory is hazy. Rebecca blocked out most events surrounding that summer."

"I understand why that would happen." Ryan knew that Rebecca had gotten away from their captor, planning to bring back the sheriff to save her little brother. She got lost and wandered in the woods for days before finally being picked up. Shane and his kidnapper were long gone by the time they found the shed he'd kept them in.

The entire town had searched for months. A decade later, Shane had been declared dead. Rebecca never gave up on finding him. Several weeks ago, Rebecca learned of a man named Thomas Kramer. She discovered that he'd been involved in her brother's kidnapping, and then she and her friends uncovered a trail that led them straight to Charles Alcorn. He'd escaped the deputy as he was being brought in for questioning. Given that he was the town's wealthiest resident, Ryan had no doubt that justice would suffer.

"I'm sure you already heard about Alcorn," Ryan said.

"About time they caught the SOB," Brody said, disgusted. "You and Lisa have been spending a lot of time together lately."

"Because I'm helping her."

Brody shot him a look that said he wasn't buying the simple explanation. "You had a thing for her once, right?"

"Don't say it." Ryan already knew what this would be about.

"Why not?" Brody asked plainly.

"Because me and Lisa aren't the same as you and Rebecca." Ryan held up his hand to stop his buddy from saying anything else. "Hey, I'm thrilled for you and Rebecca. You know that, right?"

"It goes without saying."

"And I don't think two people could be happier if they'd been matched by the big guy upstairs." Ryan motioned toward the blue sky.

"And?"

"So don't take this the wrong way when I tell you that not everyone's ready to find their forever mate."

"That's a cop-out," Brody said, shaking his head.

"What makes you say that?"

"I have eyes. I'm not stupid. There's something going on between the two of you."

"Lisa and I have been friends for a long time. She finally opened up to me a little bit recently. And I'm talking a tiny speck. That's all you're seeing." If Brody had come at Ryan with the physical-attraction thing, he wouldn't have had much to deny. Ryan could admit to himself that he felt a draw toward her. She was beautiful, intelligent and funny when she let herself be. But no relationship flourished when kept at a safe emotional distance. *Relationship?*

He was referring to his friendship as a relationship now? *Damn, Hunt.* It really was time to get a dog.

Instead of firing back a witty retort, Brody just gave Ryan that knowing look—the look that made Ryan want to haul off and punch the guy. If they weren't friends, he just might.

"Why do I have the feeling if I hang around you for much longer I'll be surfing the internet for his-and-hers bath towels?" Ryan teased. He was only half joking. It was time to change the subject to something more productive than his relationship status. "What do you think about Alcorn? Have you been following the story?"

"Rebecca hasn't turned the TV off or stopped checking her phone since the news broke." Brody shook his head. "I don't know what to think. One minute we're chasing Thomas Kramer. The next he's dead and we've shifted our attention to Alcorn. She remembers that he helped out with the search. *Shocked* isn't the word for her expression when she found out he was allegedly involved in the first place."

"You think there's a chance he's innocent?"

"Half the town is ready to march up to the jail and hang him. The other half is disgusted with those who are demanding justice before the facts have been heard."

"What do you think?" Ryan asked.

"I don't know. After talking to Dylan and Samantha, I think there's more to the whole story than just Alcorn."

"More people involved in the kidnappings? Like a ring?" Ryan asked.

"I don't doubt Alcorn's involved somehow even though Rebecca was thrown off guard when we found out it was him." Brody paused, scanning the lot and surrounding mesquite trees. "After Maribel was kidnapped, Dylan said he was taken to a warehouse on the outskirts of town and beaten by Alcorn's security team. If the guys work for Alcorn, I'm guessing he has to be involved in some way. Is he the leader? Are there more involved?" Brody shrugged. "That I don't know."

"You're thinking he's part of some kind of organized operation?"

"It's possible. Dylan's been searching the county for this warehouse. Think about it. They could house a lot of people in an abandoned warehouse on the outskirts of town."

Ryan wasn't sure he wanted to. "Whatever happened to Kramer?"

"He burned in a car accident."

"Didn't they find a boy in Kramer's house?" Ryan asked.

"They did. And it was all kinds of messed up. Turns out that years ago Kramer had lost a son around the same age as the boy, something to do with his wife neglecting the kid. Kramer believed his child was unfairly taken from him and that's how he justified taking a little boy. I think he was trying to replace his child, since he was fixated on taking seven-year-olds."

"So he kidnapped two boys years apart?"

"Yes. The first was Shane fifteen years ago and then the new boy last year. Kramer, among others, was most likely scouting kids for Alcorn or whoever is in charge. They like them younger, though, so it could be an illegal adoption ring. Taking Shane might've been this guy being greedy, taking for himself when he was supposed to keep his eyes on the prize. And that wouldn't have sat well with Alcorn."

"And then this guy ends up fried and they find a kid in his house. Sounds pretty damn sewn up to me."

"Until Samantha's father decides to come forward with what he knows and then Alcorn goes after her," Brody said.

"Plus, I can imagine that Alcorn wouldn't put up with anyone taking kids in his own backyard," Ryan agreed. "I'm guessing Shane reminded this guy of his kid and that's why he couldn't resist?"

"Me, too. And he could've been keeping an eye on Shane for a couple of years. I mean, we all went to that festival every year. Kramer was part of the cleanup crew. So he'd been watching Shane and then, and this is where Rebecca blames herself, he follows us out that night while we were playing a game," Brody said.

"That, I remember. She yelled at him and he took off. I thought she had him when she went after him or I would've helped."

"We all would've," Brody said, shaking his head. The

guilt still fresh in both of their minds based on Brody's change in demeanor. "She'll never forgive herself for what happened to him next."

Ryan knew that Brody was referring to her and Shane's kidnapping. She'd escaped, gotten lost in the woods near Mason Ridge Lake, and Shane had disappeared for fifteen years. They'd only just reunited. Since Shane had been shipped overseas on active military duty, the family still didn't have all the answers about what had happened to him. No one knew what had happened to him after the kidnapping, only that he was safe. Everyone was just relieved to have finally found him.

"There was no way a twelve-year-old could've known what was going to happen next," Ryan said.

"You and I know that to be true. I'm not so sure Rebecca will ever see it that way. Being the older sister, she always felt responsible for him."

Ryan could relate to that emotion. Even though he was the younger of the Hunt brothers, he'd always looked after his older brother, Justin. Especially when Justin had taken a wrong turn as a teenager and had gone down a path of drinking and experimenting with drugs.

"Speaking of family, how's Rebecca's mother holding up?" Ryan asked.

"She's been doing better ever since they found Shane. Rebecca said she thought half of her mother's sickness over the years was related to having a broken heart after Shane disappeared."

"I bet. After seeing what they went through, after what Dylan went through when Maribel was taken, I can only imagine the heartache losing a child would bring. Maybe that family can finally heal." The Mason

Ridge Abductor had taken so much from the town, the people.

"Rebecca never gave up and that's the only reason they found him."

"It's a shame one man can take away so much from so many." Ryan shook his head.

Brody's cell rang. He fished it out and glanced at the screen. "I better take this. It's Rebecca."

Ryan watched as Dylan pulled up and parked, leaving Brody to his call.

"Good to see you, man," Ryan said to Dylan as the two embraced in a bear hug.

"Maribel was just asking about you."

"How's baby Bel doing?" He'd bought the biggest stuffed bear he could find when she'd been returned from the kidnappers who had taken her a few weeks ago.

"This is the first time she's allowed me to leave the house since the whole ordeal." Anger flashed in his eyes as Dylan shook his head. "Her pediatrician said she'll get better over time."

Ryan's hands fisted despite the good news. "You find out what all happened to her?"

"Lucky for those bastards, they didn't touch a hair on her head," Dylan said through clenched teeth. Maribel coming into Dylan's life a year ago had turned the man's life completely upside down. Ryan shouldn't be shocked at the changes in his friend, except that Dylan had walked the line closest to ending up in juvenile detention save for Justin.

The military had helped Dylan clean up his act. He'd served his country, gone to war and come back stronger. And he was a devoted father. His relationship with

Samantha seemed to be getting serious quickly. If anyone deserved happiness, it was Dylan.

"Having a daughter changed you in a good way," Ryan said.

"It'd be impossible not to keep things in perspective every time I look into those green eyes. Seeing the world the way she does has taught me that the earth is an amazing place even though there is still evil in it."

"Evil that needs to be eradicated." Ryan nodded toward the funeral home.

"She really doesn't believe her father had an accident?" Dylan asked.

"Nope. There's no proof, but she says she knew her father wasn't drinking."

"Her word is all I need. She knew him better than anyone else. With his background, it'll be harder to convince the rest of the town," Dylan said matter-of-factly.

"She doesn't think anyone else will believe her," Ryan said. "It's her word against everyone's preconceived notion about her father."

"I can see where that would be a problem. People get an idea of who you are and it's hard to change that perception."

Ryan nodded his agreement. Both of them had lived it.

"You look good…happy," Ryan said. He'd never get over the changes in Dylan. Good changes. Changes that had Ryan thinking that if his friend could do it, then why not him? Maybe when this ordeal was over he'd recommit himself to dating. If he was being honest he'd admit to slacking off in the meeting-new-people department. The women he'd met so far could too easily be shoved into one of two categories, too boring or too greedy.

Then again, maybe he wasn't trying hard enough. Weren't those the words of the last woman he'd been interested in? When was that? Six months ago? Seven?

Sticking that thought on the shelf, Ryan motioned for Brody to join them.

"What did Rebecca say?" Ryan asked Brody as he rejoined the conversation.

"Said that Judge Matheson set bail for Alcorn," Brody said with disgusted grunt.

"Which he'll easily make," Ryan agreed. "That jerk will be right back out on the streets."

"What jerk?" Lisa asked.

"CHARLES ALCORN." Ryan's voice had an apologetic quality.

Anger burned through her at the thought that her father was dead and yet Alcorn was about to be free again. That entire family could burn if anyone asked her opinion. She'd gladly supply the match.

"The service will start in fifteen minutes," Lisa said, deciding that her family was the only thing she wanted to focus on at the moment.

"Did you want to wait for the others?" Ryan asked, scanning the almost-empty lot.

"This is probably it," she replied, masking the hurt in her voice. Of all the years her father lived in Mason Ridge, he hadn't made many real friends.

"Rebecca and Samantha are almost here," Brody supplied.

As if on cue, a sedan came down the highway, turned onto the lane and then into the parking lot.

Lori popped out the funeral home door. "Lisa, we need you."

"Okay," she shouted back, and then turned to Ryan, "See you in a few minutes?"

He nodded.

She was surprised when a second car turned into the parking lot and then a third. The fourth came as she walked inside the building.

"Who's out there?" Lori asked.

"Some of the old gang I used to hang around with when we were kids." That accounted for a few of the people. She had no idea who else was showing up. Maybe her father hadn't lived such a small life after all.

"Everything okay in here?" Lisa asked. Being inside the funeral home again sent a chill down her spine. She tried to ignore it as another emotion overwhelmed her. How was she supposed to say goodbye to her father?

"I'll be back. I need fresh air," she said. It was hard to breathe.

"Sure," Lori said, distracted with Grayson.

Lisa knew she was most likely being overly optimistic thinking that her father had friends. He worked and spent time on his small farm, trying to beat the dry soil and unpredictable Texas weather by growing a few vegetables in his garden. He'd always prided himself on his herbs. The vegetables had been finicky. Even so, every summer he'd bring in bell and banana peppers, the easiest things to grow in Texas, and cut them up to cook with eggs. Scallions had been reliable for him, too. The rest was hit or miss. He'd had some luck with cucumbers but none at all with squash.

Those were the happy memories she'd take with her and cherish.

The others, the ones involving him drinking and doing stupid things, she'd find a way to let go of and find peace. All in all, her father had tried to be a decent man. Did he fall short? Yeah. But then didn't everyone at some point in their life?

Saying goodbye to her father was going to be just as miserable as she'd expected it to be.

Pushing the door open to outside, sunlight hit her in the face. She put her hand up to protect her eyes from the bright light. She needed to go somewhere quiet to get a handle on her emotions before facing everyone again. She needed a minute to herself.

Walking out back, she noticed the small white chapel.

Inside, there was a small alter with a tray of candles, three rows of hand-carved wooden pews and a stained-glass window to allow in some light. The place could hold a maximum of a dozen people.

She kneeled in front of the alter as tears streamed down her face.

The door to the small chapel opened. A burst of light followed. She looked up expecting to see Ryan and got a shock instead.

Beckett Alcorn stepped inside.

Chapter Eleven

"What are you doing here?" Lisa shot to her feet and took a step back until she was against the altar, hating how shaky her voice was as the door closed behind Beckett. No. This was her father's funeral and Beckett Alcorn didn't get to take that away from her. Not this time. She took a few steps toward him, and then poked her finger in his chest. "Get out!"

His hands came up in surrender. "I just came to—"

Another burst of light and Ryan, Dylan and Brody filed in. The trio flanked Beckett.

Ryan put his hand out, signaling the others to stop as though he sensed Lisa needed to be the one to stand up to Beckett.

Lisa had been standing on shaky ground as it was, but seeing her friends, seeing Ryan, gave her full confidence. Her father was dead and she knew in her heart that Beckett had to be involved, even if she couldn't prove it yet.

"Your father is a scumbag who deserves to be behind bars for the rest of his life," she said to Beckett, shooting daggers at him with her eyes.

Beckett sneered, seemingly aware that he was outmatched.

"And he will be."

"My father is innocent. His lawyer will prove it and the jury will see it," Beckett countered.

"By the time I'm done with you, you'll be in the cell next to him," she bit out, poking him again until he took a step backward.

The move caused him to run into Ryan, who stood his ground.

For a split second, fear shot across Beckett's black eyes.

"What do you think you're going to do?" he sneered. "Lay a hand on me and I'll have all of you arrested."

If Lisa heard correctly, Ryan just growled at Beckett. That couldn't be a good sign.

"Like I said already, get out."

Defeated, Beckett turned, but Ryan didn't budge from his athletic stance. Instead, he and Brody held ground, blocking the door. His fists clenched, he looked ready to go if anyone said the word.

The last thing she needed was Ryan, or any of the guys, for that matter, in jail. Any one of them acted on the threat bouncing off them in waves and Beckett would temporarily gain the upper hand. His father's lawyer had already filed a motion to have his case moved to Dallas County, saying he'd never get a fair trial in Mason Ridge, not with all the news coverage surrounding the case. Lisa had heard criminals liked having their cases tried in Dallas because it was harder to get a conviction there.

Beckett must also have realized their hands were tied, because his demeanor changed. He stood tall when he pushed past Ryan, who didn't budge. Brody had to allow Beckett passage.

Lori burst in as Beckett sauntered out. "I've been looking all over for you, Lisa. We're ready to start."

Walking from the chapel to the funeral home's viewing room, Lisa watched Beckett climb into his expensive SUV.

He spit gravel from his tires as he pulled out of the parking lot.

She smiled her satisfaction on the inside. It felt good to stand up to that jerk. He wasn't so big after all. In fact, when she really thought about it, she was a hell of a lot tougher than him. She'd survived being molested by him at a young age.

Despite looking over her shoulder for years, she'd managed to put herself through college and become a teacher, a job she loved. She'd thwarted his attack and his plans to silence her.

When she really thought about it, what had he done? He'd intimidated someone weaker than himself. He'd forced himself on a little girl. No, sir, he wasn't such a big, scary man after all.

Sure, she still had the emotional scars to prove the damage from the past. However, Lisa's fear of Beckett Alcorn ended today. All she had to do was come up with a way to keep her sister and Grayson safe.

Lisa shelved that thought as she walked into the service.

A few townspeople were there. Their postman of twenty years stopped by to pay his respects, as did the town's butcher. A few others came. They were all workingmen, like her father, who lived quiet lives.

Her heart swelled as she thought that there were a few other kindred spirits in town.

The room was small but had adequate space for

them. A large picture of her father sat in front of his urn. His wishes were for him to be cremated and spread over his land, the land he loved so much. A simple man who'd lived a simple life. A good man when he wasn't drinking, which caused him to do things he later regretted. A man who'd let her sit on his lap every evening while he read the newspaper.

He'd come from a large family of nine in the Houston area. There were two girls and seven boys. He'd been the oldest, so he'd gone to work instead of high school to help put food on the table for the family. He'd been great with his hands. The handyman jobs he was able to pick up when he was sober kept the bills paid. She and her sister had had to live with their relatives a few times when times were lean or when he fell off the wagon.

As a child, Lisa had been heartbroken to have to leave Mason Ridge when her father was having one of his "episodes" as Aunt Jane liked to call them. Too many times in the middle of the night, a relative would pluck her and her sister out of bed and take them to live with them until her dad got straightened out again. He always did. Said it was for his girls.

Her dad was a mess, but she loved him. And she'd never doubted his love for her. Maybe that was why she had been able to forgive him.

When the room emptied save for Lisa, her sister and their friends, she knew it was time to say goodbye. But how would she do that? How would she say a final good-night to the man who'd tucked her into bed more nights than she could count? A man easy to love despite his many weaknesses. The one who'd put her to bed with a kiss on the forehead before tucking in her sheets.

A sob tore from her throat before she could suppress

it. She dropped to her knees in front of the table holding his urn.

Good night, Daddy.

"Everyone out!" came a frantic voice. She recognized it as the attendant's. "Now! Go!"

"What's going on?" Lisa asked as she was being pulled to her feet. She glanced up in time to see Ryan's face, the determination in his features to get her the heck out of there. His hands were underneath her arms and he was practically carrying her as he raced toward the nearest exit.

"We gotta get outside," he said, his tone stern and focused.

"My sist—"

"Is fine," he said.

She glanced over in time to see Lori and Grayson being helped out by Dylan and Brody.

"What's going on?" Dylan asked.

All Lisa heard clearly next was the word *bomb.*

The few people still inside were scattering toward exits. Doors slammed against walls as a wave of panic rippled through the room.

Her pulse kicked up to her throat, thumping wildly.

"I can run," she said to Ryan as he half carried her out of the building. "It'll be faster."

He nodded, let her legs down a little more until she could gain traction. Then he gripped her hand.

She kept pace, pushing until her chest and legs burned. Her lungs clawed for air as she and Ryan ran through the thicket.

Everyone had taken off in different directions and Lisa had lost visual contact with her sister.

Was that why Beckett had shown up? Had he meant

to distract them so one of his thugs could plant a bomb in the building, taking out Lisa and what was left of her family?

"Cover your ears." Ryan slowed down when they could no longer see the building through the thick trees.

Lisa folded over onto the ground just in time for the blast. The earth shook underneath her.

Ryan took a step for balance and grabbed on to a tree trunk.

"We're far enough away. We're okay," he said.

"Where are Lori and Grayson?" Panic filled Lisa's chest. She hopped to her feet, her fight, freeze or flight instinct having been triggered as her brain tried to process what had just happened.

Ryan's cell was already to his ear by the time she regained her bearings and looked at him.

"Come on, Brody. Answer the phone," he said. "It's gone into voice mail."

"Lori," Lisa shouted.

"Don't do that. Don't yell. Beckett or his people might be in the woods, waiting to finish the job."

She started back in the direction they'd just come from. He caught her by the arm.

"We can't go back," he said. "In fact, we need to get the hell out of here. We'll have to wait for Brody or Dylan to make contact."

For the first time, Lisa saw panic in Ryan's expression. "I can't leave without them, Ryan. What if they're hurt? What if my sister needs me?" Shock and horror filled her, making it hard to breathe.

"You're scared and I get that. Believe me when I say that I'm freaked out, too. I saw Lori with Brody and

Grayson with Dylan. We have to trust that they'll take them to a safe spot."

"Wouldn't Brody answer the phone if everything was okay?" Just thinking about the possibility of her family and friends lying hurt somewhere in a field was enough to kick off another wave of anxiety.

"Dylan has survived much worse. If he's not picking up, then I have to believe he's been separated from his phone and that's not necessarily bad. He'll take good care of Grayson. If I was out here alone with one other person, I'd want it to be him. You know his background."

Ryan was making excellent points. And that should ease her mounting panic. It didn't. Until she put eyes on her sister and nephew, Lisa's blood pressure would stay through the roof.

"Since we don't know where Beckett is, we need to stay on the move," Ryan said.

"Are you sure we can't go back and check the funeral home? The dust has to have cleared by now."

"That's the last place I want you to be," he said emphatically.

Beckett Alcorn wanted Lisa silenced. If he had his way, it would be permanent. She got that. She wouldn't argue with Ryan.

"Where should we go?" she asked, resigned to the reality that she'd have to wait for word on her sister and nephew.

"Let's keep moving until I get my bearings. I'm not sure where we ended up. Do you need help walking?" He held his free hand out.

"No. I'm okay." That wasn't entirely true. Although

she was grateful to be alive and prayed like everything no one else was hurt.

"I can use the GPS on my phone to help figure out where we are. Then we'll get a read on what's close by," Ryan said, heading the opposite direction from where they started.

If Beckett wanted to take them down, it would be easier for him to do now. He'd managed to separate Lisa from her sister. She had no idea how many men he had surrounding the area, waiting.

Ryan stopped, staring at the screen on his device.

"Looks like we need to head east to get to the main road." He paused. "But then Beckett's people could be waiting there."

"What about the sheriff? They have to believe something happened now," Lisa said.

"You're ready to file a complaint against Beckett? To tell them he's the one who attacked you last week?"

"I think I have to, don't you? I mean, I didn't want to say anything before because I was trying to protect my sister and Grayson. Now I realize we'll never be safe until he's behind bars. Maybe not even then, with his family's money. It isn't like a conviction will stick." Frustration ate through her. "I feel like I'm right back at square one. Damned if I do. Damned if I don't."

"It's not the same thing now."

"What makes you say that?"

"You didn't have all of us before," he said, taking her hand in his, spreading warmth through her. "I promise that I'm not going to let that jerk hurt you or your family. We'll have to be more careful now that we know what he's capable of. I know the others will pitch in to help. We won't let up until you can walk around without looking over your shoulder."

Lisa had to admit she had never felt this strong, not since Beckett had stolen her power when she was twelve. Well, guess what? She was no longer a scared kid. She realized she'd been acting like one by caving to his threats, but taking action made her feel strong again.

And her horrible secret had a shelf life. By keeping silent all these years, she'd fed the monster.

Tonight, when they were safe and alone, she would tell Ryan everything.

RYAN'S RINGTONE SOUNDED with his phone still in his hand. He immediately checked caller ID. "It's Dylan."

"I'm here with Lisa," he said. Lisa moved closer so she could hear.

"Thank goodness you're all right," Dylan said. "Grayson's fine. I didn't realize you'd called a few minutes ago until I got him settled down. Are the others with you?"

"No." He looked at Lisa, whose eyes closed. "It's just me and Lisa."

"We all scattered pretty good. I'm sure everyone will meet up." Dylan sounded confident and Ryan hoped that provided some measure of comfort for Lisa.

"Where's a good place for that?" Ryan asked.

"My place isn't too far from here. Plus, I have baby supplies. Where are you guys? Maybe we can make the walk together."

Ryan supplied their coordinates from the GPS on his phone.

"That's not far at all. I'll swing by and get you, and then we'll head to my place."

Sirens sounded in the distance. No doubt, the cavalry was about to arrive.

"We'll have to call the sheriff and let him know where we're headed," Ryan said.

"Good idea. Normally, I wouldn't leave a crime scene but in this case we should be okay. I'll give the sheriff a call and let him know our plans." With Dylan's security business, it was good for him to keep the lines of communication open with local law enforcement. His connections should prove a benefit.

"I'll try to reach Brody again," Ryan said.

"Try Rebecca and Samantha's phones, too," Dylan said.

"Will do."

"I've been trying to get a hold of you, Ryan," Rebecca said as soon as she answered. He'd had no such luck with Brody.

"Dylan and Grayson are safe. Lisa's with me. Who do you have?" Ryan asked.

"Samantha and the funeral director, but we're scared to go back," Rebecca admitted.

"Have you heard from Brody?"

"No. I was about to ask you the same thing." Concern laced her tone.

He already knew that Brody was with Lori. He'd seen him helping her out of the building.

"So he hasn't called you, either?" Rebecca asked, sounding deflated.

"Not yet. I'm sure he will. He might've dropped his phone while he was running."

"I haven't seen him since he made sure I was out of the building. He sent Lori running while he hung back to make sure everyone made it out okay."

Damn. Ryan was afraid of that.

"Lori's phone would be in her purse or diaper bag. I doubt she had the presence of mind to grab either," Lisa said. "There's no way to reach her now to find out if she's okay or tell her about the meet-up point."

Ryan squeezed her hand as tears rolled down her cheeks.

He finished the call with Rebecca, telling her where they were headed at the same time he heard branches crunching to his left.

Ryan spun around in time to see Dylan, carrying a baby against his chest, coming toward them.

Lisa ran to them and embraced them both. She took her nephew and Ryan could see that she was struggling to hold the baby. He also realized that she'd have to be dead for anyone to pry that child from her arms.

No matter how much pain she was in, she wasn't giving her nephew to anyone else.

Having Dylan with them increased their odds of making it out of any situation alive.

Ryan didn't doubt his own skills, but Lisa had to take it slow. Their odds of making it out of the thicket alive just doubled.

"Is there any chance we can stick around and look for my sister?" Lisa asked, the expression on her face said that she already knew the answer.

"I spoke to the sheriff. The law is nearby, so if she's anywhere near here, she'll be safe. Beckett and his men would have retreated as soon as they heard sirens. It'll do us no good to stick around. The bomb team will most likely be called in to secure the area and investigate. They might find evidence linking this crime to Beckett. That happens and they'll lock him up. I'm calling that the best-case scenario," Dylan said.

Ryan didn't voice his worst-case concern that Beckett had somehow gotten to Lori and would use her as a pawn against Lisa.

For the moment, she was preoccupied with soothing her nephew.

"What else did the sheriff say?" Ryan asked.

"That he's fine with sending a deputy over to my place to take statements. Said it was a good idea for us to steer clear of the crime scene and that he was committed to getting to the bottom of this."

It sounded as though the sheriff had given Dylan the typical party line.

The walk to Dylan's was long and hot.

By the time they arrived, the deputy was there.

Samantha and Rebecca must've been standing at the window watching for them, because the pair popped onto the porch as soon as the trio cleared the trees.

"Maribel is napping. She's completely unaware of everything that's going on," Samantha said, not stopping until Dylan embraced her.

Rebecca and Lisa exchanged worried looks.

"Do you think he's hungry?" Rebecca asked Lisa.

"He must be by now," Lisa said.

"Does he take formula or milk?"

"Formula."

"Let's go inside and fix him up with a bottle," Rebecca said.

"I'll go help." Samantha reached up on her tiptoes and kissed Dylan. He patted her bottom before she walked away.

Ryan would be lying if he didn't admit seeing them

so happy made his own bachelor life seem a little bit empty. He shoved the thought aside.

With every ticking second that went by with no word from Brody, Ryan's muscles tensed a little bit tighter.

The deputy came outside and took down Ryan's and Dylan's statements. Lisa joined them with Grayson on her hip. Babies could be intuitive during stressful times, and his clinging to her probably meant that he was picking up on the heightened stress levels. That, and the fact that he most likely missed his mom.

"Rest assured our office is committed to finding out who did this and why," Deputy Adams said before getting into his SUV and disappearing down the drive.

"Am I the only one who feels like I was handed a party line?" Lisa asked.

"I'm not thrilled with the response, either," Dylan said, and then excused himself to check on Maribel. "But then, they have a lot on their plates concerning the Alcorns and they'll have to be extra careful. If a deputy makes a mistake, the Alcorns' lawyer will chew him up and spit him out."

Ryan had the same sense. "At least we got Beckett on the deputy's radar."

"I just keep thinking about Brody and my sister out there. I'm afraid they're hurt or worse," Lisa said.

"Don't do that to yourself. We don't know what happened to them yet. They might've stuck around and been detained by law enforcement on the scene. If Brody dropped his phone along the way they'd have no means of reaching us or getting word to us that they're okay."

"That's true," she conceded but the stress lines didn't let up on her face. She kissed Grayson's forehead. He leaned his angelic cheek on her shoulder and closed his eyes. "He's tired, but I don't want to put him down yet. I don't want him waking up in a strange place without his mother."

"He has you. And she'll be back."

Lisa started pacing in the yard. "And what if she doesn't…come back? It's my fault we were there in the first place."

"There's no use beating yourself up over this, Lisa. All you'll do is make yourself sick. You had no idea any of this was going to happen. We took every precaution possible to ensure your safety. No one saw this coming." Against his better judgment, he pulled her into an embrace.

She stiffened for a slight second before relaxing.

"Does it bother you when I touch you?" he asked. The last thing he wanted was to fry her nerves even more or bring back bad memories.

"No. I'm just not used to it. And it's only for a second until I wrap my mind around the fact that you're not going to hurt me," she said.

Ryan didn't like the fact that she had to think through his touch. He reminded himself not to catch her off guard again. Or maybe it would be best for both of them if he kept a safe distance.

"I hate what he's done to me," she said, hugging the baby to her chest.

Ryan kept his facial expression neutral. He knew two things for certain. First of all, Beckett Alcorn had done something so horrible to Lisa that fifteen years later she still had to remind herself being touched was okay. Second, if Ryan saw the guy again he couldn't be certain what he'd do to him. As it was, he imagined his fingers closing around Beckett's throat.

There was a special breed of people who preyed on innocents. Any person capable of hurting a child didn't deserve to live.

Biting back the rage growing inside him, Ryan kissed Lisa on the forehead and put his arm around her and Grayson.

"Is that okay?" he asked to be sure.

"I like it when you touch me, Ryan. Even though it takes a minute for my brain to tell my body that it's okay. But I do like it."

What was he supposed to do with that? Tell her that he wanted to do more than touch her? Most of the time she acted like a spooked cat and he finally understood why. The Alcorns needed to pay for everything they'd taken from the town, the people, his friends.

Before he could ask the question he wanted answered the most, he heard a shuffling noise coming from the trees on the side yard.

"Take the baby in the house and tell Dylan that we have company."

Chapter Twelve

Lisa nodded, tucked her chin to her chest and wasted no time rushing to the house. *Good.* Ryan jogged to the edge of the yard, wishing he'd brought his shotgun with him.

A few seconds later, the back door smacked against the wall. Ryan glanced back in time to see that Dylan was coming and he'd brought reinforcement in the name of Smith & Wesson.

Thirty feet in front of him, through the trees, Ryan could see two figures huddled together. One looked to be struggling to walk. If one of them was going to shoot, he or she would've done so by now, so he forged ahead into the trees.

The sight of Brody was a welcomed relief. His arm was around Lori, who was hobbling toward Ryan.

"It's them," Ryan shouted back to Dylan. "They're okay."

He hurried to Lori's other side to take some of her weight from Brody, who was wincing in pain.

"My sister and Grayson?" Lori asked immediately.

"Both fine," Ryan replied.

"Everyone's good?" she asked.

"You guys were the only two missing," Ryan reported.

A wave of relief washed over Brody's face, and Ryan knew immediately that it was because he was worried about Rebecca.

"She's fine. We all got out okay," Ryan said to confirm. "What happened to you guys?"

"Guess we were a little too close to the initial blast. It knocked us both off our feet and into the trees," Brody said. "I must've taken a blow to the head." He felt around for the knot. "I was unconscious for a good ten minutes. Took me another five to find and wake Lori."

"Everyone's been worried sick. I've been trying to call you on your cell," Ryan said as Dylan rushed to them.

He helped Brody, who'd been masking what turned out to be a pretty bad limp.

"Have no idea what happened there," Brody said.

"I'm just glad you guys are okay. Everyone else is already here," Ryan said. "The deputy just left. I'm sure the sheriff's office will want your statements, as well."

"All I want is to see my fiancée," Brody said. "Then I'll tell the law everything they want to know."

As they approached the house, everyone else spilled out the back door.

Rebecca ran into Brody's embrace and Ryan noticed the look of adoration that passed between them.

He'd seen them together before. So why was he suddenly noticing it like it was the first time?

DYLAN HAD ORDERED pizza for pickup and then insisted everyone stay at his house for the night. After cleaning up dishes and putting the babies to bed, people dispersed. A few went out the back door to take a walk around the property before it got too late and Lisa figured Dylan followed in order to check the perimeter. Samantha's father had insisted on sleeping on an air mattress in Maribel's room and giving the others the bed in Dylan's guest room.

The day had gotten so crazy that Lisa didn't feel that she'd had a chance to remember her father. She stepped outside to get a breath of fresh air and to take a moment to think about him.

As she looked up at one of those endless starlit skies that she'd grown up taking for granted in Texas, she thought about how much her father would've loved a night like this. There were no clouds, just piercing blue landscape covered with a sea of white dots, lighting up the otherwise pitch-black night.

The back door opened and then Ryan stepped onto the small porch.

"Everything all right?" he asked.

"Yeah." She turned toward the trees, trying to hide the fact that she was crying.

"Do you mind company?"

"Sure." She wiped away the tears.

He moved closer, examining her expression. "You know, you always were a bad liar."

"I miss him."

"Of course you do." Ryan didn't make a move to hold her and she figured half the reason he was holding back was because he wasn't sure when it was okay to touch her.

"Worse than that, it just feels useless. I mean, I finally get the courage to stand up to Beckett and look what happens," she said.

"He's trying to take back control. You've rattled him and that's a good thing. He'll make a mistake and the sheriff will arrest him."

"And then what? Do you really think he's going to let me get away with sending him to jail?" Of course he wouldn't. Beckett Alcorn was going to have the last laugh no matter what it cost him. Lisa knew that the price would be even higher for her. The situation couldn't feel more hopeless. "He's most likely already planning his next attack."

"The law can't deny that someone is after you and your family now. We didn't have that protection before," Ryan said earnestly.

There was no arguing that point.

"What good will it do? A man like him has unlimited resources. He won't stop until he gets what he wants." She shivered thinking about just how Beckett Alcorn liked to take what he wanted.

Ryan's voice lowered when he asked, "Can I ask a question?"

She nodded.

"Why didn't you tell anyone about your past with him?"

"There are a thousand reasons. First of all, I was embarrassed. I was convinced I'd done something to deserve it," she said, fighting the sense of shame that accompanied the admission.

"He's a bully. There's no indignity in being picked on or threatened by someone stronger than you. I just think it was a shame that you had to suffer alone."

"Who would've believed me, anyway? I'm the daughter of the town's most notorious drunk, remember?" She'd fired the accusation, but she knew that she wasn't being completely fair. Her friends had never treated her as less than because of her father.

"I would have, for one. There's a houseful of people in there who would have backed you, as well," Ryan said, hurt lacing his tone.

"I'm sorry. You're right. I'm just off today with the funeral service and then all that happened." Lisa hadn't told a soul what really had happened fifteen years ago. She wanted to tell Ryan, to get out what had been festering inside far too many years. How did she even begin to discuss the nightmare that had paralyzed her in her sleep and made her afraid to open her eyes in the morning for fear he'd be standing over her bed? "Ryan, do you really want to know why I don't talk about what Beckett did to me?"

"I do." There was comfort in his gray eyes, compassion his expression.

And yet it was still so hard to discuss. Lisa had read countless stories over the years trying to make sense of the incident, of her own behavior afterward. Even though a shocking number of young girls and women were raped by someone they knew, very few ever reported the crime. Both of those points were certainly true in her case. The words were all there to tell Ryan, but her brain refused to form sentences with them.

"It's okay. You can tell me anything. I'm not going to think any different of you," Ryan reassured her.

Would he, though? She'd certainly put herself through the wringer, asking herself a string of questions. Why had Beckett chosen her? Had she done something to bring the abuse on? Should she tell her father?

Guilt and shame washed over her, causing her shoulders to slump forward. She suddenly felt like that same twelve-year-old girl scrubbing her skin with soap in the shower, hating the feeling of Beckett touching her.

A sick feeling of frustration had been building. The powerlessness and stigma about what had happened to her and so many others had finally reached critical mass. The need to speak out finally overwhelmed her fear.

Keep quiet and he wins, a voice inside her head said.

"I was molested." There. She'd said it. Out loud.

Something dark moved behind Ryan's eyes. Hatred? Sympathy? Both?

"What did that bastard do to you?" he asked, not bothering to mask the anger in his tone.

"He touched me. He made me do things to him. I didn't even consider it rape before because he couldn't... penetrate. He threatened it, though. Said he'd wait for me. That he'd come back when I was ready. And if I told anyone then he'd come after my sister instead." Tears streamed down her face as she said the words. Getting them out, letting them go was the most frightening and yet freeing thing she'd ever done. She didn't overthink it this time. She just said it. "Looking back, I feel like I should've said something to someone but I didn't."

"You were just a kid. And you didn't report him because of his threat."

"I tried to forget about what happened. It didn't help that I started seeing stories on the news of women being torn apart on the witness stand and treated like they were the ones who'd committed a crime. I figured no one would believe a kid and especially not over Beckett."

"The way the legal system treats victims is repulsive," he agreed.

"So I withdrew from everyone and I've been keeping this terrible secret too long." Talking about it made her feel she was taking back some of her power. "It didn't help that my sister and I were being bounced around from home to home because of Dad's drinking. I guess I thought if I told anyone that they'd take us away from him permanently and we might be separated. I know our life was hard with Dad when he drank, but it was much harder to be divided between relatives."

"Thank you for trusting me with this, Lisa."

He didn't push her away or look at her as if she were tainted. She'd felt that way about herself for so many years.

"I was so afraid you'd look at me differently. That others would look at me strangely if I told anyone."

He lifted her chin. "I'm looking at you right now and all I see is a strong, beautiful woman. If anything, I respect you even more than I did before."

Slowly, Ryan pulled her closer to him and she felt as if she'd been bathed in the sun from his warmth. He kissed the top of her head.

"I felt so helpless for so many years. Anxiety and fury had built to a level that was almost intolerable. By storing the incident inside, it was gnawing away at me like it had to get out one way or another. It feels surprisingly freeing to talk about it with you. My only regret is that Beckett is winning again. He wrecked my father's funeral. That bastard has taken away so much from me. It infuriates me that he'll get away with it."

"We won't let him this time. I promise." Ryan didn't

try to mask the threat in his tone. He bent forward and looked her in the eye. "Can I have permission to kiss you?"

"Yes." She had never felt closer to another human being. There was nothing she wanted more than Ryan's lips on hers. She reached up on her tiptoes to meet him halfway.

His kiss, tender and soft, brushed against her mouth so gently. She could feel his warm breath on her skin. He tasted like the fresh coffee he'd sipped while helping with dishes a few minutes earlier.

"You're a survivor, Lisa. And you amaze me." His mouth moved against hers as he spoke.

She brought her hand up around the base of his neck and tugged him closer. His arms encircled her waist. His strong hands on her back caused her body to tremble.

He pulled back. His eyes had darkened to steel. "Is this okay?"

"It's more than okay," she said, pressing her body flush against his. She let out a sensual moan as Ryan pulled her closer, deepening the kiss.

In that moment, she got so very lost. Nothing else mattered except the two of them under a starlit sky. The crescent moon hung low and heavy and her body trembled under his fingertips.

She could stay like this all night, except a tiny part of her brain questioned whether or not *this* was a good idea. It was Ryan, and the two of them had a long history of friendship. They'd just crossed a line. And in doing so might be putting everything on it.

As if Ryan had a similar realization, he pulled back a little.

"It's late," she said when they broke contact, reconsidering. Then she was the one to pull back a little more. Her body fizzed with awareness with him this close and one look in his eyes said he felt the same. What was really going on between them? Chemistry? Sexual awareness? A leftover childhood crush?

No matter what box she fit "it" in, the result was the same. She had no idea what to do next or even if this was a good idea in the first place. Whatever was happening between them was so powerful that the air charged around them every time they were close, and especially now. It had been such a long time since a man looked at her like that—hungry and as though she was all woman and he was all man. And she couldn't ever remember wanting one to in the way she did with Ryan.

She wasn't a virgin. And yet nothing had felt so powerful, so new, as whatever was happening between them.

"Ryan."

"Yeah."

"I don't regret kissing you and I hope you don't, either."

"Kissing you is the best thing I've done in a long time," he said, and she almost laughed again at how frustrated that admission made him sound. "It's been a long day and we should try to get some sleep."

Ryan took another step back, looking as confused as she felt and as if he wasn't sure what to do with his hands. Based on his tense expression, he'd clearly felt whatever it was buzzing between them as strongly as she did. And it almost made her laugh that he didn't seem to know what to do with it any more than she did.

"We'll regroup in the morning after everyone's had a chance to get some sleep and figure out our next move."

Sleep? There'd be no sleeping tonight for her. Not with all those confusing feelings rolling around inside her head.

Chapter Thirteen

Ryan had tossed and turned all night thinking about what Lisa told him the night before about Beckett.

Rage had kept Ryan from being able to let go of his emotions and give in to sleep. And everything inside him wanted to crush Beckett Alcorn. Lisa felt alone, but someone like him didn't stop after one victim. Ryan was realistic enough to know that it would be next to impossible to find out who else Beckett had preyed on.

Trying to figure out a solution had kept Ryan in tangled sheets.

If it wasn't for that, he would've been awake thinking about the couple of kisses he and Lisa had shared. Ryan honestly didn't know what to make of what was happening between them. There'd never been so many sparks in a room with two people or so much fire in a kiss before Lisa. All he knew for certain was that this was different than anything else he'd experienced. He chalked it up to the string of bad dates he'd had in the past year.

What dates, Hunt?

There hadn't been a real date, someone he was truly interested in, in a very long time.

For one person to be everything he needed seemed

a tall order, especially since Ryan didn't particularly *need* anyone. Had he truly been looking for a partner? Or had he given up after Maria, Chelsea and Sandy consecutively had made no qualms about caring more about what he did for a living or what SUV he drove than anything else?

Was Ryan being too hard on women? Expecting too much?

Freud would have a field day with that.

Heck if he had answers. The only thing he knew for certain was that he wasn't checking the time every five minutes or thinking about how many NBA games he was missing when he spent time with Lisa. In fact, he liked talking to Lisa more than almost every other activity he could think of. Well, except for one, and sex with Lisa was totally out of the question.

Most likely their history and a natural curiosity gave that extra pull toward her. How many times in high school had he tried to work up the nerve to ask her out but couldn't? She'd shot him down cold when he finally mustered the courage.

Looking back, he might've done the same thing if the shoe were on the other foot and she'd come up with the same lame line he had. What was his brilliant phrase? *You wanna go grab a mocha with me and do some homework?*

In all fairness, she should've laughed in his face. He remembered how uncomfortable she'd become when he moved closer to her. He'd thought it was because she couldn't get away from him fast enough. Now he knew the real reason.

Ryan untangled himself from the sheets, threw on a pair of jeans and shuffled down the hallway. No good could come out of too much thinking before a man had his coffee. He stabbed his fingers into his hair, trying to tame his curls so that he looked respectable before shuffling into the kitchen in case there was mixed company.

Lisa stood at the sink, looking out the boxed window. "Morning."

"I'm not sure yet," he teased, needing to get things back on a lighter note with her after the way they'd left it last night. They needed to focus on figuring out how to connect Beckett with his crimes and especially while his father was under scrutiny.

"This might help." She handed over what he was looking for.

"Thanks." He took the mug filled with manna from heaven and breathed in the smell of fresh coffee.

"Can we talk now?" she asked after he'd finished his first cup, refilled his mug, and then took a seat at the breakfast bar.

"Now would be a good time," he said, smiling. "Your turn to sit down while I fix breakfast."

"No way," she said, emphatically. "I've got this."

"All right. What else do you know how to cook?" he asked, noticing how uncomfortable she seemed with him doing anything for her. Even though they'd made up ground last night, there was still a huge gap between them. He could be patient and wait for her to be ready to allow someone in. Until she did, there could never be anything more than friendship between them no matter how much he was starting to think he was ready for more.

"Mostly just the eggs. I hope you're okay with that," she said, rolling her eyes and clucking her tongue at him.

"Like when you decided to cook for the group when

we were working on that project in eighth grade?" he teased.

"No. Not like that." She shot him a look. "I managed to get through college without burning down any buildings, didn't I?"

"You only set a small fire. I'm still trying to figure out how you managed to get through college fed. Meal plan?" He couldn't stop himself from laughing any more than he could keep the armor around his heart from cracking a little more. Ryan didn't want to feel this way for anyone. It was only a matter of time before they'd let him down. Life had taught him that lesson early and the hard way.

She stalked over and jabbed him in the arm.

"Ouch," he said, pretending it hurt.

"See what happens, funny man?" she shot back.

In one impulsive motion, he wrapped his arm around her waist and pulled her onto his lap. Her laugh was the sweetest music, but when she turned to look at him, her eyes glittery with desire, he couldn't stop himself. "I'm going to kiss you. If that's not okay, then you need to tell me right now."

Her answer came in the form of wiggling around to give him better access. Her movement gave him a new problem to deal with…one he didn't care for the entire house to see, especially since kids could bounce into the room at any moment. Not to mention the fact that his jeans were uncomfortably tight. Need took over and he claimed her mouth. Everything about Lisa felt like coming home. Shouldn't that freak him out?

He deepened the kiss and she tasted like peppermint toothpaste and coffee. Good thing he liked both.

"Are we the only two awake? I didn't hear anyone

else when I came down the hall." He pulled back enough to brush her lips with his when he spoke.

"Dylan took Maribel out to the playground to run out some of her energy. He's been up since before the sun, I think," she said, smiling. "And you need to eat."

He kissed her one more time before helping her up and he tried not to watch her sweet bottom as she walked to the fridge and pulled supplies.

"Having a kid keeps him on his toes," Ryan said.

"The crazy part, and I noticed this with my sister, too, is that they don't seem to mind getting out of bed at ridiculous hours and staying up too late just to get basic stuff done. In fact, I've never seen either of them happier," Lisa said. "By the time I get kids at school they can already walk, talk and go to the bathroom themselves. Spending time with Grayson has changed my perspective on how hard it is to care for kids."

"Meaning what?"

"I used to look at my college friends who had babies and all I could think of was how much work they were and how tired my friends sounded. Now I get it. You don't mind being awake for three nights in a row with a sick baby when it's your child or a child you're close to. All you can think about is making them better," she said, mixing ingredients into a bowl.

"Does that mean you want one?" he asked nonchalantly, wanting to know the answer more than he cared to admit.

"A baby?" she asked in pure shock.

"No, a puppy. Of course, a baby," he retorted.

"A puppy I can handle. I'm not quite ready for a baby. I haven't even dated anyone seriously for longer than I care to admit."

Why did that statement put a smile on Ryan's face? He clamped it down before she caught him. "I was just thinking about picking up a rescue from the shelter myself." He had no plans to share the real motivation. That anticipating the loneliness he'd feel after she left was the reason he needed to fill that void.

"I'd be happy to go with you, if you'd like. When this is all over," she said, the smile fading from her lips as her mind seemed to come back to the reality facing them.

Ryan couldn't help but think the cabin was the safest place for her. "Be careful," she said, a pleading look in her eyes.

"I will." Knowing an Alcorn had put it there made Ryan tense that much more. His family had a long history with that family, dating back to a dispute about land with Ryan's father. It was time the town knew who the Alcorns really were.

"I just keep thinking about my dad and the fact that he should still be alive. I can't let the Alcorns take away everything I care about."

Ryan had no intention of allowing that to happen.

THERE WAS A sad quality to Ryan's voice every time they talked about family, which had Lisa wondering about his mother again as she put the last of the dishes in the dishwasher.

Maybe it was the fact that she'd lost her father, but if Ryan was ever going to have a chance to heal, then he needed to face his mother and deal with his emotions.

But how would she reach Mrs. Hunt? Did she even go by that name anymore?

Lisa didn't have the first idea how to contact his

mother, but didn't he have the right to know where she was and what she was doing? How sad would it be if she stayed away because she was worried that she'd be intruding on his life?

It probably wasn't Lisa's business and a voice in the back of her mind warned her not to interfere. Losing her father made her realize how short time was and how quickly people could be taken away, and she suspected Ryan's sadness wouldn't go away until he had answers.

Lisa cleaned out her mug and tucked it away in the cabinet.

The kids were down for a nap. Lori was resting with Grayson. Brody and Rebecca had disappeared to check on their horses. Samantha was taking a nap.

Lisa sought out Dylan, finding him in his office. He was in the process of converting the detached garage in order to make more room for Samantha's father to move in with them.

She knocked and then waited for an answer.

"Come in," Dylan's voice boomed.

She opened the door to find him already on his feet, palming his gun.

"It's just me," she said, her heart jumping into her throat at the sight of his weapon. Growing up in Texas, she'd gotten used to being around guns, but this seemed different. It was a stark reminder of how dangerous their circumstances were and how ready they needed to be at a moment's notice. "Can I come in?"

"Sure." He set his weapon on the desk, motioned toward a chair opposite him and took his seat.

"This place looks great." The office was nicely set up. There was a solid wood desk in the middle of the room. The place had a comfortable Western feel to it. A large rustic barn star hung on the wall behind the desk. On a long side table sat a substantial bronze of a bucking bronco. She recognized it as work from a local artist.

She figured the potted plants had to be Samantha's contribution to the decor. The green was a nice touch to the masculine room. There were a few unpacked boxes shoved against the wall.

"If I wanted to find someone, where would be the first place to look?" she asked, wishing she could come right out and ask for his help.

His expression tensed. "I can help with that."

"It's not about this case. I'm looking into something that's not connected to the Alcorns," she said, realizing he thought she was planning to poke around somewhere that might get her deeper into this mess.

"Okay. I'm guessing this isn't something you want to share with me." He leaned back in his chair. "So, if it were me looking for someone, I'd start with the most obvious place, the internet. I'm presuming you know this person's legal name."

"I do. Well, actually, I used to know her name. She may have remarried or gone back to her maiden name."

That got his attention. "Do you know her date of birth?"

"No, but I think I can find that out easily enough." Could she outright ask Ryan for the information? He'd be the only one who would know for sure, right? She could sidestep him and go directly to Justin. Oh, but the two of them were close. Justin would most likely tell his brother and then she'd have to face him. Could she come right out and tell Ryan what she was doing? Would he try to stop her? Going behind his back didn't feel right. Except what if she got him on board with the idea of finding his mother and something bad had happened to her? Or, worse, what if she didn't want to see Ryan?

It might be safer to explore on her own first and then bring him in when she knew it was safe. The last thing he needed to feel was rejected by his mother again. His pain was palpable at her abandonment, even after all these years. She understood why he would feel that way. Lisa had been let down by her father many times over the years, but Ryan was right that his saving grace was how much her father loved her. He kept fighting his way back to his girls. It was difficult to fault him for his weaknesses when he'd tried so hard to overcome them.

The bouts when he was drinking were some of the worst times of her life. But he'd figured out a way back to his family every time. Even though he fell down, he'd claw his way back up. She knew, despite everything, that he loved her and Lori above all. And that was the reason she was able to forgive him when the cops had shown up searching for him after he'd "freed" a pack of cigarettes from the gas station. She'd found him, drunk, hiding in the shed behind the house. He'd fallen asleep with a lit cigarette in his mouth. Child Protective Services hadn't liked that move.

She and her sister had been passed around to various relatives and when no one could take them in, they'd done a stint in the foster care system where Lisa had had to defend them both from a predator in one of the houses they'd been assigned.

Lisa took a sharp breath. "If I brought you in, how much is your fee?"

"No charge."

"What about confidentiality?"

"Absolute," he said without hesitation. "But I have to

admit that it worries me you would ask. What are you getting yourself into?"

She wasn't sure how Dylan would react to her trying to find Ryan's mother, especially without his permission. She wouldn't be doing it at all if she didn't think he needed to know. In her heart, she knew that in order for Ryan to heal, to be able to move on with his life and really trust people, he needed this. Ryan deserved that.

There were those in town who'd felt sorry for Mr. Hunt, saying that a wife should never abandon her family. But when Lisa's dad had been hitting the bottle a little too hard once, he let it slip that she'd had no choice but to leave.

Others whispered about it for years and Lisa had always thought there'd been more to the story. Plus, she'd had no idea what her father meant and it was obvious that he knew something. Others must know something, too.

A new scandal had broken and people had shifted their attention to the financial crisis Brody's mother had put families in when she'd taken their investment money and disappeared.

Dylan ended the call and clasped his hands. "You know I'll do anything to help you. Professionally, I have a policy against accepting a job blindly. You're going to have to tell me who this case is about if you want my help."

"That's fair. However, if you decide not to take it then I need your word you won't tell anyone I asked." Turnabout was fair play.

"Agreed."

"I'm looking for Ryan's mother." There. She'd said it. She'd dropped the bomb.

"Are you sure this is a good idea?" he asked, concern in his voice.

And that concern had her thinking twice.

"I've considered every angle. If I tell him and he wants to find her but something's happened, then he'll be devastated," she hedged.

"I can see that," Dylan agreed.

"Then there's the very real possibility that she doesn't want to be found. How can I get him all jazzed up about locating her only to let him suffer rejection again?"

"Which makes me think that he should be the one heading this search. If he doesn't want to find her, case closed."

"Only it's not that simple," she countered.

"I can see where you're coming from and it's a good place. In your heart, you want to give him this gift. But my experience has been that people who don't want to be found really don't want to be found," Dylan explained.

"And I get that. It's a risk. I'm willing to gamble if I'm the only one who'll know. Then I can help guide him in the right direction if he brings it up again."

"I can see that you care about him and you're coming from a good place—"

"We all do," she quickly added. She didn't want her cheeks to flush with embarrassment, but they did.

"Right. So I think we have to support his decision not to look for her. He's a grown man and you might end up doing more damage than you think by acting on his behalf," Dylan warned.

She slumped in her chair, feeling that this was hopeless. "Then you're not going to help me."

"I didn't say that."

"I've gone over this a thousand times in my head, believe me. But I know Ryan. It would do him so much good to put this behind him. But he's too stubborn to make the first move."

"That's the truth," Dylan agreed with a smile.

"Maybe we won't find her and he'll go to his grave never knowing the truth. I think there's more to the story of her leaving, and if we can find her maybe she can finally tell her side."

"I see the hope in your eyes when you talk about this, but believe me, not all stories have a happy ending. Look at mine," he said.

"And that's why I thought you'd understand. Do you want to see your parents? Wouldn't you like to hear from them one way or the other as to why they never came back?"

"I can tell you why—they were selfish."

"Maybe so. Have you considered other possibilities?"

"Like?" He opened his hands and put his palms flat on the desk.

"They were young and scared, and had no idea what to do with a baby."

"I've thought of that. I'm not a baby anymore. They should make the effort at this point," Dylan said, hurt still in his voice.

And that was exactly why Ryan needed to know. That hurt would never go away until he knew the truth.

"Are you the least bit curious? I mean, we know how strict your grandmother was. Is it possible that she told them to go? Asked them not to come back?" Lisa asked.

Dylan leaned back in his chair, considering her questions.

"They didn't come to her funeral. Didn't try to make sure I was okay," he said, rubbing the scruff on his chin.

"I agree that was wrong. I'm not convinced they didn't love you, though."

He laughed. "I really have become soft since having Maribel. This conversation would've had me all kinds of riled up and ready to fight in the past. Now I'm actually considering what you're saying."

"That's a good thing, right?" she asked, not wanting to push her luck but also needing to help others see how short life really was and how little of it should be wasted on a hurt feelings or a grudge.

"It is," he said. "Now you have me thinking about finding my folks. You've brought up good points. Let's think this through for a minute. Say I locate them. Then what? I'm not ready to forgive them yet."

"You don't have to be. Do you?" she asked.

He laughed again. "I guess not."

"All you really have to be is prepared to face whatever truth comes out of it. If they don't want to see you, then you have your answer. But what if they do? What if they're the ones who are scared you'll reject them after all these years? If you can handle knowing the truth, shouldn't you try to find it?" she asked.

"You're probably right." He paused thoughtfully. "You didn't come here to talk about my situation, though."

"No, I didn't. And I'm sorry if it makes you uncomfortable. Losing my father has made me realize tomorrow is never promised to anyone. I guess I want everyone to get closure with their relationships."

"That's true," he agreed.

She waited for him to give her an answer about Ryan.

"I want it on record that I still don't agree with going behind Ryan's back," Dylan said. "Any heat comes from this and it's going to be on you."

"Does that mean you're agreeing to help?" She couldn't keep the excitement out of her tone.

"It does. Mostly because I know you're going to look anyway and I'd rather be involved so I can make sure no one leads you down the wrong path."

"Thank you, Dylan," she said, feeling extreme relief and a new sense of purpose.

"I just hope this doesn't come back on either one of us," Dylan said.

Chapter Fourteen

Ryan finished the last few bites of his dinner, looking around at the friends he'd known since he was a kid. As much as this felt like family, he'd be lying if he didn't admit that a piece of his life had always felt as if something was missing.

He dismissed the thought as being melancholy.

His brother, his friends and the people he could count on were all he needed. It was surprising just how quickly Lisa had made an impact on his thinking. She'd gotten under his armor and had him considering ideas he never would've in the past. Too bad they would part ways soon.

"We'll need to move out at first light tomorrow morning," he said.

"What's the plan?" Dylan asked.

"The cabin is safe. I'll make sure no one follows us there," he said.

"I want you to take my truck. Samantha and I will take your Jeep. We can go with you to the county line. It'd be too risky to keep going after that. The more vehicles we have, the higher the risk of being noticed," Dylan said.

"Just like the president," Ryan said, noticing that

the mood had instantly changed from light to intense when he brought up leaving. But the topic couldn't be avoided. They needed a plan.

Taking back roads was a good way to slip out of town unnoticed, but he also thought about how exposed they'd be with no one around for miles. There'd be long stretches of road in front of them and behind them with plenty of chances for ambush.

Brody leaned forward. "There's the issue of getting you there safely. Small highways have their own problems." He glanced up at Ryan, clear they'd been thinking along the same lines. "Once you get there, I don't like you being at the cabin defenseless. There's no backup around."

"Good point," Dylan agreed.

"You can't leave your horses, Brody," Ryan said, referring to his friend's horse ranch. "And, Dylan, you have Maribel. No way will she let you out of her sight. You need to be around for her."

Dylan and Brody nodded.

"We can check to see if Dawson is available. Plus, I haven't spoken to James. He might want to be involved," Brody said.

"I don't mind getting others involved if need be. I still believe we'll be fine if we make it out of Mason Ridge without being followed," Ryan said. "Nobody knows about this place, and bringing along others could make it easier to track us."

"You'll get out of town without a tail. I can see to that," Dylan offered.

"We'll all pitch in," Brody said.

Ryan raised his chin. "My shotgun's too big to handle while I drive. I'll need to borrow a weapon."

"You got it," Dylan said. "I have a few spares. Take what you need from my office."

A look passed between Dylan and Lisa. What was that all about?

Ryan knew that Lisa would be fine with guns. Heck, most everyone in Texas had grown up with one in the house along with the proper come-to-Jesus meeting about keeping them inside, unloaded, in a locked case. He'd ask her about it later.

Right now he needed to come up with a plan to keep her, her sister and Grayson away from Beckett Alcorn.

"I stopped by the sheriff's office while I was out," Ryan said. "Couldn't get a whole lot out of him about yesterday's incident."

"I've been investigating this on my own," Dylan said. "We located the warehouse outside town."

"Have you turned that information over to the sheriff?" Ryan asked.

"Not yet. I wanted to put eyes on it for a while. See what's really going on first. If I gave the information to law enforcement I was afraid they'd blast in there and scare off anyone who might be using the place. If the Alcorns know we're onto them, they'll close up shop there. And something's been bugging me. I remember a weird smell that I couldn't put my finger on. At the time, I wrote it off as nothing. Now I'm wondering if they might've been using the facility to mix chemicals," Dylan said.

"Like for a bomb?" Ryan asked. "I want to see this place."

Dylan nodded. "We can check it out later if you want. We'll have to go in the middle of the night and be very careful, though. I get caught and my relationship with the sheriff will go up in flames."

DARKNESS SURROUNDED DYLAN'S HOUSE. The blinds were closed. Lisa slipped out of the foldout bed she shared with Lori and Grayson in the living room and moved down the hallway.

Brody and Rebecca had gone home for the night. Dylan and Samantha and Maribel were in their respective rooms. Samantha's father was staying at his house in town to give them all some room.

Lisa's eyes had adjusted to the dark and she was careful not to bump into anything on her way to Ryan's room. She cracked the door.

"Ryan?" she whispered.

"Come in." He sounded wide-awake.

"What time do you plan to leave?" Lisa asked Ryan, who opened the covers to allow her to slip into his makeshift bed on the floor.

"Not for a couple of hours," he said.

"You can't sleep?" She closed the door behind her and took him up on his offer.

"No. You tired at all?" he asked, his voice husky.

"Not even a little bit. There's so much rolling around in my head. I have so many questions about this whole ordeal. I can't shut it off." The case was one thing that was keeping her up. She also wondered if she was doing the right thing by going behind his back to find his mother. All the logical reasons jumped to her defense and yet she couldn't help feeling that she was betraying him.

"You know we'll figure this out, right?" Based on his tone of voice, it wasn't a question. He pulled her closer to him and kissed her on her forehead. The move was no doubt meant to be reassuring and yet it felt incredibly intimate with the two of them lying in bed together. Only a few strips of material kept them from skin-to-skin contact.

With his strong arms around her, she settled into the crook of his neck, doing her best to ignore the pulses of electricity ricocheting between them. With every breath, the room heated. With every move, her body warmed with sensual heat.

The kisses they'd shared had occupied more and more mental space and there'd been something building between them for the past few weeks. Whatever was going on between them had pushed them well beyond friendship into a new scary world—scary because she'd never wanted to be with someone as much she did Ryan. Did that freak her out? Sure. In the past something like that would've paralyzed her. Not this time. Not with him.

The first time she'd lost her virginity jumped into her thoughts. She'd been in such a hurry to lose it in college. It had been this big fear building inside her that she'd never be able to be intimate with anyone, that Beckett had taken that from her. She hadn't been dating Timothy for long when she decided it was time.

Timothy wasn't the right guy. He was barely the "right now" guy. And yet she'd gone through with it anyway. And she had no regrets. Except that she did realize that making the decision to have sex needed to be about more than ticking a box on a to-do list.

Once she'd gotten it out of her system then she'd decided to wait until she had real feelings for a guy before sleeping with him. It seemed that her late start put her behind the dating curve and she'd ended up going out with guys who were in no way right for her or good for her, either. When Darren had forced the issue of sex after too many beers at a frat party, Lisa fought back. Even though she got away from him and he didn't get his way, she had that same feeling of shame as if she'd been molested.

Being touched and not instinctively reacting with shock was an uphill battle after that.

And yet she wanted Ryan's hands on her.

"Ryan…"

"Yes."

"I want you to touch me."

"You do know what you're asking, right?" he asked, his voice husky.

"Uh-huh." She no longer cared what this would do to their friendship. She needed him to touch her, to brand her as his, to make her unafraid again. And she wanted this to happen more than she wanted air.

Breathing wasn't proving to be a problem.

The palm of his hand flattened on her stomach, causing her to quiver. She'd lost her virginity years ago and yet this felt like the very first time all over again.

"I need to know you can handle this," he said in a low, deep timbre. He trailed his finger down her stomach and then along the lacy rim of her panties. "I want you."

Turning to face him, she could feel his thick erection pulsing against her stomach, causing need to roar through her.

She struggled to gain footing as thunder boomed in her ears. Was this really happening?

"I want this, Ryan."

"It's a damn good thing you do." He cupped her face in his hands.

His lips pressed hers with an intensity that robbed her breath.

Desire started building, reaching, climbing toward that place that needed release as he lowered his hand and ran his finger along the sensitized skin of her hip. He needed to hurry this up because her body couldn't take much more.

Rather than wait for him to decide when to raise the stakes, Lisa took matters into her own hands, literally. She wrapped her hand around his stiff length and was rewarded with a guttural groan in response. Being in control felt good with Ryan and she figured that, with some practice, she'd easily let go and let him take the lead. It dawned on her why he was taking it so slowly, and the reason made her heart melt a little more. He didn't want to spook her or do anything she couldn't handle.

"You can't hurt me, Ryan. I want this more than you do."

"I doubt that's possible, sweetheart."

She smiled against his lips before he captured hers again in a bone-melting kiss. With her free hand, she stroked him a few times.

"Hold that thought," he said, untangling their legs and pushing himself off the makeshift bed. He grabbed his jeans and returned with a condom.

There was enough light in the room to illuminate the hard angles on his face and hawk-like nose. Lisa had the startling realization that she'd never felt like this toward any other man. She'd never needed to touch anyone as much as she needed to touch Ryan right now. So she did just that. She reached toward him and outlined the ridges in his stomach, ripples of muscle.

His T-shirt and boxers were on the floor seconds before he rolled the condom down his length. She stopped long enough to admire him in all his masculine glory. He was serious hotness and she desperately wanted him.

It took her a few seconds to realize his pause was meant to give her time to undress. Her own oversize sleeping shirt and underwear joined his on the floor as soon as it dawned on her. This time, they'd make love on her schedule.

"I want you to touch me," she said, knowing he needed to hear the words. "I love the way your hands feel on my body."

She moved onto her back so that he could reposition himself inside the V of her legs. His body trembled with the need for release as he brushed his tip along her wet heat.

Palming his length, she guided him.

He dipped slowly at first, but she was already ready for him. She matched his next gentle thrust and he slid deep inside her.

Matching him stride for stride, she climbed with him toward the peak of release they could only give each other. Their bodies, now slick with sweat, moved at a frantic pace as they reached that ultimate climax together.

Tension corded her body as her inner muscles clenched and released around his length.

"Ryan," she breathed as she felt his body tighten while he climbed that same mountain, stood on that same edge and free-fell to that same sweet release.

They lay perfectly still, bodies entangled, until their pulses returned to a normal beat.

Lisa couldn't be sure she'd heard him correctly, but as Ryan rolled to his side she could've sworn she'd heard him say that he loved her.

THE AIR WAS STILL. There was a cloudless sky. The stars shone brilliantly against a black canopy.

This was a perfect night for reconnaissance.

As long as Ryan could keep his thoughts on the mission he needed to accomplish and not on the silky feel of Lisa's skin. Or just how much like home it felt to have her legs wrapped around him as she called out his name.

Ryan stood out front, waiting for Brody, as Dylan pulled together a few supplies. He strolled outside, shouldering a backpack at the same time Brody's truck rolled up the gravel drive, lights out.

"This should help you out if you find yourself in trouble," Dylan said, handing Ryan a weapon.

By the weight and feel, Ryan recognized it as a Glock.

The trio left as quietly as they could, staying dark until they'd slipped down the farm road leading to Dylan's house. There were no other vehicles on the road, but Ryan knew that someone could be watching the house.

"Even with the sheriff's office keeping watch on your place, I'm not sure I like leaving them alone," he said.

"I have electronic eyes on the perimeter," Dylan replied. "And someone stationed outside. Anything goes south and there's backup. I'm not leaving anything to chance with the people we love."

"I didn't see anyone outside, so I'm guessing that was

for a reason." Ryan didn't correct Dylan. The truth was that he did love Lisa and the past few hours had been a game changer for him. The tricky part was figuring out his next move. The answer to that was probably going to be nothing. He liked the idea that she didn't bristle when he'd touched her. And he'd allow her to take the lead.

"Exactly," Dylan agreed.

"I heard you got a colt in a few weeks ago from Lone Star," Ryan said to Brody, needing to distract himself from thinking about everything that could go wrong with their mission.

"He's a good horse," Brody said. "Or at least he will be when I finish doctoring him up and training him."

"What's his story?"

"The usual. His owner saw potential and kicked up his training routine at eighteen months old," Brody said.

"Which isn't uncommon," Dylan added.

"Nope. Didn't work out so well for this guy, though. His knees are a mess and he won't ever race," Brody said.

"How'd he end up at your place?" Ryan asked.

"Owner felt horrible for the colt. Wants him to have a chance to go to a ranch or be someone's personal horse, so he asked around and was referred to my rehab ranch."

A second chance sounded pretty good to Ryan about now. His first thought was Lisa. His second was his mother. Why did she pop into his thoughts? Must've been the recent conversation he'd had with Lisa. But it didn't matter. He had no idea how to reach his mother, and if he was being honest, he wasn't real sure he ever wanted to see the woman again.

The drive to the warehouse didn't take much more

than half an hour. The closer they'd gotten, the bumpier the roads. Dylan's jaw clenched tighter, too.

"Did you see anything when you were there before?" Ryan asked.

"No. I had a canvas bag on my head the entire time we were outside the building. I remember it being dark, but that was mainly because it was the middle of the night. There wasn't any other light source around, which was one of the signs I was somewhere on the outskirts of town. I remember waking up bound to some kind of wooden table and then looking up to see a single bulb hanging from a socket." He paused as he clenched his back teeth. "There were these plastic-looking panels on the ceiling and I remember thinking that if it was light outside, sun would stream through the half wall of windows."

Ryan nodded as he thanked his friend again for everything he was doing for Lisa and her family. Facing the warehouse couldn't be easy.

Dylan stared out the front window onto the winding road lit up by the beams in front of them. "All I could think at the time was that the place would be good for torturing people. And how much I needed to walk out of there alive if I ever wanted to see Maribel again. Later, I thought that it might be easy to hide people there, too."

"They could be doing any number of illegal activities in such a remote location," Ryan agreed. Not the least of which was storing chemicals required to make a bomb.

"Looking back, I remember a distinct smell. At the time, I wrote it off as being an old building." Dylan maintained focus on the road ahead. He instructed Brody on making a few turns before saying, "We'll need to cut the lights and walk soon."

"Say the word and it's done," Brody said.

The road became bumpier as they traveled along the clay path. A mile or so later, Dylan gave the signal to stop.

Brody pulled off the road and parked.

"I brought one of these for each of us," Brody said, and then located three backpacks from the backseat. "Let's see what's in here." Dylan held his up.

"A knife for starters. We could spend hours debating which one is best, but I like a six- to eight-inch blade with a serrated edge on the back side for sawing," Brody said. "There's also a signal mirror and gloves. There again, I like something light that gives a good grip while protecting my skin."

"With the added benefit of us not leaving behind any fingerprints," Ryan added.

"To that end, there are hair nets, too," Brody said.

"Great, we'll be rockin' the lunch-lady look," Dylan teased.

"Afraid so." Brody laughed. "I didn't say we'd be pretty, but we won't leave anything behind, either. Dylan's the only one we want identified with the scene."

"Good point," Ryan agreed. That way, Dylan could direct the sheriff to the site where he'd been held captive and there'd be evidence to prove his story.

"I brought headgear with reflective strips on the back," Brody continued, securing his on his head. "We all have cells, which we're going to want to silence, but I also brought a light source and a map of the area in case we get separated. Let's grab those and circle the spot where the truck is."

Ryan did. He pulled up their location on his phone's

GPS, and then circled the corresponding spot on the printed map.

"I didn't figure we'd be out here long enough to need insect repellant," Brody said, folding his own map and securing it in his pack.

"I have to admit it. When you told me you'd pack for us, I was hesitant. We all have different ideas of what we think we might need on a mission," Dylan said with a chuckle. "But you did a good job."

Brody and Dylan had served in different branches of the military, and that meant each one thought the other wasn't doing it right in pretty much every situation, Ryan thought with a laugh. He was basically Switzerland. Working the land had taught him how to survive if he was ever stranded. Hunting had taught him what he needed to know about using a gun. He'd fine-tuned his ability to point, shoot and hit a target.

Ryan tucked the gun in the waistband of his jeans and then he secured his hair net.

"We think this is the facility I was taken to." Dylan pointed to a spot on the map that would be half an hour's hike at best. "I encountered three men who worked for Alcorn."

"With his resources he could afford an army of men watching the place. You have any intel about others?" Ryan asked.

"My technology guy hasn't been able to watch for long. I just found the place. Under normal circumstances, I'd watch and wait," Dylan said.

"There's too much at stake now and it's only a matter of time before they figure out a way to get to us," Ryan agreed.

"Bombing the funeral home was a bold move," Dylan said.

"Beckett's got it in for her. We all know he's the one behind this, especially after his visit. But he's smart enough not to get caught," Ryan hissed.

"Did the deputy ever say whether or not they had any suspects?" Dylan asked.

"None yet. Said they couldn't imagine who would do such a thing and especially at such an inappropriate time," Ryan said. "Can't say that I have a lot of confidence in them given the fact that Alcorn's been under their nose for how many years now and look what he's managed to get away with." He shouldered his pack. "We helped them find him before and they lost him after that."

"You think the sheriff's in on this?" Dylan asked.

Brody nodded. "Rebecca seems to think so. At the very least she believes he's looked the other way a few times."

"And you?" Ryan asked Brody.

"I got questions." Brody paused. "Like how do you let someone involved in kidnapping kids live right under your nose and not have the first clue?"

"Either he's being bribed to look the other way and has no idea or he's in on it," Ryan said.

"Maybe he's looking at his pension thinking he needs more when he retires, so he looks the other way for some of Alcorn's business dealings," Brody said.

"What I can't figure out is why now? If I'm Beckett, do I really want more attention on me and my family right now?" Ryan asked.

"Other than the fact that she could come forward and damage their name even more." Brody scratched his chin. "Public opinion has been split as to whether or not people believe Charles Alcorn capable of such an act. Lisa comes forward and brings charges against Beckett and people start thinking where there's smoke, there's fire."

"That was my first thought, too. And that's most likely the reason," Ryan said.

Dylan, who had been quietly contemplating the discussion so far, leaned forward. "She's a loose end."

That thought scared Ryan the most. "Meaning they won't stop until they've tied it off."

"Did you think there was any chance they'd stop?" Dylan asked calmly, his low voice carrying anger.

"Not really. I'd hoped we could end this without putting someone in a body bag. With their money, I doubt that's possible. They can reach her even from jail. It won't be enough."

"She could go into a program, take her sister and Grayson with her and disappear," Dylan said. "I had to consider all of Samantha's options when she was a target."

Ryan mumbled something that sounded like agreement, but the truth was that he couldn't think about never seeing Lisa again. It did all kinds of messed-up things to his emotions. Instead, he looked to Brody and then to Dylan. "Ready to do this?"

Chapter Fifteen

Dylan nodded at the same time as Brody, giving a thumbs up. Dylan took the lead once outside the truck while Brody and Ryan fell in step next to each other.

The walk through the thinly wooded area became easier as Ryan's eyes adjusted to the darkness. He'd first focused almost solely on the reflector on the back of Dylan's headband but now could see fairly well as he mentally prepared for a few scenarios that they might be walking into.

First, someone could be there guarding the place, making it impossible to get what they needed. It would be a whole lot easier if no one was there. They'd be able to walk right in and check it out without raising an eyebrow or alerting anyone to the fact that they knew the location of the warehouse.

After taking Dylan there, they might've cleared it of anything that could be incriminating. So this mission could be a colossal waste of time.

Feeling that he was leaving Lisa vulnerable didn't sit well with Ryan, either. He had to remind himself that she was fine and safe and that she'd be at Dylan's house sleeping, just as he'd left her, when he got back.

Dylan stopped. His fisted hand came up, so Brody

and Ryan followed suit. Then he crouched low. Ryan was beside him in a second.

Being back to this place must bring up bad feelings for him. Dylan and Brody had personal reasons for wanting the Mason Ridge Abductor put behind bars. Both of their lives and future wives had been affected by that jerk. Both had a stake in ensuring the right person was caught and put behind bars.

A man like Alcorn would be able to twist the legal system in his favor. And his son had grown up with the same entitlement. Ryan would see to it that Beckett paid for his crimes against Lisa. One way or the other, the score would be settled.

Where they crouched, the building was about fifty yards away. There were no lights on inside or around the building, casting an eerie dark glow to the windows. The place looked abandoned and like something out of a bad horror movie, and everything about being there had Ryan's danger radar on high alert.

The strategy for now would be to wait in order to make sure no one was visiting this place on rounds. There were no vehicles in the parking lot, but that didn't mean there wouldn't be any coming or that no one was inside. Ryan couldn't imagine anyone would be, but no one in his party, including him, was willing to take that chance.

A noise came from behind them and Ryan whirled around, ready to fight in a split second.

All three stilled, waited, listened.

An agonizing full minute later, a deer sprinted through the brush. And that really was the best of possible situations. This area was known for cougars and other dangerous animals, and the last thing they needed was a battle with Mother Nature to draw attention to their location.

Even though there were no vehicles parked, that didn't mean there was no one in the building. Someone could be inside right then, watching, waiting.

There were a number of things this building could be used for. None of them Ryan liked.

Crouched in the brush, he didn't want to think about all the manner of other dangerous wildlife he could be sitting next to at the moment. Aside from the usual varieties of venomous snakes and spiders, north Texas was host to other bigger creatures that could sneak up on them, like coyotes.

Ryan didn't even want to think about all those creepy crawlies slinking around on the ground under the canopy of leaves. He'd rather face something closer to his own size. His body involuntarily shuddered thinking about how much he hated spiders.

LISA COULDN'T SLEEP and she didn't want to wake Lori and the baby, so she literally lay staring at the ceiling until she thought her brain might explode.

Nervous energy kept her heart pounding inside her chest. There was no way to contact Ryan or the guys to know if everything was okay. Her mind kept racing through worst-case scenarios.

Lisa canceled the negative thoughts, reminding herself worrying wouldn't do any good. She'd deal with whatever happened, even though not knowing was killing her.

She couldn't even begin to seriously consider the possibility that something could happen to any of them, and especially not Ryan, without pain stabbing her in the chest. She took in a deep breath and regrouped.

Thinking about everything that could go wrong wouldn't do any good. It wouldn't bring the guys back any sooner. And it would only cause Lisa to shred her stomach lining with worry.

"Are you thinking about him?" Lori whispered over Grayson, who lay sleeping soundly between them.

"Yes." Lisa would be lying if she said otherwise and she didn't want to lie to her sister.

"I miss him, too."

It was then that Lisa realized Lori was talking about their father and not Ryan. Of course their father would be on Lori's mind. Lisa hadn't forgotten him, either. He was always close to her thoughts and near her heart, and she had a moment of guilt for thinking about anything else.

Then again, she could only allow herself a few moments to think about her father before she had to focus on something else. Missing him was a cavern in her chest.

"You want me to make coffee?" Lisa asked.

"That would be nice." Lori eased away from Grayson and then positioned pillows on either side of him so he couldn't roll off the bed when she and Lisa moved.

Watching Lori with Grayson filled Lisa's heart with an emotion she couldn't quite put her finger on. It was a mix of love and fulfillment and something else. Longing?

Lisa hadn't given much thought to having children of her own. Her life was full between Lori, Grayson and the kids in her classes who felt like family. There was something magical about watching her kindergarteners successfully complete center activities or experience the joy of reading a book for the first time. The rewards of seeing those little eyes light up when children grasped a concept were as tangible today as they'd been when she first started teaching five years ago.

Lisa believed herself to be a good teacher, but was she mother material?

She let that thought rattle around while she made a fresh pot of coffee.

"You like him, don't you?" Lori padded into the kitchen.

"Yes." There was no use denying her feelings.

"Maybe when this is all over you two can spend some time together," Lori offered.

"It's complicated," Lisa said, handing her sister a mug.

"Yeah? Life's complicated, isn't it?"

"When did you get so philosophical?" Lisa teased.

"Having a baby changes your priorities, I guess." Lori shrugged and then took a sip.

Lisa motioned toward the kitchen table. She didn't turn on the light and neither did Lori.

"Remember when Dad would take us camping out by Lake Mason?" Lori asked.

"I do. He always said that you had to be made of tough stuff to camp in the summer in Texas," Lisa said.

"It would be so hot and we had those little plastic fans that squirted water to cool us off," Lori said with a smile.

"We'd stay up half the night pretending to be explorers in the African jungle," Lisa remembered.

"Discovering new lands. Watching out for lions," Lori added. "Looking back, don't you think it's kind of weird that neither one of us dreamed about being mothers?"

"I guess losing ours so early had an impact."

"Do you think about her?" Lori asked, her tone serious.

"Not as much as I should." Lisa paused. "Keeping an eye on you and Dad became a full-time job after she died."

"Thank you for that, by the way," Lori said.

"For what? We both did our fair share of watching over Dad."

"I wasn't talking about that. I was thinking about the way you've always taken care of me," Lori said.

"You would've done the same."

"Maybe. Who knows? You were a great big sis."

"If that was true, I would've been able to keep us together all the time," Lisa said. "How many times were we split up to live with relatives?"

"I didn't mind."

"Really?"

"I always knew you'd find me. I never worried about that because I had you," Lori said.

"Mom would be so proud of you with Grayson." Lisa needed to change the subject before the flood of tears released.

"If I'm a good mother to Grayson, it's because you showed me how to be," Lori said emphatically. "I don't mean any disrespect to our mother. I'm sure she was amazing. But you're the one who taught me how care for someone, how to put other people first."

Tears fell no matter how much Lisa tried to suppress them.

"But I wonder who takes care of you."

"Having you and Grayson is enough," Lisa said.

"You need more than just the two of us. I know you love your job, the kids, and I have no doubt about how much you love me and Grayson. But you need more than that. I love Grayson with all my heart, but I hope to go on a date someday, maybe meet someone who'll be a father to my son as well as a good husband to me. Someone who isn't freaked out at the thought of fatherhood and steps up for me and Grayson."

"I want that for the both of you, too," Lisa said.

"And what about for yourself?" Lori asked. "Do you ever think about sharing your life with someone else?"

"Honestly?"

Lori nodded.

"I've been too busy to think about it," Lisa said.

"Or maybe you just won't give yourself the time to," Lori countered.

Was that true? Maybe her sister had a point. For so many years Lisa had worried about making sure her baby sister was okay. And yet she was uncomfortable allowing anyone to care for her, even when she was hurt and couldn't care for herself. Frustration was written all over Ryan's face every time she forced him to sit instead of help her with something.

"I guess our upbringing taught me that if I wanted something done right I had to do it myself. I stopped relying on others," Lisa said, sipping her coffee.

"It's not a bad thing to be independent," Lori said sympathetically.

"It's hard for me to depend on anyone else, to give up that power."

"It's just that I think so many people have let you

down that you've forgotten that you *can* count on people."

Lisa thought about what her sister was saying, the truth in her words.

"When did you get to be so wise?" she asked.

"Believe me, you stay awake all night with a baby enough and you'll start contemplating the meaning of life, too." Lori laughed. She took another sip of coffee and then set her mug down. "It's different with Ryan."

"Is it?" Lisa asked, wondering if she'd ever be able to let her guard down enough to allow herself to truly rely on anyone else. Life lessons like the ones she'd learned didn't wipe away so easily on the blackboard of her psyche.

"He's a good guy."

"That much I know," Lisa responded. "I'm sure you thought Jessie was decent or you never would've gone out with him in the first place."

"Yeah, and I knew him for all of three months before I got pregnant. How much can you really know anyone in that short a time?" Lori said, twisting her mouth into a funny half smile. "Don't say I should've waited to get to know him better. I think I've already figured that one out the hard way. He was just so handsome and mysterious when he rolled through town to visit his cousin. I think I wanted something different than what I'd known my whole life, someone different than the guys in town. Boy, did I learn that something different isn't always something better!"

"So true." Lisa was still trying to sort out her feelings for Ryan, especially since they'd made love earlier, but she knew exactly what kind of person he was. It seemed that that should make her feelings for him easier to understand. When this was all over, maybe she could take some time to think about what he really meant to her. She didn't have to be back to school for a couple of weeks.

A dark thought hit her. Beckett would make sure she never returned to school or a normal life again.

For the first time, Lisa considered moving out of state. She could teach anywhere. Maybe even change her name?

No. That wouldn't work.

Not with Lori and Grayson here in Mason Ridge.

And a little piece of her heart didn't want to think about leaving Ryan, either.

"Everything is happening so fast. It's hard to know what to think anymore," Lori said.

"I was just thinking the same thing," Lisa replied. They were talking about different things, but the essential truth was the same. Life would never be the same.

Chapter Sixteen

"Let's go," Dylan said after they'd sat for forty-five minutes watching the warehouse.

The longer Ryan was away from Lisa, the more clenched his gut became. He didn't want to acknowledge all the reasons. Rather than climb on that hamster wheel again, he followed Dylan inside the building.

The air was still and it was dead quiet. He immediately smelled cleaning agents, which were common materials used in making bombs.

Inside was a long, open room. Metal bars kept the ceiling from caving in. On one end of the building was a door. All three men seemed to lock in on it at the same time. If anyone was there, they'd be inside that room.

Dylan and Brody flanked Ryan as he stalked toward it, careful not to make a sound.

There were containers shoved up against the walls and gallon jugs of rat poison. He glanced at a bucket filled with old cell phones and his immediate thought was that they could be used as remote devices used to activate detonators.

None of this was damning evidence unless he could tie the Alcorns to the building in some way. Charles

Alcorn would be smart enough to erase any paper trail leading back to him.

Ryan immediately noticed the rust on the door handle as he approached. There were two logical explanations. The first was the building's age. The second could be from chemicals used to make a bomb. They'd rust any metal nearby.

There were cords half-unraveled on the cement floor, too.

Definite signs of bomb activity.

Ryan tried the door and it was locked. He pulled out the knife Brody had packed in his rucksack. Since the doorknob was a simple push-button affair, all he had to do was jab a tiny blade into the hole and push on the locking mechanism.

He popped the lock easily and opened the door much to the wide-eyed stares of his buddies. Ryan didn't dare defend himself before he found out what was on the other side. Besides, he might be reliable Ryan but he'd had his share of reasons to pick a lock to get to his brother.

Palming his gun, he used it to lead the way inside.

The room was empty save for a wooden table that had been pushed to one side.

"The place is clear," Ryan said.

"I've been here before." Dylan focused on the table with a look of disgust. "I also saw wires out there and they tied off my head covering with something like that."

"I'm sure both of you noticed the supplies in the other room," Ryan said, leading the way back. "And the smell."

Brody stopped, his gaze locked on to something in the corner. He walked over, picked it up and held it up.

It was a toy race car.

"I don't like the look of that," Ryan said.

"Neither do I," Brody replied, setting it down gingerly in the same place. "There's so much they can do with forensics nowadays. Maybe they can lift something off it and identify the owner. Damn, that makes me think I should've left it alone."

"That's a good point. We shouldn't touch anything else we see," Ryan said. "Even though we're wearing gloves, we might smudge a print."

Dylan agreed.

They returned to the bigger room and pulled light sources out of their packs. The inside of the building was surprisingly free of graffiti, so it had been maintained or at the very least watched over by someone.

Bored teenagers generally knew every vacant building in the county because they were always looking for places to gather, drink and goof around. Another sign this place was under someone's protection.

"What's that smell?" Ryan asked.

"Could be this," Dylan held up an opened bottle of vinegar. "They have so many freakin' ways to make bombs in here. I think these are acetone and aluminum powder. Then there are these bags of sugar, nitric acid, potassium chlorate and nitrate. They've even got car batteries stacked over here."

"A good source of sulfuric acid," Ryan said. "These thermometers are a source of mercury. And this hydrogen peroxide is available at pretty much every store. One thing here and there and we have no case against the owner of this building. Put even a few together and this is worth law enforcement's time."

"How do we want to do this?" Brody said.

"We can call it in anonymously," Ryan said. "Use the tip line."

"I've got someone looking into this, as well," Dylan said. "Doesn't hurt to squeeze out whoever's involved by calling in the law."

"In the meantime, let's take pics of everything we see," Ryan said. There was dirt and sawdust on the floor. "We'll need to erase our footprints."

"You two shoot, I'll take care of our footprints," Brody said.

When they were done, they shut down their light sources and turned toward the door in time to see headlights, which almost immediately shut off.

"Spread out," Brody said.

Ryan moved near the door, behind a column so that no one could see him when they breached the entry.

He crouched low, ready to spring into action.

There were voices on the other side of the door. What was it? A police radio.

If the deputy or whoever was out there walked ten steps inside the door, he'd be face-to-face with Ryan.

He ran toward the back room. Dylan and Brody had the same idea because they both tore in the same direction.

They closed the door within seconds of the other being opened.

Dylan checked the window. "I hear two voices."

"We need to get the hell out of here. They catch us in here and we'll never be able to explain our way out of it," Brody said.

Following Dylan's lead, Ryan stealthily climbed onto the table that had been pushed against a wall. He could hear footsteps echoing louder on the concrete in the other room moving toward them.

Once the window was open, Ryan slipped out first, followed by the others.

They crouched down and belly-crawled toward the brush.

Once they found their original path, they broke into a full run and didn't stop until they were at Brody's truck again.

"What the hell was that?" Ryan asked.

"Someone must've beaten us to reporting that place to the deputy," Dylan said.

"But why? It makes no sense," Ryan said. "Unless… they wanted us to get caught. What better way to accuse us of being involved than to have us caught red-handed with bomb material?"

"You're right," Brody said. "The question is how did they know we were there in the first place?"

"It must be wired." Ryan took his seat on the passenger side after Dylan and closed the door.

"My tech guy didn't detect anything," Dylan said. "Then again, there are lots of new toys out there that can fly under the radar and we didn't have time to properly screen the location."

With Alcorn's money, Ryan figured only the best would do. And he also realized they'd walked right into a trap.

If someone in Alcorn's camp knew about them visiting this site, then Lisa might be in danger. Dammit.

"We need to get back," he said to Brody.

"I thought of that, too," Brody said. "I'm on it."

As long as Beckett Alcorn was free, none of their friends were truly safe.

Pulling into the gravel drive more than half an hour later, Ryan felt his heart sink to his toes when he saw a cruiser parked out front.

As soon as the truck stopped, he bolted for the front door.

Lisa was already coming outside, followed by Deputy Adams.

"What's going on?" Ryan asked.

She got close enough for him to see the absolute panic in her eyes.

"Ryan Hunt, I'd like you to accompany me to the station for questioning," Adams said.

"What are you talking about?" Ryan asked. What on earth could Adams want to ask him at the station that he couldn't ask right there?

Lisa's expression was complete panic by this point. "I tried to text you, but he asked me not to. He won't say what's going on."

"Don't I have a right to know why you want me to go with you?" Ryan asked, not wanting to leave Lisa alone for even a few hours.

"Like I said, I have questions." Adams was looking at Ryan as if he'd finally gotten one of the Hunt boys on a criminal charge. Ryan didn't like it one bit, and this was coming out of left field. "If you're refusing to cooperate, I can make the next visit more official."

Was that a threat?

"I'll keep an eye on things here, Ryan," Dylan offered.

Brody said he wasn't leaving until Ryan returned, as well.

At least he could count on them to take care of Lisa, her sister and Grayson until he could figure out what the hell was going on with Adams.

"Fine," he said to the deputy. "I'll go with you."

Sheer panic crossed Lisa's features. "Can I come, too?"

"That's not a good idea," Adams said.

So whatever he wanted to say to Ryan couldn't be said in front of her?

Ryan didn't like any of this a bit. It was one thing for the sheriff to look the other way and allow Alcorn free rein on the town. It was entirely something else if he knew and was pocketing money. But this screamed that Ryan's rights were about to be violated, and no Texan was about to put up with that, least of all Ryan.

He followed the deputy to the SUV and started toward the passenger side.

Adams opened the back door instead.

FROM THE SECOND the cruiser had pulled up, Lisa's panic alert had been firing on high. Never in her wildest imagination would she have figured what would come next. When Deputy Adams asked about Ryan's whereabouts, she'd been confused. Now that he was being taken in for questioning, she was flabbergasted.

"I don't like any of this," Dylan said as he ushered her inside.

Brody followed suit, sending a text to Rebecca to let her know that everything was okay in case she woke up looking for him.

Dylan pulled mugs from the cabinet and filled them with fresh coffee.

"The kids will be awake soon," he said. "I'll call in Mrs. Anderson today to help out with Maribel."

"Is it too early to call Justin?" Lisa asked.

"You sure you want him in the middle of this?" Dylan asked as a look passed between him and Brody.

"He deserves to know what's going on with his brother," she said.

"You're right. It's just that there isn't much he can do, and coming back might make matters worse for Ryan," Dylan said.

"I didn't realize that," she said.

"We all know how much the sheriff disliked Justin and I don't want to prejudice anyone else around town."

"He's not that person anymore. And it wasn't his fault when he was," she countered. "It was their father."

Dylan gave her a look and she knew exactly what he was thinking, but she couldn't let a sleeping dog lie. "He might be able to help."

Lori shuffled into the kitchen with Grayson on her hip. "He's hungry."

Lisa held Grayson while Lori mashed a banana. "You want me to feed him?"

"No, thanks. Taking care of him keeps my mind off things," Lori said.

Lisa knew exactly what her sister meant. She didn't know what to do with her hands when Lori took Grayson back.

"What else can we do?" Lisa asked.

"I need to make a few calls to find a good lawyer," Dylan said. "Until then, there isn't much."

That was about the most frustrating thing Lisa had heard tonight.

Dylan excused himself to the office out back as Samantha entered the kitchen.

"Any news?" Samantha asked.

"Nothing, I'm afraid. I just keep wondering what on earth they could think they're going to accomplish," Lisa said.

Brody finished his mug of coffee and set it on the table. "Alcorn has been after the Hunt family for years. He might be targeting Ryan, trying to make it seem like he's doing something illegal. We know the truth about him. That's what matters right now. Until we know what accusations we're dealing with, we can't mount a defense."

"So, what until then?" she asked as Samantha put her arm around Lisa's shoulders.

"We wait," Brody said.

Three excruciating hours later, Dylan walked into the house.

Lisa had been folding clothes with Samantha when she heard the back door open. She raced to the kitchen.

"What have you found out?" she asked.

"He's still being questioned. They're not finished with him yet according to Stern, his new attorney," Dylan said.

"Questioned for what?" she asked.

"Apparently, his family owns the land we visited last night," Dylan said, his tone ominous.

"What does that mean?"

"We found a warehouse full of supplies that could be used to make a few kinds of bombs," Dylan said. "Sheriff's office is saying the supplies match the material used in the one at the funeral home."

"How could he have planted a bomb there? He was with us, for heaven's sake."

"I know it. You know it. About time the sheriff's office figured it out, too," he said.

"Is that the same warehouse you were taken to?" Samantha asked, entering the room behind Lisa.

He nodded.

"That's not possible," Lisa said. "No way could he own that land. I should think he'd know about something like that."

"Not necessarily. His brother might know. They inherited it after their father died," Dylan said.

"Then we have to speak to Justin," Lisa said. "Don't stop me this time. I'm calling him right now."

She retrieved her phone. When she returned to the kitchen, Dylan was holding out a slip of paper.

"What is that?" she asked.

"Justin's phone number."

Oh. Dylan wanted her to call. Good.

"He's the executor of their father's estate. He'd know about the land. I want you to talk to him. It'll be better coming from someone like you, less suspicious," Dylan said.

She called the number.

Justin picked up on the first ring. After reminding him who she was, she asked about the land.

"It belongs to us," he said. "Why?"

"Does Ryan know?" she asked.

"I guess not."

She shook her head to let Dylan know, too.

"How come?" she asked.

"Because he didn't want anything to do with whatever Dad left behind. Said nothing good could ever come of anything connected to that man," Justin said.

Ryan had that right.

"So he never knew about the land?" she asked again.

"I never told him. After our dad died, Ryan refused to come to the reading of the will. I tried to talk to him about it a few times, but he wouldn't have anything to do with the conversation. Refused to open any mail, either."

"And what about your mother? Does she know about the land?" she hedged, following a hunch.

"I called to get her opinion," Justin said. "Do me a favor, don't tell Ryan."

"Why not?"

"He said he washed his hands of the whole situation after she walked out."

"Did she? Walk out?" she asked, unable to stop herself. "I'd heard there was more to it than that."

"I'd say. The day she left he'd beaten her within an inch of her life. She had a relative pick her up when he left to go to work and she disappeared to save her life."

"But she never tried to get in touch with you two," she pushed.

"No. For years she believed he'd find out."

"Sounds like she was scared."

"You have to understand. He broke her ribs, bashed in her face. She almost didn't make it," he said defensively as though he'd been preparing her defense for years.

Maybe he had.

"I understand. I always believed it was something more than her just turning her back on her kids."

"Much more. She wanted to come back for us, but

she was scared to death he'd track us down and kill all three of us. The only way she could ensure our safety was to leave and not try to contact us," he said. "What did you say was going on with my brother?"

"He's been taken in for questioning," she said.

"For what?" Justin sounded as shocked as she still felt.

"Turns out someone's been making bombs on your land."

"Does this have anything to do with the incident at the funeral parlor the other day?" he asked, and then it seemed to really dawn on him who she was. "That was your father."

"Yes."

"I'm really sorry to hear about that. He was a nice man."

"Thank you." Lisa was shocked to hear anyone talk about her father fondly. Most of the town seemed to want to forget he existed. "Do you mind if I ask when you first contacted your mother?"

"I hired a PI a few years ago, five to be exact. I needed to know what had happened to her and I wanted her to be able to meet her grandchild if she was interested," he said.

"And you didn't tell Ryan?"

"No. He'd been through so much and he wasn't ready to forgive her for the past. I've thought about telling him a thousand times. Every time I mention anything about her, he shuts down the conversation. I wish he would talk to her." The anguish in his voice was palpable.

"Me, too."

"It would be good for him, right?"

"I think so," Lisa said.

"Maybe you can talk to him, then," Justin said. "He sure doesn't want to hear it from me."

"Anything else about that land?" she asked.

"Charles Alcorn contacted me to buy it a few years ago."

"And?"

"I told him no dice. First of all, I can't sell it without Ryan's signature. Second, my father refused to sell that man anything."

"Is this the piece of property Alcorn had tried to buy from your father years ago?" she asked.

"It has to be. It's the only land my father ever owned. He inherited it from our grandfather, so he wanted to keep it in the family." Justin paused. "With a family now, I could sure use the money if it sold. It's not doing anything but sitting there. Apparently being used for illegal activity. Speaking of which, no way has my brother done anything wrong. He's the most stand-up guy I know."

"He is. I'm sure all this will be cleared up soon."

"I can come today if you think it'll help," Justin offered.

"No. Stay with your wife. I hear she's expecting any day now," Lisa said.

"She is. And that's important. Believe me, I want to be here for her, but I wouldn't have anything if it weren't for my brother. I can be on the next plane—"

"How about this? I promise to keep you informed. If anything else develops I'll call you and you can still grab the next flight out," she said.

A heavy sigh came across the line and she could tell how conflicted he was.

"Okay. Fine. If you promise to keep me up to date, I'll monitor the situation from here."

Lisa thanked Justin for the information and promised she'd mention the land to Ryan as soon as the dust settled. In the meantime, she said that she'd keep Justin in the loop every step of the way.

"Everybody knows that my brother is a good guy," Justin said again. "I can't believe anyone would suspect him of doing something illegal."

"It came as a shock to all of us," she said. "We're doing everything we can to get this straightened out."

"If you need any paperwork about the land, just let me know." Justin paused. "I'm more than happy to testify that Ryan didn't even know that land was ours."

"I'll make sure his lawyer knows," she said before thanking him one more time. "Would you mind texting me your mother's number? I'd like to give it to Ryan."

He agreed before they ended the call.

"I think I have a pretty good handle on the conversation," Dylan said. "I need to call Ryan's lawyer and give him the update. I don't think he's going to like the fact that Justin knew they owned the land."

"Hold on a sec," she said. "Didn't the feud between Alcorn and Ryan's dad happen because Alcorn couldn't get that land? Makes you wonder why he was so set on getting it in the first place, doesn't it?"

"I'll dig around and see if I can find anything there." Dylan poured himself another cup of coffee to take out to his office with him. "Stay inside and let's keep the doors locked. Call if you need anything."

"Okay." She didn't want to say that she knew why he'd make such a request. Because with Ryan temporarily out of the picture, Beckett could plan an attack.

"Mrs. Anderson took Maribel to the playground. Said she'd bring her back in time for lunch."

He nodded as he left, locking the door behind him.

"It'll all work out," Samantha reassured her. "Look at us. I never would've thought in a million years that I'd be planning a wedding with Dylan and becoming someone's mom all at the same time. Especially after what happened. These guys are tough. If it wasn't for Ryan's help, we never would've gotten to Alcorn in the first place."

Lisa thought about another reason Alcorn might target Ryan.

"Maybe he wants revenge."

Chapter Seventeen

Ryan had answered the same half dozen questions until he thought his brains might fall out. "I've already told you everything I know."

"Then, where were you with your friends out in the middle of the night?" Deputy Adams asked.

"We were scouting places to set up camp for hog hunting," Ryan said. Again.

With the deputy's sour look, Ryan was about to lose it.

"Are you planning to arrest me?" he finally asked.

"I didn't say that exactly."

"Then, if you don't start asking different questions I'm going home." Ryan made a move to get up.

The deputy's hand came up to stop him.

"Home to your property?" Adams asked.

"I already told you that I don't own any property other than the land my house sits on."

"I've got a deed here that says otherwise." He waved the piece of paper in front of Ryan's face. Again.

Wave it one more time and see what happens, Ryan thought bitterly. He was tired, worried about Lisa, and being separated from her was making him cranky.

The deputy had better get on with it if he knew what was good for him.

"I'm Mr. Hunt's attorney. I'd like a moment alone with my client." Higby Stern's face popped into the room.

Now this really was getting interesting. Dylan must've hired him.

The deputy looked none too thrilled to see Stern. And that made Ryan like the man even more.

Stern was five foot eleven, middle-aged and with a body that looked as though he stayed on top of his game at the gym. He was the best lawyer in town, heck, in the whole county. Ryan didn't think about calling, because he didn't think he needed an attorney.

He guessed Dylan felt otherwise.

He was probably right.

The system didn't always work. Innocent people went to jail. Ryan had read about several cases.

"Fine," Adams relented. He stood, gave a stern look toward Ryan and closed the door behind him.

"I already know you're not a terrorist, so let's get you out of here so we can talk about your case." Stern wasted no time. "They don't have any real evidence against you, so my guess is that they're hoping you'll confess. What have you told them so far?"

"I had no idea I owned the land. I still think they're sipping some crazy tea on that one for starters," Ryan said.

"Is there another party involved or are you the sole owner?" Stern already had a notebook out and he was scribbling notes.

"According to the deed, I'm co-owner with my brother." Ryan didn't like the way Stern's eyebrow went up. "Don't get too excited. He doesn't even live in town. He got out of here a long time ago. He's a family man and sure as hell isn't a terrorist."

"The sheriff's office is asserting that the materials found in the warehouse on your land are consistent with the bomb at the funeral home," Stern said.

"I'm not surprised." Ryan was about to punch a wall.

Stern's eyebrow went up.

"Not because I know what the bomb was made out of, but because I was at the funeral. Beckett Alcorn dropped by with a few of his henchmen. Not twenty minutes later a bomb exploded. Almost killing me, by the way. You really think I'd be stupid enough to kill myself or my friends?"

"I didn't say you were," Stern said quickly. "I have to know the answers to these questions so I can speak on your behalf. I don't trust any one of the Alcorns and not just because of this latest round of accusations against them. I know how they operate." The look of disdain on his dark features said more than enough. "I also know they hire the best. Alcorn has already managed to find a way to get out on bail. Word on the street is that he wasn't even in town during the kidnappings fifteen years ago and can prove it."

"Why didn't he come forward before?"

"Says he was having an affair and didn't want to ruin his marriage. He's provided an ironclad alibi. His wife is standing by him, of course."

"I would expect nothing less from a woman like her," Ryan interjected. "Her son is a scumbag who deserves to be locked away forever."

"You won't get an argument out of me on that," Stern said. "My job is to get you out of here and keep you out. It's clear to me that you've gotten on the bad side of a family with the power to squash just about anything or anyone they want. How did you get yourself in such a position?"

"Good question." Ryan didn't think it was his place to say what Beckett had done to Lisa. "Suffice it to say I'm taking care of someone Beckett is trying to erase."

"I take it this someone is a woman."

"Yes."

"Has she filed charges against him?"

"Afraid not." Ryan shook his head. "He's after her because of something that he did to her a long time ago."

Stern seemed to catch the undertone of what Ryan was saying. He nodded with a sympathetic look and made a couple more notes, mumbling something that sounded a lot like the word *bastard* under his breath.

Ryan liked Stern even more.

"Are they planning on arresting me?" Ryan asked.

"They haven't yet. And that's good. My guess is they were trying to sweat you. Get you to tell them something they could use. Doesn't sound like you fell for it."

Ryan shook his head. "Can't say what you don't know. When it comes to that property, I honestly had no idea what they were talking about."

He had every intention of calling his brother to find out as soon as he got the heck out of there and made sure Lisa was safe.

"I'll want to launch my own investigation into your case," Stern said.

"Be my guest. You let me know if you need anything from me to get started."

"Let me see about getting you home." Stern stood and extended his hand.

Ryan shook it, sizing Stern up one last time. He had that honest but tough look about him. He'd have a jury eating out of his hands with his sharp wit and good-old-fashioned looks.

"I'll be back in a few minutes. Hang tight, okay?" Stern winked before walking out the door. His dark jeans and button-down shirt gave him a surprisingly professional look. He carried himself well and that would come in handy should a trial become necessary.

Damn. Ryan still hadn't figured out when and how he'd gotten himself pinned with a possible terrorist charge.

The door opened and Stern filed in, flashing a quick smile at Ryan, with the deputy close behind him.

"You're free to go," Adams said. "Contact this office if you plan to leave town any time soon."

Ryan agreed.

The sun hit him in the face full force as he followed Stern to the parking lot.

"You need a ride?" Stern asked. "We can talk a little more about our next move on the way."

"Sure." Stern seemed to have personal feelings toward the Alcorns. Ryan wanted to know more about that.

"Dylan asked me to tell you that Lisa is fine. He and Brody have been at the house the whole time," Stern said as they secured their seat belts.

That Ryan felt relief was an understatement. He needed to talk to Lisa to tell her how he really felt about her. He had no idea if she would be game for giving a relationship with him a go, but he had no plans to go to his grave without finding out. The only thing he knew for certain was that he loved her. And maybe that was all he needed to know for now.

But there was something else on his mind that he needed to address with Stern.

"Can I ask you a personal question?"

"Yes."

"During our earlier discussion, I picked up on the fact that you have strong feelings toward the Alcorns in general but Beckett more specifically. Why?"

"Other than the fact that early in my career his father's lawyers used to eat me for breakfast?" Stern said, and Ryan appreciated the honesty.

"Yeah. This feels deeper than that."

"You don't know many good lawyers, then, do you?" Stern said. "We build our business on our reputation. We build our reputation off winning cases. Alcorn's attorneys never played fair. I'm honest. I believe in justice, in the law, in the system. You should know that about me up front."

"Good. Then it sounds like we'll get along just fine," Ryan said, and meant it.

"But you're a good judge of body language. I have personal reasons for not liking that family."

Ryan waited for Stern to decide if he was going to share more than that.

"There was an incident with my niece about five years ago." Stern stopped long enough to navigate his sedan onto the highway. "She never would discuss the details with her family or with me."

"Do you mind if I ask her age?" This sounded all too familiar. Ryan fisted his hands at the thought of any little girl being hurt by Beckett.

"She's eighteen now, getting ready to start her first

semester at Duke, but she was thirteen at the time. The only thing we know for certain is that she went to a birthday sleepover at her girlfriend's house. She came back the next morning traumatized. All we could get out of her was that her friend's much older stepbrother had a few friends over that night. She was terrified to talk about it. She'd called her mother to pick her up at six o'clock the next morning. At first, it didn't register with my sister that anything sexual could've happened. My niece was shy and she'd tried a few sleepovers in the past only to call her mom to have her pick her up early."

"And you know for sure Beckett was there?" Ryan asked.

"I can't prove it and she won't talk. My sister didn't think we should press the issue. I disagreed then and I still do. But I do understand that she was trying to do what she thought was best for her daughter by giving her time and space to speak up about it. Carolina never did. She just retreated from her friends and didn't want to leave the house for weeks."

"So how do you know he was involved?" Ryan asked.

"Every time my niece was within earshot of his voice, she tensed up. It took me two years to finally fit the pieces together. I went to my sister with what I believed to be true. Carolina was doing better and my sister didn't want to dredge up the past by forcing her to talk about it," he said. "I didn't agree with the decision. I'm convinced Katy was in denial that something horrible could've happened to her daughter on her watch. We had terrific parents and Katy always had a hard time feeling like she measured up."

His voice had a wistful quality to it.

"You think your sister would let me talk to Carolina now?" Ryan asked.

"I doubt it. However, I might be able to arrange something if you give me more to go on."

"Your niece isn't alone. He's done this before. I suspect there are many others, too," Ryan said, trying to keep his voice steady through the anger. "One of my friends was a victim of his when she was twelve. That bastard can't be allowed to prey on girls."

"My niece most likely won't talk to you about what happened," Stern said. "I wish she'd speak to someone. It isn't healthy for her to hold this inside."

Ryan wondered if he could ask Lisa to speak to her. The young woman might be more comfortable speaking to another woman. "There might be another way to come at this."

"I appreciate your concern and I would like to see all of the Alcorns behind bars. Right now, though, I've got to focus on keeping you out of jail. You can't help anyone there."

True.

"How bad does it look for me?"

"Right now? It's not that horrible. But they're trying to put together a case against you and I don't like that one bit. This tells me that they're listening to someone else and I believe that someone is Charles Alcorn."

"With enough money, I guess you can get away with just about anything." Ryan didn't mask his contempt. "We're almost there. You're going to want to take a right onto that gravel road."

"It's my job to prove you had no prior knowledge of owning the property. Have you been there?" Stern cut the wheel and turned.

Ryan didn't immediately answer.

"Let me ask that question another way, then. Will investigators find any traces of your DNA on the scene?"

"No," Ryan said emphatically. Although he couldn't guarantee someone wouldn't place his DNA there or lie about it.

"Good. It'll be tempting to go there. Don't."

"Not a problem."

"They'll mark the place off as a crime scene, anyway. Then they're going to try to link you to the scene while they're proving that the bomb at the funeral home came from the materials there." Stern parked the sedan.

Lisa bolted out the door as the two men exited the vehicle.

Dylan was already on his way to greet them from his office out back.

"Thank heavens you're okay," she said to Ryan.

He introduced her to Stern.

Then, not really caring who was watching, Ryan hauled her against his chest and pulled her in close. "I'm here. I promise that I'm not going anywhere. We have a lot to talk about when this is over."

He kissed her, a quick peck on the lips. He couldn't help himself. She felt like home and he had every intention of telling her. They could decide what to do from there.

Now was not the time. Besides, his situation didn't look promising. After talking to Stern, Ryan realized how easy it would be for a tainted deputy or the sheriff to plant evidence linking him to the scene. If Alcorn could see to it that Ryan spent some time behind bars, it would be easier to get to Lisa. All he'd have to do would be to create another "accident."

It looked as though Charles Alcorn was going to walk. That family was about to get away with another crime.

"I'll be in the house in a minute. Think you can rest?" Clearly, she hadn't slept all night.

She nodded. She had to be dead on her feet by now.

"Good. I'll be in shortly." He hugged her one more time before heading to Dylan's office, where he waited with Stern.

It didn't take long to update Dylan. Stern excused himself and left to work on the details of the investigation.

"I'm not taking any chances. I called in a few favors, brought in extra security. We've dealt with these jerks before and we know how dangerous they are," Dylan said. "This place is fortified as long as we need it to be."

"We're going to have another helluva fight on our hands," Ryan said. "I can't guarantee that they won't find DNA at the warehouse."

"It's a good thing the deputy didn't ask to search Brody's vehicle. We would've had a hard time explaining the contents of those backpacks." Dylan leaned back in his chair.

"Damn right."

"What's next?" Dylan asked.

"That's a good question. They have us on the defensive and that was a smart move," Ryan said. "I might be able to dig up some dirt on Beckett that could create a stir. We keep backing him into a wall and he's going to make a mistake."

"With you under investigation and everyone at the sheriff's office aware of our friendship, I won't get any insider information on this case," Dylan said.

"Might be best to limit our interactions with that department for now, anyway." Ryan thought about taking Lisa, Lori and Grayson to the fishing cabin to hide out. Dylan's place was really the best spot to lie low while they figured out their next move.

"I'm going to try to get some sleep." Ryan bit back a yawn. "I can hardly think straight anymore."

"I was going to tell you that you looked like a sailor who'd been at sea for a month caught in a storm," Dylan teased.

It was good to keep a sense of humor.

Ryan slipped in the back door and down the hallway. All he wanted to do was make a beeline for the bed and he hoped like hell that Lisa was there waiting. Thoughts of pulling her body against his, holding her until he fell asleep, stirred more than a sexual reaction. Being with Lisa was like going home—and that was a foreign feeling at best.

Talking to her was easy, and so much of the crazy world seemed right when they were together.

Ryan figured they could build on that feeling and create something truly special. If she'd allow it.

As he neared the door, he heard her voice. She was on a phone call.

He should've just gone straight in and alerted her to the fact that he was there, but he stopped at the door instead.

And that was a big mistake.

Because the sense of betrayal stabbing him in the gut when he realized she was talking to his mother nearly knocked him over. He backed down the hall, mind reeling. Lisa might feel like home, but since when had he ever trusted anything or anyone at home?

Chapter Eighteen

What could be taking Ryan so long? Lisa threw off the covers and went out to search for him. She was surprised to find him sleeping on the oversize chair in the living room. He looked uncomfortable with his neck held awkwardly to one side. He was too big for the space and she thought about waking him and sending him to bed.

But why had he chosen the chair over her?

She decided to let him sleep and moved into the kitchen to find caffeine and food.

The refrigerator door had barely opened when the back door flew open and Dylan burst inside.

"We gotta get you guys out of here. Where's Ryan?"

"What's going on?" Lisa asked, but Ryan was already next to her.

"Who all needs to go?" he asked.

"Lori and the baby will stay here with Samantha and Brody. I have to get you two out of here. My contact called to say that the deputy is on his way."

It didn't take two minutes for the three of them to grab their cell phones and jump into Dylan's vehicle.

Dylan fired up the engine and gravel spewed underneath his tires as he hightailed it out of there.

He called Stern and put him on speaker.

"They'd need a warrant to track you using your phones, but as soon as this call is over, turn them off just in case," Stern said. "Is there any reason we wouldn't want them to get a hold of your cell?"

Lisa's heart pounded painfully against her ribs and she desperately wanted to ask Ryan why he'd done a one-eighty on her.

"There might be," Ryan said.

"Then get rid of them completely. Make sure no one can get to them again. Are we clear?" Stern asked.

"We are," Ryan said. He was already pulling the battery out of his. He located pliers in the backseat of the vehicle and shredded the SIM card in his phone.

"Do you save any of your data to a cloud or a source that can be subpoenaed?"

Ryan cracked a smile and she immediately knew why. This was one time his being a non-techy would pay off.

"Nope."

Dylan swerved. The crack of a bullet split the air.

"Dammit. We've been set up," Dylan said, muttering another stronger curse. "There's a vehicle coming up from behind and he's about to hit us."

Dylan delivered a few evasive maneuvers, but the other vehicle kept pace, hitting the bumper and knocking them forward several times.

"Can you give me the license plate of the vehicle charging you?" Stern asked.

Ryan spun around and read off the tags.

"I'll report this to the deputy. Keep me on the line. I'll use my landline to make the call."

Ryan's arm was around Lisa, but she knew that it

was only to offer another layer of protection to guard her from a bullet or keep her head from snapping back when Dylan hit the brakes.

"I finally figured it all out. The pieces didn't make sense before, especially when Alcorn provided an alibi. All evidence keeps leading back to Alcorn, and that's on purpose. He's protecting Beckett," Ryan said, venom in his tone. "His father has been covering for him all along and that's why they'll never be able to nail Alcorn. He isn't involved. He's there to cover up for his son. His alibi will hold. Linking Beckett to the case is going to be next to impossible. Turn this thing around. Take me to Beckett."

Dylan shot a look at Ryan as if he were crazy. Lisa had the same thought.

"It's not going to end," Ryan said. "Don't you see? He'll keep coming at her. This will never be over."

"Hold on. Not if I can help it," Stern said. "Don't do anything rash. It'll only make matters worse."

"That man hurt your niece, right?" Ryan asked.

Lisa was horrified. It had never occurred to Lisa that Beckett had been hurting other girls. It was time to end this once and for all. "Is it too late to tell my story? To bring charges?"

Ryan looked at her with shock.

"Hold on, people," Dylan said as he spun the wheel.

He was too late. The Escalade slammed into the side of him, sending them spiraling into the ditch. There was a small dip that the tire must've caught on, because the next thing Lisa knew they were spinning.

They landed upright; however, the airbags had deployed and it took Lisa a few seconds to shake off the shock of being alive. Was anyone hurt?

A cut on Dylan's forehead was gushing blood. Ryan was already maneuvering out of his seat belt, looking dazed, as well.

"We're okay," she said to everyone.

Stern didn't respond. They'd lost their phone connection with him. How would he know where to send the police? Now she understood why he'd had Dylan call out street names.

Maybe the law would get to them in time.

The passenger-side door opened and Lisa felt herself being yanked out.

Beckett.

She let out a yelp that could be heard two counties away. All the anger that had been building for fifteen years exploded inside her. She was no longer an innocent twelve-year-old girl. Lisa was a grown woman who could fight back. And she had every intention of doing so.

His grip on her arm sent pain shooting down her limbs.

She twisted and dropped to the ground, breaking his grasp. She slammed her fist into his groin on the way down and then he was the one on his knees, gasping for a breath.

"See how that feels?" She threw another punch, scrambling to her knees, but it was intercepted this time.

"You just won't die." Beckett knocked her the rest of the way to the ground. She had to give it to him, he was strong. But she was just as strong. She'd survived him twice and this time he was the one going down.

Before she could regroup, he had a handful of her hair and was dragging her toward his vehicle.

Dylan and Ryan had enough to deal with. They were

being double-teamed by men who were the size of line-backers.

No way did this bastard get to win. Lisa struggled for purchase on the ground and couldn't get any. She broke free from his grasp and he spun around to face her. She curled up, twisting and thrusting her feet at him. Her foot connected with his knee. He stumbled, but it wasn't enough to take him down. She kicked a second time, harder.

With curled firsts, she jabbed at his arms and kicked with every bit of strength she possessed. She pounded him for everything he'd done to the little girl inside her.

Well, that girl had grown and could no longer be hurt by him. She realized he only had the power over her that she was willing to give him.

And he didn't get to hurt her anymore.

He managed to pull her to her feet.

Lisa fought against him as he tried to stuff her into his vehicle. He cursed and dropped her when she delivered another blow to his manhood.

Her head smacked against the vehicle, an explosion of pain in her brain followed, but she no longer cared what happened to her physically. She fought, anyway.

Just as Beckett was about to deliver a blow to her head with the butt of a gun, Ryan came out of nowhere and dove on top of him, knocking him away from her.

Sirens split the air.

Ryan fought Beckett as Lisa struggled to stay conscious.

The deputies surrounded them, ordering everyone to drop their weapons.

Ryan, hands up, backed away from Beckett.

The last thing Lisa saw before everything went black

was Beckett's arms being thrust behind his back and his wrists being cuffed as he spewed swear words at the deputy.

LISA WOKE IN the hospital and immediately asked for Ryan.

"He never leaves," Lori said. "He just sits in the hallway close to your room. But he knows that you reached out to his mother."

"Is Beckett in jail?" Lisa asked.

"Whole town says the judge is going to throw away the key to his cell. He'll spend the rest of his life behind bars just like he deserves."

Lisa took a minute to contemplate that thought. It was over. It was finally over. She looked at her sister. "Will you ask Ryan to come in, please?"

Lori, tentative, did as told.

She didn't come back inside the room with Ryan. He didn't come all the way in, either. He just stood at the door, his frame blocking out the light from the other side.

"I'm sorry I went behind your back, Ryan. I'd change it if I could. I can't. This is me. I make a mess out of things sometimes, but you should know that I have never loved anyone the way that I love you," Lisa said.

"I can put up with not being perfect. Hell, I'm the poster child for messing up," he said, and a flicker of hope lit inside her chest. "There's only one thing I can't live with, and that's dishonesty. If you go behind my back, how will I ever be able to trust you?"

That spark of hope died as he turned away from her.

"You shouldn't have lied." With that, he walked away.

Lisa rolled onto her side, pulled up the covers and

cried. She'd blown it and she knew Ryan well enough to know he'd never be able to look at her in the same way again.

THE RIDE HOME was silent. Lisa was spent. Lori had taken the day off work and left Grayson with Brody and Rebecca.

"You look so much better," Lori said as she pulled onto the parking pad in front of Lisa's two-bedroom bungalow.

"It's good to be home." The words were empty, but Lisa didn't want anyone else to know just how much she was hurting inside.

"Hold on because I'm going to help you out." Lori parked, hopped out of the sedan and ran to Lisa's side.

If anything good came out of this, it was that Lisa could finally let others help her without feeling that she was doing something wrong.

It took twenty minutes to get Lisa settled, but being in her own bed again felt like heaven on earth. How long had it been? *Too long.*

Traveling home exhausted her. She asked for a pain pill and settled under the duvet.

Lori disappeared into the other room.

"Hope I'm not too late," Ryan said as he walked into her bedroom, chewing on a toothpick.

She blinked to make sure she wasn't dreaming.

"May I?" He motioned toward the bed. He had a tray in his hands with a glass of water and a couple of pills. He looked to be in pure agony.

She nodded, trying to ignore the rejoicing in her heart at seeing him again.

She took the pills, swallowed them and chased them with water.

"Do you believe in second chances?" He set down the tray and then threw away his toothpick.

"I do." Tears were already streaming down her cheeks.

"I messed this up once already. Can you forgive me?" He brushed a kiss on her lips.

She nodded.

"Will you let me stay and take care of you?"

"Yes."

"I don't mean for a few days. I mean forever." He caught her gaze and held it. "I love you, Lisa Moore. You're home to me. And I'm lost without you."

All Lisa could do in return was take his hand. He lifted hers to his lips and kissed her fingertips.

"You already know I love you, Ryan."

"Then once you're well, I have every intention of asking you to marry me."

"And I have every intention of saying yes."

Epilogue

The heel of Ryan's boots clacked against the narrow wood porch. He opened the screen door that looked as though it had seen one too many rainstorms. It was rusty and banged up, most likely from a hailstorm.

A moment of panic had him turning to look at Lisa for reinforcements.

He'd waited until she was well enough to travel to make the trip.

Her reassuring smile gave him the strength to do what he'd been wanting to do for a long time. It was time to see his mother.

They'd talked on the phone a few times and he finally understood how much she loved her sons.

That first call was the hardest to make. Forgiving her for leaving had turned out to be the easy part.

And now he wanted his whole family together.

* * * * *

Using his foot, Oliver nudged the door open. Anger flared within him. The office had been tossed.

Oliver returned his gun to the back of his jeans. He followed Darling into the small, disheveled room. She stood in the doorway, eyes roaming over the mess. Then, like a switch had been flipped, she hurried to the other side of the desk and started to move through drawers on the floor.

"It's gone, Oliver!"

"What's gone?" But before she could answer, it dawned on him. "The security tape."

Darling nodded, clearly upset. An overpowering urge to comfort her pushed him forward. He put his hands on her shoulders, making her look up into his eyes. The moment from the night before played back into his mind.

She was close enough to kiss.

"Oliver, there's something I need to tell you."

"Yes?" His voice dropped low. Her green-eyed stare could stir up a drove of feelings in mere seconds.

"I think I know who did this," she whispered. "And you aren't going to like it."

PRIVATE
BODYGUARD

BY
TYLER ANNE SNELL

MILLS &
BOON

® and ™ are trademarks owned and used by the trademark owner and/or its licensee. Trademarks marked with ® are registered with the United Kingdom Patent Office and/or the Office for Harmonisation in the Internal Market and in other countries.

First Published in Great Britain 2016
By Mills & Boon, an imprint of HarperCollins*Publishers*
1 London Bridge Street, London, SE1 9GF

© 2016 Tyler Anne Snell

ISBN: 978-0-263-91899-1

46-0316

Our policy is to use papers that are natural, renewable and recyclable products and made from wood grown in sustainable forests. The logging and manufacturing processes conform to the legal environmental regulations of the country of origin.

Printed and bound in Spain
by CPI, Barcelona

Tyler Anne Snell genuinely loves all genres of the written word. However, she's realized that she loves books filled with sexual tension and mysteries a little more than the rest. Her stories have a good dose of both. Tyler lives in Florida with her same-named husband and their mini "lions." When she isn't reading or writing, she's playing video games and working on her blog, Almost There. To follow her shenanigans, visit www. tylerannesnell.com.

This book is for one of my best friends, Rachel Miller. Thank you for listening to everything I had to say about Darling's story, as well as every other story I've ever created! Your enthusiasm, wisdom and friendship have made my life exponentially better. Here's to many, many, many more years of staying up late and talking about books!

Also, the quickest of shout-outs to Hunter Hall.
Our friendship is also killer!

Chapter One

"It was just a little misunderstanding."

Darling Smith was standing behind the bars of one of two holding cells in Mulligan, Maine, and not at all amused.

Deputy Derrick Arrington, however, was all humor. Maybe that was due to the fact that the two had dated on and off the year before with less than favorable results. They were normally amicable if not downright pleasant, but Darling figured it wasn't every day he was able to arrest his ex. Her thoughts slid back in time for a moment.

Oh yeah, she would have loved to put a certain man from her past in the slammer and throw away the key.

"That should be tattooed across your forehead, Darling. 'It was a little misunderstanding, Officer. I'm too cute to be up to no good.'" He grinned.

"Deputy Arrington, did you just say that I'm cute?" she replied with a big dose of sugar.

He pointed at her and laughed. "See? That right there is what I'm talking about."

"Oh, come on, Derrick." Darling dropped the cuteness from her tone. She was tired. "We both know that George Hanely overreacted." Just saying the gate guard's name made her mad. He'd acted as if he was a Secret Service agent and Darling was an enemy of the state.

"He did his job. George saw a *suspicious person snooping around private property*." He eyed Darling a moment, waiting for her to confess. He'd keep waiting, too. "What's more, that *suspicious person* was found going up to his employer's garage."

"Not confirmed, just accused," she said.

The deputy shook his head. "I'd take this a little more seriously, Darling. You were caught breaking and entering into Nigel Marks's house. He's a beloved figure in this town. This will be the first time he's been back to stay for a while in years. The last time he came, do you know what he did?"

Darling let out a long breath. She had already researched the millionaire, but that didn't mean she was buying what he was selling. "He donated a new wing to the children's library."

"That's right. He was here for a little over a week, and he brought joy to an entire town's kids. Now he's coming to stay for almost a month. His visits, even if they are work related, usually benefit our community." He paused, making sure he let his words sink in before he tacked on, "We want him to enjoy that stay, not worry about some spunky private eye."

"I preferred 'cute,'" she grumbled.

"Well, I preferred starting my Tuesday morning with a cup of coffee and not picking up a criminal just as the sun rose."

"Accused criminal."

He rolled his eyes and checked his watch. Derrick was tall, had jet-black hair and the bluest eyes she'd ever seen. He was handsome, sure, but he also wasn't anywhere near her type. Though, admittedly, her type had revolved around one man and one man alone throughout the years. She stopped herself before she could picture him, angry for entertaining thoughts of a past best forgotten.

"Okay, I'm going to head back up," he said. "I just wanted to come check on you and see if you wanted that one phone call."

"But Deputy, why would I call you when you're already here?"

"Oh, Darling, how I've missed your sarcasm." They both knew that was a bold-faced lie.

It had been two days since Elizabeth Marks had walked into Acuity Investigations and asked for the twenty-five-year-old's help. Darling could recall with almost perfect precision the way the graceful woman had breezed in. She had shaken Darling's hand with a firm grip but had seemed hesitant to introduce herself. However, Darling hadn't needed to know the woman's name to understand she was important, if only financially so. It had been Elizabeth's shoes—silver-toed, red-soled, python-heeled Louboutin shoes—that had spoken volumes to Darling. Mrs. Marks came from money, and that always made a case more interesting.

"My husband is having an affair," Elizabeth had said after adjusting the Gucci sunglasses that sat atop her crown of bleach-blond hair. "I just need concrete proof now."

Darling had been taken aback. Normally when a spouse sought out a private investigator, it was to confirm a suspicion. The way Elizabeth's back had straightened and her shoulders had squared had suggested there were no doubts in her accusation.

"If you already know he's cheating, why do you need the proof?" Darling had asked.

A surge of energy had seemed to pulse through Elizabeth. Her face had become lively for a moment.

"We married when I was young, my husband, Nigel, and I. His career was just taking off, and we were so in love. He drew up a prenuptial agreement that I should never have signed, but I was foolish and naive and believed he was the man I wanted to spend the rest of my life with." She had stopped herself then, as if trying to pick the right words. "If I divorce him right now, because of the prenup, I'll receive almost nothing. Even the money I personally earned. But if I get proof that he's cheating, it will void the prenup and I can take at least half of what he owns, which will be enough for me."

So that had been the bottom line.

Darling sat on the uncomfortable cell's cot as the memory of their first meeting came to an end and a new wave of determination washed over her. She wasn't the biggest fan of the wealthy—having a past like hers left an unforgettably sour taste in her mouth for them—but she had believed in the woman's pain and anger enough to want to help. Just because Darling had fought her own personal battle against the rich, and lost, didn't mean Elizabeth deserved the same fate.

"You sure you can do this?"

Oliver Quinn looked up from the desk to see his boss leaning in the doorway. Nikki Waters's tone was light, though her demeanor carried unintentional importance. Since she not only founded the Orion Security Group but also ran it, he decided that importance was deserved. He certainly respected it.

"Excuse me?" he asked, half of his mind still going through the travel details in the open folder between his hands. He was twenty minutes away from heading to the airport to start a three-week contract and, since Oliver was the lead agent of Team Delta, he was triple-checking their route. He wanted to avoid as much traffic as possible—a goal made easier by the somewhat remote location.

"Maine," she replied, staying in the doorway. It was almost seven in the morning and she was dressed in her workout clothes, her dark red hair slicked back in a short pony tail. Most likely she was headed to the twenty-four-hour gym across the street. There were several of them spread throughout downtown Dallas. "In April, no less."

Oliver raised an eyebrow at her.

"Oh, come on," she continued with a smile. "Every time I checked in on you during that stint in Montana two years ago, you talked about how crazy you were going from being in the cold."

If he had been a rookie like Thomas, the newest addition to Delta, or even someone who had been around a year like Grant, he would have thought she was serious in questioning whether he could do the job or not. However, if there was one thing he rarely doubted, it was Nikki's faith in his abilities. If she hadn't believed in them, she wouldn't have sought him out when Orion had only been a name.

"What can I say? I'm from California. We tend to love the sun and heat. I don't think Maine will be too bad, though. I'm just glad we aren't going there a month earlier. I can handle April."

She laughed. It was clipped. He knew something was bothering her and waited until she spoke again.

"Listen, I wanted to thank you for not giving me grief about this client," she said. "I know Mark and Jonathan think taking him on is unnecessary." She was referring to the lead agents of the other two teams and Oliver's closest friends. They had worked together before Orion, sharing a past that had been fused together by tragedy.

"They don't like thinking about the big picture," he said, trying to lighten the mood. He knew she had been struggling with her decision to accept millionaire Nigel Marks as a client.

"It's just…" She hesitated. "We've spent the last few years claiming to protect those who need it but can't afford it. That's the Orion Group's bottom line. We provide security and guarantee safety to those who don't have bottomless pockets. And now we're taking on an almost monthlong project with a millionaire?" She sighed. "I feel like I'm selling out."

"But if we don't occasionally pick up an elite client, then we can't continue to be Robin Hoods. Right?"

Nikki snorted. "Robin Hoods, huh?"

"Well, we don't steal from the rich, but you get the idea."

She seemed to like that way of thinking and nodded. "You're right. I need to be firm in this decision. You're heading there soon?"

Oliver pulled out his plane ticket. "Since he insisted on us meeting him there, I want to head up there a little earlier to make sure everything is okay," he said. "The rest of Team Delta will follow but might be a bit late since their flight last night was cancelled."

"Team Delta. It still sounds as corny as it did when Mark suggested the name."

"Says the woman who named her security group

Orion," he replied. Though as he said it, he glanced past her to a picture framed on the wall. The real reason behind the name.

The picture weighed less than an ounce, but it left an unbelievably heavy weight on his heart.

Nikki didn't have to follow his gaze. She knew what he was feeling. Her pain had turned to anger over the years. His had only drowned in guilt.

"Well, be careful," she said after the moment passed. "And, Oliver? Keep this client happy. We need him, as much as I hate to say it."

Oliver needed to ensure everything was on the up and up since Nigel had been clear he didn't want to start the contract until Wednesday morning. He still didn't understand why the man had hired a security group to protect him while he traveled if he didn't want to use them as he traveled *to* Maine. He'd been cautious enough to hire Orion after he'd earned a few nasty anonymous letters at work. He clearly had felt threatened. Oliver didn't think about it too much, though. He'd learned the hard way that most of the upper class was stubborn, and arguing with them did little to change their minds.

Oliver tried not to dwell on the past as he arrived at the airport and then boarded his plane.

Nigel Marks had been transported by way of his private jet; Oliver's long legs were pressed against the back of a snoring man's chair in coach. When he finally landed, stretched and turned on his cell phone, he wasn't in the mood for the voice mail from Nikki.

"Oliver, I received a call from the security guard who watches Nigel's house. I think his name is George? Anyways, he found a woman lurking around early this morning and had the cops come pick her up. They are holding

her on trespassing and potentially breaking and entering.
George didn't give me all of the details. He seemed too
excited. I already talked to Nigel. He's actually at work
in the next town over and will be delayed until later this
afternoon. He liked the idea of you going to talk to her
to see if she's a threat. Call me after you do." She didn't
say goodbye. She was in business mode. Nikki the boss,
not Nikki the friend.

He hung up, aggravated.

"Great," he grumbled, making his way to baggage
claim. "Not even in town and already having problems."

The town of Mulligan—a name that Oliver found
humor in—was thirty minutes away from the airport via
one dust-covered SUV. Oliver hated rentals. Due to the
company's track record, no agent was offered the rental
insurance that was an option with each vehicle. In his
line of work, there was a high chance they would receive
damage in some form. Oliver knew from experience the
rental companies were a pain to deal with when that happened, and as team lead, he was the one who dealt with
it. The man he'd rented the car from had taken his sweet
time passive-aggressively warning Oliver about how it
would be unwise to bring it back in anything less than
pristine condition. Every pothole he bumped through
made him cringe.

Thinking of the uptight man only dampened his darkening mood. He mentally ran through a list of questions
he would ask Nigel Marks's intruder as the vehicle's GPS
directed him to Mulligan's police department. It wasn't
until he was nearing Main Street that his phone blared
to life.

"Quinn," he answered, pressing the speaker button.

"It's Nikki." There was no mistaking the annoyance

in her voice. "I wanted to warn you that our intruder is a private investigator."

"A private eye?"

"Yep. I finally got the chief on the phone, and he said she's a local. And she's feisty. Try to figure out why she was snooping around, but don't make her too mad. If she's a local, it might make the next three weeks unpleasant."

"Okay. Don't tick her off. Tread lightly. Yada yada."

"The sheriff also made a point to warn me not to let her name fool you."

Oliver raised an eyebrow to no one in particular. "Her name? What is it? Candy? Bunny?"

Nikki laughed. "No, even better. Darling."

Oliver almost swerved off of the road.

Before he could stop himself, the image of a woman popped into his head. Dirty-blond hair, round green eyes, a button nose and a set of soft, curvy lips.

"Come again?" he asked. He was already certain he'd heard Nikki wrong.

"Her name is Darling. Darling Smith."

A silence followed before Oliver found his voice again. "I hate to say this, but I can almost guarantee she's already pissed at me."

FOOTSTEPS SOUNDED FROM the stairs, bringing Darling out of her haze of absolute annoyance. Derrick had been coming down a few times each hour to talk her ear off. She wished Nigel Marks's lackey would hurry up and question her. Anything was better than staying any longer in the mildew-scented cell. As the steps got closer, she ducked her head and rubbed her eyes. She didn't think she could take another round of Deputy Derrick.

"If you're going to keep bothering me, the least you could do is bring me a coffee," she called when the footsteps stopped outside of the bars.

"Well, I haven't been in town long, but I'm sure I could find some somewhere."

Darling's heart skipped a beat. Slowly she raised her head to look at the new speaker. She could only stare.

Out of all of the town jails in the world, Oliver Quinn had picked hers to make a grand appearance in.

It had been almost eight years since she had seen him, yet she recognized him instantly. Brushing six feet, the twenty-eight-year-old had broad shoulders and a stocky but muscular build, giving him the look of a well-toned soccer player. His blond hair was cut short but not too short, still covering the top of his forehead with a golden swoop. His amber-colored eyes and ridiculously soft-looking lips only added to the attractive angles of his tanned face. Not to mention a jawline that simply begged to be touched. For a moment Darling wondered why she ever had ill feelings toward the man who looked like an angel. But then, all at once, she remembered not only who he was but also what he had done.

No matter how handsome he was, Oliver Quinn had crushed her heart. A fact Darling wouldn't forgive or forget anytime soon.

"Miss Smith, this is the security agent Nigel Marks sent," Deputy Derrick said, coming up behind Oliver. "His name is—" He stopped, noticing Darling's deer-in-headlights stare. "You okay?"

Oliver, with a small smile attached to his lips, was about to interject, but Darling found her voice. Though she had to tamp down several less-than-pleasant responses.

"Deputy Arrington, this is Oliver Quinn," she said, standing. "We used to make out in my father's Ferrari." Derrick raised his eyebrow before looking at Oliver.

"What can I say? Fast cars and pretty girls equal a winning combo in my book," Oliver shot back with an easy laugh. It was not the response she had expected, but Derrick thought it was funny enough. When Darling didn't show signs of joining in on their shared mirth, the deputy sobered.

"Do you want me to stay down here during the questions?" Derrick asked her directly. They might not have had the best romantic relationship, but they did consider each other friends.

"I can handle this one," she answered. It earned another little laugh from Oliver.

"When you're satisfied she isn't a threat, let me know," Derrick said, turning to leave.

"She isn't a threat. You can let her out now." Oliver moved aside and motioned to the lock. Derrick and Darling exchanged a confused glance.

"You don't want to question her?" Derrick asked.

"I do, but unfortunately, I have to get back to work." He looked at her. "I was thinking we could pick this up tonight?"

Alarm bells as loud as the Monday-morning trash pickup rang in her head.

"Like on a date?" she blurted, heat rushing to her cheeks.

Oliver gave off another short laugh. "More like catching up with a few pointed questions concerning my client," he said. Then, when she was about to decline fiercely, he added, "I need to make sure I was correct in saying you aren't a risk. If you are, my client will press charges."

Both men looked at her, waiting for an answer.

If Oliver was the only thing that kept her from receiving the potential wrath of Nigel Marks, she'd have to take up his offer. She sighed, thinking about her bad luck so far on this case.

"Fine, but you're buying."

Oliver produced a business card as Derrick opened the cell door. He handed it to Darling, never dropping his grin.

"Would it be okay to stop by your office around seven?" he asked.

"Do I have a choice?" she replied with one of her sweet, yet not sweet at all, smiles.

"Of course you do, but it might be better if we could have that dinner."

"Then I guess that's what will happen."

The three of them went back upstairs. Oliver the Bodyguard didn't even hesitate to get into his car and leave, while Darling got into her car that had been brought to the station. She sat in the driver's seat, trying to process all of what had happened in the past ten minutes. Fate? Coincidence? A cruel joke? She couldn't decide which category her situation fell into.

She might have kept wondering had her phone not buzzed with a text she had been hoping to receive. Looking at the caller ID, she couldn't help but feel better.

Darling pulled up to the Mulligan Motel a few minutes later with excitement coursing through her. Her caller was Dan Morelli, a transplant from New Jersey and the owner of the less-than-ideal motel. There was a Holiday Inn fifteen minutes south of Mulligan, but those who participated in not-so-legal extracurricular activities often stayed at the Mulligan Motel.

Or people who wanted to meet someone in secret.

"Hey, Dan," Darling greeted him, walking into the lobby with her camera swinging around her neck. Dan had been a valuable contact throughout the past few years, keeping an eye out for certain persons Darling had cases on. Though since she had tried to stay away from the dirty-laundry spectrum of stereotypical private-eye jobs, she hadn't seen him in a good few months. She'd paid him in cookies, movie rentals and the promise of an exciting bust in the past. There wasn't much else to do in Mulligan for a man who hated the cold. Plus, he'd confessed once that Darling reminded him of his little sister, which apparently worked in her favor.

Dan didn't look up from his paper when she stepped inside.

"Room 212," he responded, intent on his crossword. "And you figured that out all on your own."

"Of course I did. You know nothing—everyone knows that, Dan."

He laughed but didn't say anything more. Darling went behind the desk and grabbed the key with the chain marked 212. Some people might have felt guilty for what she was doing, but Darling could justify it easily enough. Nigel Marks had spent a few hours in the Mulligan Motel's room 212 last night. And what's more, he hadn't been alone. The millionaire had left while the sky was still dark, but his mistress hadn't checked out yet. It was time Darling paid a visit.

She walked up the stairs and down the length of the second floor until she came to a stop at the last door. A TV could be heard on the other side, but no voices. Darling, using a method her former boss had applied in the field before, adopted a high-pitched voice and knocked.

"Room service," she sang. There was a Do Not Disturb sign hanging from the doorknob. If she kept nagging, the woman would answer, annoyed yet visible. Then Darling would do what she did best and question or trick her into confessing. Who needed pictures when the mistress would admit publically to the affair? Sure, it was a little brash of her and maybe not what she would have done under normal circumstances, but she felt oddly off-kilter after seeing Oliver. Even though they'd barely had a conversation.

She knocked a few more times and waited.

And waited.

"Room service. I'm coming in," she sang again in a lower voice. She slid the key into the lock and turned, an excuse for her intrusion ready on her tongue.

But no one yelped in surprise or yelled in anger. Aside from the TV, the room was still and spotless. Maybe Dan had gotten it wrong, Darling thought. There was no luggage or bags of any kind, the trashcans were empty and all the lights were off. She walked past the two double beds and peeked into the bathroom, hoping for some kind of clue that would prove Nigel Marks's mistress had been there.

However, the proof she found was more than she had bargained for.

Lying in the bathtub was a woman wrapped up in the shower curtain. Blood was everywhere.

Chapter Two

"And you're sure she won't be a problem?" Nikki asked after Oliver more or less summed up his visit to the police station. He had admitted to knowing Darling, just not *how* he knew her.

"I'm sure. She was just curious, that's all," he said for the third time. Nikki might not have been fond of taking on Nigel Marks as a client, but now that he was under contract, she was going to make sure nothing bad happened. "Listen, I don't blame her. This place is impressive. I'd have done the same thing. If it makes you feel better, I'm catching up with her when Thomas and Grant relieve me tonight. I'll bring it up again and if she lies to me, I'll catch it."

"Well, just try not to tick off the long-winded gate guard, George, while you're there. I'd really like to avoid talking to him again."

Oliver agreed and they ended the call. He looked through the window to the gatehouse down below. George Hanely had been like a kid on Christmas as he recounted the story of how he had saved the Markses' home from the more-than-suspicious private investigator. Oliver had been at Nigel Marks's home for less than ten minutes, and in that time he had watched George re-enact what had happened.

He had led Oliver from his post in the small one-room, half-bathroom house that sat at the front of the drive around to the garage. It, like the house, was large. It could easily fit several cars. Darling had been spotted next to the side door. Her story of just being close to the gate that surrounded the property was hard to believe. The iron gate was a good forty to fifty yards away. If she had been trying to get back over the fence, then why come so close to the garage?

Oliver could guess the answer. She was trying to get *into* the garage. But why?

Ever since he had seen Darling, he had been assuming that she was still the same girl he'd known before. The fact that she was in jail to start off with had proven the opposite. And a private investigator?

He smiled to himself. *That* he could believe. Darling had loved the challenge of a good mystery.

He remembered the first time he'd met her. She had been butt up in a Dumpster behind an office complex, rooting around in discarded papers and files. At the time he'd assumed it was a part of some weird bet. She hadn't looked homeless with her designer clothes and perfectly manicured nails. Then, when she found exactly what she didn't want to find, she had opened up in a burst of emotion to the nineteen-year-old him. Her world wasn't over, but it had changed. Through the next few months the once-spoiled, once-naive teenager transformed into a thoughtful, compassionate young woman. The people around her hadn't appreciated the changed Darling, and slowly she had become isolated. Oliver, however, had formed a bond with her, staying by her side until…

Self-loathing pulsed through him at the memory of the last night he'd seen her. *Time can heal all wounds, but seeing the girl whose heart you shattered only breaks out the salt and pours it into the gashes*, he thought with a frown.

Seeing her after all those years had been a shock to his system. One he wasn't sure was entirely good or entirely bad. As he tried to clear his mind, he marveled at the fact that he still felt so strongly about what had happened almost a decade ago.

Oliver left the guest bedroom Nigel had assigned to him and started to go through each room of the house. He checked windows, catalogued all exits and got his bearings of the Markses' second home. Its large size didn't surprise him in the least.

After finishing his sweep, he made his way back over to the gatehouse. George, a slight man in his thirties with dark hair and a pasty complexion, could barely keep his excitement at bay at having someone to talk to. Oliver didn't blame the man one bit. Even though Nigel Marks hadn't been at his house in years, it was still George's job to watch the gate daily. If it had been Oliver's job, he would have hated it. However, George seemed to take pride in his tasks, and Oliver spied a movie player and several movies under the front desk, which must have made sitting in one room day in and day out a little more bearable.

"So, have you ever met Mr. Marks in person?" George asked when Oliver was satisfied with each part of the property. Aside from the gatehouse, garage and house, there was nothing but open land surrounding the acres the Markses owned.

"No," Oliver admitted. "My boss handles the client

interactions before the contract start date," he explained. "Do you see him often? I was under the impression he didn't come visit much."

George shrugged. "He calls to check in from time to time and ask about things," he said. Oliver noticed the gate guard puffed his chest out a bit. "I keep him informed on what's going on in Mulligan." There was no mistaking that George definitely took pride in working for Nigel. Oliver could respect that, even if he wondered what kind of social life the guard was left with after the hours he worked. Having a good boss was an absolute must for Oliver, especially after the nightmare of what had happened with his last. "That's how I knew that woman was up to no good."

They had just stepped outside the gatehouse and were facing the private drive. It wasn't as cold as the Montana case had been, but there was a chill in the air that moved with the breeze. Oliver tilted his head as another gust pushed against his clean-shaven face, and he thought about his next words carefully before speaking.

"You mean the private investigator? She seemed harmless enough," he said, not believing himself as he said it.

George snorted. "Private investigator. Yeah, that sounds a lot better than what she really does."

Oliver raised his eyebrow. "What does she really do?"

"Sneak around, break the law and ruin lives. Just like the rat of a man she got her office from," he explained with a surge of anger.

"From what I could tell Derrick seemed to like her," Oliver added.

"Deputy Derrick and her are close, if you know what I mean."

A quick burst of jealousy flashed through Oliver. The

idea that Darling was with someone romantically hadn't yet breached his thoughts. Not that it should matter either way.

"And as for the chief, he's one of many people here that have fallen for her charms. If you ask me, she uses her looks to get what she wants. It's repulsive. She should be using her time better, you know? Get married, have some kids."

Oliver's brief jealousy turned to a not-so-brief anger. It was true he couldn't claim to know this new, older version of Darling the same way he had known the younger one, but he seriously doubted she was this repulsive person George was claiming. He was about to set the man straight when his cell phone beeped.

"They're almost here," Oliver said instead. "I want you to call me if anyone other than my team and Nigel comes to this gate. No matter the time. Are we clear?"

George straightened his back and almost looked as if he was ready to salute. "Yes, sir," he barked.

Within minutes a black SUV came up the drive, followed by a sleek silver two-door Audi. Originally, Nigel was supposed to be escorted from his home in California to Mulligan, but a week ago he had changed this detail, much to Nikki's frustration. He had spent two days in the neighboring city, working to put out business-related fires due to his company's newest merger while he stayed at a four-star hotel less than a block from that branch of Charisma Investments. The other two members of Team Delta had been ordered to pick Nigel up that morning, officially starting their contract time frame.

Oliver nodded to Thomas Gage, Orion's newest recruit, as he rolled down the SUV's tinted driver's side window just before the gate. His build was on the lean side, with narrow shoulders and arms toned but not as built as the rest of Team Delta. He had light brown skin, dark hair and bright blue eyes that Nikki had commented on more than once. Thomas never sported facial hair, and that decision often got him mistaken for younger than twenty-five. This was his third job as a Delta agent. Oliver liked his humor and lingering innocence.

"Hey there, Boss," Thomas greeted Oliver with a smile. He motioned to the backseat, where Nigel Marks sat with a laptop on his lap and a phone to his ear. He looked up and gave a quick wave before turning his attention back to his work. "He had an emergency call that couldn't wait," Thomas explained.

Oliver motioned through the gatehouse window for George to open the gate. George didn't hesitate, and Thomas moved the SUV the rest of the way up the drive, parking in front of one of the garage doors. Grant Blakely arrived next, driving Nigel's high-end rental. He was already grinning as he paused next to Oliver.

"This assignment may not completely suck after all, especially if we get to play with his toys," he said as soon as the window was down. He petted the dashboard.

Oliver chuckled. He missed working with his old team of Jonathan and Mark, but he had grown fond of Grant. The thirty-four-year-old was the epitome of intimidating without even trying. Tall, wide and thick with muscles, the dark-skinned bodyguard never looked as if he couldn't win in a fight.

"Just wait until you see the house," Oliver said. "Any problems getting here?"

"No, sir. It's about a thirty-minute commute with no traffic. How about on your end? Did you deal with the private eye?"

"The threat wasn't as threatening as we thought, but just to make sure, I'm going to ask a few more questions after my shift." Grant nodded, and Oliver once again told George to open the gate.

"The man driving Nigel is Thomas, and the one in the Audi is Grant," Oliver explained to George. "You have all our numbers. Don't hesitate to use them if you need to. At all times there will be two of us with Nigel."

George took the three cards with their numbers and put them in his pocket. Although he said he understood, Oliver could tell his attention had moved toward the cars, where his true boss had just exited.

Nigel Marks was over six foot, of average size and dressed in a proper suit. His salt-and-pepper hair was cropped close to his head, with a pair of reading glasses resting on top. The file Oliver had been given said Nigel was fifty-three, though he looked years younger. The file also said he was an avid runner, competing in marathons and triathlons in his spare time. That would account for the toned body his suit did little to hide. As Oliver approached, Nigel ended his call and extended his hand.

"Sorry about that," Nigel said with a smile. "This merger has made everyone forget how to do their jobs. You must be Mr. Quinn."

Oliver shook. "Call me Oliver."

"It's nice to meet you, Oliver. Nikki spoke very highly of you and your team. Hopefully you won't get too bored on this job."

"It's a good sign when a job stays boring," Oliver replied.

Nigel seemed to consider this and laughed. "I suppose you're right. Well…" Nigel waved to his house as Grant and Thomas joined them. "As I told Nikki, feel free to treat this as your home while here. There are no off-limits areas, but I do ask my office be left alone unless I'm with you. I have a feeling that my free time will be spent in there." He paused as his phone rang. His pleasant mood seemed to slide away in an instant. Replacing it was the look of a tired man. "My work is never done."

DARLING FELT AS if she was frozen yet couldn't stop everything around her from moving. It wasn't until her vision started to tunnel that she realized she was about to pass out. With a quick dose of good sense, she backed out of the bathroom and crouched, flinging her head down between her legs. In the moment she couldn't remember why that stopped a person from fainting, but she knew she needed to try it nonetheless.

So there she was, crouched just outside of room 212's bathroom and its body in the tub, trying to calm her stampeding heartbeat and erratic breathing.

This case was nothing but bad, bad luck.

A car door shut in the parking lot some time later. Whether it was seconds or minutes, she wasn't sure. The room hadn't been the only aspect of her reality that had warped when she had seen the body. However, instead of sending her into a bigger fit of worries, the sound of the outside world started to make her focus.

She took two deep breaths and slowly righted herself. The camera around her neck slapped against her chest, reminding her of the reason she had been there in the first place.

Nigel Marks and his mistress had been in this room the night before. He had gone, but his mistress hadn't checked out. It wasn't a stretch of the imagination to guess it was her unfortunate fate that she was the one wrapped up in the tub. Darling knew she had to call the police, just as she knew that once she left the room, she'd never be allowed back in.

At the moment, it was a thought that didn't sit right with her. So, blaming the impulse on her desire to solve mysteries, even ones seemingly cut and dried, she took her camera from her neck and walked back to the bathroom doorway. With hands she let shake, she snapped a few pictures of the bathroom and its deceased guest before she turned back and took a few of the bedroom. Another car door slammed shut in the distance. She glanced once more toward the bathroom.

Darling felt a mixture of anger and sadness pull at her heart. Nigel Marks might be a powerful man in the business world, but by killing this woman, he had unwittingly stepped inside Darling's domain.

Darling hurried to the main office and was thankful that Dan was still alone. He didn't look up when she came in, he just raised his hands.

"I know nothing," he said, still in a bubble of humor. It was a bubble she was about to pop.

"Dan, you need to call the police. There's a dead body in room 212."

Dan laughed, thinking it was a joke until he finally met her eyes. Darling figured she must have looked as serious as the situation was. She watched his face and mood sober.

"Where?" was all he could manage.

"Wrapped up in a shower curtain in the tub."

His lips thinned, and his brows pulled together. "You better give me the key and leave, then," he said after a moment. He pulled the only landline phone the office had from the second shelf of his desk. Darling felt a quick wave of fondness for the man. He was always trying to cover for her.

"I don't want you to lie about how you found the body," Darling said. "I'll tell the deputy the door was already open." She handed the key back to him. "We don't have to tell anyone about the key. Though I don't think they'll care either way." It seemed obvious to her what had happened.

Dan nodded and pocketed the key.

"Then you call them," he said, already shrugging into his coat. "I want to go see it for myself."

Darling sat behind the front desk with a very loud, long sigh and did as she was told. Deputy Derrick wouldn't be happy she had managed to get into this mess, but at least this time she wasn't guilty. Not that she would have admitted she had been guilty that morning. Instead of dialing 9-1-1, she called the man directly. In a small town like Mulligan, where the members of police force could be counted on two hands, Derrick had the dual duty of being their trusty investigator as well as deputy. Instead of puttering around with someone else in the bull pen, Darling went straight to the source.

"Deputy Derrick," he answered on the second ring.

"Derrick, it's Darling. I hope you're not busy right now."

She heard him snort. "Is that your way of trying to ask me out? We both know how well that works," he said, all humor.

"Well, not quite."

"Where are you calling from?" he asked after a pause. She knew him well enough to recognize something close to suspicious concern creeping into his tone.

"The Mulligan Motel," she paused for a moment and

then dove in. "There's a body in room 212, wrapped up in the tub."

"A body?"

She nodded. Then, realizing he couldn't see her, she said, "And Derrick? The last person seen leaving the room was Nigel Marks."

There was silence on the other end.

"Stay there and tell Dan don't let anyone else in that room," he finally said. "And I mean it, Darling. No one else goes in there."

Darling agreed to his no-tampering-with-a-crime-scene rule. Suddenly her morning indiscretion didn't seem as bad. She even bet Oliver's need to question her would disappear when he found out.

Oliver.

She pulled his card out of her back pocket and looked at his number.

If Nigel did kill whoever it was in the tub, where did that leave Oliver?

Chapter Three

Oliver didn't answer when Darling called him.

Somewhere in the back of her mind, she felt she owed it to him to give him a heads-up that the man he had promised to guard was about to need a lot more protection than he could offer. Oliver had said she wasn't a threat, vouching for a woman he no longer knew. Plus, it was no fun to be blindsided. She knew that from experience.

"This is Oliver Quinn. Leave a message and I'll get back to you as soon as possible," his voice mail recording answered. Darling felt her face heat up after the beep to leave a message came and went. She realized then that giving him a heads-up might also give Nigel one before the cops were even able to see the body in the tub. She didn't want to be the one responsible for giving the number one suspect time to lawyer up or possibly run. Although he probably had already done one or the other. It wasn't as if the body could have gone unnoticed for too long.

"Um, hi, it's Darling," she floundered. "I need you to call me as soon as you get this. Something's happened. Thanks." She let out a long sigh as she ended the call. She liked to believe she was a very confident and sure woman, but mix any part of Oliver into her life and she suddenly felt off her game.

Darling went back up to the second floor to find Dan, trying to push thoughts of her ex clear out of her head. She had walked into the crime scene that, most likely, her current client's husband had created. That gave her a new set of problems and concerns without adding the complication of the man from her past.

"I talked to Deputy Derrick," Darling told Dan, who was standing in the doorway to room 212. "He said no one else needs to go in there until they get here."

Dan didn't answer right away. His eyes were stuck on a point somewhere in the main room. She wondered if he had peeked in the bathroom yet. When he met her gaze, she knew he had. He looked haunted.

"Do you think he really did it?" he asked. "Nigel. Do you think he really killed her?"

Darling shrugged. "I can't say for certain, but I can make the leap and say I think there's a pretty good chance he did. You said yourself that he stayed the night here."

Dan nodded, but there was no enthusiasm in it.

"Do you want me to wait in the lobby and send the cops up when they get here?" she asked when it was clear Dan wasn't going to talk. He nodded again and returned to staring into room 212. She patted him on the shoulder and made the walk back, thinking a dead body in your hotel couldn't be good for business.

Darling sat behind the desk again but didn't let her mind wander. Instead she thought about Elizabeth Marks, the only other woman who knew about her husband's affair. Or, at least, she had thought so. If Nigel went to jail for murdering his mistress, she'd be in the clear to take what was hers, and possibly his, and leave without any strings attached.

A coldness seeped into Darling's heart.

She pulled her phone out and went to her email. Searching through discount offers and social media updates, she found the itinerary Elizabeth had sent to her after she had signed on to the case. During the duration of Nigel's work trip, Elizabeth would be with her mother in the Bahamas. She claimed that if she were far away with no chance of accidentally spotting Nigel and his mistress, he might get careless. It would be easier to catch him, she had said with vigor. If the schedule Darling was looking at was correct, the two women would have left for the trip on Sunday, two days ago. That meant Elizabeth wasn't even in the country when the woman had checked in.

Plus, why would you hire a private investigator if you were just going to kill the problem?

All at once, Darling realized there was an easy way to figure out who the mistress was.

Jumping up, she hurried to look out the door to make sure no one was coming. Derrick had been at the police station when she had called, which meant she had very little time left before he arrived. She ran back behind the front desk and pulled a big leather-bound registry book out. Dan hated leaving it on the desktop because he claimed it got in the way of his crosswords. He only pulled it out when a new guest had already handed over the money. It was also the only way he kept tabs on the people who checked in and out. Darling could have slapped herself. She couldn't believe she hadn't thought of looking at the registry as soon as she had come in.

She flipped through a few pages until she found the

entries from the night before. Three people had checked in. All were after 6:00 p.m., and none of them were Nigel Marks. A car door shut in the parking lot, and for the second time that day, Darling took a picture of something she probably shouldn't have. This time it was with her phone, but that reminded her she needed to hide her camera or else Derrick would take it from her. He was always suspicious of her, which, she guessed, was deserved in this case. She grabbed the camera, put it in the bottom drawer of the desk and replaced the registry seconds before Deputy Derrick came into the office.

"Two times in one day, huh?" she greeted him. Derrick didn't think it was funny. She sobered. "Sorry, it's been a weird day."

Whatever he had been about to say, he must have changed his mind. His face softened.

"What room?" he asked.

"Room 212. Dan is waiting outside. I told him not to go back in, like you said."

Derrick nodded. Behind his knitted brows, he was probably running through police procedures.

"You okay?" he asked when she kept staring. "I mean, like emotionally," he tacked on. He had never been that great at talking about feelings, so the question surprised her.

"Yeah, I didn't really see much."

He nodded and turned for the door that led to the stairs outside. He paused long enough to add, "And Darling, don't leave. I have a *lot* of questions for you."

"I know."

"I NEED YOU to call me as soon as you get this. Something's happened. Thanks." Oliver hadn't recognized

the number, but he sure did recognize the voice and the oddness behind it as he listened to Darling's message. He didn't have long to think about it, though, before his phone rang again.

This time it was George.

"Oliver, the police are here," he started. "They want to know if they can come in."

"The police?"

"Yeah, they say they need to talk to Mr. Marks."

Oliver looked up as if he could see his client through the ceiling.

"Let them in," he answered, ending the call.

He left his spot in the kitchen next to the back entrance and walked down the long hallway to the front. Grant, off duty until seven that night, was sitting in the dining room, reading one of the many books he had brought with him. He looked up as Oliver opened the front door.

"Something is up," Oliver said over his shoulder. A police cruiser was parking next to his rental SUV. Two male cops got out. "I need you on duty right now," he added, seeing their facial expressions. This wasn't a courtesy visit.

"Good afternoon, officers," Oliver said when they were a few feet away.

"Afternoon," the first one responded. He was in his upper fifties and had almost no hair left on his head. He was built strong but didn't look intimidating with his short height. "I'm Officer Barker and this is my partner, Officer Clay." He motioned to the much younger black man next to him, whose lack of hair looked more intentional than his partner's. "You must be one of Mr. Marks's bodyguards."

"Yes, sir. How can I help you?"

Officer Barker looked considerably more uncomfortable than Officer Clay. They shared a glance before Barker straightened his back and answered.

"We need to talk to Mr. Marks," he said. "Now."

"Okay," Oliver said. He turned to nod at Grant, who had been hanging back in the dining room to listen. "Can I ask what about?" Oliver ventured as Grant walked out of the room, heading for the stairs.

Again Oliver caught the feeling of unease that passed between the officers.

"Something's happened," Officer Clay answered. Oliver instantly recalled Darling's voice mail. "We shouldn't say anything more until we've talked to Mr. Marks."

Oliver wanted to push for more answers but had to remind himself that he was the bodyguard, not Nigel's personal assistant. He let the officers stand in silence until the man of the hour made his grand appearance.

"Officers," Nigel said, a question already in his tone. "What can I do for you?"

"We'll give you some privacy," Oliver said, falling back into the house with Grant but maintaining a sight line. Nigel didn't seem to notice, and as soon as they were out of earshot, the officers began to talk in lowered voices.

"What's going on?" Thomas asked. He had come down the stairs with Nigel, face filled with curiosity. Not that Oliver could blame him.

"The cops are here," Grant answered. He turned to Oliver. "Do you know what's going on?"

Oliver watched as Nigel's entire body visibly tensed.

"No," he answered. "But I can guess it's probably not good."

Probably not good was an understatement. In less than

five minutes, Nigel Marks was in the back of the cop cruiser and as mad as a hornet. Before they had driven away, the businessman had asked Thomas to call his lawyer.

"About what?" Thomas had asked.

"I'm being accused of murder," Nigel had bit back.

All three bodyguards didn't have time to hide their surprise.

Oliver had had many interesting things happen in his line of work, but he could definitely say a client being accused of murder was a first. No matter the new unique circumstance, he couldn't forget he was team leader. He sent Grant and Thomas—who had followed Nigel's directions and was calling Nikki to get the man's lawyer's information, and also an earful of confusion from her—to the police station. There they would continue to work as his bodyguards until Nigel was officially convicted of the crime or cleared of it.

Oliver made sure George knew he needed to keep an extravigilant eye on the gate and jumped into his rental, already calling Darling. It wasn't a coincidence she had called. She knew something.

She always did.

Minutes later, Oliver pulled into the lot of the Mulligan Motel. The coroner's van along with two police cruisers were parked next to the entrance, while a few guests stood around, but he had eyes only for one woman.

Darling was sitting on a bench next to the lobby's front door, concentration aimed at her phone. She had been brief during their call but had admitted they had found a dead body. Though how it was linked to Nigel, he wasn't sure yet.

"Apparently my questions are going to have to be

asked a little earlier than planned," he said by way of a greeting. It made the woman jump, but she didn't appear angry when she met his eyes. His body tensed at her gaze.

"Believe me, you aren't the only one who has questions." She stood and stretched. He was acutely aware of her five-five height, having to incline his head down slightly to look at her. A memory of how easy it was to pick her up into his embrace flashed across his vision. "Where is Nigel, and why aren't you with him?"

Since Nigel was a client, what went on in the man's private life was confidential. Oliver was under contract, which meant, unless it was public information, he couldn't divulge the fact that the businessman had been taken to the jail. Even if the person asking was Darling.

"Grant and Thomas are with him," was all he gave her. "Now, what's going on here, and how is it connected with Nigel?"

Darling was visibly trying to hide her anger at not being given a full answer, but she reined in the emotion along with any words born from it. She pushed her shoulders back when she was no longer actively trying to hide her displeasure.

"A body was found in the room your boss was staying in last night," she answered. Oliver didn't correct her with the difference between boss and client. His interest level had jumped off the charts instead. He was about to push for more when the Mulligan Motel's front door swung open and the deputy walked out. His mouth was set in a grim line, one that thinned when he saw Oliver.

"I'm surprised you're here," the deputy said, coming over. "I thought you'd be at the station."

"So Nigel was arrested?" Darling cut in before Oliver could comment.

"He was picked up a few minutes ago," Derrick said, relieving Oliver of having to withhold the information. Even though Darling kept her face guarded, he didn't miss the satisfaction that the cop's words brought her. "Which is why I didn't think you'd be here," Derrick said to Oliver.

"The rest of the team is with him," he repeated. "I came here to find out what's going on." Oliver sent a pointed look to Darling. "And how you're involved."

Darling crossed her arms over her chest.

"I was actually about to ask the same thing," Derrick said. The two of them focused on the private investigator. She shifted under their collective gaze. A long exhalation escaped between her lips.

"I was working a case," she admitted. "It led me here and, to my surprise, right up to a dead body. But as soon as I found it, I called you," she said to Derrick.

The cop outdid her earlier sigh and pinched the bridge of his nose.

"What's your case?" Oliver had to ask.

Darling set her jaw. "I'm not at liberty to say."

"Dammit, Darling, a woman is dead. You need to tell me everything you know," Derrick said with tried patience. Oliver guessed murder wasn't a normal occurrence in Mulligan.

"So it is a woman, then?" she asked. Derrick nodded. It was her turn to skate around a direct answer. "I didn't look hard enough. How was she killed?"

"And how is Nigel connected, again?" Oliver tacked on.

The deputy wasn't happy about the questions. "It's my turn to say 'no comment.'" Darling opened her mouth to argue, but he held up his hand. "This is an ongoing murder investigation, Darling. I can't give you anything right now. Not even for old times' sake."

Oliver didn't like the way he said the last part or the way the deputy brought up their shared past. The past that Oliver's past few years didn't even touch. However, a small part of him did feel a sort of odd joy to know that whatever relationship they'd had was now seemingly over.

"Now, please go wait inside so I can take your statement," the deputy said to Darling before focusing on Oliver. "And I suggest you head to the station. We're going to need to talk about that client of yours."

He was gone after that, leaving Oliver and Darling speechless on the sidewalk.

"You said Nigel was the last to see the woman alive?" he asked, voice low and serious.

"He spent the night with her, Oliver."

"Are you sure?" Nigel had said he was in his hotel in the city until the morning. Neither Grant nor Thomas had said otherwise. "It could have been a mistake."

Darling's lips turned down. "It looks like Nigel Marks isn't the saint you thought him to be." There was no mistaking the undercurrent of anger that coursed through her words. He was a step away from a dangerous territory with her.

"This isn't how I pictured running into you after all of these years." Silence stretched between them as neither had a response ready for the topic of their past. Oliver then continued, "I'd still like to catch up, but it looks like tonight might not be good." He had already started a mental list of things he needed to do. "Can I treat you to breakfast tomorrow instead?"

Darling seemed to be thinking it over. Eventually she

nodded before she, too, disappeared back into the building. Oliver retreated to his SUV, pulling his phone out to call Nikki along the way.

The job was officially no longer boring.

Chapter Four

Darling chewed on her bottom lip, not stopping until she tasted lipstick. She was standing in the lobby of Acuity the next morning, staring into a folder, confused beyond belief.

The afternoon before had blurred by after she'd given a statement to Derrick and then been ushered home. He wasn't happy with her investigating, or the fact that she wouldn't say for whom, and had in so many words let her know that she wouldn't keep that secret for long. So instead she had tried to reach Mrs. Marks. The resort manager she had spoken with had taken a message and promised to give it to her when she returned.

It had eaten Darling up as she lay awake in bed, fuming that Oliver knew more about what was going on with Nigel than she did. Here he was, stepping into her town, and he had already managed to be on the inside loop with the infamous Mr. Marks. She could have called Oliver, sure, but her pride had shut that idea down quickly. Admitting she needed the fair-haired man in any capacity was something she refused to do ever again.

After only a few hours of rest, she had opened Acuity to find a folder filled with curious things lying on the hardwood floor, slipped under the door as an unmistakable greeting.

Now between her hands were four eight-by-ten pictures of Nigel Marks with a woman who wasn't his wife. Each picture—printed on glossy card stock and dated—was focused on the businessman and a red-haired woman in four varying shows of affection. The first two had them in an intimate embrace, while the third and fourth were of the two sharing meals. In one of those, Nigel was even holding the woman's hand, a smile splitting his lips. None of the four pictures had a clear shot of the female's face, but there was no denying it was the same woman in each and that the couple was happy. All pictures were dated from the previous December up until March, the month before.

Elizabeth Marks had been looking for proof that her husband had been seeing another woman in secret. From what Darling could tell, she was holding that proof.

But why?

She stood there, cycling through each picture again, when a knock at the door made her jump. The folder fell to the floor. She hurried to pick it up when she noticed there was something still inside it.

"Knock, knock. It's me," called Oliver from the other side of the locked front entrance. "You in there?"

Darling didn't immediately respond. Her eyes were glued to a newspaper clipping that had been stuck to the inside of the folder. It was a picture of her parents that she knew to be almost nine years old. However, it was the words written in red across it that grabbed all her attention.

Do the right thing this time.

"Hold on," Darling said after another knock sounded. She hoped Oliver didn't catch the waver in her voice. She put the pictures, including the clipping, back into the folder and tucked it under her arm to unlock the door.

"You okay?" Oliver asked immediately. Perhaps her poker face wasn't at its best today. He wore a zip-up black jacket over a black shirt that looked good contrasting with his lighter hair. Staying away from the all-black body-guard stereotype, he'd donned beige cargo pants with more pockets than she cared to count. She didn't recognize the brand of tennis shoes, but she bet that he could run fast in them if needed.

"Yeah, just tired," she lied, leading him into the lobby. "Let me just freshen up and I'll be ready to go." She stuffed the folder into her purse and excused herself to the bathroom. There she turned on the faucet and took a deep breath.

What had briefly felt like a gift that could close her case against Nigel now felt tainted and wrong. As far as she knew, no one in Mulligan was aware of her parents' past, especially the quiet part she had played in the background.

Do the right thing.

She didn't need to wonder what that meant.

Whoever had sent her the folder wanted her to turn it in to the cops. But why not just do it themselves? If the red-haired woman was the same one who had been left in the tub, that meant the pictures definitely linked the two before the hotel room. Why would they give them to her?

Darling ran her hands under the cold water but didn't splash her face. For the first time in a long while, she had taken pains to look nice. She wore a pale pink blouse that dipped down into a V—not enough to be seductive, just feminine—a pair of comfortably tight light blue jeans and dark brown boots that folded down at the ankle. Her hair was twisted up into a purposefully messy bun so the yellow daisy earrings she loved so much could be seen with ease. A subtle coral tinted her plump yet small lips. They were downturned at the moment.

She'd convinced herself that Oliver's presence in Mulligan was a good thing. What Oliver had done in the past had broken a big part of who she was, but she liked to think she had come out stronger because of it. As soon as she had turned eighteen, she had left California, her family and all of those bad memories behind. There was no reason to dredge them up now. If she could keep her head up while Oliver was in town, then she could get through anything.

That thought alone pushed a wave of new purpose through her bones until it made her stand taller. Putting away the man behind the murder of the woman in the tub was more important than her failed love life. Nigel Marks's mistress deserved better.

Darling eyed her purse before nodding to herself in the mirror.

She *did* need to do the right thing.

"You ready for some breakfast?" Oliver asked when she emerged. He was talking to her but looking around the office's lobby. Pride swelled in her chest.

Acuity Investigations was housed in an old strip mall that predated half of the other businesses in Mulligan. Acuity was at the tail end of the shops, next to a narrow road that deposited drivers back on Main Street. The reason Jeff Berns, Darling's former boss, had rented the particular space was its proximity to traffic yet its back-door access so clients could be as discreet as they wanted.

Darling remembered the first time she had walked into Acuity. The cream-colored walls, leather and oak furniture, pictures of boats nestled in calm water and slightly musty smell had been a sharp contrast to what she referred to as her former life. Instead of turning her nose up at Jeff and his place of employment like her parents would have, Darling had embraced it with vigor.

Acuity wasn't fancy or elegant, but it was important to her. As Oliver's eyes traveled along the hardwood floors to the heavy oak door that led to her office, in the back of her mind she hoped he felt that truth ring through his bones as she did.

"Actually, would you mind if we swung by the police station really quickly?" Darling asked when his eyes finally moved back to hers. "I need to give something to Deputy Derrick." When he didn't immediately respond, she tacked on, "If you don't have enough time, we could reschedule."

"No, it's fine," he answered. "Just as long as we actually eat afterward."

Darling slipped into her black faux-leather jacket and smiled inwardly at its comfort before ushering Oliver out and locking the door behind her. They walked in silence up to his SUV. She was oddly saddened when he didn't open the door for her. The Oliver from younger years had not only opened the car doors for her but also occasionally put on her seat belt, laughing and mock-admonishing her about the importance of car safety.

The memory tugged at long-forgotten heartstrings. Now as they settled into their seats, the disconnect between the present and the past stretched between them.

"Is this visit for business or pleasure?" Oliver asked as the SUV pulled out of the parking lot.

She gave him a sideways glance. "Business."

He nodded to the road. "Does it have to do with Nigel?"

"It does," she admitted.

"What is it?" he ventured.

"Something very important."

She didn't elaborate and he didn't push.

"I don't think he did it, Darling," Oliver said. "I don't think he killed that woman."

Darling couldn't help the reflex to tense up, her body readying automatically for a verbal spar. It was a response she had picked up out of necessity as a young female investigator. She rolled her shoulders back to ease the new tension and answered with a controlled voice.

"Did he admit to being at the hotel last night?" she asked.

She knew Oliver sensed the mood change. He shifted in his seat and lost his smile.

"I didn't get a chance to ask. As soon as he was released, he locked himself in his study with his lawyer and son. They were still there when I left."

Darling's control cracked. "They *released* him?"

Oliver nodded. "I don't think there was enough evidence to hold him."

"But he was there," Darling exclaimed. "He spent the night with her!"

"Just because he spent the night with her doesn't mean he killed her, Darling." Instant anger filled her veins at how he said her name, as if she was some confused child.

"So, what, it's just a coincidence, then? You can't comprehend that a man like him, an adulterer, could ever do something like kill his mistress?"

She watched as his jaw hardened. "We don't know for

sure he was having an affair," he said. "The visit could have been business-related for all we know."

Darling laughed. "Oh, you're right. They probably just sat around and talked business all night."

"It's possible," he tried, but Darling wasn't having it. Defending men like Nigel, bending to their wills, was unforgivable in her book. Heat rose from the pit of her stomach, but it wasn't embarrassment. It was the force of an old wound breaking open. She yanked the pictures from her purse right as they turned into the station's parking lot.

"He seems to like to talk to women in secret," she said, barely able to keep her voice level. Oliver took the pictures from her hand and cycled through them just as she remembered the clipping was on the bottom. Operating on the assumption that Oliver knew he was dealing with an angry Darling, she snatched the pictures back and threw open the door. "I'll right back."

She marched into the weathered, blue-painted building without looking back. Her head was almost spinning with the range of emotions she had experienced in such a short amount of time. It amazed her how Oliver brought out the worst in her, no matter what attitude she wanted to convey. Instead of seeming put together, she had come off as truly childish in the end. Her cheeks heated; this time it was all shame.

The Mulligan Police Department was poorly insulated. Derrick had liked to joke that was one of the reasons the town's crime rate was so low. No one wanted to spend the night in the cells. She hadn't even liked spending the morning in one. Darling wondered how Nigel Marks's act would shake the community's relative peace and quiet. She made a mental note to grab a newspaper after her breakfast date was finished to see how the media had handled it.

"Hey, Trudy," Darling greeted the bundled-up secretary. She was the first and only barrier between the front doors and the bullpen.

"Darlin' Smith, I hope you're not in trouble again," she said. Her tone was laced with disapproval. Trudy had more grandchildren than most people had fingers. She was proud of this and often acted as Mulligan's mother hen, believing she had earned that right even more with every relation that had come from her and her children.

"Not today," she said with a small smile. "But I do need to see Derrick. Is he in?"

"No, ma'am. He should be in soon, though. Do you want to wait?"

"Um, no, but can I just leave something on his desk?" Darling flashed the woman the folder, though the pictures were in her other hand. Trudy nodded and let Darling around her to the rows of desks. Another cop sat focused on his computer and didn't seem to notice or care as she went to Derrick's space in the corner. Glancing at a picture of Derrick's niece and nephew positioned next to his keyboard, Darling felt as if she was making a good decision by turning the evidence in. Derrick wasn't her Mr. Right, but he was a good, just man.

However, in true Darling fashion, she quickly snapped pictures of each individual image and their corresponding dates before slipping them into the folder, minus the newspaper clipping. She stuffed that into her back pocket.

A source dropped these off at my office today.
Darling.

She scribbled down the lie and was suddenly glad that Derrick and his questions weren't there yet. He'd call her, no doubt, but not until after he had investigated the evidence. If he caught her now, it would be the other way around, a thought that made her hightail it out of the station.

Dodging one ex only to get into the car with another.

THE RED LEAF was one of two local coffee shops in Mulligan. Like the town, it was quaint, yet endearing in its own right. They also made a mean coffee, Darling said after she had returned from the station. She hadn't apologized for her outburst, but he hadn't expected her to, either.

Bailing Darling Smith out of jail had never been on Oliver's list of scenarios for when, and if, they ever met again. Sure, he'd thought of the possibility of crossing paths when he went home to California to visit family. Maybe even a random encounter in an airport as he traveled for work. But never like this.

Occasionally, he'd wonder what he would say to her during a chance encounter. *How have you been? Isn't the weather nice? Have you cut your hair?* They weren't good greetings, but how else could he skate around the topic of their past? Now, as they sat across from each other in a worn leather booth, he doubted such a thing could be accomplished. Darling hadn't forgotten or forgiven what he'd done, and he couldn't blame her for that.

He hadn't forgiven himself yet, either.

"Expecting a call?" he asked as she took care to adjust the volume on her cell.

"Expecting? No. Hoping? Still no, but I can't ignore it." He raised his eyebrow so she explained, "Work-related."

"Ah, I know the feeling." He pulled his phone from his pocket and placed it on the table, as well. With the recent changes in the job, Nikki had made it clear she wanted all guards to have their phones on at all times, even when they were off the clock.

"So, I have to ask. You didn't seem at all surprised to see me yesterday… Why?" she asked, getting the conversational ball rolling. Darling had never been a fan of silence.

Unlike the seventeen-year-old he had left behind, this Darling was all grown and all woman. Oliver couldn't deny she was beautiful—she always had been—but now there was something more as he really looked at her. The way her dark green eyes bore into his, trying to figure him out, was so fierce it almost shook his resolve to leave the past just where it was.

"My boss told me the name and I couldn't imagine it being a coincidence," he said honestly. "Though I wasn't a hundred percent given the circumstances."

"Ah…circumstances. You mean the trespassing accusation."

Oliver made a gun with his hand. "Bingo."

"Well," she said, "given recent developments, I'd say that *accusation* is the least of everyone's worries. Wouldn't you agree?" she finished, crossing her arms over her chest. That movement meant Oliver needed to tread softly.

"We wouldn't have taken on this case if he was a bad man, Darling. I stand by what I said earlier. Just because he was there doesn't mean he did it, and I'd like to ask you to drop whatever case you might still have that involves him," he said. And, apparently, it was the wrong thing to say. Almost instantly the color in her cheeks rose, her brows lifted and her lips thinned. Knowing a storm was brewing, Oliver made a second conversational mistake, hoping to pacify her. "For old times' sake, Darling."

He might as well have kicked her beneath the table.

"I can't believe you're still simply rolling over for the big dogs," she bit out, angry. "Nigel Marks is a millionaire, so that makes whatever he does justifiable? Is that why you do what you do, Oliver? Do you get some kind of thrill from protecting the rich? Did you ever stop and wonder why that's even necessary? No, you probably don't, because all you care about is pleasing the elite, just waiting for them to yell 'jump.'"

She stood so abruptly that the booth's seat pushed back and scraped the tile. The waitress and few patrons looked over, but Darling seemed oblivious. Like them, Oliver looked at her, but in a state of awe.

"You know what?" she said. "I'm not going to sit here and be talked to like I'm still the girl you used to know." She grabbed her purse and started to leave, pausing for a second to finish her tirade. "And Oliver, if I still had a case, I certainly wouldn't drop it 'for old times' sake.'"

And just like that Darling Smith became the one who left.

Chapter Five

There was a reason Darling had picked the café as a place to talk with Oliver—it was only a block away from her office. He watched her through the café's front windows as she walked in an angry huff down the street, turning into the strip mall's parking lot and disappearing around back. Each step had been rigged with tension, each movement forced.

The waitress waited until Darling was out of view before coming to the table. She also didn't look so pleased with him.

He let out a long breath.

"Can I place a to-go order?" he asked, glancing back out the window.

For the first time in years, Oliver let the past wash over him, bringing in the flood of memories that pieced together the last conversation he had had with the younger Darling.

She had been wearing a white dress with daisies printed across it, a stark contrast to the tears that had streaked her cheeks.

"They're horrible, Oliver," she had yelled. "They'll never change! They of all people have no right to tell me what I do and don't deserve. So, please, let's just leave. Let's run away together and never look back!"

"We can't."

"Oliver, I love you," she had said, taking his hands in hers. They had been soft and warm. "And if you love me as much as you say, we *can* make it." There had been so much hope in her eyes, despite the tears she had shed because of her parents. Despite everything she had gone through in the past year. So much hope that Oliver could still see it clearly today.

"But, Darling," he had whispered. "I don't want to."

Just like that, the hope had died, and the memory of breaking Darling Smith's heart had burned itself into his mind, becoming another moment he could never forget.

It still amazed him that such a brief conversation had made such a big impact.

"Order's ready," called the waitress, holding up a paper bag and a cardboard cup holder. Oliver pulled himself out of the hardest conversation he'd ever had and paid for the food.

Instead of climbing into his rental, he followed the same path Darling had taken until he was, yet again, at Acuity's front door. He didn't knock this time. She wouldn't have let him in if he had.

The private investigator was standing behind the lone desk in the front room, a scowl still attached to her face, when he pushed into the lobby. Her hair billowed around her head, a crown of dark blond that seemed to crackle to life as the rest of her grew angry at the sight of him. Before she could get on a verbal roll again, he held up his café spoils in surrender.

"I'm sorry," he said, smile wiped from his face. He let his hands fall and took a step closer. "After all this time, I shouldn't have asked, and certainly shouldn't have expected, you to listen to me. It wasn't fair." Her lips parted to talk, though he wasn't sure which emotion was trying to push through. He continued before he could find out. "Although you weren't fair, either. It's clear you've made a few assumptions about me—some I'd like to correct—and, again, I can't quite blame you for that. But the fact remains that it's been eight years since we last saw each other. Our lives have changed—we've changed with them." He took one last step forward, testing her waters. "Give me the chance to set a few things straight, Darling."

"You don't have to answer to me," she replied. Her voice was low.

"You're right," he agreed. "I don't have to, but I need to."

Darling's expression—brows drawn together, lips thin, jaw set—slowly changed to a more pleasant mask. For the first time since he had walked in, she looked at his peace offering. She didn't smile, though he knew she could smell the delicious chocolate-covered confections, but she didn't continue to frown. If he wanted to find a safe ground with Present-Day Darling, he was going to have to come to terms with the fact that she might not warm up to him again. He would have to settle for whatever she gave him and ignore how the idea of never being in her good opinion hurt deeper than he'd like to admit.

"I'm surprised Carla still served you after the scene I caused," she finally said. "You must have done some quick sweet talking."

Oliver smiled. Dangerous Darling was gone. He'd get a chance to explain everything now. Well, at least the real reason behind his love and respect for the Orion

Group. That explanation meant more to him than she could fathom. The desire to tell her what had happened three years ago had been replaced by the need to explain the past the moment she had stormed out of the café.

"I told her I needed to score some points with you." He motioned to the bag in his hand. "Hopefully freshly baked chocolate donuts and a coffee with two creams and three sugars will do just that."

Joy flashed through him as the corner of Darling's lip quirked up.

"You're lucky that my breakfast preferences aren't one of the things that have changed over the years."

Darling walked forward, grabbed the bag and led him into her office. It was a much smaller room, but Oliver instantly liked it. Exposed brick walls, once painted white and now chipping, were decorated with certification plaques, black-and-white pictures of Mulligan scenery and a rusted sign that said Acuity across it.

"So you actually own Acuity, then?"

"I sure do. Expenses and all." Even as she said it sarcastically, he saw the pride in it. She was comfortable behind her desk. He was sure her ease was subconscious. Darling Smith had found her place in the world after all. He wondered how her parents felt about it but knew he'd never ask her that. If he was a gaping wound, they were bottomless caverns. "I interned here when I was eighteen. Jeff didn't tell me then, but he was ready to retire. So, he started to groom me as his replacement. When I was done with all my certifications and schooling, he split. Now it's just me." She bit into her donut and her eyes fluttered closed. "And more than occasionally the sweet, sweet Red Leaf pastry."

"Sounds like a good setup. I'm happy for you."

Darling flashed a small smile. "Thanks," she said. "Now, what about you? What assumptions do you need to clear up?"

"I feel like you have the wrong impression of me."

"I still stand by the fact that you don't need to explain yourself to me. You could be married with kids and living in the suburbs of Canada for all I know. Not that it would be bad if you did. I just want you to know that you don't owe me anything, Oliver."

This made him laugh. He lifted his left hand to show ringless fingers.

"No marriages, children or suburban Canadian living. Just an apartment in Dallas, where Orion's located." It might have been his imagination, but he thought she looked pleased at this information. He had already done his research on her. She wasn't and hadn't been married. Although he wasn't sure if she was attached currently. He decided against asking her that, too. "I know you aren't forcing me to explain, but I'd still like to do it."

"All right, then, I'm listening." She set her pastry down and laced her fingers together on the desktop. Oliver took a deep breath and began.

"I know you think I've sold out by working for a company that caters to the rich and privileged, but that's only partially true. Before I worked for Orion, I was hired as an agent at another security agency called Redstone Solutions out in California. I was excited—thrilled—with the offer because, one, I needed the money, and two, I was good at what I did. A lot of people think bodyguards just stand around and occasionally have to tackle someone, but the truth is there's a lot more to it. Strategies and problem solving, for instance. Redstone let me lead an exciting life of travel and leisure while also challenging me at every turn." Oliver felt pride and nostalgia surge through him. Though it didn't last long. It never did. He felt his smile sag and his face harden. Darling leaned in closer. "But then Morgan Avery was killed, and everything changed."

Darling's eyebrows rose in question, but she didn't interrupt.

"Redstone is a large company with more connections and funding than you can imagine. Its reach isn't limited to the US, either. I was based in the California branch as a part of a three-man team when Morgan Avery first came in and asked for our help. She was twenty-one and an astronomy student, utterly brilliant. She'd been competing for a spot in an elite university program in the UK that, if she made it in, would make her career. But when she was invited to the final round of the competition in England, she started getting these really nasty letters. Anonymous letters that threatened her life. So, she came to Redstone Solutions asking for a team to escort her while she traveled there. The only problem was, she didn't have enough money to come up with the minimum payment. My boss turned her away after she practically begged us to reconsider." Oliver's jaw tightened and his fists balled. "For a week straight, she tried to convince us, and for a week we had to turn her away. The day before she was scheduled to fly out, she was found dead in a ditch near the airport—beaten and almost unrecognizable. The police were able to find the killer—a competitor—and send him to prison for life, but it didn't matter. The damage was done." Oliver took a long pull from his coffee before continuing, finding a better place in his mind. "Morgan's death was an eye-opener for us."

"Us?"

"Nikki, the secretary, was the person who talked to Morgan the most. After Morgan's death, she became furious and left Redstone to start her own security agency. She asked me and my then-team to join her." He smiled. "We did, and that's Orion's origin story."

"Secretary to boss, huh?" Darling sipped her coffee. "I like the sound of her."

"Nikki was and is a beast in the business world. When she left, she already had a few connections willing to fund Orion. Since then, she's kept it going *and* growing with no issues."

"She sounds like my kind of woman," Darling replied with a smirk. Oliver laughed.

"She's something, all right." He sobered. "We've spent the last three years offering our services to those who can't afford it but need it, specifically when traveling. Without her connections and the occasional sponsor, we'd never be able to take on our clients for basically free."

He watched as Darling's ears seemed to perk right up.

"Basically free?"

Oliver smiled, but he was sad. "We'll never turn away another Morgan."

"Wow," Darling breathed. "And Nigel Marks is one of those sponsors you have to take on occasionally?" she guessed.

"Bingo. Team Delta was assigned and now, here I am."

"Team Delta?" She snorted. "What are you, five?"

Oliver held his hands up and grinned. "Hey, don't look at me! My bud took the Orion Belt theme and went with it. He got a kick out of Orion Belt's three stars also being referenced as Delta, Epsilon and Zeta."

Darling's eyes widened as she understood the meaning behind the name. Her voice softened. "Morgan was in astronomy. The name Orion was chosen to honor her memory," she said.

Oliver nodded. "It was her favorite constellation." A warmth that was equal parts fondness and sadness pooled in his chest as he remembered Morgan. "Darling, I know I have no right to come into your life and start trying to call the shots, but I have to state this again. I don't think Nigel killed that woman, and unless he's convicted or decides he doesn't need us, he's my number-one priority while in Mulligan." Oliver wanted to put his hand out to touch hers, to show her that she should trust him. To show that even though Nigel was his top priority, he still cared for her. Even though he shouldn't.

Darling, to his surprise, seemed to choose her next words carefully.

"I understand," she said in almost a whisper. "But, tell me, why are you so sure that he's innocent?"

"The surprise on his face when he found out about the body," he answered.

Darling huffed. "Surprise can be faked, Oliver. I do it every Christmas when Trudy gives me a can of peanut brittle wrapped in reindeer-decorated paper."

"True, he could have faked the surprise," he conceded. "But not the pain." Oliver replayed the moment when he'd watched as the cops had told the wealthy man about the body. He didn't need to hear the man's response to know it had caught him completely by surprise...and hurt him.

Darling hesitated, brows pulling together, but she didn't have time to respond. Her phone blared to life, a cute jingle that felt out of place within the conversation. She let out a long sigh as she read the ID.

"Excuse me a second," she said, standing.

"No problem."

Oliver was able to drink the rest of his neglected coffee, pairing it with one of Darling's chocolate-covered circles of delicious sin, before the private investigator came back. The look on her face made him stand.

"What's wrong?"

Darling bit her lip. "Do you want a list or a long-winded sentence?" It was a less-than-halfhearted attempt to lighten whatever mood had erupted around her. Oliver answered with an equal lack of mirth.

"List."

"One, the medical examiner believes our Jane Doe was killed yesterday morning," she ticked off. "Two, that puts Nigel in the clear since he was apparently eating breakfast with your team while you were bailing me out." Oliver wanted to feel relief at her words—that he had been right about Nigel's innocence—but Darling's grim expression had every part of him on guard. "Three, they haven't been able to identify the woman yet." There was a hesitation after the words left her mouth.

"Couldn't Nigel identify her? If he met with her he had to *know* her."

She held up four fingers. "Four, Nigel is denying that he was ever even at the hotel, let alone in Mulligan, last night. No one has stepped forward to prove otherwise, and it's Nigel's word against Dan's. There are no security cameras at the hotel, either. None that work properly, at least."

Oliver's instinct was to question Dan's claim of seeing Nigel in the first place, but he felt an irrational loyalty to him, because it was obvious that was how Darling felt about him.

"I don't think prints take that long to process," he said

instead. "Surely they'll figure out who she is within the week and go from there."

Darling's face darkened. She held up her hand. "Five," she said, voice shaking despite her calm exterior, "all of her fingers and teeth are missing. Someone removed them."

Chapter Six

Any chance of normal conversation disappeared at the grim news.

"Removed?" Oliver repeated.

Darling let her hand drop to her side and settled back behind her desk. Her half-eaten donut wasn't as appealing as it had been minutes before.

"Postmortem, but yes," she confirmed.

Oliver also sat back down, though he didn't relax.

"Who told you all this?"

"Derrick," she admitted.

"You two must be close if he'll disclose information about an ongoing murder investigation."

"We used to date, but now we don't," she said matter-of-factly. "I think he told me to warn me."

Oliver's eyebrow rose at that. "Warn you? Of what?"

"That my case against Nigel isn't safe anymore," she said. "Considering the murder."

"So he thinks Nigel is still connected even though he's denied being in town?"

"I'm not the only one who trusts Dan. Just because Nigel has an alibi for where he physically was at the time of the murder doesn't mean he isn't connected." Darling recalled the pictures of the millionaire and the red-haired woman. Derrick had confirmed their Jane Doe also had red hair. If they could prove it was the same woman, Nigel would have no choice but to offer her identity up.

"You think he's denying knowing her because he had someone else kill her," Oliver summarized. Darling didn't nod or shake her head. She was trying indifference. "Why would he go through all of that trouble?" he asked.

"Something tells me he can't afford an affair right now."

Darling froze. She was being too candid with Oliver, though she wondered if it even mattered anymore. Soon the town of Mulligan would hear the rumor that Nigel had been at the hotel and the woman who had been with him was dead. With or without denials, the idea that Nigel was an adulterer would cross each resident's mind at least once. The beloved Nigel Marks was about to have his image tested with or without her saying a word.

"Ah," Oliver said with a slight nod. "The prenup loop-hole. If he cheats, the wife can take at least half of everything Nigel owns."

"What?" She feigned ignorance but barely concealed her surprise. Oliver wasn't buying it.

"You aren't the only person with connections," he said. "If working for Redstone Solutions taught us anything, it was to be thorough in knowing the clients we take on. That includes the threats to them. Orion may be small and less well funded, but that doesn't mean our analysts are anything to laugh at." That piqued Darling's interest, but she didn't interrupt to follow up. "If Elizabeth Marks wasn't in the Bahamas right now, she would be the first person I would suspect. Although, like you said about Nigel, she could still be connected even though she wasn't physically there."

"But, even if what you say is true about this prenup

thing," she said, "why kill the mistress when you can expose her?"

"Why expose the mistress when you can kill her?"

"Ah, casting blame on the jilted wife. An overplayed card, don't you think?" Darling quirked her lip up into a grin.

He laughed. "I'm assuming the case you have against Nigel is about infidelity. Why else would you be snooping around his house and then the hotel he was at?"

"Nigel Marks is almost a legend in Mulligan. Who's to say I'm not his number-one fan?" Darling had her eyebrow raised high, a smirk across her lips to match. She knew Oliver wasn't dumb, but she wasn't going to admit to her deal with Elizabeth yet. There were a few questions she needed to ask the millionaire's wife first.

"Last time I checked, you weren't the biggest fan of the upper class," Oliver said. She couldn't deny that. "That's why I assume you asked the hotel owner to keep an eye out for Nigel, just in case."

Darling held up her hands. "Okay, you got me," she said. "I am Nigel's number-one fan. I have a poster of him over my bed and everything."

Oliver laughed, and the mood around them softened. They lapsed into small talk while picking up and finishing their food, avoiding the topics of murder and blame. They were delving into their individual pasts, while the one they shared wasn't brought up. Darling silently marveled at how the Oliver that sat across from her was so similar to the one all those years ago, and yet completely different. She couldn't quite put her finger on it, though she didn't want to, either. Trying to define Oliver Quinn would be a slippery slope—if she found she liked the new one, then what? It was better for everyone if she just played nice and treated the man as an old friend, nothing more and nothing less.

"Speaking of the job," Oliver said, "I need to go relieve Thomas. He worked well past his hours last night."

"Not to pry into your work, but where does the whole murder accusation leave you with Marks?" she asked, standing with him and ignoring the small part of her that wanted him to stay.

"Innocent until proven guilty." He shrugged. "The fact that he was with my team during the woman's death is an ironclad alibi, in my mind. The only way we'll stop working for him now is if Nigel terminates the contract or Nikki calls us off. Considering he already signed a contract, it'll cost him more to get out of it than to stay in it, and last time I talked to Nikki, she said we continue to do our job. She's a good person, Darling. There's a reason we all trust her to make the right call."

Darling nodded, not wanting to point out that everyone at some point was wrong. If this was Nikki's time, it meant Oliver and his team were protecting the man behind a woman's murder. But she let that thought slide. She wasn't Oliver's mother or wife or even his girlfriend. Darling couldn't dictate his choices just as he couldn't dictate hers.

"It *was* nice catching up with you, though," he added, meeting her eyes and holding her gaze. "Even the bumpy parts."

Darling couldn't help but smile back. "It certainly has been interesting."

Oliver picked up his coffee and slid his phone back into his pocket. Darling didn't know if she was supposed to hug him or shake his hand as a goodbye. It wasn't as if they had done either in greeting the day before when he had strolled into the town jail to get her out. As she struggled with trying to figure out what to say to the man who had broken her heart, Oliver saved her the trouble.

"I would say goodbye, but I have a feeling you'll pop back up in the middle of wherever you aren't supposed to be. So I'll just see you then." She returned his smile with a mischievous one of her own and watched as he walked out of her office.

He was absolutely right.

An hour passed without any new leads, evidence or answers. Darling was feeling unbelievably restless. She half expected Derrick to call or stop by with a no-nonsense attitude about her case, but Acuity's door remained closed and her phone remained quiet.

So Darling, unable to cope with the fact she wasn't making progress, made a list of all the evidence and facts she had. It reminded her that her camera was still beneath Dan's desk at the hotel.

"Better than sitting here and doing nothing," she said to the office.

Despite yesterday's discovery, the Mulligan Motel looked as normal as it ever did. No one was in the office, but Darling preferred that. She hurried to grab her camera, hoping to avoid explaining to Dan why she was back.

It took a few seconds to register that there was no camera to grab.

"What the?" she asked herself, squatting to make sure it hadn't been pushed out of view.

Darling's blood ran cold.

There was a piece of paper where her camera had been. Written across it in red ink was a message.

You already did the right thing, Darling. Now stop.

Chapter Seven

He wasn't tall, he wasn't big and he wasn't intimidating. His shoulders weren't wide, either, but he still held himself up straight and proud. With dark hair, muddy-green eyes and a surprisingly hard jaw, Jace Marks was sculpted with equal parts his father and the most average of people.

Oliver shook the twenty-six-year-old's hand and couldn't help but compare him with Nigel.

While his father dressed to impress, Jace wore a blue flannel button-up, jeans and tennis shoes. Instead of having a cropped haircut like Nigel's, Jace slicked back his short hair with a pair of sunglasses resting on top. Despite the past forty-eight hours, he looked rested enough.

However, one detail that matched his father to a tee was the trademark smile he wore easily. It spoke of wealth, privilege and many, many secrets.

"It's good to properly meet you," Jace said. He shook Oliver's hand. He had a firm grip, which also surprised Oliver. "A passing hello at the police station isn't the same thing, if you ask me."

"No problem. I didn't realize you would be in Mulligan during our stay," Oliver admitted. All clients were asked to disclose pertinent information. That included their travel companions.

"When the merger got complicated, Nigel called me in," he answered. "I hadn't planned on staying, but given recent events, I feel I should be here to support him."

They were standing in the kitchen, Oliver next to the back door with a clear sight line to the front. Nigel was still upstairs in his study with his lawyer, Stan, while Grant was stationed outside the door. Oliver had sent Thomas to rest as soon as he had come through the door, considering the new recruit hadn't slept yet.

"Nigel," Oliver repeated the name. Had he been informed wrong? Was Jace a stepson and not the millionaire's blood relation?

"He doesn't like when he's referred to as Father in a work setting," Jace answered with an apologetic smile. "He doesn't want anyone to think he's partaking in favoritism. So we keep to a first-name basis when working, but I guess it's become a general habit."

Oliver supposed that made sense. He didn't call Nikki by her first name in front of the new recruits or clients, but that was more of a show of respect. Members of Orion earned the right to be familiar with the head honcho by doing a good job and remaining humble. Nigel having his son call him by his first name might make sense, but Oliver couldn't deny he didn't like the informality of it. If he'd ever called his dad by his name, Jacob Quinn would have been fast to correct him.

"So you work at Charisma?" Oliver asked when it was apparent Jace wasn't leaving the kitchen anytime soon.

He sat down at the island and faced Oliver. "It's the only place I've ever worked," he said with notable pride. "I oversee the company's support specialists and deal directly with the more complicated clients, walking them through every part of the investment process. With this merger going through, however, I'm hoping to make the move up in the ranks. But now, with this…" He looked up at the ceiling and shook his head. "I just hope it all gets taken care of before it does any damage to the company."

Oliver couldn't help the raise of his eyebrow or, he was sure, the look of slight disgust that contorted his face. If Darling had been in the room, she would have flown right off the handle at how crass the millionaire's son was being. She would have pointed out in no uncertain terms that he was referring to a human being who had been murdered and that finding justice for her was much more important.

But Darling wasn't there.

"Hopefully it will be sorted out," Oliver offered.

Jace nodded, oblivious to Oliver's thoughts. "You know, I told Nigel he shouldn't have even come back to Mulligan for the merger. I could have handled it and stayed in the city, but he's getting stubborn in his old age." He frowned, and his brow creased. "If he had listened to me, this whole ordeal could have been avoided. But he loves this place, the small town he came from and the people who love him. I wonder, though, if they'll love him after all of this."

Oliver didn't have an answer to that.

"I should get going now. This merger won't happen by itself." Jace grabbed a water from the refrigerator and started to leave. "In case Nigel didn't tell you or your boss, my mother will be here by the end of the week."

"No, I haven't been told that yet," Oliver said, already cursing in his head.

"This family is all about supporting one another," Jace

said. "You accuse one of us of murder, you accuse all of us of murder." He said it with sarcasm, meant to be an offhand joke, but Oliver saw the irony in it. Jace's parents were, in fact, the top two suspects.

For the next three hours, Oliver did the more boring parts of bodyguard work while his mind kept running. If a thought wasn't about his current client, it was undoubtedly about a petite, sandy-haired woman with more attitude than even she probably knew what to do with. Darling Smith was incapable of ignoring what was wrong in the world. It was an infuriating and endearing quality that he hadn't realized he missed.

He moved through the first floor, scanning his surroundings with tried interest. Oliver liked to memorize each piece as if he hadn't done it the previous day. That way, if something was off—if something had changed—he'd be more likely to notice.

The smaller details often ended up making the most impact.

THE LONGER DARLING stared at the note, the harder she willed it to explain itself.

"Who wrote you?" she asked it for the tenth time. "And why?"

Like the nine times before, the note didn't answer. Instead, it stayed frustratingly still against the top of her desk, its red ink blaring across the surface.

You already did the right thing, Darling. Now stop.

There was no denying the message had been intended for her.

So, Darling had gone back to her car with the hairs on the back of her neck standing at salute, also confused.

She had driven back to Acuity and pulled the newspaper clipping with the first note out to compare the two.

The handwriting and color had matched perfectly.

Whoever wanted Nigel's affair out in the open was not only was watching Darling but also had taken her camera. Why? The cops had seen everything in that room plus more once they had gotten there.

Darling growled to her office.

It felt like a threat.

Had Nigel caught wind of her case against him, or had he figured it out like Oliver had? But then why give her the pictures of Nigel and the red-haired woman, and urge her to turn them in to the police? And why tell her to stop?

Stop what?

Darling cast a long look at her empty coffee cup. It was nearly five, and she had put off calling Derrick for hours. Just as her resolve to disclose everything began to dissolve, her phone chirped to life with the name Liz across the screen.

"You're very hard to get a hold of," Darling greeted her, no humor in her voice.

Elizabeth didn't waste an excuse.

"We both know I'm a suspect in this murder. I'm having to cut my vacation short while recording my recent movements to send over to my lawyer. All under the ever-watchful eye of my mother. Be thankful I was finally able to step away from her."

"Does she not know about your case with me?"

"No. I love my mother, but I don't love her tendency to run her mouth. Give her enough wine and she'll tell you every secret she's ever been told." Elizabeth was tired, that much Darling could tell. She pictured the woman's impeccable posture slightly bent, makeup pulling double duty to hide the stress in her face. "Have you told anyone about our case yet?"

"No, ma'am. I wanted to at least talk to you first." There was a silence, and Darling used it to her advantage. "Did you hire another private investigator to trail Nigel before me or after me?"

"No," Elizabeth responded. "Truthfully, hiring you was a last-minute decision. The less people know about my plans to leave Nigel, the better. That being said, I want you to go to the police and tell them everything."

Darling had to take a beat to process that. "About the case?"

"About the case, the reason why I hired you, what you've found, everything." There was a change in her tone. Elizabeth had moved from tired to determined in a breath. She brooked no argument with her words. "Give them total disclosure. I don't want them looking at me as a suspect. I didn't hire anyone to kill that woman, and I don't want anyone to think I did. I will ask, though, if you think the police could keep my desire for a divorce on the private side of the investigation?"

Darling thought this over. "I can't promise anything, but I think they would. Nigel has denied knowing the woman or even seeing her, so right now, I think they are just trying to figure out who she is. I don't think they would take the time to publicize your marital problems."

"Good. Then, please, could you tell them everything while still trying to keep it from Nigel?"

"Yes, I can do that." Darling wanted to exhale in relief. Elizabeth didn't know it, but if she hadn't called before six, Darling would have told Derrick everything anyway.

"Great. Now, one last thing," Elizabeth said before her

voice dropped to almost a whisper. "I don't care how you do it, but I want you to find out who that woman is. My husband may be a cheat, but he's no killer. Something isn't right, and now my family is suffering for it. I will not stand for that."

Darling didn't doubt for a second that anyone who crossed Elizabeth Marks would regret it. She just hoped Jane Doe hadn't been one of those people.

Darling accepted the job, though she didn't tell Elizabeth she had already decided to pursue the woman's identity. She marveled at how straightforward Elizabeth had been. It was refreshing in a way. She wasn't sugarcoating anything, and she wasn't trying to get Darling to lie about their involvement. No, she knew she was in a compromising position and was trying to get out of it. Full disclosure to the police. That hadn't been what Darling had expected, but she was happy to comply. Grabbing her coat and cell phone, she began dialing Derrick's number as she closed up Acuity for the night.

The sun was setting, leaving a light glow hanging around the parking lot. It was serene and almost calming. A feeling Darling tried to hold on to as she approached her car and saw the door was cracked open. On the driver's seat was a paper bag.

In it was her camera.

Chapter Eight

Darling's body went on high alert. She turned her head from side to side, scanning the parking lot for her mystery figure. Her hair slapped her cheeks at the movement, and a chill found its way into her bones.

She was alone.

"Hello?"

Darling was so startled she nearly threw her phone. She had forgotten she had called the deputy.

"Hey," she exclaimed into the phone. Her nerves pushed her voice into a high octave. She tried to tamp down her fear. "We need to talk again." She checked the back for any unwanted passengers, then climbed into the driver's seat. Her grip on the phone had gone tight, as if talking to a police officer made her instantly safe. She knew this was not the case.

Derrick said some not-so-nice words before answering.

"More evidence, I'm guessing."

"Something like that," she hedged. "I'm coming to the station now."

"Unless you know for certain the identity of either the deceased or her killer, can we meet at Carter's? I'm just now going off duty and haven't had a lick of food since this morning."

At the mention of food, Darling's stomach let out a loud growl.

"That actually sounds good, but you think you could pick me up from my place? I'd like to change. It's getting cold." Even as she asked, Darling started her car and backed out of her spot. What had been a cute outfit that morning was now feeling like a poor choice. April in Maine might have warmer days, but its nights could get nasty quickly. It helped that her apartment was midway between the station and Carter's. The return trip would also have them passing by her place on the way to his work.

Plus, she was hoping he'd be chatty when boxed inside a car.

Derrick agreed, and within fifteen minutes Darling was dressed in a long-sleeved royal blue sweater and a heavier coat. Her ankle boots were swapped out with a pair of black boots that laced up her shins, keeping her calves warm. She didn't bother with refreshing her makeup or checking her hair. Impressing Derrick was nowhere on her list of things to do.

Darling lived in a large house built in the 1900s that had since been converted into four apartments. Hers was apartment number three and tucked away on the left side of the second floor. In her years of living in Mulligan, she had found she loved the two-bedroom, one-bathroom dwelling. She jogged down the community stairs and wondered if Oliver would like her home.

It amazed her how complicated life could become within two days.

"Whatever you're about to say or ask, I'd like you to hit your pause button until we've sat down and at least have drinks in front of us," Derrick said when Darling had situated herself in his Jeep. So much for Chatty Cathy. "A man can only take so much on an empty stomach."

OLIVER PULLED ON his beer, looked around Carter's Bar and Grill, and wondered what it was like to live in Mulligan. It was such a small town compared with most places he had visited through the years. A giant leap different compared with Dallas, especially. The fact that Darling had settled in Mulligan made him question the town even more. Was it that great a place, or had Darling's need to distance herself from her old life driven her to settle for the exact opposite?

Now off the clock, Oliver took his time finishing his beer. The noise level in the restaurant had risen considerably. He turned to survey the new crowd. Should he get a table or stay at the bar?

"Evening, Deputy," he heard one of the waitresses call. He cast a quick glance toward the door and was surprised to see Deputy Derrick holding the door open for none other than Mulligan's private investigator. The couple didn't see him as they were seated.

Couple.

Darling had already told him—of her own accord—that she and the deputy were no longer an item. Either way, it wasn't Oliver's business. He had been in town for only two days and had spent no more than an hour or two with her during that time. Feeling a connection that wasn't there was a distraction he didn't need and one he was sure Darling didn't want.

When he'd left home—and Darling—eight years ago, he had been firm in his decision. What Darling didn't know wouldn't hurt her…at least, he had hoped it wouldn't, not forever. He had watched the younger Darling change into an independent, clever young woman within the year they had spent together. She'd had so much potential at such a young age. He had never doubted her future would be bright. His, however, had always been in question. When he left Darling behind, he hadn't ever planned on returning to her.

He laughed to himself.

Now he was in Maine, sitting a few feet away from the same woman and her ex, the deputy.

In a way, Oliver was glad she had dated Derrick. He hoped that, even though it hadn't lasted, she had been happy. He hoped she had opened up to Derrick—or to some other man—letting him in to her carefully guarded world. Because even though he had purposely broken her heart, Oliver had hoped it would one day mend.

He watched as Derrick pulled out her chair, and the two settled into their seats. Darling had changed clothes but kept her yellow daisy earrings in. She had always loved daisies.

"Want another?" the bartender asked, pulling Oliver's attention away. He was thankful for it. He needed to give Darling and her life the privacy they deserved.

"Yeah. Can I also get a menu?"

The bartender tossed a laminated menu over and slid him a replacement beer.

"Our steak dinner is a favorite," he said, pointing out the item listed under Entrees before going to tend another patron. Oliver didn't keep looking. George had said the same. If a Mainer praised it, then that had to mean it was good, right?

"It's a lie."

Oliver sloshed his beer in surprise at the new voice to his left.

Darling was amused.

"A lie?" he questioned, regaining his composure.

Darling took the menu from his hands and set it on the bar. "The steak dinner is good but not amazing," she continued. "You'd be disappointed."

"Your friend George the Gate Guard would beg to differ."

Darling snorted. "Well, George is a liar. Didn't we already establish that yesterday?"

It was Oliver's turn to laugh. "We didn't, actually."

Darling waved her hand through the air as if to shoo off such trivial thoughts.

The bartender made his way back over, but before Oliver could put a word in edgewise, Darling had caught his attention.

"Hey, Benny, Oliver here will take one of your fantastic lobster rolls," she said. "And can you send it over to our table?" She pointed back to where Derrick was seated, talking on his phone. Bartender Benny nodded.

"Well, looks like I'm eating some lobster, then. And not alone."

"You can't just come to Maine and not have one of its best dishes. Plus, if I remember correctly, you're a fan of fresh seafood." Oliver nodded, conceding that. "And as for the whole eating-alone thing, that's just sad." There was a teasing tone in her voice, but when she spoke again the humor was gone. "I need to tell Derrick something about the case. I have a feeling I'll cross your client's path again before this is all over. I'd rather keep you in the loop." She held up her hand to silence any questions Oliver was about to ask. "But first, I also *really* need a drink."

Chapter Nine

Derrick greeted Oliver with a nod that picked up enthusiasm only when he saw the beer Oliver had gotten for him. The past two days had been long for Darling, but she knew they were nothing compared to what Derrick was having to deal with.

"I hope you don't mind dining with an out-of-towner," Oliver said. He took the outside seat next to Darling. It wasn't a long booth, and their thighs touched as he got settled.

"Listen, as long you don't go on a killing rampage before we get our food, I'll be fine."

"I'll see what I can do," Oliver responded.

Derrick had stayed true to his plea to keep shoptalk out of the picture until he at least had a drink. He and Darling had done almost no talking on the ride over to Carter's. Then she'd seen Oliver sitting alone at the bar after they were seated. The act of including him had been impulsive.

Why? she wondered.

She waited as each got his fill of his respective drink. Darling found that her lips wanted to remain shut, also, until her drink arrived.

"So, how are you enjoying Mulligan so far?" Derrick asked.

"Well, aside from the Marks residence, I've only had the pleasure of visiting a few places." He tipped his beer toward Derrick. "The police station was my favorite, by the way. I'm a sucker for being colder inside a building than I am outside it." Derrick let out a laugh. It seemed genuine. "But Mulligan has its charms. I don't know if I'd be singing the same tune year-round once the snow comes in, but for now I can see the appeal."

"The appeal. You've traveled around the world and you think Mulligan is appealing?" The deputy held up his beer. "That's mighty generous of you." They clinked their bottles together, and Darling rolled her eyes.

She listened to them talk a bit longer before her drink arrived. She had readjusted her attention to the small glass between her hands.

"Is that milk?" Oliver asked, peering at the cream-colored drink.

"This, my friend, is another part of Maine you should partake in." She took a long sip. The creamy goodness of Allen's Coffee Flavored Brandy mixed with milk created one of Darling's favorite after-hours drinks.

"It's cheap and delicious," Derrick supplied. "This one here can only take so much before she turns into a puddle of giggles."

"A puddle of giggles?" Darling said. "Is that even a thing?"

"I think I get what he means," Oliver defended the deputy. He turned his attention to Derrick. "Right before her eighteenth birthday, Darling got ahold of the key to her father's liquor cabinet and called me after she did a few taste testings. She laughed for almost the entire conversation. I caught maybe one or two words the whole time."

The two men laughed, and even Darling found herself smiling. In the time that she had met and fallen for Oliver, a lot of bad had happened in her life. However, when she was able to step back from her pity party, she could remember the good times, too.

"Okay, so I may turn into 'a puddle of giggles' when I drink a little too much, but at least I don't cry or yell!" As if they had planned it, the two men shrugged. "But, just in case, I think I better go ahead and talk shop." Darling took a large gulp of her drink and dove in.

"Elizabeth Marks hired me last week to get proof— pictures—of Nigel with another woman while he stayed in Mulligan. She believes he's been having an affair for quite a while." None of this information fazed either man, so she continued right along. "She planned her trip to the Bahamas with her mother for the duration of his stay because she thought the fact that there was no way she could accidentally catch him might entice him to philander."

"That's a different spin on reverse psychology if I ever did hear one," Oliver observed.

"The Markses have a prenup that—in the foolish throes of young love—Elizabeth signed without question. If she divorces him now, she forfeits money she thinks she deserves, including the funds she actually made herself."

"But if he cheats and she can prove it…" Oliver started.

"Then that prenup is void, and she's free to take, at minimum, half of everything he owns," Darling finished.

Derrick leaned forward. "Which gives her one hell of a motive to hurt both her husband and his mistress. This is the kind of thing you tell the police who are investigating a murder," the deputy bit out.

"We both know you already checked her alibi, and it's as clean as Nigel's. I knew from the start where she was and that she couldn't physically do it."

"Did you see her in the Bahamas?" Derrick pushed her. "Do you know for a fact that she actually went?"

Darling sighed. "Derrick, I had Dan keep an eye out at the hotel just in case Nigel stopped by, and that's exactly what happened. Nigel spent the night with Jane Doe. Dan saw him. We both know that now Nigel's lying about even being there. We also both know that Elizabeth Marks was checked in to her resort at the time of Jane Doe's death."

"Then why are you telling me this now? Why not keep it to yourself if you think it's not a big deal?" Darling knew Derrick was angry with her for withholding information. She didn't blame him for it, either. If she had been a cop, she would have been angry, too.

"Elizabeth wanted me to disclose everything to you because she realizes she's a top suspect. She wants me to tell you everything we've talked about and everything I've found," Darling explained.

"Just like that?" Oliver asked, clearly impressed.

"Just like that. Sure, she wants discretion—if Nigel finds out she's wanting to divorce him, he could do it first and leave her with nothing—but she isn't stupid. Hiring a private eye to follow your cheating husband and then running off to the Bahamas for an airtight alibi? Yeah, she's smart enough to know how that looks."

The men thought that over, and Darling used the silence to take a few more sips of her drink.

"Have you had any luck with figuring out who Jane

Doe is?" she ventured when they appeared too involved in their own drinks. "Any new leads?"

The deputy rested his bottle on the table. He began to thumb the label off as he answered. He seemed to be considering each word he spoke.

"We have hit a few…snags."

"Snags?" Darling and Oliver asked in unison.

"We're still searching several avenues in an attempt to identify her, but as of right now, we're no further than we were when you found her." Derrick wasn't much for sighing, but his body sagged with the weight of frustration. "As far as we can tell, no one has reported her missing. We've sent her picture and description out to other departments to see if anything catches, but so far it's been one dead end after another. We even checked with cab companies and car rental agencies since we still can't locate the car she went to the hotel in. If we don't find something soon, we'll have to take this to the media."

Darling shifted in her seat, as if she could move away from the bad information.

"Has anyone reported on the death yet?" Oliver asked. It was a question that Darling hadn't answered, either. Meaning to buy a newspaper wasn't the same as actually buying one.

Derrick shook his head and pulled a long strip of the beer label off. "Nigel's name might be in the clear because of his alibi, but word has already started to spread that he was possibly at the hotel with Jane Doe. Covering a story, even without his name directly in it, is still getting too close to insulting Mulligan's golden child," he said. "I don't expect that to last much longer, though. The chief has a meeting with a local reporter first thing tomorrow morning." He shot a look at Darling. "Rebel Nash."

Darling let out a whistle. Rebel Nash was a Mulligan transplant who was the embodiment of unwavering determination and absolute stubbornness. If anyone was going to break the story *with* Nigel's name in it, Rebel would be the one to do it.

"From the little I know about her," Darling explained to the out-of-towner Oliver, "Rebel values the truth more than the consequences of losing Mulligan's hero. Which, I have to say, I like about her right now."

Oliver smiled. "Just what everyone needs, another you in a different profession."

Derrick laughed and Darling picked up her glass. "I'm going to take that as a compliment, thank you."

"I knew you would," Oliver replied with a smirk.

The food arrived shortly after, and their conversation all but died. Well, the one in which Darling was included. Derrick and Oliver went back and forth, sharing their war stories about law enforcement and personal protection before switching gears to sports. Darling watched her exes with interest as she sipped away her drink.

When Derrick was tense, it was hard for him to ease up. Finding the humor in a case, if only for a brief stretch, was a task in itself. Darling knew that emotionally, it was hard for him to get out of his head long enough to enjoy his surroundings.

Oliver, on the other hand, knew when to laugh and did it with no issues. He was lighthearted but could slip into a more serious tone when needed. She watched as he laughed and slowly began to remember all of the sweet moments they'd had together. Sure, age had changed Oliver—he was more confident and there was no denying he had more muscles beneath his shirt—but Darling still could see the boy she'd once loved.

Darling let out a laugh at the thought. Both men paused their conversation but didn't comment. She ordered another drink and thought back on the case.

"What about the ledger?" she asked suddenly. She'd interrupted the men, but Derrick knew what she was talking about.

"We didn't think about looking until this morning," he said with obvious disapproval. Whether it was of himself or the other deputies, she didn't know. "When we went back, someone had torn out the last three pages. We grabbed it for prints, but nothing so far."

Darling brought up the pictures on her phone and slid it over to Derrick. "I took these yesterday, after I found the body." Derrick's eyes went wide. "I swear I would already have given it to you had I remembered," she hurried on. "But with everything that has happened, it slipped my mind." The real reason being the mysterious letters. It had knocked her off her game, along with the amber-eyed man sitting next to her.

"You took a picture of the check-ins from the night Jane Doe checked in?" Derrick wanted clarification, but with his free hand he was already waving over the waitress.

"Yes. I wanted to use it as evidence against Nigel that he was having an affair. At the time, I didn't realize Jane Doe would stay a Jane Doe."

"Check, please," Derrick called to the waitress. "And you haven't searched these names yet?"

Darling shook her head. "I didn't even think about them until just now."

"Send me this picture. I'm going to go back to the station and run them."

Darling took her phone and did as the deputy said.

"I'll take care of the food," Oliver chimed in. "You go ahead and get outta here."

Derrick might have reconsidered had he not been given a new lead, but instead he just left.

"Looks like my snooping comes in handy sometimes, huh?" Darling said after she'd sent the picture. Oliver laughed and gave the waitress his card when she came back. "You don't have to pay for me," Darling added.

"Consider it a reward for your snooping."

"I'll finish my drink to that."

And she did just that.

Oliver not only paid for dinner but also extended his gallantry to offering Darling a ride home. They settled into his rental, each pushing through the cold of outside, before Oliver started the engine and its heater.

"I have to say, Mulligan keeps on surprising me," Oliver said.

"Do you mean Mulligan or its murder mystery?"

"Both," he admitted.

"I still can't believe that no one can tell us who Jane Doe is," Darling dove in. Her lips were a little loose and her body was a little warm, and not from the heater.

"Yeah, you would have thought that the cops would have found a witness by now. Even someone who had seen her at least driving through town." Oliver clapped his hands together. It made Darling jump. "On the way in from the airport, I only passed one gas station," he said, eyes bright. "I'm assuming that on the other side of town there's a gas station leading into Mulligan?"

Darling thought for a moment, then nodded.

"So there's a chance she might have stopped at either one of these gas stations, depending on which direction she was coming in from? We even checked with cab companies and car rental agencies since we still can't locate the car she went to the hotel in."

"That's a slim chance, but yes."

"Why don't we go check it out, then?" He started the car, suddenly energized. "A slight chance is better than anything you have right now."

He was right about that. Even if Derrick was able to identify her, getting video of Jane Doe could make all the difference in the case.

"Okay, so let's assume she did drive in but not from the city side."

"Why not?" Oliver asked. He had his hand on the gearshift, ready for direction.

"If she was already in the city, why would Nigel *and* Jane Doe drive out here to Mulligan to meet? I'm sure there are plenty of places they could have done it there," she reasoned.

That was all Oliver needed. He backed out of his parking spot.

Once again, they were a team.

Chapter Ten

The clock read nine fifteen when Oliver cut the engine in the parking lot of Zippy's Pump & Pour. Its two pumps were positioned in what they hoped was the front security camera's range.

"Okay, that's Connor-something," Darling said, pointing through the windshield to the clerk inside.

"Looks young. How do you know him?"

"Just from getting my gas here on occasion." She gave him a quick wink that made him wonder if she was feeling her two drinks yet. "They're the only place in town that carries the candy bars I really like."

"Do you think he'll let us see the security footage?"

Darling bit her lip as she thought. Oliver couldn't deny it stirred up some feeling within him. He readjusted in his seat.

"Maybe," she answered. "I don't know enough about him to make that call yet. We're going to have to find out."

Oliver nodded and they entered the station. It was small, and Connor was undeniably bored. When they walked to the counter, he stood from his stool and smiled.

"Hey, hey," he greeted them. His eyes slid over them, stalling on Darling. "Whoa! You're the private eye."

Darling's cheeks tinted red, but Oliver didn't know if that was another aftereffect of brandy or surprise at Connor's obvious admiration.

"Private investigator, but yes," she said with a smile. "That's me."

"Awesome! I was telling my buddy the other day I wouldn't mind doing what you do," Connor said, excitement only mounting. "You wouldn't happen to be hiring right now, would you?" He lowered his voice and leaned closer. Oliver and Darling leaned in, too. "Because working here kind of sucks."

Oliver couldn't help but chuckle.

"We aren't actually hiring at the moment," Darling said. Connor looked supremely disappointed. "But you might be able to help us now if you're not too busy."

Connor's disappointment was short-lived. He smiled, and it was downright mischievous.

"I'll do anything you want!"

Darling cut a quick smile to Oliver. "Well, great!"

Oliver wondered how the private investigator was going to approach the topic at hand. If he was a betting man he would have put his money on the honeypotting approach. Being sweet to lower the boy's defenses, getting information with a nice tone and even nicer words. Or would she try to trick him into giving up what they needed to know? He leaned against the counter and watched with interest.

"Were you working here two nights ago, by chance?" Darling asked.

"Oh, yeah, I've worked night shift for the last week and a half." Connor lowered his voice. "My boss is out of town 'on business,' but I think that's a load of crap." He made finger quotes to show what he must have thought was a lie.

The private investigator took a beat before responding, no doubt noting the employee had some obvious disdain for his employer. "That's gotta be a drag." She let her body droop a bit as she said it. Oliver realized it was because she wanted Connor to feel as if they were on the same page as him. It was an approach somewhere between honey-potting and straightforward. She wanted to be relatable.

"I told him I'll quit if he keeps me closing every single night. I mean, I can do it once and a while, but I have a life, you know?" Oliver nodded in unison with Darling. A different thrill than the one he'd felt in the car filled him as he realized they were in secret cahoots, working together toward the same goal without any friction from their past breaking in. He wondered if she felt it, too. They had always made a good team.

"I don't blame you," he said to show his empathy further. Conner nodded again, giving them both a look that clearly said he liked them. Darling must have realized it, too. She straightened slightly. She was going in for the kill.

"Well, the thing is, two nights ago, a woman might have stopped here." She paused and pulled out her phone. She scrolled to one of the pictures she'd been given of Jane Doe and Nigel. "This woman. Do you remember her, by chance?"

Connor squinted at the phone's screen for a few seconds before snapping his fingers.

"The redhead, yeah! She was here." Oliver and Darling shared a look. They had gotten supremely lucky. "She didn't come in, but I remember her getting gas."

He winked at Darling. "I don't forget a pretty face, especially a new one in town."

"Do you remember if anyone was with her? In the car?"

"No, she was alone," he answered, brow wrinkled as he thought. "Why? Is she in some kind of trouble? Is she a criminal?"

Darling raised her hands and laughed. "No, no, she's—" Oliver could tell she was looking for the right thing to say.

"We're worried about her, is all," he interjected. "She came to town for a visit but hasn't checked in for a few days, and we thought she might have stopped by here."

"She isn't from around here, so we're really worried," Darling added. "You said she didn't come in, but that camera outside would have seen her, right?"

Connor was emphatic as he answered. "Oh yeah! You two want to see it? We still have tapes from a week ago." He lowered his voice again. "I may have fallen behind on changing them out, but, hey, it's not like I get paid out the yin yang to keep up with it all." Oliver raised his eyebrow at Darling as Connor ushered the two of them to the back room. Oliver couldn't tell if he was being so lax with security because he seemed to dislike his current boss or if he was trying to show off for the woman he wanted to be his new boss. Either way, after throwing around several VHS tapes, the clerk popped in the right one and hit Play.

"You can fast-forward as much as you want," he said as a ding sounded from the front door. "There's no sound—the boss is too cheap, ya know—but everything else works okay. I'll be back!"

"We seriously lucked out that the boss isn't around,"

Darling whispered, already hitting the fast-forward button. She kept her eye on the time stamp in the corner of the screen. "I think we also lucked out that our Jane Doe stopped here.

"Good call, by the way. I hadn't even thought about the possibility of her coming here." Darling turned to give him a quick smile. It made his breath hitch for a split second. When they were younger, sometimes Darling would look at him and the world around him would slow. A candid moment from the woman that reminded him how beautiful she was in every way. It caught him off guard as he realized that all the time that had passed hadn't changed that feeling.

Her lips turned up, her cheeks rosy, her eyes unrelenting as they searched for the truth. Darling Smith was determined, and Oliver knew nothing would get in her way.

"Just trying to get the town PI on my side," he ribbed her.

She turned her attention back to the television monitor with a laugh.

They quieted as the footage's time ticked by, leaned in and focused. The footage wasn't in color and, at best, only a step up from unrecognizably grainy.

Oliver pointed to the pump farthest from the security camera. Partially hidden by the pumps was a young woman exiting the driver's side of a car. She disappeared behind the pump before reappearing to put the nozzle in her gas tank. Her hair was shoulder-length and wavy. Wearing dark pants and a light button-up blouse, she rubbed her hands together before walking to the trash can between her car and a van closer to the building. An older woman stood against it as she waited for her vehicle to fill up.

"Is that her?" Oliver asked, still uncertain. Darling's eyebrows drew together, her eyes squinting at the screen.

The woman in question was all smiles as she caught the older woman's eye. Her mouth began to move, but without sound, they couldn't hope to decipher what the two were saying.

"Yes," Darling answered. "That's our Jane Doe. Her smile is identical to the one in the pictures. Working on the assumption that the woman in those pictures *is* our Jane Doe. Which is what I'm doing."

Oliver continued to watch as Jane Doe held a conversation with the older woman at the neighboring pump. There was no denying she was happy about something, almost bouncing as she talked. The conversation didn't last long. Both women finished their pumping and paused to say goodbye to each other before getting back into their respective vehicles. Jane Doe drove off first. Darling paused the tape as soon as the car was out of view.

Oliver kept silent as she rewound the tape and they watched it for a second time. The van at the next pump and the angle of the security camera made the scene difficult to decipher. Only the driver's side door and seat, and the back end of the car where the gas tank was could be seen around the van and pump. The color of Jane Doe's car was dark, but aside from that, the black-and-white footage didn't give anything away.

"It's clearly a four-door, and a smaller one at that. I'd say it's an older model, too." He scooted closer as if that could help him figure out what the model was. The new proximity didn't help. "I'm not a car guy, so I can't make this call. Pause it as she drives off."

Darling did as he said, but the picture was blurred.

"They may have a security camera, but it sure isn't that high-tech," she muttered.

"The boss is a lot of things, including cheap," Connor said from the doorway. Darling jumped.

"Sorry, we just need to figure out what kind of car this is." She put her finger up to the blurred spot that was Jane Doe's car. If Zippy's had had a camera at the pumps, they would have been able to see the make and the license plate. But that wasn't the case.

"Ew, yeah, sorry about that." He, too, squinted at the footage, as if that could suddenly make it clearer. "The farther away from the camera you are, the worse it comes across on the tapes."

"Do you remember anything about the car she was in?" Oliver asked.

The question turned Connor's cheeks red. "No," he said with the shake of the head. "I wasn't really focusing on anything else after I saw her." There were no perverted or salacious undertones in his statement, just honest appreciation for the woman's beauty. It earned a sincere smile from the private investigator.

"Connor, would you mind if we borrowed this?" she asked. "I'd like to take a closer look at it."

The clerk shrugged but nodded. "You can keep it for all I care," he said. "The boss man doesn't ever look at them unless we've been robbed."

"Great! Well, if he does happen to find out and isn't happy about it, tell him to give me a call. I'll set him straight."

"Yes, ma'am."

"This was surprisingly productive," Darling said when they were back in the car.

Oliver gave her a questioning look at her new level of excitement. He was betting she was definitely tipsy.

"Because we know where she was the night before she was killed?" he asked.

Darling laughed. "No," she exclaimed with a grin. "Because for the first time, we have a witness who talked to Jane Doe."

THREE OF THE FOUR names from the hotel ledger checked out. Derrick guessed the fourth was a fake. Darling could hear the stress in his voice as he said he would be tracking down the other three people to see if they saw anything at the time of check-in. Even though he was sure he had already questioned each the day the body was found. Darling had been hesitant to give their new information over to the deputy, but Oliver had urged her on. Plus, she supposed she owed it to the main investigator on the case.

"And you're sure it's her?" Derrick asked.

"Yes, but we can't figure out the make of her car," she said. "But, if you let me, I can track down the woman she spoke to and ask her tomorrow if she saw anything…"

She waited for the backlash from suggesting she help in the murder investigation, but it never came. With an exhalation so loud that Oliver chuckled in the seat next to her, Derrick relented.

"I'm only saying yes because we're swamped…and I know how crafty you can get." Darling smiled at the windshield. Being called crafty was a much nicer descriptor than what private investigators were usually given. "Call me if you get something, and try not to do anything illegal."

"He acts like I do illegal things all the time," Darling said once the call was over. Oliver raised his eyebrow.

They were still seated in his rental, parked at the curb outside her apartment. "I don't, I should add."

"Of course not." A wisp of a smile trailed across his lips, suddenly bringing her attention to his mouth. His lips were thick, yet entirely masculine. And, when pressed against hers, made the world feel whole. Darling cleared her throat and reached for the door handle at the thought. Fantasizing about the bodyguard in any way was dangerous. Considering there was a murderer on the loose, there was enough danger for all of them without reigniting old feelings. A monumental distraction that could cause either one of them to slip up at their jobs.

"Well, I guess I should turn in for the night," she said, hoping her heated cheeks weren't visible in the darkness of the SUV. "I have a feeling tomorrow's going to be a long day."

Oliver nodded and started to get out, too.

More heat ran up her neck. Did Oliver want to come up to her apartment? There wasn't much they could do other than watch television, talk or get *reacquainted*. However, Oliver didn't seem to care about any of that.

"I'm going to walk you to your door, if you don't mind," he said, coming around to her side. "Mulligan is a little too surprising for my liking at the moment."

"And it's appealing, too, right?" she teased.

He cast her a sideways look as they walked up the sidewalk and to the front door. "It has its perks."

If she hadn't been blushing already, she would have blushed then. Or maybe it wasn't a blush at all. Maybe it was the alcohol. Either way, she led him into the foyer and up the stairs to the left. When they stopped in front of her door, she turned with every intention in the world to say good-night, but he had stopped much closer to her than she had realized. Having to tilt her head up to meet his eyes, Darling's thoughts scrambled.

The world became quiet. It didn't make a peep as she held Oliver's gaze. She imagined the feel of his lips against hers—soft yet rough, full of desire and passion—and almost rocked up onto the pads of her feet to close the space between them. The rest of her body tingled in anticipation of such a bold move.

The bodyguard had been in town for two whole days. Almost a decade spanned between now and their past. Even though they had gotten to catch up on the major life changes they had gone through, they were still swimming in a sea of unknowns.

Yet at the same time, Darling felt as if they had picked up right where their old lives had ended. Fitting together without resistance like two pieces in a large, complicated puzzle. Could it be that easy? And if it was, did that mean they *should*?

Darling felt weight settle in her feet, declaring they weren't going to support her pushing up to make an impulsive decision. It was time to break the news to her brain that kissing Oliver—although almost every part of her wanted to—wasn't going to happen.

"Thanks for coming with me tonight," she said, almost whispering. She took a step backward and grabbed the doorknob. "I should probably get some sleep now." She unlocked the door and opened it wide, breaking eye contact for a moment so she could cool slightly. "Thank you for dinner, too. Next time is on me."

Oliver blinked a few times before simply nodding. He didn't hesitate as he turned and headed for the stairs.

"Let me know if you need anything," he called over his shoulder. But he didn't stop, and he certainly didn't turn around.

Chapter Eleven

Harriet Mendon lived in a tiny yellow cottage surrounded by one hundred or so other tiny, brightly colored cottages. Darling parked at the curb and waved to a mother and her young girl who were walking past. They smiled and waved back, their minds already returning to the beautiful day.

Darling wished she could follow suit. Not have to worry about talking to a stranger about another stranger who had been murdered. She could—get back into her car, drive to the coast and relax next to the water—but she was too invested in Jane Doe's case to stop now. Finding her body had somehow given Darling a sense of protectiveness over the case, deeply investing her into the pursuit of truth in what had happened. Sure, getting into the car and leaving would have been easy, but it wasn't an option her heart could reason was good.

The cottage's front door was baby blue and sounded thin as Darling rapped her knuckles against it. After taking the security tape from Zippy's to Acuity—and watching it a few more times—Darling had plugged Jane Doe's pump mate's license plate number into her computer. Using a private investigator database she paid for monthly—a tool that often came in handy when searching for a name—Harriet Mendon had been the result. In a town as small as Mulligan, it wasn't hard to find her address thanks to a stack of old telephone books Darling's former boss had left behind. Now, waiting for Harriet to open the door, Darling wondered if she should come up with an alternate story for how she'd tracked the woman down. One that sounded less calculating.

As far as broaching the topic of Jane Doe, Darling wasn't going to dance around the reason for her visit. She was going to ask Harriet to tell her about her conversation with the young woman and hope it was enough to identify her. Or damn her killer.

However, Harriet didn't come to the door. Darling knocked again and listened for any noise from inside the house. It remained quiet.

"Great," she muttered. She took out one of her cards and quickly wrote a note across the back before placing it into the jamb next to the doorknob. Hopefully Harriet Mendon's interest would be piqued enough to call.

Darling drove back to Acuity with her mind somewhere else entirely. The day might been beautiful, but the temperature was already dropping. She wondered how Oliver was faring with the chill but then decided it wasn't safe to think about the man. Thinking of him in any capacity—no matter how innocent—pushed thoughts of his lips and their almost-kiss right between her eyes. Would it be a familiar feeling or some new sensation since the last time their lips had touched? Her parents would get a kick out of how, after everything they had said and tried, Oliver Quinn had found his way back into their daughter's life after all.

The thought of her parents brought on another set

of memories she needed to stay away from, but it also helped her trail back to what was important.

Jane Doe had tangoed with the wealthy, too.

She just hadn't survived the dance.

Darling recalled her silent laugh and jovial attitude when talking to Harriet at the gas station. "I need to find you, Harriet," she said aloud. "I will find you."

A handful of cars were parked in the lot behind Acuity, all of which Darling recognized as belonging to the strip mall's tenants. Still, she kept alert. It was best to not forget about her mystery note writer and the fact he or she had been watching her. With caution, Darling swept her eyes all around her as she went to Acuity's door. Her mind dropped to the next task on her mental list. She wasn't the most patient person. Waiting for Harriet to see her calling card was beyond Darling's current capabilities. She was going to have to find her at work and go from there.

All she needed was to search a little longer on the internet until—

"Whoa."

Acuity's front door was cracked open, the top window pane broken out. Through the hole, Darling could see shards of glass littering the lobby floor. Her hand went to the doorknob on reflex, but fear caught up to her. What if the culprit was still inside? She pictured Jane Doe wrapped up in the tub.

Maybe she needed to call in some backup.

NIGEL WAS ACTING STRANGE. There was no doubt about it.

"Are you okay?" Oliver asked when the businessman came down from his office. He was visibly shaken. Eyes too wide. Face taut. Oliver glanced up the stairs where he knew Thomas stood guard next to the office door. Grant wasn't on the clock for another few hours. Oliver had rotated between perimeter checks and standing guard at the two entrances to the house's main floor. He'd looked out at the gatehouse each time he made an outdoor pass but kept his distance from it. He appreciated the loyalty George had for his job, but he didn't want to get caught up in a conversation with the man. Aside from the three bodyguards and their client, Oliver knew they were alone. The lawyer and Jace were at the new Charisma branch's office. Which was why his concern was so acute. There was no reason Nigel should look as off-kilter as he did.

Nigel blinked several times, clearing his throat when the words still didn't come.

"Yes. I just got off of the phone with Deputy Arrington." His voice wavered as he answered. It put Oliver on even higher alert. Why would Derrick call Nigel if Nigel alibied out? What was the point? "He told me how the young woman was killed. I don't think he believes I had nothing to do with her death." He gave Oliver a weak smile and went to the refrigerator. Unlike his son, instead of a water, he went for a beer. "I didn't kill her, but that doesn't mean I don't feel sympathy for her..." He dropped eye contact for an instant. "Bludgeoned to death with a hammer seems barbaric."

"A hammer?" It was the first Oliver had heard about it.

"Yes."

"Seems cowardly."

Nigel gave Oliver a look that questioned him and agreed simultaneously. The older man wanted to say something—Oliver could feel it—but he didn't. Instead he nodded and made his trek back up the stairs.

A few minutes went by before Oliver decided to check

in on their client. Thomas was standing in the hallway next to the door. When he saw Oliver, he shook his head.

"What?"

Thomas lowered his voice to a whisper. "I don't know what you said to him down there, but he's really upset." Oliver raised his eyebrow and the younger bodyguard shrugged. "I heard a weird noise and looked in and he was crying."

"Crying?"

Thomas nodded. "He stopped when he got a call but, man, I hope he doesn't do it again. I wasn't trained to handle all of that."

Oliver didn't know what to say to that, so he left the bodyguard to go back downstairs. He didn't know if he should feel sympathy for the man. Had he been crying for the loss of Jane Doe? The woman he claimed to not know?

His phone started to vibrate in his pocket. When he saw it was Darling, he knew she'd find the information interesting.

"Quinn," he answered.

"Oliver, can you come to the office right now?" she asked in a rush.

"Why? What's wrong?"

There was worry in her voice. "I—well—the thing is…" She sucked in a deep breath before another gushed out with her words. "I think someone broke in to Acuity and might still be here but I don't want to call the cops just yet."

"Wait, where are you now? You aren't *in* there, are you?" He could imagine the spunky private investigator hiding in the office bathroom as the culprit went through her things a few feet away.

"Of course I'm not in there! I'm sitting in my car, watching the door from the parking lot," she defended herself. "If they are still inside and decide to leave, I'm going to catch them on film." Again, it wasn't hard to imagine Darling sitting in her car, looking through the lens of her camera at her office.

"You need to call the police, Darling. This isn't some kind of game." As he said it, he was walking upstairs to Grant's temporary room.

"I know it isn't a game, but the police have a lot on their plates already. I'm not going to call them until I've personally assessed the damage. If you can't come, though, I'll wait a few more minutes before going in myself." Every word held a stubborn edge.

"No. Don't go in." He knocked on Grant's door. "I'm headed that way now."

If Grant minded stepping in for Oliver while he "attended to a personal matter," he didn't show it. Oliver didn't like up and leaving during his shift, but he took solace in the fact that Nigel planned on working from home for the rest of the day. Just in case, though, he paused at the gatehouse as he was leaving.

George took his time coming out. He looked ruffled, as if he had been caught napping. Oliver didn't have time to admonish the guard for sleeping on the job. Not when he was leaving in the middle of his own shift.

"Hey, George, I'm running out for a bit," Oliver said. "Until I get back, call Thomas if anyone shows up here. Okay?"

George nodded, and Oliver left before the man could get a conversation going. He had a private investigator to worry about.

Minutes later, he pulled into the strip mall's parking

lot, next to Darling's car. He was relieved to see her face bob into view when he walked up. True to form, her camera was in her hands.

"No one has come out," she said in lieu of a hello. "I didn't hear anything when I first was at the door, either. I just wanted to be on the safe side."

"Caution isn't a bad thing," he pointed out. "You stay here and let me go check it out. If you hear anything, take off and call the cops." He could see an internal battle wage across her face. Why had she called if she was going to argue about him going inside without her? She must have been really nervous.

"Okay," she agreed after a moment.

Oliver adjusted his shirt to keep his gun covered as he walked to Acuity's entrance. He didn't often carry it—Orion's bodyguards used nonlethal weapons as much as they could—but it was never too far away from him, either. If someone had broken into Darling's office—in his opinion—that showed malicious intent for her. Oliver wasn't about to go easy on someone who had shown that level of disregard for the investigator. Especially when she was in the parking lot, yards away.

The door was cracked open. Whoever had broken the glass had snaked a hand through the window to unlock the door. He wondered if anyone else in the strip mall had heard the break. Pulling his gun out, he quietly pushed the door open enough to get a good look at the lobby. No one was inside. He moved into the room, gun raised and ready. Whoever had broken in was either being really quiet or wasn't inside anymore. Oliver moved slowly to Darling's personal office. The wood was splintered; the door was ajar. He paused to listen again for any movement.

Nothing.

Using his foot, he nudged the door open. Anger flared within him. He stood alone in the office.

It had been tossed.

Desk drawers were on the floor, the filing cabinets had been toppled over and pried open, papers were scattered around and—the detail that made Oliver's blood run hot—every framed picture on the wall had been smashed.

He went back out into the lobby and made sure to check the small bathroom before going outside to wave Darling in. She was more than ready and hurried over. Oliver returned his gun back to the back of his jeans and frowned.

"I hate to say it, but someone trashed your office," he told her before she could move through the lobby to her personal space. Oliver didn't like watching her face fall at the news.

"Is it bad?"

"It's not pretty."

He followed her back into the small, disheveled room. She stood in the doorway for a few seconds, eyes roaming over the mess. Then, like a switch had been flipped, she hurried to the other side of the desk and started to move through drawers on the floor and their spilled contents.

"It's gone, Oliver!"

"What's gone?" But before she could answer, it dawned on him. "The security tape."

Darling nodded, clearly upset and stood straight again. An overpowering urge to comfort her pushed him forward. He put his hands on her shoulders, making her look up into his eyes. The moment from the night before played back into his mind.

She was close enough to kiss.

"Oliver, there's something I need to tell you."

"Yes?" his voice dropped low. Her green-eyed stare could stir up a drove of feelings in mere seconds.

"I think I know who did this," she whispered. "And you aren't going to like it."

"YOU SHOULD HAVE told someone—told me—about this note writer, Darling," Oliver fumed. He hadn't liked her story about the warnings—plus the mention of her parents and the news article—she'd received from her anonymous stalker one bit. He'd already called the station and talked to Derrick directly, recounting everything she had told him.

The doubt she had harbored that the note writer was trying to help had left the moment she'd seen her office and found the security tape gone. She wasn't dealing with a third-party player anymore.

Darling believed they were dealing with Jane Doe's killer.

Oliver paced back and forth in the lobby, face reddened with emotion. His words were angry, but she knew he was worried. However, that didn't mean she liked being scolded by Oliver, of all people.

"You can't keep making these decisions," he continued. "It's reckless and stupid."

"Stupid?" Darling asked, voice pitching high.

"Yes, stupid." He put his hands out wide, exasperated. "How am I supposed to protect you if you don't give me all the facts?"

In the back of her mind, Darling knew it was concern that made his tact disappear, but it triggered the deep-rooted pain Oliver Quinn had left all those years ago in her heart. Their camaraderie from the night before vanished.

"Protect me?" She laughed. "News flash—I don't need you to protect me, Oliver. I've taken care of myself for the last eight years just fine. Thank you for coming over here, but I realize now that it was a mistake." Once she said it, she felt a twinge of regret, but her pride wouldn't let her back down. "So, if you don't mind, go back to work and protect the person who actually wants it."

She walked to the broken door and held it open for him. The sound of a car door shutting derailed whatever he was about to say. They both looked out to see Derrick walking toward them.

"Darling, I—" Oliver started.

"Please, just leave."

"But I wanted—"

Darling heard the strain in her voice as she pleaded one last time with him. "Oliver, you owe me that much."

The bodyguard's brow creased, but he didn't have time to answer.

"I have some words for you," Derrick called, coming closer. He looked exhausted.

"Oh, I know," Darling said, trying to sound annoyed rather than wounded. "Mr. Quinn was just leaving. He has to go back to work now."

"Yeah, I guess I was," the bodyguard said, not meeting Darling's gaze. Instead he looked to the deputy. "But first, can I grab a quick word with you?"

Derrick must have liked Oliver, because he didn't give him any snark about the request, but Darling was done with the fair-haired man. She excused herself to the bathroom and took a long look at herself in the mirror.

How could one man make her feel so crazy?

THE SKY WAS dark by the time Oliver decided he couldn't take it anymore. His shift had ended an hour earlier, but he had stayed on the house grounds, going over Elizabeth Marks's itinerary. She was set to be in town in two days, which meant Oliver and his team would have to scout out routes and try to foresee any vulnerabilities that their trip to pick her up might cause.

Vulnerable.

What Darling had looked like when she had told him to leave.

He balled his fist.

He didn't want to leave her side, but she had been right. It wasn't his job to keep her safe. He had given up that privilege eight years ago when he'd left her without so much as a backward glance.

The idea that someone had been watching, following and threatening Darling put fire through his veins. Despite their past and her present wants, Oliver wouldn't have left her side had Derrick not convinced him she'd be safe.

"Listen, we're at a point in this case where we're waiting on results and information to come in," Derrick had said when Oliver had pulled him to the side at Acuity. "Whoever is messing with Darling won't get away with it. I'll make sure of it."

Derrick had promised he'd keep an escort outside her house that afternoon and through the night. Until they caught the culprit, he wasn't going to let her be alone. Oliver might have been wary of the deputy when he'd first come to Mulligan, but now he was grateful for his presence. It was true they weren't currently dating, but that didn't stop Derrick from being zealous about keeping his friend safe.

Still, Oliver couldn't ignore the worry that ate at him.

He would at least check in with Derrick, even if Darling didn't want his concern.

The temperature had dropped considerably since the sun had gone down. He wondered how he would handle Mulligan's true winter. Just the thought of the massive amount of snow made him turn the heat on high. By the time he pulled up outside of the old house, he was downright toasty.

It was a feeling that didn't last long.

All lights were off in Darling's apartment, from what he could tell. In fact, the entire building was dark save for the foyer light, which could be seen through the front windows of the common area. It was there on the front steps, in the faint glow of that light, that Oliver saw the outline of a body.

He swung his car into the parking lot between a police cruiser and Darling's car, all feeling of warmth gone from his body. For the second time that day, he grabbed his gun from his console. This time, though he didn't pretend to not have it.

No one sprung from the cruiser as Oliver hurried from his rental, gun in clear view. But he wasn't expecting anyone to. If they hadn't seen the body from this close, chances were no one was in the car.

The body belonged to a man lying on the top step and porch. He was on his side, face away from the parking lot. Oliver pulled out his phone and used the flashlight to see that the man was Derrick.

Blood was caked on the back of his head, and his left leg was bent at a weird angle. Oliver checked for a pulse. It was weak.

Adrenaline began to pump through him. Dialing 9-1-1,

he ran through the entryway and took the steps two at a time to Darling's door. It was shut but not locked.

"Darling?" Oliver called into the apartment. He didn't bother knocking, and he didn't worry about her privacy when no one responded. He quickly searched each room, gun raised. There was no sign of struggle inside.

Oliver ran a hand through his hair and went back to the front door.

"What's the nature of your emergency?" the operator finally answered.

"Deputy Derrick Arrington was attacked and needs immediate medical attention," Oliver bit out. He was angry at himself. "And private investigator Darling Smith has been kidnapped."

"What is your location?"

Oliver repeated the address as he checked the door. It wasn't broken, and there were no scratch marks to suggest someone had tried to pick the lock. He kicked the bottom of the door. Pain exploded in his foot, but he didn't care. He shouldn't have left Darling in the first place. He pulled his fist back this time, ready to let the door know the anger and regret flowing through his blood when he noticed a piece of paper sticking out from under the doormat.

He moved it out of the way, careful not to touch the actual paper. Its neat red writing made Oliver growl in absolute anger.

One more strike and you're out, Darling.

Chapter Twelve

Cold.

Seeping, slithering, unrelenting cold.

It didn't just push against her body. It invaded. Twisting and turning around every inch of her skin. Darling repeated her first waking thought.

"Oh, my God."

She was sitting outside in what was a clearing, as best she could tell. Whether it was night or early morning didn't matter. She couldn't see a thing. Darkness and the freezing air had combined and were currently conquering her. In the back of her mind, she calculated the normal temperature after the sun went down. It could drop to anywhere between forty to fifteen degrees. She certainly felt as if it was more like fifteen.

And that's when she realized why she felt the chill so acutely.

She was naked.

Fear, panic and slight hysteria rose up into a small scream that bubbled from her lips. With shaking hands, she clamped her mouth shut, afraid that whoever had put her here was still around. That's when the pain around her neck registered. Between deep breaths, she recalled her last memory of walking out of her apartment.

And then strong hands wrapping around her neck and squeezing until darkness came.

Before she could even replay the memory again, she had to entertain a new, terrifying one first. Tenderly she got to her feet and focused on the lower parts of her body. She nearly cried with relief when she found there was no pain or soreness south of her waistline. Whoever had tossed her into the freezing unknown without a stitch on had at least not taken advantage of her in such a horrible way.

It was enough of a silver lining to put a little light back into her dark situation.

A breeze picked up, and Darling wrapped her arms around her chest. Closing her eyes, she listened.

Deafening silence.

No noise from the town. No cars. Nothing.

A picture of a territorial moose or bear happening upon her made Darling's eyelids flutter back open. She prayed right then and there that her demise wouldn't be by some hungry animal. Though dying of exposure also wasn't fun. Before her mind could fill up with images and stories of lost hikers and stranded civilians who couldn't outlast the cold, Darling put one foot forward.

Standing still wasn't going to save her.

She walked in small strides, feeling dead grass and dirt between her toes before putting her weight down. Mulligan was a small town surrounded by enough rural land that she could have been anywhere within the town's limits. That included a stretch of land south of the town center that was reserved for hunting. Just as Darling didn't want to be eaten, she didn't want to stumble across an old hunting trap.

What if she was no longer even in Mulligan?

Minutes crept by and nothing seemed to change. Just grass and dirt—no trees or asphalt—pressing against feet she was slowly losing feeling in at each new step. Worry and panic, which Darling had decided to push clear out of her head when she took her first step forward, were using a battering ram to get back in.

Someone had knocked on her door. Thinking it was Oliver, she had flung it open, ready to fight. Yet no one had been there. Curious, she had moved down the stairs and out to the front porch. That's when she had seen Derrick.

Darling's heart squeezed as she remembered him sprawled on the steps. Had there been blood or any obvious wounds? She hadn't found out before someone had decided to choke her out.

Darling let out a humorless chuckle.

With its battering ram taking another charge, panic got one step closer to getting in.

What felt like ages later—though realistically she bet it had been only an hour at best since she had awoken—Darling's steps faltered. Her body ached and shook from the cold. Her mind had become blank. Slowly she angled her gaze down to question the change in her walking. A cloud must have finally passed by, because the blessed moonlight broke through and created a hazy glow around her. For the first time since she had opened her eyes, she could see. Pale skin stretched downward—too pale—and a dark spot that looked suspiciously like blood covered the grass next to her left foot.

Panic hadn't given up. She felt it hoist its battering ram back up for one last attempt to break down her emotional barrier.

Darling bent to investigate but lost her balance and

toppled over. She repositioned herself into a better position and felt a thrill of happiness that she could still feel anything in her almost-numb limbs. Pain meant she was still alive. The moment she couldn't feel at all was the moment she would lose it.

The blood—because it was blood and not her imagination—was coming from her foot. Her left one, to be exact. She wiped at the cut on her sole, but more blood replaced what was now smeared across her hand. There was nothing in the cut and nothing in her immediate area that looked sharp. Yet as she wiped another layer of blood off, the wound kept bleeding at a good clip.

How could she not feel the large gash in her foot?

The answer didn't matter. Panic took three steps back before rushing the door that was made to keep her sane and rammed it clear off its hinges.

Darling Smith finally hung her head and let out a sob. It shook her body more than the cold.

"WE'LL FIND HER. I promise you that," the chief said.

Chief Sanderson was a tall, thin man in his fifties with cropped gray-white hair and a clean-shaven face. His badge and gun were visible on his belt, but it was his demeanor that spoke of authority. He and Oliver stood outside Acuity's office, retracing Darling's steps for the second time. Looking for anything that might lead them to who was behind her disappearance.

Her phone was off—all calls going straight to her voicemail—and no one from her building or the strip mall claimed to have heard or seen anything out of the ordinary.

Oliver wanted to believe the chief was right—needed to believe him—but it had been hours since he'd found the empty apartment and the injured officer. Derrick had been alive but hadn't woken up before his surgery. Chief Sanderson had said that even though he temporarily was out of the woods, they wouldn't know the extent of the damage from his head injury until he was conscious. They didn't know if the same hammer that had killed Jane Doe had been used, but they did know the same method had been.

Hit from behind to knock them out of commission.

Though it looked as if Derrick hadn't gone down without a fight. His leg had been broken in two places, and his knuckles had been bloodied.

Oliver hoped Darling was putting up a better fight.

"This case…it's all theory and no conclusive, hard evidence. This note writer, a possible affair and now our own kidnapped private investigator," the chief ground out. "We're missing something big here."

"Whatever it is, I think Darling must have gotten close to it."

"It's time we get closer. Excuse me." The chief stepped away to answer his phone.

Oliver had been surprised when the chief had personally accompanied him in an attempt to find out what had happened. He could have sent other deputies but hadn't hesitated in getting his hands dirty. Oliver was finding he liked Sanderson just as he liked Derrick. Both men were fond of Darling and, instead of seeing her as a nuisance because of her profession, seemed to respect her. Sanderson wanted her to be found. It helped that the popular opinion had changed about the connection between Derrick's attacker and Darling's note writer.

Which also meant the chances were high that the mystery person was directly connected to Jane Doe's murder.

Oliver's stomach dropped as his mind jumped to the worst possible outcome for Darling. He needed to find her. Whoever was behind this couldn't have been this careful. There had to be a trail he could follow somewhere.

Like water to the face, Oliver knew for certain there *was* one person who knew more than they did.

Nigel.

Pulling out his phone, he scrolled through his contacts and went straight to the number of Orion's senior technical analyst, Rachel Delvough. Although he'd brought Grant and Thomas up to speed on the situation, he hadn't yet made a call to Nikki. As far as he was concerned, they were still doing their job correctly with the other two members still protecting the client.

The client he was about to target.

"Hello?" Rachel answered after a few rings. It was almost ten in Dallas, but she didn't sound as if he had woken her. Though he wouldn't have cared if he had. Darling's life was more important than being polite.

"Rachel, it's Oliver."

"What's wrong?" Orion operated with a handful of people. Everyone knew everyone else. Rachel was more connected at times than the rest, considering she handled all the behind-the-scenes affairs of each agent.

"I need a favor," he said, turning his back on the chief. "And I really need you to do it, Rachel." He wasn't as close to the quiet analyst as he was to Nikki, but he liked to think she'd help him out. Even if what he wanted was illegal.

"Okay...what is it?"

"Can you remotely look through someone's phone?" Nikki had hinted that Rachel's technical background might not have been wholly on the up-and-up. She hadn't used the word *hacker*, but he was taking a shot in the dark.

"Look through? Anything specific?"

"The incoming and outgoing call logs."

Nigel was lying about not knowing Jane Doe. If Oliver could see the numbers he had called or been called from, maybe he could find out who Jane Doe was. And if Nigel *had* hired someone to kill her and take Darling.

"Yeah, I can do that. But Oliver, it's illegal."

Oliver's fist balled. He wasn't angry at Rachel but at himself.

"Listen, I wouldn't ask unless it was absolutely important," he said.

There was hesitation. "Do you need it tracked, too?"

"No." He knew Nigel was still at his house.

"Whose phone?"

"Nigel Marks's."

More hesitation. Rachel knew exactly who Nigel was. She knew he was Orion's ticket to keeping afloat.

"Does Nikki know about it?"

"No," he admitted. "Listen, I wouldn't ask unless it was necessary. Please, Rachel."

He could hear movement on the other end of the phone.

"I'll have to head back to the office. I'm assuming you need this now?"

He let out a breath of relief. "As soon as humanly possible."

"I can do it. And Oliver? I won't lie to Nikki." Her voice was resolute. He didn't blame her. Everyone at Orion respected their boss. "But I won't bring it up to her unless you do."

"Deal."

The called ended, and Oliver was left feeling helpless. His job was to protect people, and yet he was invading the privacy of the client he had been hired to guard and had let down the only woman he had ever loved.

Oliver blinked.

Was that true?

And did he love her still?

Chapter Thirteen

Debrah and Andrew Smith had both come from money, but that didn't stop them from wanting more. They took to the business world, becoming a force many respected. Debrah and Andrew were inspiring. The perfect role models for a child with a growing mind like Darling.

So when Darling's childhood friend Annmarie Moreno's father accused the tycoons of running a string of Ponzi schemes, everyone including Darling couldn't help but not believe him. It was absurd, she had thought, but Annmarie's father didn't back down.

So Debrah and Andrew made sure to prove him wrong, in a very public way. A newspaper article and a televised interview painted a picture of their innocence, and their accuser's jealousy and greed.

It ruined his career and social standing in the community. He left the city with Annmarie and life returned to normal.

Until Darling received an anonymous email claiming the evidence that her parents were lying was about to be thrown out. She was given an address and told what to look for, and less than thirty minutes later, Darling's entire world had changed.

That was also the first time she had ever met Oliver—

standing in a Dumpster, holding the first clue in a series that would prove her parents had lied.

And destroyed a man's life because of it.

Since then she'd gone down the rabbit hole and found nothing but corruption. Bold-faced lies that built up until the moment she realized they would travel great lengths to ensure their fame and fortune were never threatened. That was the moment she asked Oliver to run away with her. Little did she know as she stood there watching him walk away, tears blurring her vision, that within the month, she would be on a plane to Maine, to a small town named Mulligan.

Now, as Darling pressed her hands to her cheeks, unable to feel her tears, she mused how her end felt intrinsically connected to the beginning of her adulthood.

Corruption.

Despair.

Oliver.

The last point—the man with golden hair—didn't hold the same dark weight as the first two points. Even if he had denied her all those years ago, she couldn't find the heat behind her anger for it. In fact, she realized the anger wasn't there at all anymore. She liked the life she had made since. She liked to think she had made a difference and left a mark in the lives of those she had met and helped through the years.

All Darling felt now was a needling of regret.

She should have kissed Oliver when she had the chance.

Thinking of kissing him replaced an ounce of cold with an ounce of warmth. She hoped she could hold on to it for a long while.

Darling closed her eyes, took a deep breath and stood.

It wasn't the most graceful of movements, and she did struggle, but in the end she was back on her feet.

The moonlight hadn't waned while she had reveled in her breakdown. She let her eyes adjust and started to turn in a circle to see if she could make out anything else. She stopped halfway through the cycle.

She was in a field of short, dead grass. A tree line darkened the distance, giving her no bearings for where she actually was. However, it was the hunk of black metal to her direct right that made her heart flutter. Without the moonlight, she might not ever have seen the car.

With an extreme amount of caution, she dragged her heavy feet and closed the space between her and her possible savior. Darling wasn't sure if she wanted someone to be in the car or not. Her rising grief and fear had kept the idea of her attacker being nearby from her mind. What if this was her attacker's car? But why would the attacker still be here? If her body hadn't been numb, she would have felt the hairs on the back of her neck stand as the idea of someone staying behind to watch her crept in.

No one jumped out from behind the car to grab her as she neared it. She circled it anyway. Better to see the attacker now than drop her guard and be surprised later. It wasn't as if she had much of a chance to defend herself either time, though. When she was satisfied she was alone, she peered into the car to find it was empty save for some clutter in the front seat floorboards. She tried the driver's door handle and let out a shaky breath. It was locked.

The other doors also wouldn't open. Scouting the immediate area, she found a rock that fitted in the palm of her hand. Squaring her shoulder, she approached the backseat's right window.

She threw the rock and watched as the window only cracked.

"Co-come on!"

She scooped the rock back up and threw it again. This time it missed the window completely. Trying to aim when you couldn't feel your throwing arm or hand was definitely difficult. The third time she was able to widen the crack. At this rate she would freeze where she stood.

I can't feel my face, she thought with a new sense of determination. *I need to get into this car.*

This time she gripped the rock and took a deep, shuddering breath.

Go through the window.

The sound of glass shattering cut through the silence.

She dropped the rock, ignoring how the new cut across her hand dripped blood, and unlocked the back door. Reaching around the front seats, she hit the unlock button for the rest of the doors. It felt like so much work, but she finally managed to sit behind the wheel with a slight feeling of accomplishment.

There were no keys in the ignition or anywhere else in the car, as far as she could tell. Her inner optimist hung her head. The center console had CDs in it, and the glove compartment was filled with napkins. Food wrappers littered the floorboard. A silver watch stuck out from under one. but Darling had little use for that. The small hope that she would be able to drive away or, at the very least, turn the heater on, withered away as the rest of her search turned up empty.

She would have to wait it out until the sun came up. The car was a few degrees warmer than outside. If the wind was kept at bay, she might survive the night. In a last-ditch effort to find something to save her, she hit the button that popped the trunk. Once more she pushed back out into the cold.

The trunk contents didn't give her any relief. A bag of tools and a greasy, balled-up hand towel. Darling cursed but grabbed the towel and, after a quick thought, the yellow-handled hammer. She settled back into the driver's seat and locked the doors. She pulled her knees to her chest and rested her head on top, draping the hand towel over her shins. It didn't warm her, but at least it was something.

A few minutes went by. Exhaustion was trying to drag her into sleep.

Leaving her naked in the cold Maine darkness sent a pretty clear message. Someone wanted her to die but didn't want to get their hands dirty.

Darling just hoped she could make whoever that was regret it. She might have been naked, hurt and as cold as a Popsicle, but she wasn't dead. Debrah and Andrew Smith had passed on the drive that kept Darling from cracking again.

With a small smile, Darling formed a thought so clear she wondered if she had actually said it out loud.

You should have killed me when you had the chance.

OLIVER WAS SECONDS from calling Rachel for the third time when the chief jogged over to him. There was no mistaking he was excited.

"We tracked her phone!"

"What?" Oliver followed him to the cars when he didn't stop. "I thought you couldn't if the phone was off."

"We can't. It just came back on." Oliver's mouth opened in surprise.

"I'll follow you."

He left no room for the chief to mistake his statement as a request. For the first time since he had met the man hours before, the older man laughed.

"I knew you would."

Chapter Fourteen

Oliver drove, white-knuckled, in a convoy to the point where Darling Smith's phone was located. The sun was starting to rise, creating a crisp blue landscape without a cloud to blemish it. Under different circumstances, he would have called it serene and even beautiful. However, his heart was in his throat, terrified of the possible outcomes when they found Darling's phone.

In front of him was Chief Sanderson in his four-door pickup. Bringing up the rear was a deputy named Casey Heath in her patrol truck. Oliver raced along the asphalt between them with no worry about what the cracked road might do to his rental. Finding Darling had become his top—no, his only—priority the second he'd found Derrick unconscious. Everything else was on the back burner.

The chief braked for a second. The action bit into Oliver's nerves. They didn't need to stop. They needed to keep going until they found her. After a few beats, Sanderson flipped on his left turn signal and drove off-road. Without hesitation, Oliver and Heath followed.

He made a left onto the new road, and they whizzed down it, away from town. He didn't slow until they had gone past trees on either side. He braked, and Oliver followed suit. They were on a dirt road, dense tree lines surrounding them.

"It's coming from around here," Sanderson called after he swung out of his truck. His hand rested on the top of his piece, a silent gesture that Oliver didn't miss.

His security experience had already tensed up his body but not enough to hinder the fluidity of his movement. He didn't have his gun out, but he didn't think he needed it, either. His adrenaline was too high. He would use his strength to overcome whatever obstacles the unknown was about to throw at them.

"Spread out," Sanderson barked. They all fanned out. "Darling?" he called.

Silence.

Less than a minute later, Deputy Heath yelled.

"Over here!"

The phone was on the ground just inside the tree line a few feet from their cars. It was on but unattended. Deputy Heath shooed Oliver's hands away when he went to grab it and instead threw on a pair of latex gloves.

"We don't know who has been touching this," she said.

"Check the recent calls and texts," Sanderson ordered. Oliver looked over her shoulder.

"The last call she made was to me yesterday when she found someone had broken in," he confirmed.

"And the last text...was from a week ago." Heath quickly browsed the last few pictures. They were of the photographs she'd received at the start of the case.

Heath pulled a plastic Baggie from her pocket and dropped the phone in.

"The phone was placed here," Chief Sanderson said when the bag had been returned to the patrol truck. Oliver agreed.

"It wasn't thrown from a car when they realized she had it. It wouldn't have landed like that," he said. The phone had been on the other side of a tree. "It was purposely placed here."

"But why was it turned back on?" asked Heath.

"For us to find," the chief said at the same time Oliver said, "So we'd find it."

Silence didn't have time to fall around them. Oliver bet that the same sick feeling had exploded within the chief.

"We need to find her," Oliver said, voice hard. "Now."

"Agreed. Heath you go through there," the chief said, pointing to the trees behind them. "Just in case." Heath went back to her truck and pulled her rifle out and did as she was told. "Oliver, follow the road in your car until you are on the outer perimeter of these trees." He held up his hand before Oliver could complain. "We know we won't find her in the direction we just came from. If she was on foot, there's a chance she came out on the other side. Darling doesn't seem like the kind of woman who would hide. Follow the tree line. If you see anything, call my cell." He reached in his pocket and produced his card.

"But if she's in there—" Oliver started. He didn't get far.

"Deputy Heath and I know these woods. You come, you'll slow us down." There was no more discussion as Chief Sanderson began his trek. Oliver saw the reasoning, but he didn't have to like it.

The road extended south for another mile before the trees thinned and open fields replaced them. A quick scan showed no sign of people. Oliver cut the wheel and took his rental off-road. He followed the outside of the woods as the ground sloped uphill and down, but he did so at a slow clip.

An emotion he couldn't quite place clung to his mind and body like a second skin. Fear and longing. Regret and anger. They were mixed in with the unfamiliar feeling, causing a calm before the storm. It was the only way for him to stay focused.

Oliver slammed his hand against the steering wheel.

He had hoped beyond hope that Darling would be with her phone. Being the stubborn woman she was, he'd hoped she had taken down the bad guy and would be waiting for the cops to come. She'd make some wisecrack about Oliver being a day late and a dollar short, and then life would become simple again.

Finding Darling's phone—one that had most likely been purposely placed there—without the private eye at its side brought on a flood of thoughts Oliver didn't want to entertain.

He focused on the trees that he drove past, occasionally scanning the land to the left. He was so intent on the woods he almost missed the spot in the passenger's side mirror. Slamming the brakes, he turned and looked through the SUV's back window. A black car sat a few yards from the woods, its hood angled away from view.

Oliver threw the SUV in Reverse and sped toward the car. He put the SUV in Park and dialed the chief's number. The chief picked up on the first ring.

"I followed the tree line and found a car in the middle of nowhere. Going to check it out. Hold on," he said, not giving the chief room to respond. Oliver's body was even more tense than before. If caution was a tangible material, it would have been dripping off him by the bucketload. He slipped the phone, still on, in his back pocket and approached the car from the rear.

The car was an old Mazda and seemed to be in good

condition minus a dent in the fender and a broken back window. The tires, as far as he could tell, weren't deflated, either. So why was it out there?

Oliver snatched his phone out and yelled into the receiver.

"It's Darling!"

He didn't hear if the chief responded. He had come around the passenger side of the car and had seen her through the windshield.

She was curled up in the driver's seat with a small towel around her feet. Blood was streaked across her face and, he realized with anger and concern so poignant he almost stumbled, she was completely naked.

Oliver pulled on the door but it didn't budge. It was locked. Darling didn't stir. He ran back to the open window and unlocked it before opening the door and unlocking all doors from the passenger side. Then he was back at Darling's side.

She was leaning against the back of the seat but slumped over toward the center console. Her knees were pulled against her chest, her arms slack at either side. Her cheek was pressed against the top of her knee. She was pale.

So pale.

"Darling?" Oliver's voice came out in a whisper. A harsh yet faltering sound. He placed his hand on her blood-stained cheek. He felt the cold all the way in his heart.

A feeling he would never forget.

"Darling, please…"

With his free hand he pressed his fingers to check her pulse. For one horrible moment there was nothing. Then, like a storm in the distance, Oliver felt a soft beat.

He backed up and tore off his jacket. It wasn't thick or long, but it fit around her front easily enough. Oliver put one hand around her shoulders and the other under her knees. There had been a time where an entirely naked Darling in his arms would have made him happy in every way possible, but as he pulled her limp body against his chest, Oliver felt no glee.

"Keep beating," he whispered, as if her heart could hear him.

"Okay."

Oliver looked down, wide-eyed, at the woman in his arms. She tilted her head back and gave him the smallest of smiles.

"God, you're beautiful," he said.

Her smile didn't disappear.

"You found me," she whispered.

"You bet I did."

She made a noise that almost sounded like a laugh, but she didn't speak. Oliver cast a quick glance back into the car. There was no blood on the beige seat, he was happy to see.

"Are you hurt?" he asked anyway. He turned, trying not to jostle her too much, and walked toward his rental.

"No," she answered, voice still low. "I'm cold."

Oliver held her tighter.

"How long have you been—" He was cut off by the sound of a vehicle approaching. Darling tensed so quickly that Oliver had to look down to make sure she was okay.

"Who?"

"Chief Sanderson," he answered as the four-door raced toward them. Deputy Heath wasn't far behind.

"Keep me covered," was all she said.

Oliver angled his body to the side so the chief couldn't see Darling's skin that wasn't covered by the jacket. It was an absurd thing to worry about in the moment, but she sounded so weak. The protective side of him needed to do this for her. It was his fault he hadn't kept her safe in the first place.

The chief kept his truck running and jumped out. He waved Oliver over and flung open the back door.

"It's quicker to drive to the hospital than to wait for an ambulance," he said. Oliver nodded and realized there wasn't a way to shield Darling's body from the older man.

"Could you step aside for a sec?" Oliver asked, a few feet from him. Sanderson sent him a confused look.

"We don't have time to waste," he shot back.

"I'm naked," Darling spoke up. The chief's eyes went skyward at the news. Oliver hurried to get her into the backseat, repositioning the jacket after setting her down. He was thrilled to see she was able to sit up on her own.

"I found her in that car—driver's side—unconscious," Oliver said. "I need to go with her."

The chief nodded his approval, and Oliver slid in next to Darling, shutting the door behind him.

Deputy Heath ran up to the truck and was given quick instructions. Sanderson was inside the cab seconds later, already reversing and heading back to the road.

"Any serious injuries?" the chief asked, eyes not moving to the rearview mirror.

"She says no, but there's blood on her face."

"My foot," she replied. "I cut it."

"And your hand." He caught her wrist and followed the dried blood to her palm. Her skin was still so cold.

"Were you outside all night?" the chief asked.

"Yes," Oliver answered for her when she nodded. His

anger almost boiled over at the realization. In one fluid movement, Oliver took off his shirt.

"Let's put this on you," he said, already moving her to face him.

"No," the chief cut in. "Put her against you."

Oliver raised his eyebrow. "What?"

The chief was all business when he answered. "She'll warm up faster from your body heat. Just putting your shirt over her—although it's a kind gesture—won't work fast enough. Sit her on your lap and let her hug your bare chest. Your warmth will become her warmth."

Never did Oliver think he would see the day that a cop told him to hug a naked Darling, but it wasn't time to marvel. Darling didn't argue. She must have been a lot colder than he'd thought. She didn't resist as he pulled her onto his lap. She slowly moved her legs around him while he helped guide her arms into his jacket to cover her back.

Oliver made sure to keep eye contact with her as he wrapped his arms around her torso and pulled her down until her bare skin was pressed against his.

Darling's eyes fluttered closed for a moment before she returned the embrace. He waited as she settled her cheek against his shoulder. There was no denying she needed the warmth. Her skin was as cold as ice.

"How long to the hospital?" Oliver asked when Darling relaxed against him. Absently he began to rub her back beneath the jacket.

"Ten minutes. You still with us, Darling?"

Oliver felt her nod against his shoulder.

"What happened to you?" Oliver didn't want to push her, but he also needed to know. Whoever had done this was still out there. "I went to your place and saw Derrick on the ground and you nowhere to be found."

"Derrick okay?"

"Just a nasty bump on the head is all," the chief supplied. "He'll be back to it in no time."

Darling nodded into his shoulder again. As her cheek moved across his bare skin, he had to repress a shiver.

"Someone knocked. I thought it was you," she said, voice a bit louder than before. "No one was there. I went downstairs and then—" She let out a shuddering breath. Oliver looked down to see tears shining in her eyes. She tilted her head to the side, and Oliver cursed.

"What?" Chief asked.

Oliver let out another string of obscenities before he answered.

"Someone choked her," he bit out. "There are marks on her neck. I don't know how I missed the bruising before."

"I didn't see a face," she said after the chief also voiced his anger. "Flat chest. Male. Then woke up outside."

Oliver returned his hand to her back, satisfied she hadn't been hit over the head like Derrick.

The cab of the truck became silent as their individual thoughts formed faster than their mouths would let them. Oliver was trying to keep his growing anger under control. To put hands around Darling's neck until she had passed out, and then to strip her and leave her in the cold to die were two acts that painted an unsettling picture of a man with nothing but bad intentions. The idea that he had been watching Darling and waiting for her to leave her apartment was one that crawled under Oliver's skin and simmered. But at the same time, a thin yet strong layer of guilt covered it.

He shouldn't have left her alone after someone had ransacked her office. Even if Derrick had consoled him with promises of her staying safe.

Darling sighed, and Oliver felt the movement go from her chest to his. Despite the fact that she was completely naked—and pressed against him—Oliver noted that the overriding emotion he felt was protectiveness.

Sure, he could admit that what he had seen of her today was all woman and all beautiful. Her curves, her breasts, her hips, her legs. But instead of overpowering feelings of lust and desire, he had instantly felt the need to keep that body safe.

To guard it with his own body.

In that moment, Oliver realized the only person he wanted to be a bodyguard for was wrapped up and shivering in his arms.

Chapter Fifteen

The chief took charge of the entire hospital when they came in. He barked orders no one questioned. That included giving Darling privacy until she was placed in a room with a nurse, a doctor and a gown.

"We need you to step out of the room for now," the nurse told Oliver after he'd made sure she was situated on a bed. He started to argue, but Darling silenced him.

"It's okay," she tried to assure him. "I'm safe."

He didn't want to point out that she'd thought that before. Instead he kept his mouth shut. She'd been through enough.

"Heath found something," Chief Sanderson said, bustling over. "Call me if you learn anything new or she remembers anything. Give me your keys and we'll have someone bring your car over."

"Thanks." In truth, he hadn't even thought about the rental.

"And tell Darling we'll get the bastard who did this."

"You bet your ass we will," Oliver responded. The chief gave him a quick nod and was gone.

Now that Darling was safe, Oliver was able to think about the rest of the world. Grant and Thomas were having to stretch themselves thin to cover Oliver's day shift, but he couldn't see a way around leaving Darling.

He let out a long exhalation and slumped against the wall. There wasn't enough time to rest.

"You look tired."

Standing next to him in a black pantsuit and matching heels, Nikki Waters was the last person he had expected to see. At least, not this soon.

"It's been a long twenty-four hours," he said. Nikki didn't smile.

"How is Miss Smith doing?"

He glanced back at the shut door.

"Cold," he said. "Scared, but won't admit it. I don't think there's any permanent or life-threatening damage."

"I'm glad to hear that."

"How do you even know about all of this?" He motioned around them.

"Thomas told me about the break-in when I called for a status update." She shrugged. "With all these unknown variables continuing to come into play, I thought it best to jump on a flight and come out here." She was waiting for Oliver to say something, but he didn't want to start a conversation he knew wouldn't end well. Nikki must have realized this. She turned her body toward the empty room across from them. "Can we talk in private a moment?"

Oliver followed without complaint. He moved himself so he could see over Nikki's shoulder to Darling's room. If anyone who wasn't hospital staff tried to get to her, they'd soon find out they would have to go through him.

"I don't know where to begin, really," she started. Her posture was stick straight, her arms across her chest. "But I suppose I'll start with this. What were you thinking,

Oliver? You asked Orion's senior analyst to *hack into an active client's phone to take information.*" Disbelief and blatant disappointment blanketed each word. "Do you have any idea how much trouble we would be in had I not stopped Rachel when I called to tell her I'd landed?"

Oliver was taken aback.

"It was necessary—it still *is* necessary—to find out what Nigel's hiding," he said, frustration pouring out. "Nigel is connected to all of this. We have to know how, and that call log could be the key."

"Then let the police get a warrant for it," Nikki snapped back. Her cool composure cracked. "Did it ever occur to you that getting evidence illegally would hurt your case more than it would help it? Courts would dismiss whatever evidence you found. Plus, what makes you so sure he's involved with that woman's death or Darling's abduction? You told me yourself that in your gut, you didn't believe he killed the unidentified woman. What changed?"

That gave Oliver pause. She was right. Oliver knew in his gut Nigel hadn't had anything to do with the death. When he didn't come up with a good answer, she continued.

"Just because there isn't another obvious suspect doesn't mean you should jump on one of the only suspects you *do* have. This is one bad judgment call I can't overlook, Oliver. You didn't just jeopardize Rachel. You jeopardized us all. Every agent—their families—and every person we ever would protect in the future. You put us all—including yourself—in danger."

Oliver was about to protest. Finding a kidnapped Darling didn't compare to the remote possibility that Orion could be held accountable for the breach in security. He had already decided that if it came down to it, he would shoulder all of the blame. However, Nikki didn't give him a breath to say any of that.

"All of it—all of this—could have been avoided had you just come to me directly," she said, voice cooling. "Instead you went behind my back, asked an analyst to go against her ethical code and broke the law. You should have come to me, Oliver."

"You'd already made it clear I wasn't supposed to get close to Darling," he reasoned, thinking back to his first day in Mulligan. "I thought you would have shut me down and then out. I didn't want to take that chance."

"That chance? Oliver, I started Orion because I believe that every life deserves the basic right of safety, no matter that person's financial situation. For three years I have busted all of our collective asses to make sure we offer virtually free services and every client who comes to us can rest a little easier. What makes you, Oliver Quinn, think that I wouldn't have done everything in my power to help when I knew a woman's life depended on it?"

Oliver's mouth slid open, but no words came out. Like a fish out of water, he stared at her. She had him there.

"I—I wasn't thinking straight," he admitted. "I'm sorry, but I couldn't take the chance."

"And *that* is why I'm taking you off this case and sending you home." Whatever anger had been within her was seeping out. Her resolve, however, was absolute. There was no reprieve to be had. As he responded, he hoped she could see his level of intensity, as well.

"She's more than just a friend. I can't leave her, Nikki. Not until this is all put to rest," he said, voice low, unyielding. "I won't leave her again."

For an instant Oliver thought he saw Nikki's body sag. She let out a low breath and shook her head slowly.

"Then I'm afraid I'm going to have to ask for your resignation."

"HE TOOK MY EARRINGS."

Darling rubbed at the smoothness of her ear lobes. They were warming up, as were her fingers, but she didn't feel any yellow daisy earrings beneath them. "Doesn't that seem oddly personal?"

"Excuse me?" Nurse Jones looked up from the end of Darling's hospital bed. Her glasses slipped to the tip of her nose.

Darling shifted her weight. The readjustment moved her foot, which earned her a glare from the nurse. She put her hands around the top Darling's foot to hold it still.

"Never mind," Darling said.

Nurse Jones finished her evaluation in silence. Considering she was inspecting the stitches on the bottom of her foot, Darling didn't want to annoy the woman. Even though she had been one of the handful of people who had seen Oliver carry her in wrapped around him naked, she hadn't questioned Darling about the situation when they were alone.

Not that she felt the need to talk to the older woman about it. Darling still had to sort her through her own thoughts.

"Okay, looks like your little stunt didn't tear open your stitches," Nurse Jones said, standing with her hands on her hips. She was a stern woman in her fifties and didn't care for any excuses. So Darling didn't give her one.

"Next time I need to get to the bathroom, I'll hit the

call button," Darling promised. "And not try to get there without my crutches."

Nurse Jones nodded and turned her attention to the rest of her patient. "And how do you feel now?"

It had been almost an hour since she had been passed off to the doctor. Hot water bottles and blankets had been applied to her body in an attempt to make her warm as the cut across her foot had been stitched. The doctor had confirmed she was suffering from hypothermia but, lucky for her, taking shelter from the wind had helped her more than anything. Also, Oliver's body temperature had begun to put warmth back into hers on the ride to the hospital. It was a great starting point, the doctor had exclaimed.

Some of the warm water bottles were still placed across her stomach and thighs while Darling kept buried beneath three thick blankets.

"I wouldn't say cozy, but I'm not cold anymore," she answered. Darling held up her bandaged hand. "This doesn't hurt anymore, either."

"And your throat?"

On reflex, Darling's hands flitted to her neck. She could still imagine the strong grip that had brought her to unconsciousness wrapped around her.

"It doesn't hurt as much when I talk," she admitted.

Nurse Jones wrote on the clipboard in her hand without commenting. The woman showed no signs of sympathy. The nurse had obviously seen a lot working in a hospital. Darling wasn't going to hold it against her that her bedside manner was lacking.

"Okay, I'll have to get the doctor to sign off on it, but I think you're good to leave just as soon as that young man brings you your clothes. You still need to take it easy, though." The nurse tapped Darling's big toe. "No pressure on this for four or five days. We'll set up a time for you to come back and get the stitches removed." She pointed to the set of crutches leaning against the bed. "Use those. Understand?"

"Yes, ma'am."

"Good."

The nurse left without another word. Darling let out a long, deep sigh and pulled the top blanket up to her chin. She imagined the cloth was a nice, hot bath. Her body submerged in water that would stave off any cold the night could bring. Scented candles along the lip of the tub, all combining in the epitome of a relaxing atmosphere.

"Should I come back later?"

Darling jumped and turned to see Oliver standing in the doorway. A duffel bag thrown over his shoulder, a smirk attached to his lips.

"Sorry. You looked like you were enjoying your thoughts."

Darling laughed. "I was actually dreaming of a bath," she said. "Cheesy, right?"

He walked over and put the bag next to her. "After what you've been through, I'd say you have every right to a bath. Heck, I'd even go so far as to say a bubble bath."

She followed that with another laugh but cut it short. Something seemed off about the bodyguard. He was smiling, but the expression didn't reach his eyes.

"What's wrong?" Darling asked with such intense concern it almost moved her. Oliver looked surprised.

"What do you mean?"

"Your smile doesn't reach—" She stopped herself and then amended, "Your smile seems off. Fake."

He crossed his arms over his chest. His eyebrow rose. "My smile seems fake," he repeated with obvious mockery.

Darling felt a flare of frustration lick to life inside her. When would Oliver realize that she could read him as easily as he could read her?

As if on cue, Oliver's face softened, and his voice lost all contempt. "I'm tired. I haven't gotten much sleep recently."

It was Darling's turn to soften. She reached out and took his hand. She had thought her skin had warmed considerably since she had been brought in, but where Oliver's hand touched hers, there was nothing but brilliant heat. Instead of pulling away, she squeezed.

"Thank you for finding me. I didn't get a chance to say it earlier."

Oliver squeezed back.

"Thank you for not freezing to death," he replied with a new tilt to his lips. Together they laughed and dropped hands. The moment passed, and Darling opened the duffel.

"Now, the question is, are you as good at finding a decent outfit?"

"If your idea of a good outfit is a white tank top, skintight jeans, and a red thong…" Darling's face heated before she could stop it. "Then that's not a good outfit. And on that note, I'll leave you to change." He started to leave but paused to add, "Unless you need help?"

"No, thanks. I think I can do it."

He shrugged and closed the door behind him. It wasn't as if he hadn't seen *and* felt her naked body only a few hours before. Heat flared up her neck and into her cheeks.

Oliver had picked out a sweatshirt, jeans and tennis

shoes. It meant he had grabbed the first thing he'd seen in her closet and chest of drawers. As for undergarments, thankfully he had gone sensible and picked a no-lace beige bra and a pair of black cotton bikini-cut panties. Darling spent the time putting on each item trying to recall what all he had seen when going through her underwear drawer. He had to have seen every type of underwear she owned. From the see-through special occasion lace to the long, unattractive pieces meant for a Maine winter. Within the past few hours, she had lost a lot of privacy points with the bodyguard.

Nurse Jones came back in just after Darling had wrangled on her pants, taking care not to disrupt the stitches on the bottom of her foot. Dr. Williams had signed off, and she was officially being discharged.

"Will the young man outside be taking you home, or do you need a ride?" the nurse asked after she had put some ointment on Darling's foot and wrapped it up. "It's the end of my shift, so I could drop you off." She shrugged to show indifference, but Darling smiled. Apparently the nurse wasn't completely apathetic.

"Thank you for the offer, but I suppose I'm with him."

Nurse Jones mimicked her smile for the first time. "That's not a bad lot to have."

"I suppose not."

Darling turned down a wheelchair to help her to the car and instead put a crutch beneath each arm and began an awkward gait down the hallway. Oliver carried her bag and kept close. He still seemed off somehow, but she was going to believe it was because he was tired. She couldn't deny she was in the same boat. The sleep that she had gotten in the car hadn't been sound or comfortable.

And she hadn't been too sure it wasn't the beginnings of death by exposure.

"Should I go see Derrick before we leave?" Darling asked. "The nurse said he should be waking up soon."

"It might be a better idea to let him rest for now," he answered. "I checked in on him before I went to your apartment, and he was still sound asleep. I think it's his pain meds."

Darling nodded. Guilt outlined with a sad edge cut inside her. If Derrick had not been watching out for her, he never would have been attacked. If she had only listened to Oliver and taken his offer to help protect her... Darling paused in her thinking. Whoever had taken her was determined. Hospitalizing an officer was a great testament to that fact. If Derrick hadn't been there but Oliver had, then it would have been Oliver hurt. Or worse.

Her guilt ebbed away.

Another feeling tore through her at the thought of a horrific fate befalling the bodyguard. She glanced sideways at him. When the chaos around her died down, she would have to think about why her heart and mind always seemed to clash when the topic of Oliver Quinn was put on the table.

Chapter Sixteen

The bathwater stopped running, and a few seconds later, a splash sounded.

"You okay?" Oliver couldn't help but call out.

They were back in Darling's apartment. To celebrate, Darling had indeed drawn herself a bubble bath.

"I'm fine," she answered through the door. "You can stop hovering now!"

Oliver fell into the couch when he was finished with another security sweep. He settled his back against the armrest so his sight line to the front door wasn't obstructed, a habit. The conversation with Nikki started to replay in his head.

He was no longer a bodyguard.

All to save Darling.

He hadn't fought Nikki after she had asked for his resignation. It was a choice he didn't resent. Funny, he thought, how once upon a time he had left Darling to protect her, and now he was staying to do the same.

Why was it so easy to sacrifice everything for a woman who would never trust him again?

"Oliver!"

In a flash he was off of the couch and standing at the bathroom door. "Are you okay? What's wrong?"

"I'm fine! I was just going to see if you were hungry?"

"Hungry?" he repeated, his adrenaline on the brink of spiking.

"Yeah, I haven't eaten in—" She stopped. Oliver almost opened the door all the way to make sure she was okay. "Breakfast yesterday, I suppose. So, I thought we could maybe order something? There's a pizzeria on Main Street that delivers. Unless you need to go back to work?" She had hesitated before her last question had slipped out. It made Oliver wonder if she knew about his conversation with Nikki. He pushed that thought away.

"No, I can stay," he answered. That was a conversation he didn't want to broach through a partially opened bathroom door. "And pizza sounds good."

"Wonderful," she almost sang. "I don't have anything here to eat. There's a magnet on the fridge with the number. Order whatever you want. Just make sure there's a lot of whatever it is."

Oliver shut the door and did as he was told.

Instead of sitting back down to swim in his deepest thoughts, he looked around the living room. Like the rest of the small apartment, it was filled with character. He found he liked it more than his apartment.

The bathroom door opened.

"Need any help?"

"No," she replied, frustrated. "But I sure do hate crutches." They clinked against the hardwood floors as she started to go for her bedroom. That gave Oliver an idea.

"Wait, are you dressed?" he asked, though he was already moving.

"Yeah, why?"

He held up his finger to get her to wait and walked

past her into the bedroom. Going straight for her mini-office in the corner, he grabbed the chair and rolled it back into the hall.

"It's no wheelchair but, really, isn't it a chair with wheels?" He cracked a smile and Darling laughed. She wore a long-sleeved white robe that fell to her ankles and tied around the middle. Her hair was wet and wound up into a bun atop her head. It was the first time in eight years he had seen her without a lick of makeup on, and he had to admit she was still as beautiful as ever.

He helped her angle herself into the chair and placed her crutches against the wall.

"Where to, madam?" he asked with little bow. She laughed again. He liked the sound.

"I heard the couch is all the rage this time of the year," she said playfully. "A five-star destination second only to the kitchen bar."

"Then that's where we'll go." He did another quick bow and began to roll the chair toward the living room. He kept an eye on her foot, careful not to jostle it. They reached the living room, and without letting her stop him, he lifted her from the chair and placed her on the couch, her back against the armrest and legs stretched out. He sat on the edge of the coffee table right in front of her.

"Are you comfortable?" he asked.

"My foot is sore, but I guess that's normal for having it split open and stitched back up. I didn't get it wet in the bath. I was too afraid," she admitted, rotating her ankle. As she spoke, Oliver's gaze went to the bruises on her neck. "It doesn't hurt that much," she whispered, tone changing with her mood.

Oliver couldn't help it. He reached out and traced

the skin around the bruise on her right. It made Darling shiver. He stopped but didn't pull away.

"I thought you were dead," he breathed. "When I found you in that car…for a moment I thought you were—"

"But I wasn't," she interrupted, voice soft. Her hand covered his. They sat still, both caught in a moment that couldn't be summed up in words.

Oliver leaned in. "I'm glad," he whispered.

Darling searched his face, but he only had eyes for those lips. Careful not to spook her, he slowly closed the space between them, giving her plenty of time to move away. His heartbeat sped up when he realized she wasn't going to.

The kiss was soft and warm. A ribbon drenched in sunlight. He wanted it to continue—to get lost in a moment that could be so much more—but he let it end.

After everything that had happened, Darling was vulnerable, whether she wanted to admit it or not. And he couldn't deny he wasn't in the best spot, either. He didn't want to take advantage of her. He was finding that she still meant too much to him.

He pulled back and smiled. The private investigator's cheeks were tinted red, her lips a shade of dark pink.

"Better than I remember." As the words left his mouth, Oliver feared he had overstepped their relationship by bringing up the past. However, Darling didn't seem to mind it. She mimicked his smile and opened her mouth to speak. Her response was cut off by a knock at the door.

"If that's not at least a large pizza, I'm going to be so upset," she said instead.

"I did you one better. I ordered two." Darling thrust her fist in the air in victory, and just like that, they returned to normal.

Ten minutes later, they were seated at the kitchen bar, plates covered in pizza slices and minds set to work. The question about who they were together was put aside for a time when one of their lives wasn't in danger.

"You know what I don't get?" Darling asked after putting down another large bite. "Why take me in the first place? I mean, I realize that stripping me down and dumping me in the cold is a pretty clear way to kill me without having to actually kill me, but why *take* me?"

"You must have gotten too close."

"But why not warn me instead?" It must have been a question she had been wondering about for a while. She put down her food and angled her body to face him. The top of her robe opened a fraction, giving him an uninhibited view of the top of her bare chest. She didn't notice his glance downward. He tried to refocus. "I get a folder of pictures of Nigel and Jane Doe with a note telling me to do the right thing—plus the article with my parents—and I follow those instructions. Then I go to get my camera with pictures of the hotel crime scene and there's another note, warning me to stop snooping. The camera is returned before I go to the police, but this time with no note."

"Then we take a trip to the gas station, confirm Jane Doe was there and get the security footage. You find out the woman Jane Doe talked to was Harriet Mendon. The next day Acuity is ransacked and the security tape is gone," he continued.

"But *with no note*." Darling said this with a punch, as if it held more importance than all of the rest.

"Yes, but then you come back here and get taken. There's a new note with a threat saying you have one more strike left. Though you didn't see that note." Anger began to build within him once more. He pictured her sitting in that car again, motionless.

She kept on, not noticing the tension. "Right! One more strike. Implying that I hadn't yet crossed whatever line had been drawn." Darling lowered her voice. "So, I ask again—why take me less than two hours later, and why not leave the note at Acuity?"

"Whoever it was, they got sloppy."

"You're right," she exclaimed. "*They* did!"

"Wait, what?" Oliver tried to follow the train of thought she was already on but came up short.

"Oliver, I think we're dealing with two killers. Hear me out," Darling began. "Two people are trying to frame Nigel. Note Writer enlists my help to make the case seem more valid. He—or she—is observant, smart. He knows what to say and when to say it. He's careful. But then he trashes my office without a note? Then *kidnaps* me? What's the point in leaving a threat on my door and then taking me after I clearly hadn't left the apartment or done anything else on the case?"

"You think that like all the good crime-fighting and crime-committing teams, one of them is the brains and the other one is the hothead," he finished for her.

"What's more, I don't think they're communicating all that well, either. I think the brains wrote the last-strike threat without knowing about Acuity being ransacked or vice versa. The note writer wanted to scare me. The other one wanted to hurt me."

"If this is all true, then our problems just doubled. What's worse than one killer? Two."

Chapter Seventeen

Darling was trying to put all the clues back together but couldn't help but see them now as two separate lines, running sloppily parallel next to each other.

"Two people would make killing and cleaning up after Jane Doe easier," she said aloud. "A rich man like Nigel wouldn't have a problem finding a killer for hire with his wealth."

Oliver didn't skip a beat. "I know you are keen on thinking Nigel is behind this, but I'm telling you, it's not him. Thomas caught him crying yesterday, just after Derrick called to tell him about how Jane Doe was killed." He knew now that had been an attempt to shake whatever truth Nigel had about the woman free. "Do you really think Nigel Marks would cry over a mistress he'd killed? If it's anyone in that family, I'd bet it's the wife. They share the wealth. She just as easily could have fronted the money for a contract killer."

Darling held in her rebuttal. Her desire for Nigel Marks to pay for all of his indiscretions was great, but she was finding the idea of him being behind Jane Doe's murder didn't quite sit right with her anymore. Although she wasn't ready to point the finger at Elizabeth, either. She still believed the older woman was too smart to do something so stupid. And if she really thought about it, if Elizabeth was going to kill anyone, it would probably be her husband.

"We need to figure out who our Jane Doe is," Darling said instead.

A booming knock sounded at the front door. It was so unexpected that Darling almost fell off her stool. Oliver's reflexes were a lot more productive. He was off his stool and standing in front of Darling, using his body as a human shield. He had even reached back to help steady her.

"I'm not expecting anyone," Darling whispered. "If you were wondering."

Oliver nodded and reached over the bar to the kitchen counter. He pulled two of the steak knives out of their wooden holder next to the toaster. He passed one to Darling and brandished the other. She grabbed the handle of her knife and watched wide-eyed as the bodyguard silently crossed the room and sidled up to the front door.

The knock sounded again. Oliver waited for it to stop before calling out.

"Who's there?"

Darling marveled at how controlled he was. He looked like a man about to go to war. Calm, calculating and also ready for whatever what was about to happen.

"Chief Sanderson!"

Darling relaxed, but when Oliver didn't, she tightened her grip on the knife handle. Slowly the bodyguard cracked open the door. He must have been okay with what he saw. He straightened his back and opened the door wide. The knife in his hand remained there, but the chief didn't seem to mind it as he looked between them.

"Sorry to intrude, but I have some new information

I'd like to talk to you about," Chief Sanderson said. Darling hadn't been too focused on the chief when she had ridden in his truck that morning, but now she could see as clear as day that he hadn't been getting much sleep, if any. Dark circles hung beneath each eye, and there was a droop to his shoulders as he moved to the chair next to the couch. Darling swiveled her stool around to face him while Oliver took point, standing between the two.

"Is it about Derrick? Is he okay?" Darling asked out of the gate. If anything happened to Derrick, it would be her fault. Derrick was one of the few friends she could claim as her own. She might not have been in love with him, but that didn't mean she wasn't loyal to him.

"No, he's fine. Sleeping last time I checked in," he assured her. "You two expecting company?" The chief looked at the knife in Darling's hand. Heat rose in her neck, and she put the weapon back on the counter. Oliver relaxed his hand but didn't put his knife down.

"We weren't, and that was the problem," he said with a nonapologetic smile.

The chief let out a chuckle. "Better safe than sorry," he said.

"So what's the news, Chief?" Darling asked. For him to personally visit was out of character.

"Well, we finally found what we believe to be Jane Doe's car."

"That's wonderful," Darling exclaimed. Surely they could find out who she was now. That was a break they all needed. The chief, however, didn't seem as enthused. She shared a look with Oliver. He didn't understand the chief's current emotion, either.

"The car was stripped. No plates. No insurance."

"Then how do you know it belongs to Jane Doe?" Oliver asked.

Chief Sanderson's face was absolutely stony when he responded. "We found the murder weapon on the front seat. A blunt object that fits the indention in Jane Doe's skull with trace amounts of blood on it."

"So—if you can get her prints—you should be able to ID her now. At least faster, I hope, than sending her blood off?" Oliver supplied.

The chief shook his head. "She isn't in the criminal database, so unless she's been printed at some point in her life, it'll still be difficult to see who she is. The system isn't perfect and sometimes, no matter how hard we try, it doesn't work." He cracked a smile. It wasn't happy. It was downright malicious. "So we're going to get Nigel Marks to tell us who she is."

That surprised Darling.

"Why?" Oliver asked.

"We found evidence that suggests Nigel was in that car recently, which means he knew our victim. Not even his fancy lawyer will be able to deny it. He's now physically connected to her."

Darling couldn't believe it. "What is the evidence?" she asked.

"I can't disclose that information." Before Darling could complain, he held up his hand. "But I'm sure if you think really hard about it, you'll remember."

"What do you mean, I'll remember?"

"You were in the same car, too."

Darling felt her eyebrows slam together.

"Wait a second." Oliver held up his hands. "You mean the car we found her in this morning belongs to Jane Doe?"

The chief nodded.

"Oh, my God," she said, drawing both men's attention her way. "The watch! It was Nigel's watch? It *did* look expensive. I didn't really think too much about it, given the situation."

"Well, some people should think twice before they get their names inscribed into their accessories."

"And the hammer," Darling exclaimed, realizing what the blunt object the chief was referring to was. "It's the murder weapon." Darling's raised her eyebrows when the chief nodded. She looked down at her hands and cringed. "I picked that up. It was in the trunk and I—I wanted a weapon! Did I mess up the evidence?"

The chief gave her a sympathetic smile. "No," he said. "We were able to tell the older blood versus the blood left from your hand. As for her prints, I'm betting the hammer will be wiped down like the car, save for yours. But I'm trying to remain optimistic."

"What about Nigel's alibi?" Darling asked.

"It still holds. We're just accusing him of hindering a murder investigation now. He's lied to us, and now we have physical evidence that ties him to the victim. It's enough to hold him until we get some answers. I'm sure his lawyer is already earning his keep right now." The chief stood to signal the conversation was over. "I also came by to make sure you were okay." He didn't smile, but she could hear the concern in his voice.

"I'm much better, thanks," she replied. "I would have been worse had you two not found me."

"Don't look at me," Chief Sanderson said. "Blame this guy. If he hadn't been so concerned about you, we wouldn't have gotten to you when we did."

Darling turned to Oliver. He shrugged, trying to look indifferent.

"Well, I need to get back to it. I'm going to have an officer stop by later to take down your official statement and also take your prints so we can know which are yours in that car." The chief turned to Oliver and put out his hand to shake. "Thanks for not giving up. Not everyone can keep their cool in these situations. I suppose I'll see you and your boss around the station since we have Nigel in custody now."

Oliver shook back. An emotion that Darling couldn't place flared to life across his face.

"Actually, I'm no longer on the case," he said, surprising Darling. "I might have said and done some things I shouldn't have when I couldn't locate Darling. I personally don't regret it, but professionally it wasn't the best call to make. Though I can't complain at the moment." Oliver looked pointedly at Darling.

"I can't, either," the chief agreed.

The chief said another quick goodbye and left. Darling waited until she thought the older man was out of the building before she turned on Oliver.

"You were taken off the case?" she asked with concern. "What does that mean? Does Orion lose the money now?"

"No, my team is still working with Nigel. Only I was taken off." He sat back down at the counter. Darling held her hands wide in question. "Though I don't know if even they will be working on it now that Nigel has actually been linked to Jane Doe. He might not be guilty of killing her, but this new evidence will make Nikki take a long second look. Do you think he'll admit to the affair now?"

Darling decided to put a pin in the issue of him getting dropped from the case and instead went along with this thoughts. Because, truth be told, the new information hadn't made the case any easier. Every clue was another layer of confusion. It was as if they were looking over a map and everything was a fraction off. They needed a key that would show them the correct way to decipher it all.

"I would imagine Nigel will either come clean about everything or give an alternate version. Something that covers him," she answered. "Elizabeth should be in town soon, right? To admit to the affair now would ruin everything for him. He's a smart man. He has to know he's got his back up against the proverbial wall."

"Nigel *is* a smart man." Oliver was looking at the wall, but she doubted he was seeing it. Concentration mixed with confusion were two expressions she could pick out with ease. Darling knew the feeling well. "So, why would he leave a watch with his name in his mistress's car?"

Darling had already picked up on that thread of thought.

"It could have been an accident." She didn't feel the certainty in it as she said it.

Oliver cast her a questioning look. "But…"

"But, I can't get over the fact that I was the one who found the car. Me being taken and then left to find it couldn't have been a coincidence, could it?" Like with the car, Darling tried to recall with new attention the moment after waking up in the darkness until her trek to the car. "If I hadn't had walked that way, it's true I might not have found it, but now that I think about it, there was no other place for me to go."

"What do you mean? You could have walked off in any direction. You just lucked out and happened to go the direction the car was already in." Darling knew Oliver was playing devil's advocate now. She knew the idea of her finding the car being a coincidence wasn't sitting well with him. However, he wanted her to work for her side of the argument. He was challenging her as he always had. Normally it would have made her angry, but she realized it was helping her work her own thoughts out, as well. Oliver Quinn, annoying her into being a better person.

"No, I think that was the only place to go," she said. "I heard the chief tell the doctor at the hospital that he guessed I had to have been left a few yards away from the Pinketts' property line." She envisioned the aerial shot of the land she had once seen framed in the police-department lounge. It, along with other land reserved for hunting, was showcased in the room. "If that's true, then if I had decided to walk in the opposite direction, I would have run into their woods." Without meaning to, she shivered.

"Okay, so you could have walked into the woods."

"But I wouldn't have. Not with its hunting traps and animals galore," she rebutted. "Plus, it somehow felt creepier to be trapped among the trees instead of out in the open."

Oliver's frown deepened. He made to grab her hand but then changed tactics and put his own around his cup instead. Darling felt a twinge of sadness. Whatever moment they had had earlier seemed to have been lost in the muck of all the questions regarding Jane Doe's fate.

"You wouldn't go into the woods, but that doesn't mean whoever took you knew that. What about the road that cut through it all? If you had found that, you could easily have missed the car."

She didn't have a response for that. If she had found the dirt road Chief Sanderson and Oliver had come in on, she *would* have followed it one way or the other. She never would have seen the car. Maybe it *was* a coincidence. "Then why turn my phone *back* on?" she asked with a tilt of her head. "Why take my phone, turn it off, then turn it back on later so the car and I could be found?" Oliver didn't have an answer to that, either. She let out a frustrated sigh. "We need fewer theories and more facts," Darling muttered. "I'm so tired of guessing. What if we're just grasping at straws?"

"Well, let's look at the facts, then." Oliver got up from his stool and disappeared into her bedroom. Moments later he was back with a pen and one of her notebooks. He flipped it open to a blank sheet and started a numbered list. "Nigel Marks spent the late night and early morning at Mulligan Motel with Jane Doe."

"Which he denies having done."

"Jane Doe was killed while Nigel was eating with Orion agents. Giving him a valid alibi."

"Elizabeth Marks also has a confirmed alibi," she added. He quickly wrote that down.

"Jane Doe's fingers and teeth were removed, meaning the killer didn't want her to be identified, or maybe the killer wanted some trophies." Oliver hesitated before writing the last part down. Darling tried not to picture the body in the tub. "Then a mysterious person gives you pictures of Nigel and Jane Doe over the course of several months this year. Nigel's lawyer reasons it could be anyone or the images could be doctored. Without the original files to be tested, the cops can't keep him or get him to reveal her identity. You get another note saying to stop investigating, and they take your camera only to return it. Acuity gets ransacked, you get another note and then you're taken. You find Jane Doe's car stripped car with Nigel Marks's watch in it."

When he was done, she looked down at the short-hand list.

"I feel like we're just talking in circles now," she breathed out. "We're missing something."

They lapsed into a thoughtful silence. Maybe it was time to leave the case alone. Maybe they were hurting it instead of helping. It was already her fault that Derrick, the lead investigator, had been hospitalized. If she hadn't kept digging…

"Oh, my God, that's it," Darling exclaimed. Oliver met her wild stare with skepticism.

"What?"

"Let's stick with the theory that there *are* two people involved in the killing of Jane Doe. So far they've shown up whenever I discovered something new. The office was tossed looking for the security tape. They got it, so that should be it, right? But then they grab me two hours later? Why?" Before Oliver could answer, she beat him to it. "Because I found Harriet Mendon."

"Wait, what do you mean you found her?"

"Before you and I had it out at Acuity, I looked up where she worked."

Oliver's features seemed to reanimate.

"Oliver," she continued with new enthusiasm. "I think Harriet Mendon is our key."

Just as quickly as excitement at a new lead flashed across his face, a darker emotion replaced it. When he spoke, it made the hair on the back of Darling's neck stand up.

"Then we'd better find her before they do."

Chapter Eighteen

Darling found the number of the boutique where Harriet Mendon worked and left an urgent message with the owner, a friendly woman named Barb. She also left a new message on Harriet's home machine. One way or the other, she wanted to cover all her bases.

"Okay, it's time I change out of this robe," Darling said when she was done. "Make yourself at home."

Oliver looked around the living room with a new perspective after she went to her bedroom. He imagined his recliner in the corner, the picture of his parents next to the one of Darling and friends on top of the bookcase, his shoes tossed off next to the front door and the fight that would always come from him leaving them there.

Holiday get-togethers, quiet nights spent in, loud meaningless arguments that would never last long and makeups that would certainly last longer. There they were, moving around the small space without an ounce of regret or anger or guilt.

He pictured the two of them finishing something they had started when they were basically kids.

And loving every moment of it.

"It just isn't my week," Darling said a few minutes later, interrupting his thoughts.

"What happened?"

"Do you want a list or a long-winded sentence?"

He gave her his full attention. "Let's go long-winded sentence this time."

She took a deep breath.

"Elizabeth called because she's at the police station with Nigel—who apparently finally realized it was a good idea to tell the truth about knowing Jane Doe. But Elizabeth wouldn't say the name—and because of everything that happened, she terminated my contract," she said in a rush. "Finding Jane Doe's killer isn't her top priority anymore."

"Or she wants the police to handle it since you were *kidnapped* and left for dead by the same person or people," Oliver pointed out. Darling frowned and sent him a pointed stare. He held up his hands in defense. "It's guilt, Darling. She doesn't want to deal with it if something happens to you while under her orders." His thoughts turned to Nikki. "It has nothing to do with your job performance."

"I know," she admitted. "But the way she spoke…" Darling's brow furrowed and she sucked on her bottom lip, thinking of the right words. "She didn't sound upset at all. I guess I just assumed that finding out the identity of her husband's mistress might hit a nerve, even if she already knew about the affair." She shrugged. "Either way, I've been fired, so the case doesn't matter anymore."

The private investigator tried to look nonchalant. She leaned on her crutches in the doorway of her bedroom, gaze going through him as she focused on some thought in the distance. Oliver didn't point out that neither of them was ready to let the case go without getting justice for those who had determined Jane Doe's fate *and* hurt Darling. He crossed his arms over his chest and waited. It didn't take long.

"Who am I kidding?" Darling exclaimed. "Like being fired is going to stop me."

Oliver clapped. "That's my girl!"

Darling smiled. He could see how tired she felt.

"But first, coffee?" he suggested.

That earned a bigger smile. "That sounds wonderful, Mr. Quinn."

"DEPUTY HEATH, I never got a chance to thank you for helping to find me."

They had already gone through an entire pot of coffee waiting for the deputy to show up to take Darling's statement.

"It's no problem," she replied, wasting no time in getting down to business. She pulled out her printing kit, and Darling offered her hand. The older woman looked as if she also needed some coffee. "I can't wait until we catch those sons of b—"

"Those?" Darling interrupted. A wild kind of excitement crossed her face. Oliver bet she was ready to call out every clue she had that connected to two killers rather than one. "As in more than one?"

Oliver watched as the deputy's cheeks tinted pink. "I *meant*," Heath said, "whoever is responsible. We have a very promising lead and I—personally—am confident we'll have this case closed up soon."

The private investigator held her comments back while Deputy Heath finished the prints. Her gears were turning. That much Oliver could tell from his seat at the kitchen counter. With a bit of distance between them, he tried to look at her from an objective viewpoint.

Tired yet determined. Hurt yet unperturbed. Curious yet cautious.

"I can't disclose that information right now," Heath said after everything was done. "Give us tonight, Darling. Everything will make much more sense in the morning."

Oliver was ready to point out that after what Darling had been through, she deserved at least the name of Jane Doe, but the investigator shot him a silencing look. Neither pressed the issue as the deputy left.

"A sane person would probably take all of this—" Darling waved her arms around "—as a sign to change professions, huh?"

Oliver came around and took a seat next to her. "I don't know if you've noticed, but you aren't like most people." He patted her knee on reflex. She didn't pull away.

"I guess you really dodged a bullet back in the day."

Oliver tensed. Whether it was an off-the-cuff remark or a pointed comment about him rejecting her, he didn't know. What he was sure of was that he didn't like that she seemed to be blaming herself for what had happened. He cleared his throat.

"Darling," he started, but he was cut off when she touched his hand with hers.

"I don't want to talk about it," she said, voice resolute. "What you've done in the last week is more than most would have done for me. You saved me and it cost you. I'm sorry for that, Oliver." She meant to pull her hand away, but he held it fast. Darling's green eyes were calm as they searched his.

"Don't you dare apologize to me after what I've done," he said, voice filled with grit. "And I'll never regret what

I did trying to find you. Never." Unlike their kiss earlier that day, the atmosphere darkened. There was lust—he was certainly feeling it—but there was also pain. Had he gone too far when he left her? Had he changed her life for the worse instead of for the better? These thoughts pushed Oliver off the couch as if he had been burned. Darling let go of his hand, eyes wide. He didn't miss the flush across her cheeks, either.

"Well, thank you," she said in a rush, also standing. "I—uh—think I'm going to dry my hair." She reached back and took her crutches leaning against the couch. Oliver didn't respond. Guilt and regret were slamming against his rib cage. He shouldn't want her—shouldn't imagine a life with her—after deciding to cut ties with no explanation. She had a life. She deserved better than him. Always had, always would.

He watched as she awkwardly began her walk back to the bedroom. The crutches clinked in the silence. However, she didn't make it far. Oliver was in front of her in an instant.

Her eyes were red, tears waiting on each rim. His last image of the younger Darling had been with tears in her eyes, but his mind didn't connect that vulnerability or memory to the woman standing in front of him. He didn't connect it the day she found out what her parents had done, and he didn't even think to compare it to the cold, naked woman he had held in his arms that morning.

Bringing his hands up, he cradled her face and moved closer.

There was the difference. Between his fingers and the heat of her skin was an electricity he couldn't ignore. It coursed through each of them before crashing together. Rapid, shocking, sensational.

And it was begging him to not let go.

Before the world could catch up to them, his mouth covered hers.

Chapter Nineteen

Hunger. Passion.

Pain. Lust. Desire.

Everything exploded in the kiss. Darling didn't know which thought to rest on as Oliver's lips pushed and pulled at more than just her body. There were a million reasons they shouldn't be intertwining and yet she couldn't recall a single one.

Darling's eyelids fluttered closed, and she let herself enjoy the moment. Oliver's lips pressed against her with an undeniable hunger that ate its way right into hers. Her crutches clattered to the ground as she wrapped her arms around his neck, seeking a new anchor. A new lifeline. His tongue found hers, and they tasted each other for the first time in eight years.

Their painful past melted away. They were finding their way back to each other. Back to the home they had made all those years ago. Darling moaned against his lips. She had missed this.

Oliver deepened the kiss, moving his arms around her and pulling her flush against him. It forced a new proximity that woke up every part of her body. She arched against him and he grabbed her hips. She felt him push against her and a new thrill began to pool below her waist. Another moan escaped against him. Oliver silenced it with his own. Instead of raw hunger, Darling could feel the control in it. He deepened the kiss only to break it off a moment later.

Darling looked up at him, confused and breathless.

His face was flushed. His lips red and swollen. Those amber eyes searched her face in the quiet. For once, Darling dared not speak.

There weren't a lot of things in life she felt she absolutely needed.

But right then, she knew she needed Oliver Quinn.

"Darling," he whispered, voice husky. Another shock of pleasure pulsed through her at the sound. He closed the space between their lips again. It was a soft kiss that burned slowly.

He didn't speak again.

With one quick movement, he picked her up and put her legs around his waist. Darling gladly hugged his body back, not breaking their connection. Then they were moving down the familiar path to the bedroom.

Though as she began to unbutton his shirt, she realized that where they were going was a place neither had visited before.

THE SOFT CARESS of cotton against her bare skin.

The mattress that molded against her every curve.

The warmth of a man around her heart.

A wisp of a smile trailed across Darling's lips.

She stretched out, feeling for her bodyguard beneath the sheets. Her hand found the edge of the bed instead. Slowly her eyelids opened.

Fear made her heart beat against her chest. For one awful moment, Darling thought she was back in the clearing, naked and in the dark. However, as panic tried to claw its way through her, common sense blocked its path.

She could feel the bed beneath her, the sheets around her. She smelled the citrus that had attached to her skin after her bath. The scent of Oliver's body wash that mingled with it.

No, she wasn't in danger here.

She waited as her vision adjusted to the low light of the room. From where she was, she could see out into the hallway and to the stools at the kitchen counter. Light filtered across the floor from the TV. She closed her eyes again, still tired. She couldn't lie there and think about what had happened between them *and* keep her eyes open. There wasn't enough energy to sustain both acts.

So she burrowed back beneath the covers and let her smile widen. When she was younger, she would often imagine what it was like to be with Oliver. Would he be gentle? Would he be rough? Or would he be a man who walked the line in between?

It was as if she had been holding her breath for years, waiting for Oliver. Now that she had let him back into her life, into her home and her bed, she felt she could let that breath out.

She drifted back to sleep, thinking of the bodyguard, only to wake up a while later, looking at him.

"Hey there," he said.

Darling stretched and smiled. "Hey back." She glanced to her alarm clock to see it was still late. Before she could ask what was going on, Oliver answered her.

"They're running a news story about the murder. I wanted to make sure you saw it, too."

That made her sit up.

"Yeah, I really do want to see it."

Much like before, Oliver carried her across the apartment. The heat of his bare chest against her was a welcome reminder of that afternoon. However, this time, once they reached their destination, he set her down and let go. She marveled at how badly she wanted to stay in his arms—to be wrapped up in his touch—but told her brain to focus.

Which wasn't hard when she looked at the television. On its screen was a local news reporter standing in front of the Mulligan police station. A spotlight from her camera crew was positioned on her face, trying to keep viewers' attention on her and not the crowd behind. Even in the dark, Darling could make out reporter Rebel Nash and a handful of others in a semicircle around Chief Sanderson and a few of his deputies behind her. The woman who filled the screen, however, looked excited about whatever story she was reporting on. Oliver turned up the volume on the TV.

"—a corporate conspiracy that is connected to the death of a Jean Watford, found dead in a bathtub at the Mulligan Motel. One of Charisma Investment's board members and its interim CEO, resident Nigel Marks, has refused an interview at this time. His attorney issued the following statement—'My client cannot confirm or deny at this point in time that Ms. Watford was guaranteed a top managerial position within the company, but she was being seriously considered. The fact that this could have been the cause of her death is abhorrent, and the Marks family wants nothing more than to see those responsible brought to justice.'"

A picture of a red-haired woman—apparently their Jane Doe—popped up in the corner next to the reporter's head.

"Jean Watford, age twenty-three, resided in Miami, Florida. She was visiting Mulligan on business."

Her picture was replaced by an image of two men talking to each other by the side of a building. They stood in the shadows and didn't seem to be aware someone had been taking their pictures. Darling didn't recognize either of the older men but knew by their outfits alone they were high-level businessmen.

"CFO Lamar Bennington and executive assistant Robert Jensen are being held for questioning after an anonymous tip led to the discovery of controversial emails about Ms. Watford, including one that contained information pertaining to what police believe to be the murder weapon. Both men are currently denying these charges."

The reporter changed gears and gave viewers some background on Charisma Investments and their merger, which was almost complete. Darling already knew this information. She muted the television and gave Oliver a questioning look.

"So, Jean Watford wasn't a mistress?" she asked. Her entire investigation had been based on that one assumption.

"I suppose he—" Oliver's phone began to ring, cutting him off. "I don't know who this is," he muttered before answering. "Oliver Quinn here," he answered. Darling watched as his face hardened. He held up his finger to ask her to wait and headed to the bedroom for some privacy.

Darling sighed. She wished the police would give her phone back soon. Surely there would be no reason for forensics to keep it now that they had men in custody. She didn't like being without it.

The local news cut to a weather segment, so Darling turned it off. She reached for her office chair and hopped into it. Pushing herself with her good foot, she went to the kitchen counter for a pen and paper. Before she could forget the two men's names, she wrote them down. There was no need to pen Jean Watford. Now that she could put a name to the body in the tub, she knew she'd never forget either for the rest of her life.

"Well, looks like we have more of a story to go with," Oliver said when he came back into the room a few minutes later. "That was actually our friend Deputy Derrick. He's fine, by the way. Should be discharged in a few days." He grabbed the arms of the chair and rolled Darling over to the couch, sitting in front of her. He placed his hands on her thighs as he continued. "He was brought up to speed right before the news segment aired. He figured we were watching or, at the very least, deserved a bit more than what they had to offer."

Darling knew that the only reason they were getting the special treatment from Derrick was that the case had become personal for the three of them. Once he had been attacked, Darling had been taken and Oliver had helped save them both, Derrick had mentally put them on the same page. A task he wouldn't have done otherwise.

"Tell me," was all Darling could manage. Something akin to hesitant excitement had started to flow through her. The case felt as if it was almost over, even if it had taken a turn she didn't expect.

"Nigel admitted that he had been seeing Jean in secret for the past year. He met her at a business conference when he was in Miami and was impressed. Apparently Jean was a very smart cookie. Nigel was beginning to finalize the merger but wasn't happy with the people who were going to be in charge. He wanted some new blood and decided to start grooming Jean in secret."

"Why in secret?"

"He was afraid that if he publicly acknowledged he was about to restructure the new business, stocks would suffer and he'd have to deal with unnecessary backlash. No one was supposed to find out until the end of the month, but apparently word got out somehow."

"To the CFO and the assistant?"

Oliver nodded. "Nigel told the chief that the CFO had formed not-so-beneficial friendships with those who worked for him. He didn't care that they weren't doing their jobs anymore."

"And Jean was going to take one of their jobs at the new company?"

"Bingo. Nigel wasn't sure why the executive assistant was involved. He only guessed Bennington offered something in exchange for his help. They had emails about the rumor that Jean was going to replace someone, and the CFO was furious about it. They flew in the day before Nigel, and neither of their alibis can be confirmed for the time of death."

Darling leaned back, trying to take it all in.

"Robert, the assistant, also can't provide an alibi for the time Derrick was attacked and you were taken," he added, voice dropping to a whisper. "But they found a long blond hair on his jacket that the chief thinks might be yours."

The excitement she had been feeling at shutting down a case left in an instant. She recalled the picture of the two men, trying to place a face with the body that had choked her. Oliver took her hands in his and rested them against her legs again. It was enough to ground her emotions and make her able to ask another nagging question.

"What about the murder weapon? Surely they weren't stupid enough to *email* about it?"

"Bennington asked the assistant if he had some tools they could use for a secret project."

"The hammer!"

"He didn't ask for one specifically, but he did mention they needed to make sure they had pliers."

Darling's mouth dropped open. "To pull out her teeth," she said, horrified. "They put all of that in emails?"

Oliver shrugged. "Derrick said the chief thought Bennington was under the influence of some narcotics when they picked him up, so that definitely could have made him sloppy. Plus, I think this is a man who usually gets what he wants. Having a loyal follower—like Robert Jensen, who had access to Nigel's entire schedule, emails and probably calls—helped him pull off the murder without leaving anything behind."

"If all of this was business related, then why didn't Nigel just tell the cops about it all when Jean was found?" Darling didn't understand why the man had preferred to look guilty rather than coming clean in the first place, especially if the link would be easy to make when everything was out in the open.

Oliver's eyes lit up. "Get this," he almost sang. "He thought his wife was the one behind it. That she had hired someone to take care of a woman she thought was his mistress."

Darling didn't speak for a moment. "Wow. If they stay married, they definitely are going to need some counseling about trust."

Oliver agreed. "That's all Derrick knew. They were getting search warrants to go through each man's hotel room and belongings, but the way it sounds, both men are in trouble."

Darling nodded. "So, it's over, then?"

"It looks that way. The killers are in custody, and Jane Doe now has a name." Oliver squeezed Darling's hands. "No more looking over your shoulder. Unless I'm walking behind you and you just want to see all of this." He motioned to his chest and abs. A smile had stretched his lips, changing the mood from dark to playful. He felt relieved, and she knew it. But did she feel it, too? The motive, means and suspects made sense even though she had never even known about them until now. Logically, everything had fallen into place. However, her gut felt as if something was off.

Oliver brought his hand up to her chin and pulled her face forward.

"I know that look," he whispered, an inch from her lips. "You took the entire day off, remember? That means the night, too." He brushed his lips across hers, sending a wonderful thrill from her stomach downward. "That means no overthinking."

"But that's what I'm good at," she defended herself with no real weight behind the words.

He passed his lips across hers again, pausing only to speak. "Not tonight, my Darling."

Chapter Twenty

Everything felt so right.

Darling opened her eyes and didn't want to move. She could feel Oliver's even breathing against her back. His arm was thrown over her, pressing the warmth of their naked bodies together.

It was perfect.

She didn't want to leave the bed, but her mouth felt dry and she desperately needed to use the bathroom.

So, as carefully as she could, Darling slipped out from underneath his arm and grabbed her crutches discarded on the floor. Oliver didn't move once. It made her wonder how much sleep he'd skipped the past few days.

Once she was up and moving, Darling decided to go ahead and start the day. It was almost ten in the morning and she felt wildly energized. She knew that was greatly due to the naked bodyguard in her bed. With each step she took, her body reminded her just how close they had become the night before. Though in the light of day, she wondered what that meant for their future. Did they have one, or had it been a one-day event?

The bodyguard had promised to stay by her side as long as the threat of her kidnappers was still out there. Now that they had been caught, she didn't need protection. Why would he stay in Mulligan when his life—his home—was two thousand miles away?

She tried to push the troubling thoughts from her mind as she took a quick shower, awkwardly hopping around to avoid putting too much pressure on her foot. It took the attention from the potential heartbreak she might have to endure again from her fair-haired bodyguard.

Darling managed to dress herself without falling over. She chose a red, long-sleeve top that plunged low to show some cleavage, and a pair of dark jeans that hugged her nicely. It was a more flirty outfit than she usually wore but, as she looked at Oliver's still-sleeping form, she had the urge to break out of her boring wardrobe habits. Not that he seemed to mind when she was and wasn't dressed up.

Oliver stayed asleep throughout the next half hour as she got ready and made breakfast, confirming her suspicion that he had been seriously lacking sleep. She tried to be as quiet as possible but found that when her food was gone, a restlessness was beginning to replace her feelings of contentment. Her gut was back to telling her something was off about Jean Watford's death. But what was it?

"Do you really think Nigel Marks would cry over a mistress?"

Darling snapped her fingers as Oliver's words replayed in her head. That was it.

She went back to the bedroom and grabbed her laptop, putting it in a bag so she could avoid dropping it while using her crutches. Moving to the living room, she powered it on with new vigor. Working on a hunch, she opened an internet browser and searched Jean Watford's name. After some digging, she found the young woman's public social media profile. It had all the information Darling needed.

She did some quick math and typed in a new search.

A few minutes later she found a picture that nearly confirmed her hunch. The picture was from the early '90s and showed a young Nigel Marks at a Christmas party. He stood tall—and rather handsome—amid a large group of people. The quality wasn't the greatest, but Darling got the break she needed when she saw the name of each person printed across the bottom. It didn't take long to find the last piece of the puzzle.

Standing next to Nigel was a red-haired woman with a giant smile.

Her name was Regina Watford.

Darling's mind began turning at such a fast pace she almost felt dizzy. This was why Nigel hadn't admitted to knowing Jean. He *did* have an affair. It was just twenty-three years and nine months earlier.

If Darling was right, she was looking at the night the businessman had strayed from his wife of twenty-six years with the red-haired woman at his side and produced a child—Jean.

Darling thought about the pictures she had been given of Nigel and Jean from the past year. Everyone had thought the two happy people were having an affair, but that was because the daughter angle had never entered their minds. Now, the pictures of the two laughing, hugging and dining in public fit the scenario of a father and daughter meeting. Had they been seeing each other in secret for years or had they just reunited?

Before she could talk herself out of it, Darling went back to the bedroom and grabbed Oliver's phone. She went into the bathroom and shut the door. Scrolling through his contacts, she found Nigel's personal cell phone number.

For some reason she couldn't quite place, she needed to confirm the truth. She hit Call and waited with bated breath.

What was she going to say?

"Nigel Marks's phone," a man answered after two rings. "This is Jace Marks."

That put a kink in Darling's plan. Did Jace even know about his half-sister?

"Um, hi," Darling stuttered out. "This is Darling Smith. I, uh, just had some information for Nigel I thought he might like to know."

"Darling Smith? The woman who was kidnapped?"

"Yeah," she responded, uncomfortable.

"How are you?"

Surprised at the concern, she answered on reflex. "I'm okay. My foot is sore, but I'm alive."

"That's good. It would have been another senseless tragedy had that bodyguard not found you."

"I'd have to agree there." She cleared her throat. "Is there any way I can speak with Nigel, though? It won't take long."

"I'm sorry but no. He's currently unavailable. The best I can do is pass along a message."

"No," she said a little too quickly. She tried to sound calm as she continued. "It's personal. I'd really like to talk to him myself." She wasn't about to announce the real reason behind the call.

"Hold on, then," he said. She didn't hear anything on the other end of the line and looked at the phone to make sure the call hadn't dropped. "We're about to leave the police station and head home. You can meet us at the house, but we have to ask that you keep this meeting and whatever information you have private until Nigel has talked to you. This family has had enough false accusations and rumors started lately."

"Sure thing. I completely understand."

"Thank you. We'll see you soon."

Darling ended the call, shocked at how easy it was to get a meeting. She supposed it made sense that the Markses wanted to go ahead and squash any remaining gossip within the town or general public. Charisma Investments was going to suffer thanks to the actions of Lamar Bennington and Robert Jensen. They didn't need any more bad press.

She returned Oliver's phone to the nightstand and watched as the bodyguard continued to sleep. He looked so peaceful, she decided not to wake him. She wasn't a child. The danger was gone. She could go tie up this loose end without him. Her kidnappers weren't out there to get her. She could be back within the hour.

Bending low, she pressed her lips to his temple. He didn't stir.

She wrote a quick note and left.

Laughing at the fact that the last time she had been at Nigel Marks's home she'd been arrested, she thrummed her fingers against the steering wheel as she drove. It was amazing how a week could change everything.

The gate to the Markses' house was shut, but Darling could see a car parked in the driveway beyond it. She pulled up to wait at the gate and rolled down the window. George Hanely had never been one of her favorite people. He might not even let her in.

However, he never came.

She sat up straighter to see into the gatehouse. No one was inside.

"Getting lazy, George?"

She put the car in Park and opened the door. Pulling her crutches from the backseat, she made her way to the window. George was probably lounging, watching one of his daytime soap operas or whatever it was the man did all day. She looked inside, ready to scold the gate guard but stopped short.

George was sprawled out on the floor, facedown.

Darling tried the doorknob and let out a breath of relief when it opened with no resistance. She knelt beside the unconscious man, almost falling in the process.

"George?" She felt for a pulse and was happy to feel the beat against her fingers. "Hold on. I'll call for help."

She got back up and looked to the phone on the desk. Oliver was going to be upset that she had yet again found herself connected with the police in such a short span.

"Don't move."

Darling froze, hand hovering above the phone.

Turning slowly, she felt her stomach bottom out.

George Hanley was not only coherent but also sitting up and smiling. A gun was in his right hand, pointed at her, but that wasn't what put ice in her blood.

In the palm of his left hand were her two daisy earrings.

"Just so you know how serious I am."

AN ANGRY CHIRPING pecked at the haze of sleep around Oliver until, finally, he had to make it stop. Rolling over, he grabbed his cell phone and gave it a stare that could kill before turning off the everyday alarm. It was meant to make sure he was wide-awake by noon, which, to him, was a time that no man should sleep past. Even on his days off. Although, given recent events, he had meant to deactivate it the night before. But then a beautiful private investigator had let him into her bed, twice.

All thoughts of the alarm and pretty much anything else had gone out the proverbial window the moment their lips and bodies met.

Afraid he had woken her, Oliver rolled back over, ready to laugh that they had slept in. He was disappointed her side of the bed was empty. The rest of the room was, too. In fact, he couldn't hear any movement in the apartment.

"Darling?" he called, swinging his legs over the edge of the bed. He stretched wide and noticed a note on the nightstand.

"'Tying up a loose end with Nigel. Didn't want to wake you. Be back by lunch,'" he read aloud.

He read it again as if it would make more sense. It didn't. Of course the maddening woman wouldn't give him more information than that. What loose ends were left?

Oliver picked his phone back up and went to his recent call list. He sighed and made a mental note to take her by the police station to get her phone back. Now there wasn't a way to reach her directly. He was about to put the phone down when he noticed the most recent call was placed earlier that morning. Darling had used to his phone to call Nigel.

It was a bold move. One she wouldn't have made unless she had a solid lead on something.

Suddenly Oliver's calm wasn't as resolute. A sinking feeling of apprehension slunk in.

He dialed the number again and put it to his ear.

It went straight to voice mail.

"Okay," he said to the empty apartment. "Time to get dressed."

Five minutes later Oliver was in his rental and driving toward Nigel's vacation home. He could have called Thomas, Grant or Nikki to let him talk to Darling if she was with Nigel, but after his talk with Nikki the previous day, it didn't feel right. Darling wasn't in trouble. He was just being overprotective. Jane Doe's, or rather Jean Watford's, killers had been caught. The men who had taken Darling were being held...or were they?

He rolled his shoulders back. The seed of doubt that had sprouted in his mind was growing, but there was no need for it, he tried to reason with himself. Yet it was a pill he couldn't seem to swallow. The closer he got to the vacation home, the more his nerves pricked. Why, he wasn't sure, but he knew he wouldn't shed the sudden restlessness until he set his eyes on a certain sneaky private investigator.

Oliver was sorely disappointed that no one seemed to be home when he arrived outside the gatehouse. No cars were in the driveway minus one he believed to belong to George. His aversion to calling Nikki was starting to ebb. He pulled his phone out just as it buzzed against his palm. It was a Maine number but not one he recognized.

"Oliver Quinn," he answered, getting out of his SUV to look into the gatehouse for its guard. He mentally snorted at its emptiness. He was probably goofing off somewhere, not doing his job.

"Hello. I think this is the number I was supposed to call. Barb said some people were looking for me?" a female responded, uncertainty clear. There was a blanket of noise in the background.

"Harriet Mendon?" Oliver guessed.

"Yeah, that's me! Now what's this about?" She didn't sound mad or scared. Only curious. An older Darling, he quickly mused.

"The woman at the gas station you stopped at on the way out of Mulligan the other night—the one with the red hair—was—" Oliver paused and changed where the statement had been headed "—she died the next morning." There was a tiny gasp, but she didn't interrupt. "There was a guy—a bad guy—who thought whatever it was you two talked about might have been something that could have hurt him. We just wanted to make sure if you saw him to call the police, but you shouldn't have to worry about that anymore. He's with the police now."

"Oh, wow, I leave Mulligan for the first time in ten years and suddenly it gets exciting," she answered after a beat. "I am sorry about that young woman, though. She was so happy and vibrant. Made me feel young again just talking to her. How did she die?"

"I'm not sure," he lied. Jean's death was probably already splashed across the local paper. Harriet would be able to read about it all when she got back. Oliver didn't want to rehash the details.

"What a tragedy. I can't imagine what the man thought she told me. We only talked for maybe a minute. Nothing out of the ordinary. She was just excited to meet up with her dad and relax for a few days."

Oliver stopped, his hand against the SUV door.

"Her dad? I thought she was in Mulligan on business," he said, recalling the reporter's words from the previous night's news.

"I don't think so. I remember her specifically saying she was going to spend time with her dad and enjoy some downtime," Harriet said. "She was smiling ear to ear. Does that sound like she was about to work to you?"

"No," Oliver answered. "It doesn't sound like work had anything to do with her visit to Mulligan after all."

Oliver didn't extend his conversation with Harriet Mendon past the new information. He also didn't question the validity of what the woman had gleaned from her chat with Jean. The security footage had shown a happy young woman, not someone about to dive into a stressful, secretive business world.

No, Jean Watford was about to go to meet up with her father.

She had been on the way to meet Nigel Marks at the Mulligan Motel.

All at once, the clues and lies made sense. The pictures of Nigel and Jean over the past year—meeting in secret—with the two of them enjoying each other's company without any sexual or provocative contact. The pain and surprise Oliver had picked up on when Nigel had been told about Jean's death.

In Orion's research on the Marks family, Oliver couldn't recall a single detail about a daughter. Half, step or otherwise. Jean Watford must have been one of the best kept secrets of Nigel's life.

That's what Darling was referring to as her loose end, Oliver realized. That's why she had called Nigel. She had figured it out, and the always curious Darling needed confirmation.

But where was she now?

Oliver took another look at the house. His feeling of unease had grown so strong, he felt as if it was a tangible object he could wield to cut open the gate. Had the entire story of Jean Watford joining Charisma Investments been a lie? If so, where did that leave the motive for her two supposed killers?

A new puzzle was coming together just as the old one was falling apart.

Oliver flew through his contacts until he found Grant's number. He hesitated and passed the name, going straight for another. He pressed Call next to Nikki's name, not willing to make the same mistake twice. Knowing her, she was still in town and would remain there for the duration of the contract. "Yes?" she cut right to the chase. Oliver could hear several voices in the background.

"Are you still with Nigel?"

"Oliver, you know I can't divulge information like that on a current—"

"Is Darling with him?" Oliver's voice had dropped to an almost icy plane of existence. Nikki picked up on it immediately.

"No. We've been at the new Charisma building since this morning." He could hear her moving away from the group of people next to her. She spoke louder. "Why?"

"She called him while I was asleep and then left a note saying she was coming here to talk to him. I'm at the vacation house now."

"Unless she called him before five this morning, she didn't talk to him," Nikki said with certainty. "He's been in board meetings all day, trying to clean up this mess. He literally hasn't left the room in hours. The room has a glass wall and everything. We've been able to see him at all times, and not once has he made or picked up a call."

"Could he have done that when you looked away?" Oliver reasoned.

"Here, he's coming out now. Let me just ask." He could

hear her annoyance at not being taken at her word, but Oliver needed to know what had been said during that call.

It could be nothing.

It could be everything.

Muffled voices filled his ear. It was a white noise that did nothing to break the silence of the outside world around him. He stood back from the gate and wondered if Darling had come here at all. If George hadn't been at the gate, she would have had to leave. Why wasn't George there to begin with? It was paramount he be at his station when the house was empty. To make sure it stayed that way.

Oliver went to the gatehouse and tried the door. It was locked. He cupped his hand and looked inside. Everything seemed normal.

"Oliver," Nikki said, bringing his focus back. "Nigel said he never talked to Darling. He can't even find his phone."

"He's lying, then," Oliver responded with grit. "My phone said the call was made." He didn't need to look again to know that was true. It not only was received but also lasted almost a minute.

"Well, Nigel didn't speak with her." Nikki kept talking, but Oliver didn't hear it.

"I need you to get Rachel to track George Hanley's cell phone," he ground out. Oliver tried the doorknob again, and when it didn't budge, he took a step back.

"What? Why?"

Oliver didn't answer as he threw his shoulder into the door. It splintered at the lock and swung open.

"Oliver?" Nikki's confusion was turning into anger.

"Because I'm pretty sure George Hanely took her."

"How do you know?"

Oliver had scanned and rescanned the gatehouse each time he had made a sweep while on duty. George was a neat person. Every item in the small room had always been in a specific spot and order. His DVDs all were stacked nicely next to his television, his books were ordered next to his security tapes, and even his chair had always been pushed beneath the desk when he was occupying it. Now Oliver saw a room out of order. A few of the books were strewn across the desktop, the chair was on the other side of the room and one of the DVD cases lay in the corner, cracked open. However, it wasn't the unusual state of the space that caught his eye. It was the set of crutches poking out from beneath the desk that coaxed a concerned Oliver into the gatehouse. The blood on one of the pads only threw fuel onto the burning fire within him.

"Her crutches are here. Nikki, I need you to track him now," Oliver repeated, more urgent than before. "Please."

This time Nikki didn't hesitate.

"Give me five minutes," she answered. Her voice had taken on the calm of the determined woman he knew her to be.

"Let me talk to Nigel," he added. Again she didn't even pause.

"What's going on?" Nigel asked a few seconds later.

"George Hanley took Darling," Oliver said. "I need you to tell me why."

"What? He took her?"

"Yes. Now, what the hell would he want with her?" Oliver was moving around the room, looking for something that might clue him in to where the gate guard had gone.

"I have no idea!"

"Come on, Nigel. I talked to the man. He seemed to worship you, said you two were great pals. Think!"

"You're mistaken," Nigel said hurriedly. "Mr. Hanley is close with my son, Jace, not me."

Everything stopped for a moment.

"Hello?" Nigel asked, bringing Oliver out of his icy thoughts. He only had one question left.

"Did Jace know that Jean Watford was your daughter?"

As if he was standing in front of the millionaire, Oliver could see the older man had reached the same conclusion as he just had.

"Oh, my God."

Chapter Twenty-One

It was a three-story building with cracked gray siding and a crumbling roofline. There was a workshop in the back, attached by a makeshift walkway that hadn't fared well against the weather. The several acres around each were untouched and gave clear sight lines to the road in the distance.

Darling took in all of these details as George drove up the long dirt drive. She had been to this abandoned house hidden near the heart of town before with Derrick who had said knowing its location might help with future cases considering the amount of criminal activity that happened there from time to time. It was dubbed the Slate House and hadn't been occupied in almost twenty years. The local teens really liked it as a location to drink in private, considering its next neighbor wasn't even in shouting distance.

A shiver ran up Darling's spine.

Perhaps that's why George was taking her there, as well.

"Why?" Darling asked the gate guard for the third time. Her chin was throbbing, but with her hands bound behind her back, she couldn't touch her face to assess the damage. She took solace in the fact that before George had managed to wrestle the plastic zip ties around her wrists, she had been able to do some damage of her own. Her crutch had made an excellent bat. The bleeding gash on his forehead was a testament to that.

George didn't slow the car until they were next to the workshop's outside door at the back of the house. He cut the ignition without answering her yet again. Never had she hated the silence more.

"George, why are we here?" she asked, expanding her earlier question in hopes he would answer. Instead he opened his door and got out.

For one wonderful moment, Darling thought he'd leave. That he would just walk off and give her enough time to figure out an escape route. But George didn't do that. He turned to the back door and opened it, and for the first time since he'd yelled at her to get into the car while simultaneously shoving her, he spoke.

"Someone wants to talk to you."

He reached into the car and grabbed for her. Darling tried to shrink away, but George was faster than he looked. He caught her jacket sleeve and tugged hard. "Don't fight it, private eye," he snarled as he struggled to pull her out and up. "You brought this on yourself."

"What are you talking about?" Darling yelled. He shut the car door and held her by the tie on her wrists, bending her slightly so she couldn't stand at full height. Without her crutches, the weight she put on her foot made her wince.

"Have you ever heard of the story where curiosity killed the cat?" He started to walk to the door, pushing her in front of him. She stumbled and considered making a run for it, but no sooner had the idea popped into her head than she felt the gun poke into her back. If anyone would shoot her without warning, it would be George. Whatever anger he was harboring for her, it was malicious. He stopped in front of the door. "In this story, you're the cat."

George let go of her wrists long enough to open the workshop's door, then pushed her inside. Darling wasn't sure what she had expected to find in the tiny room, but she hadn't foreseen the lone two chairs and freestanding electric lights in the least. The chairs faced each other between the white peeling walls and the concrete floors. It felt cold and sterile.

And terrifying.

Whatever was about to happen, Darling was positive she didn't need to be a part of it.

George shoved her into one of the chairs and stepped back while she righted herself. He didn't take the seat opposite.

"You don't even remember me, do you?" he asked, voice pitching higher than normal.

Darling was confused by the question. Surely he wasn't referring to the trespassing incident that had just happened. Apart from that, she had seen the man only in passing. Nothing that would earn her the death stare he was giving her now.

"What do you mean?" she asked instead.

George laughed.

"Of course you wouldn't bother remembering what you did."

"Just tell me," Darling snapped. She was afraid, but she didn't want George to see it.

"Wow, you ruin a family's life and you don't even remember it," he said, surprising her. The gun in his hand stayed trained on her as he spoke. Darling glanced at the door they had just come through. If she managed to escape she would be out in the open. She hoped he wasn't a good shot, because he could hit her easily. But if she could somehow make it into the house, there was a chance she could find something to defend herself with or, at the very least, hide until Oliver found her.

Because he would.

He had done it before.

"Then tell me about it," Darling said. She wanted him to talk, get distracted and waste time.

The gate guard kept the gun pointed at her. Standing behind the chair opposite, he would not miss if he wanted to shoot her.

"You know, when you first came to Mulligan, I thought you were cute. Young, new, interesting." Darling searched her memory for George when she was new to Mulligan but was drawing a blank. Whatever memory he was in, she wasn't sharing it. "Even when I heard the rumor you were working for Jeff as an intern, I still thought that made you more interesting than the women I had grown up around. But then you stuck your nose where it didn't belong, and I realized you were no better than your scum of a boss." He waved his gun at her in a sudden burst of anger. Without meaning to, she yelped.

"My father skipped out on my family when I was a kid," he said. "My mother worked her fingers to the bone trying to give us a good life. When I graduated, she hurt her back on the job at the woolen factory. For the first time in years, she was able to take a break, and she deserved it." Recognition started to prick against Darling's memory. "So, I encouraged her to tell a little white lie and say she was still hurt. Have herself a little vacation."

Darling could almost feel the color drain from her face. George must have seen the change.

"Ah, you do remember me," he said.

"Workers' compensation fraud," Darling responded as if she was reading the file Jeff had handed her years ago. She hadn't put together that George had been Carmen's son. Their last names were different, if she recalled correctly.

"That's it."

"It was more than just a little white lie," she said with an even tone. "She was collecting it for a year and a half."

George grabbed the chair and hurled it into the wall. The echo it made rocketed Darling's fear skyward, but it was nothing compared to what she felt when she realized where the gun was. George held it level with her face. His hand was calm. His eyes were filled with rage.

"You watched and followed her like she was some kind of criminal when all she was, was a woman who worked herself into the ground to provide for her family," he roared. "She had to spend a year in jail and pay almost fifty thousand dollars! It broke her, it bankrupted us and it was all because you and your boss wanted to make a little cash!"

Darling wanted to say that, although she could sympathize with his mother, her actions had been illegal. Darling had done her job the correct way, observing an energetic woman with no issues and reporting back to the insurance company that had hired Acuity. But she didn't say anything. George was enraged. He had already cast the first stone and didn't seem to regret that one bit. Anything she said now would only fan the fire. She didn't want to give him any more reason to use his gun.

"All out of questions?" he spat when Darling still

didn't speak. Her back was ramrod straight. Her heart was racing.

"I wouldn't talk to you right now if I was her, either."

Darling gasped as a voice spoke from the doorway. She hadn't heard or noticed the door open, and she hadn't expected that particular man.

"You're too passionate, George. It's terrifying." Jace Marks smiled a perfect smile at the gate guard. His eyes slid to Darling's look of surprise, and he laughed. "After all of his obsessing over how bothersome you can be, I'm kind of shocked you didn't put the dots together much sooner."

He grabbed the discarded chair and set it up across from her. In the process of sitting down, he took the gun from George's hand and pushed the man gently aside. Darling watched the interaction with new attention. George was being obedient and took the spot behind Jace with obvious pride. She had never known the two even knew each other, yet the loyalty George was exuding for the younger Marks was concrete.

"The dots," was all Darling could manage at first.

"Yes, the dots." He crossed his legs and leaned back in his chair. As if they were in a meeting making small talk. "About Nigel's little secret. His tryst from younger years."

"You mean Jean," she said, finding her voice. "Your sister."

"Half-sister," he corrected. "*Secret* half-sister."

"But you knew?" Darling was going back over all the events that had taken place. This time she was inserting the two men before her. Finally what felt off about the arrest of Lamar Bennington and Robert Jensen made sense. "Nigel told you?"

"Of course he didn't tell me," he said. "Perhaps that

would have been the right thing to do, but Nigel doesn't always operate with the best morality."

"Then how did you find out?" Darling didn't know why he was opening up to her, but if it bought Oliver more time to find her—which she prayed he was already trying to do—then she'd keep the conversation going. Although she couldn't pretend that Jace confessing to everything was good for her health. Trying to tie up the loose end with Jean Watford's identity had turned Darling into Jace's loose end.

"A very inebriated family lawyer let it slip that Nigel wanted to make some changes to his will. At first I thought it was to give Mother and me what he had set aside for leaving this pathetic community after his death, but then Mother made an odd comment about Nigel's extracurricular activities. So I followed him, and there she was." Every time he referred to Jean, he acted as if it left a bad taste in his mouth. Darling didn't wonder which of the men had actually killed her. She would bet everything she owned Jace had been the one to do it.

"At first I thought it was an affair," he said, "but after watching them, I realized the affection wasn't sexual. That's when I really did some digging. I even went so far as to steal her hairbrush for a DNA sample to make sure, but when I went to get something of Nigel's, he caught me." He rolled his eyes. "He didn't deny it but had the audacity to ask me to keep it a secret until he could figure out how to tell Mother."

"And you did, didn't you?" Elizabeth hadn't known about Jean. Darling was sure of that. If she had, it would have been more than enough to get out of the prenup.

Jace shrugged as if keeping his father's illegitimate child a secret hadn't been a big deal. "It was just another job in a long list of jobs he had already given me. I really didn't mind the new development."

"But?" Darling wanted to know what had changed.

Jace smiled wide. It didn't last long. His words became low, dangerous. "But then he tried to give her money, and when she wouldn't take it, he promised her a job at the new branch of Charisma." He paused and uncrossed his legs. Moving his head side to side, he cracked his neck. The calm exterior of control he had been trying to exude was beginning to flake off. When he was ready to speak again, however, George put his hand on Jace's shoulder.

"He'll be looking for her soon, Boss," the gate guard said.

Jace didn't look as if he enjoyed being interrupted, but he shrugged the irritation off with a nod.

"Go," he commanded. "And don't waste any time. Shoot to kill, as they say."

It was George's turn to nod. He took the gun from his demented friend and began to leave.

"Shoot to kill? Who?" Even as Darling asked, she knew the answer. George left without a word. She turned her wide eyes to the man in front of her. "Who is he going to shoot?" she almost yelled.

Jace's smile came back. "Your bodyguard, of course."

Darling's breath went shallow. She felt her nostrils flare, and her eyes became slits. Every fiber of her being was warring between anger and fear.

"Why? He doesn't know anything," she ground out. "I didn't tell anyone. There was no need to, since the murderers were already thought to be in custody."

"Oh, Darling, we both know that Mr. Quinn won't stop until he saves you or avenges your death." A shiver shot up her spine at that, but she tried to hide it. "Either way, he's a problem, and I don't need any more of those."

Darling heard her car drive away, picturing it going around the side of the house.

"If we were such problems, then why even involve me in the first place?"

"You mean the pictures," he guessed.

"And the notes."

"When I realized my mother hired you to prove Nigel's infidelity, I checked up on you. With all that happened with your parents, I assumed you had some guilt I could use to my advantage. Plus, considering your relationship with the police here, I figured you'd want to do the right thing and turn in any evidence. The hope was that you being so adamantly against Nigel would help put a nail in his coffin." He made a *tsk* noise. "By the way, I must ask. After you got all of that evidence on your parents and their extracurricular activities, why didn't you turn it in to the authorities?"

Anger was starting to win against the fear she felt at being so vulnerable in front of a killer. She lifted her chin a fraction.

"I would think someone like you would understand," she answered. His eyebrow went up in question, so she explained. "Being the children of powerful people isn't easy, especially when you see how far they will go to protect themselves. Like you, I was afraid." It was the first time she had ever admitted that to anyone. In a small way, she felt a sense of relief at finally saying it out loud. It was a shame the admission was wasted on Jace Marks.

"I'm not afraid of my father," he spat.

"Then why do all of this?"

Jace cracked his knuckles. More of his calm fell away.

"I wanted to be a painter, once upon a time. Travel the world, find beauty in everything, set up shop in Europe and start a family with a woman with dark hair and an accent." His voice trailed off for a moment before clear anger started to shine through. "But Nigel already had plans for me. He had high expectations, and I wanted to meet them all. I graduated at the top of my class in high school and college—where I pursued a degree he picked out—and when it was all done, I went straight into Charisma. I didn't even take a break.

"I rose up through the ranks the right way. No special treatment from Nigel…and no appreciation or approval, either. I gave up the life I wanted to live for the only one I thought would make him happy. Not once has he ever given me a 'good job, son' or 'I'm proud of you.'" His fists balled. Darling readied herself for whatever outburst she was sure was coming. "Then Jean shows up after all of these years, and suddenly Nigel is laughing and smiling? Changing his will to include her even though she didn't want a dime? Giving her a job in the company without her having a college degree? All of it finally helped me come to the most important realization of my life."

Darling gave him a questioning look when he didn't continue. He opened his fists and rubbed his palms against his pants. A small smile lifted up the corner of his lips. He looked as if he had mentally checked out.

"I realized that I could never please my father. So, I found a way to hurt him instead."

Darling swallowed. The bravado she had started to feel stalled at the callousness in his words. "But she was your sister," Darling started.

Whatever thread of calm he had was severed at her statement. He stood so fast that his chair toppled over.

Less than second later he was in her face, hands on the arms of her chair.

"She was a stranger," he roared. Any facade of a sane man vanished as his anger reverberated off the walls, making its way around the small room. He was seething, chest heaving. It wasn't until that moment that Darling felt absolute fear. Jace managed to calm himself enough to keep talking. But when he spoke, his tone was nothing but ice. "And you're about to find out how little sympathy I have for strangers."

Darling didn't try to hide her new fear. Instead, she let it show clearly across her features. There was no hope for Jace. There was no turning back. He had chosen his path, and there was no doubt in her mind that he would kill her when his story finished. Though Darling didn't want the end of it to be the end of her. She also refused to let an angry gate guard be the end of Oliver.

Darling gave the man in front of her a quick once-over. She met his gaze when she spoke.

"You don't have a gun."

And then Darling threw her entire weight against the man who dared threaten her happiness.

Chapter Twenty-Two

Jace was taller and heavier than Darling, but she had the element of surprise on her side. He let go of her chair, and together they fell to the ground.

He let out a moan as his back met the concrete. With her hands still tied behind her back, Darling fell against his chest. She didn't want to lose her momentum, so she brought her knee up hard against his groin. He cursed loudly and swung up, his fist meeting her jaw. The blow was hard enough to make her see stars but also had enough power to push her off him.

Trying her hardest not to pass out, she managed to rock up into a crouching position and, using the wall, eventually stand. Jace wasn't fast to respond, still writhing in pain. It gave Darling all the time she needed to get to the door. She backed against the door and was thankful she could still move her wrists enough to grab and turn the doorknob.

"There's nowhere to go," she heard Jace yell out as she ran through the poorly made hallway to the next door that led into the house. With adrenaline pumping through her body, she opened the door and immediately backtracked to shut it. The task of throwing the deadbolt took precious seconds, but she managed it by getting on tiptoe to lift her hands up. She heard Jace laughing from the workshop but didn't let it slow her down.

The Slate House had three stories. The basement was dark and damp, and had one half bathroom in it. Its stairs were located next to the kitchen—the room she was currently in—but Darling refused to enter a room with only one exit. Without any lights on, the natural light that filtered in through the upper stories' windows wouldn't touch the lower level. The main floor, if she remembered right, had four rooms and no real place to hide since there was no longer any furniture. That left the top floor and its three bedrooms and attic space.

Darling had started to move through the kitchen when a shot rang out behind her. Unable to stop the scream that tore from her throat, she looked, terrified, at the bullet hole in the door she had just locked. Jace had a gun after all.

With more urgency than before, Darling hobbled down the hallway and turned at the stairs. Quickly yet quietly, she took the steps two at a time until she was at the landing. The pain in her foot was incredible, even though she was trying her best to only put pressure on the very edge of her foot, but she knew she had to keep going, If she could find a place to hide, maybe it would buy Oliver enough time to get to her.

She just hoped Oliver would see George Hanley coming.

OLIVER RACED DOWN the road, determination pushing him. The pleas from Nikki to wait for the police replayed in his mind, but he paid them no heed. This time he wasn't going to count on them to guide him to Darling. She had been gone too long. Every second counted now.

He glanced at the gun on the passenger seat. Rarely

did he find a good excuse to bring it out, but he couldn't think of a better reason.

Rachel had traced Jace's cell phone to a piece of land in the middle of Mulligan. George's phone had last been used at the gatehouse, so that had been a quick dead end. Oliver was betting that Jace believed no one else had figured out his connection to the murder or the kidnapping. He had the confidence of his father. Though when Nigel had come to the realization that his son was one of the two behind everything that had happened, Oliver could hear the man crumple.

He had no time to sympathize.

If Darling had been hurt or worse…

He crushed that thought. The private investigator was strong and clever. She wouldn't let someone like George or Jace end her life.

Oliver pictured the two men trying to hurt her, and anger instantly filled him. It took him a few seconds to realize his phone was ringing on his lap. Not recognizing the number, he answered on the second ring.

"Darling?" he asked, hopeful.

"It's Derrick," the deputy replied. "I heard you're going after her by yourself."

"If you're going to tell me to wait, you can—"

"I'm not," Derrick interrupted. "You're driving up to a house that's three stories. There's a front door, a side door that leads to the attached workshop from the kitchen, and a back door that leads off of a second sitting room." Oliver didn't stop the man as he continued to give him a quick layout summary. After detailing the rooms on the main and top floor, he said, "There's also no cover driving up to the house. Whoever is in there will see you coming a mile away. So I suggest you go in fast and hot."

"No problem there," he assured the cop.

"Good luck, Oliver. Backup should be there a few minutes after you."

They hung up without any more comments. Oliver visualized the house from the deputy's description, already forming a plan for entry.

Crash.

A car from the opposite direction slammed into the side of the SUV.

Oliver tried to keep the vehicle from going into the ditch, but the impact was too great. The SUV went to the left just as the airbags deployed, and the SUV flipped before he could do anything to stop it. The windshield blew out and an awful metal crunching sounded before the world stilled.

Oliver gasped, trying to suck in some air while getting his bearings. His seat belt kept him upside down but still in his seat. Below him he could see the ground where the windshield should have been. He tried to look out the driver's side window, but the door was too damaged. When he could catch his breath, he undid his belt. The fall to the car's roof wasn't graceful, but he was glad when he didn't feel any broken bones. Though his left shoulder didn't feel the best.

He tried to open the door, but it wasn't budging. As quickly as he could, Oliver crawled to the passenger's side door, grabbing his gun as he went. He wouldn't have left the vehicle without it. Whoever had hit him had done it on purpose. That he was sure of, at least.

He had been hit about five minutes from his destination, which meant that on either side of the road there was nothing but open fields with trees in the distance. That meant no cover. Oliver kept that in mind as he exited the flipped SUV and moved around its side to the back to get a view of the road he had just been on.

The car that had hit him was in the middle of the road, the front right side dented but mostly intact. Oliver checked his gun, wincing at the pain in his arm. It was Darling's car he was looking at, but it was empty.

"You're harder to kill than I thought."

Oliver spun around, gun raised.

George Hanley met him with his own raised gun.

"Where's Darling?" Oliver yelled. The gate guard was bleeding from his forehead and shoulder.

"Does it really matter?" he said with a smirk.

Oliver pulled the trigger and jumped to the side before George could do the same. The bullet hit the gate guard in the shoulder, and he dropped his gun in surprise. He hadn't expected Oliver to act that quickly.

George tried to bend down to get the gun, but Oliver wasn't through with him. He closed the space between them and punched the sleazy man for all he was worth. George crumpled to the ground.

It was an instant knockout.

"I don't have time for you," Oliver said to the unconscious man. He didn't give him any more thought before jogging back up to the road. The keys were still in the ignition of Darling's car. He hopped into the driver's seat and sighed in relief when the car started. Although the door didn't shut all the way and the window was gone, it did the job of turning around and speeding down the road.

George had been dispatched to take care of him, which meant that Darling was alone with Jace. It was a thought that kept his adrenaline running high.

Derrick had been right about the house being in the middle of nothing but open space. Minutes later, Oliver was speeding up its drive. Darling's car was quiet, but anyone looking out of the windows would see him. Pain went through his shoulder as he cut the engine and opened the dented door. He knew he'd feel more of the crash's damage as his adrenaline wore off and he was able to rest, but for now he needed to find Darling. Thinking of losing her tightened his chest. He pushed the feeling away. He needed to focus.

He hurried to the back door and moved beside it. It was locked. Derrick had said there were two more ways to get into the house. As much as he wanted to burst through the door, he didn't want to give up his location until he had a better handle on what was going on. If he went in, guns blazing, he might spook Jace into doing something he would seriously regret.

Oliver would make sure of that.

Following the wall closely, Oliver crept along its length until he turned the corner to see the workshop extension. He held the gun firm and listened for a beat. Nothing. He turned the knob. It opened with ease. With gun raised, he went inside.

There had been a struggle but thankfully no blood. Two chairs were knocked over and Oliver could see through the open door, down the walkway and into the kitchen. He imagined Darling running into the house and hoped his mind wasn't inventing a wishful scenario instead of a plausible one. He moved quickly through the windowless pathway and into the kitchen. The house wasn't as well-lit as he would have liked—shadows stuck to the corners—but Oliver was thankful the house was devoid of furniture. Only a random assortment of bottles and trash was scattered around. He sidestepped a glass bottle and moved into the adjoining room.

It was empty, and so was the room opposite.

"Here, here, little Darling," Oliver heard Jace taunt.

Oliver pushed himself against the living room wall, looking out through the double-framed archway to the base of the stairs.

"Come out so we can get this over with," Jace called in a singsong voice. "You can't hide forever."

Sweet relief swept through him. Darling was alive.

But where was she?

Oliver looped around the archway, and instead of going for the stairs, he went to the front door. He threw it open, making as much noise as he could, before retreating to the living room again. This time he positioned himself with his gun held high and steady.

Footsteps sounded against the landing and then the stairs as Jace ran down them. Oliver waited until the man was in his sights before he spoke.

"Don't move or I'll—"

Just as Oliver had done to George, Jace raised his gun and shot before Oliver could finish talking. The bullet hit the wall beside him, and he returned fire.

But nothing happened.

His gun jammed.

Oliver pulled back deeper into the room as another bullet struck the wall. He could hear Jace move back up the stairs in a hurry. Oliver cursed under his breath and ejected the jammed bullet from the chamber. Now that Jace knew he was in the house, he might get more desperate to find Darling. Oliver couldn't have that.

Readying his gun, he swung around into the hallway and started to run up the stairs. He didn't expect Jace to keep shooting blindly. Oliver had already made the judgment call that the younger Marks lacked courage unless he was confident everything was on his side. Less confidence, less control. Stepping out to gun Oliver down on the stairs would mean that he would have to put himself in a compromising position. No, Jace was probably already setting himself up in one of the hallway's corners, waiting for Oliver to step onto the landing. The question was, was Jace to the left or the right?

Taking a deep breath, Oliver stepped past the last stair and pointed his gun to the right. It was the wrong way. A bullet whizzed by his ear and shattered the top portion of an already broken window at the right end of the hallway. Another noise filled the air, but he didn't have time to register it before turning and shooting to the left. Jace ducked into one of the bedrooms to avoid the hit. That's when he realized the noise he had heard had been Darling's scream.

He turned his head back to the now fully broken window. Standing on the outside of the house—on what must have been the workshop walkway's roof—was his private investigator. She was bleeding across her chin and her hair was wild, but she didn't seem to be in any major physical distress. She watched him with wide eyes as he ran over to her. Had the bullet hit her?

"I'm okay," she answered his unasked question. "It scared me."

Oliver looked over his shoulder, expecting Jace to pop back out. He needed to get Darling out of the way. She must have been reading his mind again. She ducked to avoid a low-hanging shard of glass. Her hands were bound, so he helped guide her through the window until she was standing inside.

"Oliver!" she yelled before he could usher her to safety. He spun around, gun raised, but it was too late.

Oliver put his body in front of Darling's and felt an explosion of hot pain searing into his stomach. Only on reflex was he able to return fire. It put Jace back into the bedroom, giving Darling enough time to drag Oliver to the left.

"No, no, no," Darling chanted, putting her body under his arm to help him walk. The pain was excruciating. It took all he had not to fall to the floor. The bedroom was empty save for a dark oak bed frame in the middle. Darling guided him to the side farthest from the door. They all but fell to the ground next to it. "Oh, my God, Oliver."

He looked down at the bullet wound and winced at the sight. A bullet in the stomach wasn't good—though most bullets anywhere weren't—and he knew he was in a bad situation.

"You need to put pressure on it," she whispered. "I can't. My hands are tied."

Oliver put down the gun and reached into one of his pockets. The movement made him see stars.

"Lucky you," he said, pulling out his pocket knife. Darling turned and scooted toward him. He cut through the ties easily enough. As soon as her hands were free, she surprised him by taking off her jacket and putting it against his wound. He couldn't stop the yell of pain at the pressure.

"We need to get you help," she said, not apologizing.

"The police—" he said between his teeth "—will— will be here soon."

"You need them now."

Her voice shook as she said it. Oliver wanted to let her know everything was going to be okay, but the truth was, it wasn't. He looked down at his wound again.

He was losing too much blood, too fast.

He was going to pass out soon.

He dropped the knife and picked up the gun again. "There are ten shots left," he said, handing it to her. "Just pull the trigger if you see him."

If Jace thought Oliver was down for the count, he wouldn't hesitate in underestimating Darling and trying to finish her.

Oliver watched as a myriad of emotions crossed the woman's face.

"You shouldn't have jumped in front of me," she said, matching his tone.

"It's part of my job description."

"It's not," she whispered, "but thank you." Oliver didn't miss the red in her eyes. The pain in his stomach intensified. He was sure his own eyes were starting to tear, too. He reached out and took her free hand.

She was beautiful.

"I wanted to, Darling," he started, pausing once again to make sure he didn't hear Jace moving around. Maybe his bullet had also found its mark. Darling raised her eyebrow. He was happy to see she kept control of the gun in her right hand. She could defend herself if push came to shove.

"You wanted to what?" she asked.

"I wanted to run away with you," he continued. "When you asked me, there was nothing I wanted to do more, but—" Oliver sucked in a breath. Darling squeezed his hand.

"Don't."

The pain tripled from his wound. He couldn't hide it. Darling's face softened in acute concern. He needed to finally tell someone—finally tell *her*—the reason he had left the girl in the daisy dress all those years ago.

"I didn't want to hold you back," he whispered. "You would have given up everything for me, and I didn't want you to have to do that. I'm no good for you, Darling, but —" he took his hand from hers and placed it against her cheek "—I'm no good without you, either." His vision started to tunnel. He was on the cusp of unconsciousness. Before Darling could respond, Oliver let his hand drop. "Now focus. I can hear him coming."

Without much furniture in the house, Jace's attempt at stealth echoed off the walls and down to their room. Oliver half hoped he would leave them and make a run for it, but he knew the millionaire's son had too much to lose. In his mind, Oliver and Darling were the only two people who knew about his connection to Jean. Their deaths could ensure his continued freedom, especially since two men were already in custody for it. Although if Jace really stopped to think about it, he'd realize running was his best option.

However, he didn't.

DARLING FELT AS if she was having an out-of-body experience, watching the horrible scene unfold from somewhere else entirely. Jace was almost to the door—all caution apparently abandoned—and the life was visibly draining from Oliver. His revelation had touched a deep part of her, but it had also been terrifying. The bodyguard's breathing had shallowed. She knew he was giving it his all just to stay conscious.

Darling could feel the urge to distance herself and wait for the inevitable to happen. Wait for Jace to make it to them and finish the job while Oliver bled out. To give up and give in. She bit down hard on her lip. She didn't need to distance herself. Oliver needed her now.

She tightened her grip on the gun and took two deep breaths. Jace was nearly at the door.

"I love you, Oliver Quinn," she whispered.

And then she was up and shooting.

Chapter Twenty-Three

Darling was uncomfortable but trying her best not to show it. She was sitting in the hospital hallway with her foot propped in the chair next to her, waiting for Nurse Jones to come back out.

The older woman, along with the doctor on duty, hadn't seemed surprised when Oliver was rushed through the ER doors with Darling limping by his side hours earlier. The chief or Derrick must have given them a headsup, which was fine by her. It had meant Oliver had gone into surgery almost immediately.

An ache had crossed her heart at seeing him go limp in the Slate House's bedroom. His state hadn't changed in the ambulance, either. There had been so much blood...

"I thought you might need this."

A woman with dark red hair, wearing a smart burgundy pantsuit, took the seat to Darling's left. She held out one of two coffee cups. Darling's eyelids fluttered closed for a moment. The coffee smelled like heaven.

"You must be Nikki," Darling responded once her coffee euphoria was over. The woman nodded and handed the second cup over. It warmed Darling's hands. "You came into town to fire Oliver."

Nikki let out a chuckle. "I've been warned you say

what's on your mind." She smiled. "I have to tell you, I like that in a person. But yes, that's why I came. I won't apologize for it, though. I have an obligation to protect all of my agents, even if it's from themselves from time to time."

Darling nodded. Oliver still hadn't told her what he'd done that was so bad when he was trying to find her, and she didn't care. He had saved her. Twice. She wasn't going to nitpick him about it.

"Which brings me to this point," Nikki continued, leveling her gaze with Darling's. Her expression softened as she spoke. "Thank you for protecting him when no one else could." It was an admission Darling hadn't expected. She bet it was a rare show of emotion for the founder of Orion. Especially with a stranger. "Starting Orion and trying to keep it afloat have left me little time to do much else. I have few friends, and Oliver is one of them. So, thank you."

It was Darling's turn to smile. "I don't know if I did the best job at protecting him. He did still get shot."

"Don't sell what you did short. You shot and then disarmed a man hell-bent on killing you both before the cops even got to you," Nikki pointed out. "If that's not protecting someone, then I don't know what is."

Darling replayed the moment after she had told Oliver she loved him. Jace had been right outside the door, and she hadn't taken any chances on him getting past it. Shooting through the wall, she had hit her target. She rushed him when she heard his gun clatter to the ground. Like Oliver, Jace had passed out from his injury. Unlike Oliver, Jace's wound hadn't been serious. He was currently handcuffed to a hospital bed on a different floor, surrounded by cops.

"I suppose I should listen to the owner of a bodyguard service," Darling said with a smile.

"You've got that right."

They lapsed into a mutual silence as they appreciated their coffees. Darling took the moment to marvel at the past week. It would be a while before Mulligan returned to normal. The gossip alone would carry them into the new year.

"You should let Oliver come back to Orion," Darling blurted after a minute had passed. "I can tell he really loves working there." She expected some kind of push-back, but Nikki kept smiling.

"I'm going to offer him his old job," she said. It made Darling happy and sad at the same time. She wanted to be greedy. She wanted to keep Oliver in Mulligan, to stay with him and live out the rest of their lives together. But she also wanted him to be happy. Orion was a big part of that. "However, I have a feeling he won't take it."

Darling raised her eyebrow. "Why wouldn't he?"

"Have you tasted this coffee?" Nikki shook her cup. "I wouldn't want to leave this place, either."

"The coffee is good but not *that* good."

"Something tells me Oliver feels differently." She paused, letting her double meaning sink in. Darling didn't want to smile, but she couldn't stop it. "On a completely unrelated note, since there is no issue with Nigel paying Orion for its services, we now have enough money to start expanding."

"That's great!" Darling was glad something good had come from everything that had happened.

"I'm thinking of creating a new analyst division. One that would cover finding and assessing threats, and build-ing strategies for the more complicated cases. I wouldn't start it right away, but I do think creating a freelance position now would only help Orion in the long run. So whoever took the job could work from home. Wherever that might be." She winked at Darling. "It would only make sense that that someone would need to have a thorough knowledge of the group as well as an unwavering loyalty…"

"You know, I think I might know someone who fits that description," Darling said, already picturing a certain bodyguard wrapped up in winter clothes, grumpy at the Maine temperature. The thought warmed her heart. "But don't get your hopes up," she said more to herself than Nikki. "This person might be fine staying with his old job."

Nikki took a long pull from her coffee and smirked.

"I think we both know that isn't true."

"I can't believe you crashed your rental."

Orion Zeta team lead Jonathan Carmichael, Oliver's closest friend, was shaking his head at Oliver. It had been a week since his surgery, and he was finally being okayed to leave the hospital. Oliver had been surprised when Jonathan had shown up instead of a certain private investigator to give him a ride. Though he wasn't going to question his friend. He knew the man had been worried.

They all had, including Oliver.

"I'm telling you, it wasn't my fault," he said. "There should be a clause in those contracts that says if a crazed idiot is trying to kill you by using a stolen car, then the rental place can't get mad at the renter."

Jonathan laughed and helped Oliver into the car. Although no long-lasting damage had been done by Jace's bullet, Oliver was still mighty sore.

"Nikki said the cops thought you had killed that idiot and left him on the side of the road," Jonathan said as he got behind the wheel.

Oliver smiled. It wasn't sweet.

"After what he had done to Darling, I would rather he rot in jail for years and years to come." George had been released two days before with a straight shot to jail. Jace Marks was right behind him. After Jace had awoken in the hospital, he had cracked under Chief Sanderson and Deputy Derrick's unrelenting questioning. Jace had admitted to murdering his half-sister as punishment for his father after convincing his old friend George to help. The two of them had tried to pin the murder on Nigel but hadn't expected the millionaire to have such a great alibi. Then, when Darling started to figure out Jean Watford's connection—which would have shown Jace had a great motive to kill her—they had panicked. George had jumped the gun and, instead of dropping Darling off next to Jean's car with evidence showing Nigel was lying, he had tried to kill her through exposure. It had just been a happy accident the private investigator had found the car. Another accident that ended up benefiting them was Jace's knowledge of CFO Lamar Bennington's and executive assistant Robert Jensen's drug addictions. Framing them was easy, especially when both businessmen were picked up under the influence of narcotics.

Now Jace and George were going away for a long, long time.

Nothing made Oliver happier.

Well, almost nothing.

"I still can't believe that girl of yours tackled a killer to keep him from getting to you *after* she shot him,"

Jonathan observed. "Sounds like you got a good partner in crime there."

"I can't complain," Oliver responded with a smile. Right before passing out in the Slate House, what he thought would be the last thing he ever heard had been Darling saying she loved him. He had been ready to die happy at those three little words.

However, now that he wasn't on his death bed, he was ready to make those words into something much more.

FOR THE FIRST time since Elizabeth had hired her, Darling had no trouble walking up to the front door of the Markses' Mulligan home. Since George was no longer on the payroll, and Grant and Thomas were still doing their Orion bodyguard duty until the end of the month, the front gate was left open, and the gatehouse was kept dark. All it took was one knock on the heavy front door and a smile to be welcomed inside the mansion.

"Which Marks invited you?" Thomas greeted her. He had met Darling while Oliver slept in the hospital. Both he and Grant had made sure to check that their former partner was okay.

"Elizabeth, but I'd like to talk to Nigel for a quick second if that's okay."

Thomas and Grant hadn't hidden their new respect and appreciation for Darling keeping their friend alive when she'd talked with them in the hospital. Thomas wasn't hiding it here, either. Without a question he led her to the second-floor office and through its open door.

"Sir, Darling Smith would like a moment," he said to the millionaire. His tone had gone almost stern, as if warning Nigel that declining her presence wasn't a good idea.

Nigel looked up from the papers on his desk and nodded. Darling bet the man hadn't slept well in days. Everything about him sagged. Only his eyes remained strong, no doubt holding the confidence he had garnered over a lifetime of experience.

"Thank you, Thomas," he said. The bodyguard left but didn't go far, standing on the other side of the open door. Darling wasn't afraid of any more attacks, but she was grateful for the watchful eye. "I'm sorry it's taken so long for us to meet, Ms. Smith. Life has been…" He ran his hand through his hair and let out a long sigh.

"I hadn't expected you to want to meet with me in the first place," she said honestly. From the brief phone conversation she had had with Elizabeth earlier that day, she knew the millionaire's wife had admitted to her husband that she had hired Darling to prove his infidelity. Beyond that, Darling didn't know where that left the couple. What was more, if Darling hadn't kept digging, his son wouldn't be in jail.

"I admit, at first I was angry, but then I realized it was at myself," he said, guilt ringing clear in his words. "I could list the things I should have done differently in my life, but there's no point now. My son killed my daughter, and the simple truth of it all is that it was because of me."

"When did you find out about Jean, if you don't mind my asking?"

"A year ago she approached me at a business convention in Miami. Her mother was a good friend of mine in college. Our paths crossed one night while she was on business. It was only a one-time thing, though I know that doesn't make it right—I was with Elizabeth—but I didn't see her again after that. She passed away a few years ago, and Jean decided to start looking for me. Her mother never told her who I was, and she certainly never told me who Jean was." His brow furrowed. "I would have been there for her growing up if she had." Darling had just met the man, but she felt in her heart he was telling the truth. Finding out he had a daughter had seemed to soften a big part of him. "When we met, I thought maybe she only wanted money, but the more time I spent with her, I realized she just wanted family."

"You tried to set her up with a job in Charisma?"

He nodded. "Her mother was sick for a while, and that drained almost all the money they had. Jean dropped out of school to take care of her but couldn't afford to go back. She was smart—very smart—and I told her that if she did well at her job, after a year the company would pay for her to get a degree. It was the only way she'd let me help. A lot of good it did in the end." Nigel averted his gaze, and Darling pretended not to notice his eyes rimmed with red. He was a strong man but, like everyone else, had a breaking point.

Darling cleared her throat. "I should go talk to Elizabeth now, but I wanted to stop by and give you this." She handed him the folder she had been carrying and stood. "I did a little more digging the past few days and found something that you should know about." Confused, Nigel held up the picture of a little girl that was attached to the file. "Her name is Isabella, she's five and I've been told she is a ball of energy." Darling smiled. "She's your granddaughter."

Nigel's mouth opened to say something but words never formed. He looked back at the picture of the red-haired girl.

"But Jean never said…"

"According to Jean's best friend—who is taking care

of Isabella right now—Jean was going to use this trip to tell you about her. She wanted to get to know you a bit before she included her. Just in case."

"She looks just like Jean," he whispered. Nigel's reddened eyes were now shining.

"I can't stand here and tell you that everything is going to be okay. That the little girl's existence is going to help make everything that has happened better," Darling said. "But maybe someday it will help."

Darling left Nigel with his new revelation without another word. There wasn't anything more to say.

LESS THAN AN hour later, Darling walked into Acuity in a much better mood. It only intensified when she saw Oliver lounging on the lobby's couch. She hadn't seen him since the night before, having visited him every day since he had been admitted. Though they had talked, neither had brought up the topic of their future.

"Well, don't you look better," Darling said as she sat down next to him. "I'm sorry I wasn't the one to pick you up, but Jonathan insisted he could handle you."

Oliver laughed. "That's funny, because he insisted that I couldn't handle you," he said. "He told me any woman with that much fire would just burn me up."

Darling smirked. "That doesn't sound too unpleasant, if you ask me."

Oliver's eyes widened. His smile grew.

"So, how did your meeting with Elizabeth go?" he asked, slightly defusing an escalating moment. A part of her didn't want to answer. Telling him about the last interaction she'd had with Elizabeth in a professional capacity, officially ending her case with the woman, cut the last thread that had in some way attached them while

Oliver was in Mulligan. She wouldn't need his help any-more. There would be no shoptalk left to hide behind to avoid talking about their future.

"Surprisingly well," she said almost reluctantly. "She started by telling me she didn't blame me for what hap-pened to Jace. She understood he needed to be punished for what he'd done. Though you could tell she was hurt by it all. Who wouldn't be? She also paid me because, in the end, I proved that Nigel had an affair *and* I discov-ered the identity of Jane Doe." Darling left out the part where she had refused Elizabeth's money the first two times it had been offered.

"Is she going to file for divorce?"

Darling shrugged. "She wasn't too clear about that, and I certainly didn't push it. If she does decide to do it, I don't think it'll be for a while. They have a lot to talk about." Elizabeth had been upset—obviously—at what had happened but, as with her husband, there was strength holding her up. Darling was confident that no matter what happened in the future, Elizabeth Marks would be fine.

"So, it's all done, then?"

Darling didn't want to, but she nodded. Fear that she had misjudged their reconnection filled her. But it was only fear that he didn't feel the same.

Darling knew without a doubt that she loved Oliver. She hadn't *stopped* loving him, no matter how many years had gone by.

"Well, I guess it's time to get to work, then." He got up from the couch and walked to the lobby's lone desk.

Darling looked on, confused. "Work?"

Oliver grinned. "You're looking at Orion's first free-lance strategy-and-threat analyst," he paused. "Well, I don't know if that's my official title, and technically it won't be live for a few weeks, but I figured I'd go ahead and check out the available office." He made a show of inspecting the desk.

Darling's heart filled with happiness.

"You're staying?" She stood, unable to contain the mounting joy.

Oliver's grin widened.

"Why would I leave?" He closed the space between them. Taking her chin in his hand, he tilted her head up so their eyes met. "Unless that's a problem."

"Not on my end," she whispered.

"Good, because there's nowhere else I'd rather be than by your side."

Before Oliver had a chance to say any more, Darling pressed her lips against his.

In that one moment, all of the pain from their past turned into beautiful hope for their future.

* * * * *

MILLS & BOON®
INTRIGUE
Romantic Suspense
A SEDUCTIVE COMBINATION OF DANGER AND DESIRE

A sneak peek at next month's titles...

In stores from 10th March 2016:

- **Trouble with a Badge** – Delores Fossen *and* **Deceptions** – Cynthia Eden
- **Navy SEAL Captive** – Elle James *and* **Heavy Artillery Husband** – Debra Webb & Regan Black
- **Texan's Baby** – Barb Han *and* **Full Force Fatherhood** – Tyler Anne Snell

Romantic Suspense

- **Cavanaugh or Death** – Marie Ferrarella
- **Colton's Texas Stakeout** – C.J. Miller

Available at WHSmith, Tesco, Asda, Eason, Amazon and Apple

Just can't wait?
Buy our books online a month before they hit the shops!
visit www.millsandboon.co.uk

These books are also available in eBook format!

MILLS & BOON®

Why shop at millsandboon.co.uk?

Each year, thousands of romance readers find their perfect read at millsandboon.co.uk. That's because we're passionate about bringing you the very best romantic fiction. Here are some of the advantages of shopping at www.millsandboon.co.uk:

✳ **Get new books first**—you'll be able to buy your favourite books one month before they hit the shops

✳ **Get exclusive discounts**—you'll also be able to buy our specially created monthly collections, with up to 50% off the RRP

✳ **Find your favourite authors**—latest news, interviews and new releases for all your favourite authors and series on our website, plus ideas for what to try next

✳ **Join in**—once you've bought your favourite books, don't forget to register with us to rate, review and join in the discussions

Visit **www.millsandboon.co.uk**
for all this and more today!